A Lullaby o

Copyright © 2022 Grace Terry
All rights reserved
ISBN: 9798754308916

A Lullaby of Lies

Grace Terry

*For the tragic heroes who aren't so heroic,
You will be remembered.*

World Map

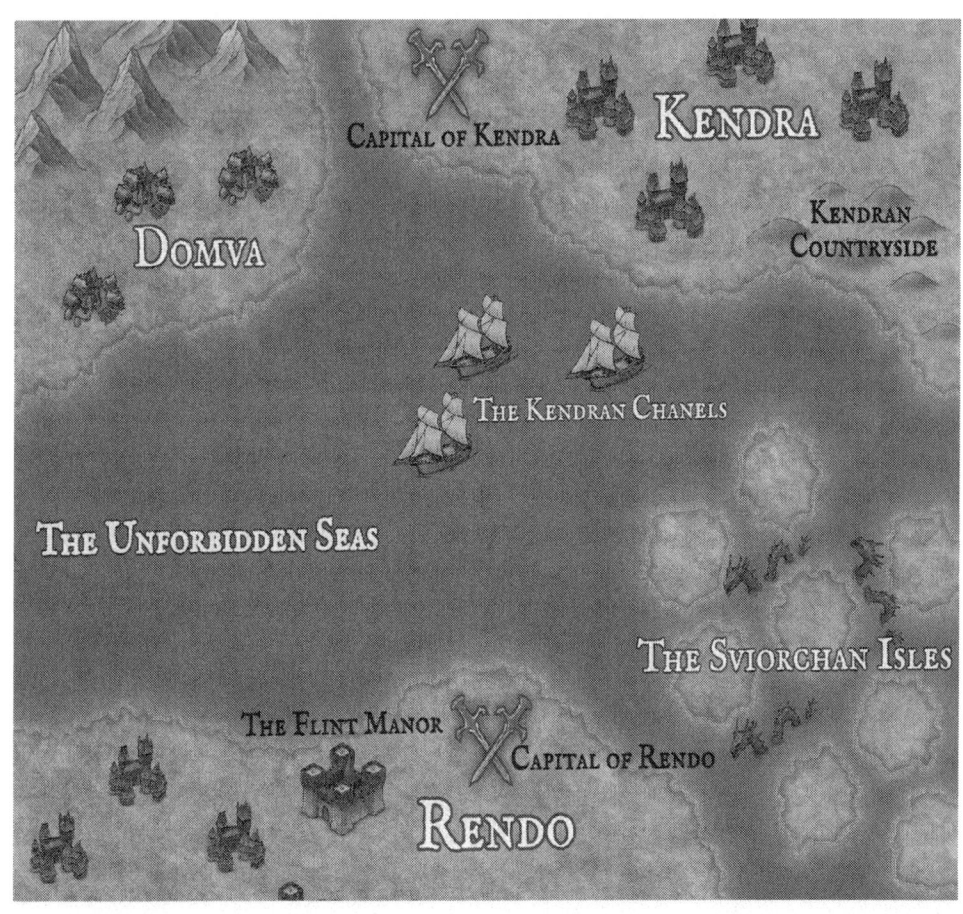

'Tell me what to do to make it
All feel better.
Maybe it's a cruel joke on me.
Whatever. Whatever.'

> Pity Party
> Melanie Martinez

⚔ Prologue ⚔
TEN YEARS EARLIER

DARK RED BLOOD RAN like rivers in the corners of Kendran streets, acting as a plague to young children walking along the pavements.

A declaration of war against Kendra had been made the night before, and it was difficult for most people to figure out why.

The people who did know wished they did not.

The few people who did know also knew that the Rendan streets were not bleeding.

A certain Rendan family was licking the blood off their hands, laughing, drinking, mimicking.

A tall man with cold eyes and dark skin.

A small boy with a warm smile and messy hair.

An infant girl, imitating her older brother's facial expressions.

A far off woman, awaiting the return of her daughter.

But the final member of the laughing and bloody family did not laugh, did not drink, did not mimic.

A boy with black hair and eyes like thunder, skin deathly pale

A boy with a sword at his thigh and a dagger in his pocket.

A boy made of death.

A boy made of war.

⚔ Chapter One ⚔

I WAS THROWN INTO the arena for the second time when I was 12 years old. My fingernails were already bloody from picking them in anticipation; I had been told that, this time, my opponent would have no mercy, unlike the first time. And I knew it would be a fight to the death.

I pulled my sword from its sheath as I waited, it's blade glinting in the dim sunlight. It was a cheap sword; it had to be. Nathaniel wouldn't waste his money on expensive handles and steel for a 12 year old boy who could barely shoot an apple with a bow. Instead I had a bronze sword with a wooden handle. It wasn't much, but I loved it.

Dread started filling me, bones and all, when the clock struck 11:30; it was time. And, from what I'd heard, the person I was up against was never late. I swallowed the lump in my throat. It was too much; I was still a child. But I didn't have a choice.

A big man burst through the doors, his long hair tied back and his armour shining. I thought, at first, that it must've been a mistake. He was twice as large as me! How could I possibly best him? But Nathaniel came in behind him, beckoning for me to come down, and I knew I was doomed.

Hesitantly I stood up and made my way to the middle of the arena, my heart pounding as if it were going to burst from my chest. The man must have noticed, because he smirked slyly at me before joining me in the middle of the room.

I waited, vexatiously, for Nathaniel's signal. Apparently he didn't need to give one, because the man was jabbing at me before I knew it.

People often say that adrenaline gives you the strength to win a fight; well, let me tell you now- it doesn't. As soon as I felt it I had to force it back down. Adrenaline makes you crazy, I suppose. It makes you irrational and it makes you forget everything you've learnt. I couldn't afford that in a life or death situation.

I took a hit of my own as soon as I saw the opportunity. It would've been a great hit, if I had been a little older or if my muscles had fully grown. But the man saw it from a mile away and blocked it with ease.

'You're pathetic.' he snarled. I frowned. I was a very petty person, and didn't take insults very well. Because I knew I wouldn't be able to touch his skin before he was worn out, I sliced off his long hair.

'You little fu-' It seemed I had hit a nerve.

'What's your name?' I asked, my movements quickening. I had been taught that keeping the rival distracted was, sometimes, the best option.

'Felix. You better remember it in the afterlife, because you just cut off my life's work.' Felix said harshly. I snorted, catching him off guard and sliced his arm. Felix cried out in pain but his movements weren't deterred. He was quite good, I had to admit.

'Well I'm Maximus, Felix. It means the greatest.' I responded. Felix huffed out and tried to trick me, by aiming for my throat and landing at my chest. I blocked it and sighed. 'That's no way to treat a preteen, is it?'

Felix was positively livid. At that point, I had hit more than a single nerve.

'Oh, I'm going to kill you, kid.' he growled. His sword arm started going faster, trying for more vulnerable places. The corner of my lip quirked up; he was being clumsy. He wasn't good enough to fight so quickly, and he knew it.

I took my chance the moment it opened itself to me. His legs were perfectly still- a big mistake- so I latched my foot around his knee and kicked him to the floor, watching in triumph as he yelped.

'Do shut up; you sound like a dog.' I said, pushing the tip of my sword to his neck

'How did you do that?' Felix demanded. The remaining strands of his hair were stuck to his forehead, which was glistening with sweat. I wasn't even scratched, but he was gasping for breath.

'I suppose I'm just better than you.' With that, I pushed the sword through his throat and back out again, so I could stick it into the floor.

When I looked up at Nathaniel, I didn't notice how impressed he was; I, a 12 year old, had defeated a man who had been sword fighting longer than I'd lived. Perhaps if I knew how much of a feat it was, I would've felt better. But all I could think about was the silently pleading look in Felix's eyes as I opened his neck and watched him bleed out. I shivered. The whirlwind of battle had caught me, and it made me afraid of myself.

The icy winter wind made the memory even more disturbing. I had always relished taking the lives of others; it was after I felt the heat of my actions. Most people thought I was a psychopath. I wasn't.

The remorse I felt was so strong it drowned me every minute of my existence, over and over again until it was unbearable.

'Good afternoon, Maximus.' I jumped and turned sharply to see none other than Nathaniel Flint, leaning against the wall of his house. He looked like a statue, his skin pale and his poise perfect.

'Nathaniel.' I responded, 'Is there anything you want?'

'Yes, actually. I want you to go through the story with me before you leave, because we both know that George won't make you.'

That was the other thing.

I was being sent to the countryside of Kendra to spy on their princess.

I had no idea as to how Nathaniel had managed to get them to let me stay; if I was honest, I didn't want to know. But my task was simple; deter the princess, their greatest warrior, and find out what the Kendran army was planning on doing.

The Rendan's and Kendran's had been threatening war for the past 10 years, but neither armies had good enough soldiers to fight. The new generation was different. I was destined to be the Rendan's best warrior, the princess the Kendrans. Neither of us were supposed to know that, but Nathaniel had his ways.

'I was kidnapped by the Rendan army as a child. They were planning on sending me to slavery in Sviorch, but you and your team managed to get on the boat and change it's path to the countryside of Kendra. Of course, the Rendan's found out and tried to take control back over the ship, but it ended up crashing and killing most of us in it.' I said. I had the whole plan memorised, and had for a while now.

'Perfect. But I'm not on *Leomaris*. Remember that.' Nathaniel said.

'Yeah, I will.' I said. There was a pause. 'Wait, since when was this boat called *the lion of the sea*?' I asked.

'Since my grandparents were young. It deserves to go down as a hero, for how much it has done for our family.' Nathaniel said wistfully. I doubted that heroic was the best way to describe what I was doing.

'Erm, yeah.' I responded. I was quite awkward for someone who could kill people like it was a sport.

'Remember not to die in the crash.' Nathaniel said.

'I don't think that's something that I just *remember*. It's based on luck. Besides, George will get me to shore. That's always been the plan.' I said.

'I know that that's the plan. I bloody *made* it. I'm just reminding you not to do anything stupid.' Nathaniel said. I laughed humorlessly; I was known for my recklessness in Rendo, as well as my skill with a sword. To be honest, I had built quite the reputation for myself.

'I still don't see why our prince couldn't do this. It would make so much more sense, what with Emile being a princess.' I countered.

'He couldn't use a sword to save his life and we all know it. Besides, there isn't any possible false backstory you could give for a prince spying on a rivalling princess. You're our best option.' Nathaniel said. He was being strangely patient.

'I'm flattered.' I said dryly, an eyebrow raised. Nathaniel might have been acting like he cared about me, but he didn't. It hurt, sometimes, but for the majority of it, it only enticed me to come up with more plans on how to murder him.

'Don't be insolent, kid. We're going to the boat so I can send you and George off.' Nathaniel said before striding off. I blew out a breath of air before following him to the water's edge.

'Keep up, will you?' Nathaniel called. So much for the patience.

'I'm here!' I said back. Nathaniel turned around to check, and I could've sworn he looked disappointed.

We arrived just before the ramp going up to *Leomaris*, and Nathaniel turned to stare at me. I squirmed under his gaze.

'What?' I asked, tilting my head. Nathaniel didn't answer; only narrowed his eyes.

There was a few minutes of silence.

'I'm just making sure you look like someone being shipped off to slavery.' he said, eventually.

'I should hope that I do.' I said, affronted. I hadn't spent an hour finding old clothes for no reason.

'You don't look too bad, I suppose. The dirty water will make it more believable.' Nathaniel said. I didn't like the prospect of having to go in that river; I had heard of all the diseases and filth that lay within it.

'Well, we're getting you sent off as soon as we can, so get on the boat now.' Nathaniel said, stretching his arm out for me to shake his hand. I did; his skin was as cold as it had always been.

'Don't mess it up.' Nathaniel said as I started to walk away.

'Me? Mess something up? Why, you must be thinking of the wrong person; I would never.'

If I was on land, Nathaniel probably would have broken my ribs.

I got on the deck of the ship and walked over to the rail, leaning on it and watching the people I shared a house with talking and laughing below me. 5 minutes passed and I was being waved off, leaving Rendo for the longest I ever had. It was strange to think about, but I was ready. Nothing could stop me.

The water didn't look so bad, where I was at the moment. It was shining and blue, rippling softly in the breeze. Bubbles were everywhere, signalling that there were creatures there. I hoped there wouldn't be any when we crashed.

The sky was a grey that would rival my own eyes. I could see dark clouds in the distance, but I wouldn't be there to see the rain being poured from them. Where I was going it hardly ever rained.

After about 10 minutes, I registered the quiet tap of feet as someone came up behind me. Well, I knew who it was; I could tell from how he came up to me so easily, how he wasn't frightened by me.

'*Salve*, George.' I said, turning to face him. His hair was a mess of light and dark blonde, and he clearly hadn't brushed it. Saying that, neither had I. But I had a reason; he, on the other hand, was supposed to be Nathaniel Flint's son.

In case you hadn't realised, this was the same George Flint that was Nathaniel's heir. He didn't seem like it, with his lanky limbs and too-big feet, but when he wanted to be, he was rather cunning. Although, it was an unlikely event that he actually did want to use his brain for something good. Most of the time he used his skills learning how to do circus tricks.

George had an uncanny resemblance to his *mater* rather than his father, with his dark skin and warm eyes. She'd been sent away with Adelaide, George's younger sister, to the south of Rendo after her birth, and I hadn't seen her since then.

'How did you know it was me? I swear, you're a sorcerer.' George said with a frown. I felt my lips tug upwards.

'To start, sorcerers aren't real.' I said. George crossed his arms over in feigned annoyance.

'Then you must be a wizard.' he said. I only shook my head, chuckling lightly; George was my first, and only, friend in Rendo. Yes, I was Rendan from birth, but I was antisocial and unpredictable; who would want to be friends with that? The answer was George, apparently.

'If I was a wizard I would be far more skilled than I am right now.' I said. George looked sceptical.

'Is it even possible for you to get better?' he asked.

'I should think so.' George didn't look convinced. If he had any common sense, he would know to pretend to believe me, as to not inflate my ego. But, lucky for him, I had the smallest ego out of all the great warriors, so his lack of wit could be excused.

'Alright but seriously now, how *do* you always know when I'm near?' George asked, genuinely interested.

'You're the only person with footsteps so light who dares come straight to me, without hesitation.' I said. George grinned.

'I suppose I'm just fearless!' he declared. I stifled a laugh as he jumped around in circles.

'More like mad.' I said with a lifted brow. George glared at me through his spins; I considered saying everyone was staring at him, but he wouldn't care.

'You can't say much. You'd fight a dragon if they didn't love you so much!' George yelled.

Well, he wasn't wrong…

'And I would win, too.' I responded loudly, voice smooth. It was rare that I could keep a conversation going for so long; normally I would have ran out of things to say, by that stage.

'Yes, yes, we all know, there's no need to show off.' George said as he came to a stop, barely out of breath.

'How do you have so much energy?' I said.

'I have energy levels that would rival even yours, Maximus.' George said, running a hand through his hair.

'That doesn't answer my question, you big baboon.'

George stared at me for a second before bursting into laughter.

'Did you actually just call me a big baboon?' he asked between wheezes. I felt my cheeks heat up.

'It just came out! I couldn't help it! You call me a slug all the time, so leave off!' I said defensively.

'Yeah, but you're all prim and proper. You should call my father a big baboon, see what he says!'

That set him off laughing all over again.

I hated the word 'father'. We had grown up having to speak this language, but I didn't grow to despise it any less. The Rendan language... well, it spoke to me, as terribly cliched as it sounds. It rolled off my tongue in a way these words didn't.

'Finished yet?' I said. A few more minutes passed and it seemed George had finally calmed down, although he was quite red in the face.

'Okay, okay, change the subject before I laugh so hard I die from not being able to breathe.' George said solemnly. I blinked.

'Um... there are dolphins in the Kendran waters?' I said. George raised his eyebrows at me, unimpressed.

'That's boring. I think I might go to sleep for a little bit. You should, too; save your energy for what's ahead.' George said. I merely nodded and waved as he walked away.

I was standing alone, my eyes fixated on the sun as it set behind the now white clouds. I must've been watching it for at least 10 minutes before heading to my own room on the ship and laying in the bed.

I fell into a dreamless sleep as soon as my head hit the cushion.

'Maximus! Maximus, wake up, you lazy little swine!' I woke up with a start, jumping out of bed and rushing out. The captain of *Leomaris*, a woman called Jane, was pacing outside of my door. As soon as she saw me, she grabbed my wrist and pulled me to the deck.

'What? What's going on?' I asked dumbly. Jane looked at me as if I were stupid; I felt stupid, anyway.

'Exactly what should be going on; we've crashed. You slept through it, even though you're the key to this whole thing!' she snapped. Oh. That made more sense.

'Hold on, so how long was I sleeping for?' I asked, rubbing my forehead. It felt like I had barely dozed for five minutes.

'At least two hours. I don't know how; Nathaniel said you slept nine hours last night.'

Nathaniel lied. I'd barely slept one.

'What do I need to do?' I asked. For some reason, I felt... calm. I should have been panicking, running around, screaming, but I was utterly relaxed. I came to the conclusion it was a result of actually having more than half an hour of sleep.

'Jump off.' Jane said, much too casually. I looked over the rail; the water was considerably more murky. It must have been brimmed with dirt and chemicals.

'Right now?' I said. My calmness hadn't lasted very long.

'Yes, right now! Unless you want to go down and drown! George is waiting for you; do you want him to catch his death?' Jane said irritably. I bit down on my lip until it bled. 'I said now!'

I had nothing to lose.

With a deep breath, I squeezed my eyes shut and jumped in. The coldness hit me like a train.

I had thought I was dead as soon as I was in. I couldn't swim; Nathaniel never felt the need to teach me. I tried desperately to float, but I just kept sinking. I tried and I tried and I tried, until my muscles ached and my vision blurred.

My sweat was mingling with the river water as I made one last attempt to stay on my back. I didn't even get my head out.

Instead of trying to resurface until I killed myself, my hand flung itself above, wildly shaking around before falling back in.

Whatever I had done must have worked, because George was catching me from sinking any further within seconds.

It didn't really make a difference. My head felt like it was going to implode from the pressure or being so far under water. When my eyes shut again, they didn't open, and I let myself pass out.

⚔ Chapter Two ⚔

I WAS IN THE arena, again. This time, it looked different; Nathaniel was there, yes, but there was something odd. Something I couldn't quite put my finger on...

It was embarrassing how long it took for me to figure it out. There was a small, metal box in the middle of the room, the heat radiating off it.

I turned around to look at Nathaniel, who was at my left side. He didn't look back; he was scrutinising the little box as if his life depended on it. I frowned and averted my gaze back to it, unable to find what was so interesting.

'It's perfect.' Nathaniel said suddenly. My frown deepened. I hadn't said anything to induce that answer.

'Then put him in.' came a voice. My heart dropped at the sound of it; I searched and searched, but couldn't find the owner of it; it was simply there.

'What good would it be for me?' Nathaniel asked. He sounded different... he sounded empty. I felt chills run down my spine. Something was going on, something I was quite obviously excluded from

'You know what his future holds. Put him in, now. It'll kill him. Kill him!' The voice gradually became more aggressive as it carried on with its apparent desire to kill someone.

'It's different, now; I made sure of it.' Nathaniel said. I was listening so intently that I didn't notice a boy coming out of the shadows.

'There he is! Put him in, before you lose your chance!' the voice seethed. My head snapped around to the boy who came out of the shadows; and my pulse stopped thumping.

The boy was me. An exact replica of me. He had the same hairstyle as me, the same uneven nails, the same freckle just under my right eye. I gasped out loud, but nobody heard me. I should have noticed before that that they didn't know I was there; I was invisible, I must have been. There was no other explanation.

'What's wrong?' my twin asked. My throat felt dry at the sound of my own voice being spoken by someone else.

Nathaniel did not answer. He stalked over to my twin, grabbed him by the ear and pushed him in the box.

Sweat broke out on my brow.

The door slammed shut and an obnoxiously loud laugh could be heard; the sweat was building up by the second.

'Yes! Now, he will suffer!' the voice said darkly. I would've found it pretentiously funny if I hadn't been drowning in my own sweat.

I rolled up the sleeves of my shirt and stumbled forward. I hadn't been so hot in my entire life.

What shocked me even more was when it became hard to breathe. I could feel my mind racing, trying to figure out what was going on. It was only when Nathaniel's eyes locked on mine that I realised.

'Can you hear me?' I asked carefully. Nathaniel laughed mockingly.

'Of course I can hear you; well, the real you. The fake one's in there, and the temperature is going up as we speak.' he said, his eyes glinting. I took a long, shaky breath in.

'Why- why is i- i- it hurting m… m-me?' I stammered, stomach churning. Somehow, he must have linked the 'fake me' to the real me, and everything that he felt, I was feeling, too.

'Don't ask me; ask him! How does it work?' Nathaniel said loudly. There was a minute of silence.

'Did you hear him? He's a genius.' Nathaniel said in awe. If I had been in the right frame of mind, I probably would've punched him, then.

'You're crazy.' I said harshly. Nathaniel's eyes hardened.

'For that, I'm going to close the walls in early.' he snarled, pulling a strange button with an antenna out of his pocket.

'What do you-' I cut myself out as I felt something pushing in both of my sides. I moved forward, I moved back, but there wasn't an escape. I was going to be crushed to death by some weird invisible force.

'Hey! HEY! Wake up!'

My eyelids snapped open. It was a dream. It wasn't real. I wasn't being squished inwards.

'I was worried, there.' My eyes darted over to where the voice was coming from. There was a man with dark skin and honey-coloured eyes crouched at the side of the bed.

'Who are you?' I asked. The man looked increasingly concerned.

'I'm Desmond. Do you know where you are?'

Desmond. The name seemed familiar… Desmond… Desmond! *Your trainer, for while you're there, will be a man called Desmond Axel; make sure you pay him respect. He's well known, and loved, among Kendra*, I remembered George telling me.

So I was in Kendra, then. I made it. I hadn't drowned and I was on the right path to making this mission work. That was good. That was really good.

'Kendra… right? I- Gods, I'm in Kendra.' I whispered. Desmond smiled at me; he looked extremely kind for a Kendran. But, saying that, I couldn't judge their whole population based on a few bad people. A few bad people whose names I didn't even know.

'I thought you had amnesia, there, lad.' Desmond said, 'Your name's Maximus, right?' I liked being called 'lad'. It was better than 'kid' and 'boy'.

'I- yeah, Maximus is right. Is George okay?' I sounded frantic when asking the last part, but I had to know. If he had sacrificed himself for me then I'd never forgive myself.

'Is George the tall one with brown eyes?' Desmond inquired.

'Yeah.'

'He's perfectly fine, so don't worry. So are quite a lot of your… friends. We got them a ferry back as soon as possible.' Desmond said.

'Oh… um, thank you.' I said, scratching my arm. I realised that I felt fine, even though I'd nearly died hours before. I was still tired, though; but when was I not?

'How am I not, like, vomiting or something?' I asked. Desmond's eyes were warm and homely, and it was rather comforting.

'Unless you gained any injuries from the wreckage, you shouldn't have any symptoms of illness.' Desmond said. My eyebrows raised; it was rare I got normal medicine, nevermind medicine that healed my illness immediately.

'Oh.' It didn't feel right to say thank you.

'I'm assuming you want to go to your own room and rest?' Desmond said. I didn't want to sleep, even though I knew I should. I felt like I'd slept too much in the past 24 hours.

'Erm, I'm actually wide awake. Could I still go to my room, though? I'm curious as to what it looks like.' I said, trying not to sound as cruel as I usually did.

'Of course, of course; but do you not want to look around the house, first?' Desmond said, inclining his head. I thought about it for a moment; it did seem quite intriguing...

'I suppose it won't cause any harm.' I said, eventually. Desmond beamed at me.

'You seem awfully kind, you know. I'm sure Emile will gladly show you around. Wait here while I retrieve her.' Desmond left without giving me a chance to object.

I wasn't necessarily scared; I was simply uneasy. I had been training for years for this moment; I was going to meet the princess of Kendra, my rival, and I was going to speak to her and walk with her as if she were my comrade. It was fairly surreal.

I got out of the bed, for some reason, and stood as still as I could while I waited. There was a strange tickling sensation at my tonsils, making me feel even more queasy.

After an age, Desmond returned, holding the door open for Emile. Immediately, I bowed; I did not want to be killed on my first day.

'Oh, no, you don't need to bow. Please, stand up straight.' Emile said, laughing lightly. Her voice was soft, soft in a way that was still so loud that it filled a room, but also in a way that it felt like some sort of a blanket.

I looked at her properly, regarding her. Her hair was a flaming red, deeper than the blood that had stained my hands many nights, and her eyes a blue so dark it held a stark comparison to her pale skin. She was quite tall, only shorter than I by perhaps a few inches. She looked like a princess even in the clothes she wore now, an old sweater and baggy jeans.

'Your Highness.' I said. Emile's dark eyes flickered all over me and I struggled as to not squirm.

'Please don't address me as a princess while we are here. I would like to see what it feels like to be normal, for once.' Emile said with a small smile.

It seemed she was regarding me, too.

'Of course.' I responded. Emile looked as if she were going to laugh again, barely visible creases forming at the corners of her eyes.

'Another rule will be that you treat me as you would anyone else; don't be afraid to disagree with me. I'll only be offended if you don't.' Emile said. 'And, also, treat these rules as if they are laws; don't break them. I mean it.'

'It is strange to tell a killer not to break a law.' I said after a beat. Desmond looked at me, his eyes wide; I didn't pay any attention. I was giving her what she wanted. Trust didn't have to just come from respecting her as a princess, but from respecting her as a real person with real feelings and a real life, too.

'I quite like you. Maximus, isn't it?' Emile said.

'Yes. Maximus is right. And you're Emile, I suppose.' I replied. For once, I didn't stumble over my words, and I didn't feel the need to run away. It was always like that when I was with people of authority; I knew I wouldn't have to control the situation, and it eased me.

'I wouldn't be anyone else, would I?' Emile's grin was like a cat's; wide, cunning and positively gleaming with wit.

But it was a rhetorical question, so I simply returned the smile with one of my own. My awkwardness was starting to peek through; manipulation was moderately difficult.

'Will you two be going?' Desmond said, cutting in. It dawned on me that we were all in his room.

'Oh, sorry, of course we will.' Emile said. She walked out without waiting for me, earning me a pained look from Desmond as I quickly followed her.

'Right, where would you like to start?' Emile asked. I looked down the corridor; there were only 3 other rooms. It seemed quite small for the lodgings of a princess.

'Anywhere.' I said with a half-hearted shrug. Emile considered it for a minute.

'Well you aren't allowed in my room, and I'll show you to your own bedroom last, so the only one left, on this floor, is the bathroom.' Emile said, 'So we'll go there.'

The bathroom was in the room opposite Desmond's. It was quite simple; the walls were grey, the floor tiled, a mirror above the sink. However, it had to be the largest bathroom I'd ever seen. The bath itself wasn't even a bath; it was one of those peculiar 'wet rooms', where it was like a separate room just to wash.

'What do you think?' Emile asked. She was sitting on the counter next to the sink.

'It's big.' I said stupidly. I mentally kicked myself; how stupid could I be? Who describes a bathroom as *big*?

'Well, that's a new one.' Emile said in amusement. I could feel my face heating up from embarrassment; luckily, she turned away and left before she could see the red tint on my cheeks.

'We'll go to the second floor, then. It's my personal favourite.' Emile said, running down the stairs. I raised an eyebrow and ran down, too; she reminded me of George in some ways. Constantly happy. But, aside from that, she was totally new.

The second floor had 3 doors. But the roof was much higher and it felt... it felt different. Emile didn't even ask which one to go in first; she went straight through the first door to her left.

I felt a rush of cold air hit me as I walked through. The floor of this room was stone, the walls not even painted. It seemed there was a reason why; I recognised the room from it's layout. It was the weapons room.

On display there were two swords; the longer one had small engravings in the handle, in a language I couldn't understand. That creeped me out; I knew most languages.

The shorter one, on the contrary, was like nothing I'd ever seen before. By the looks of it, the handle was made from pure gold. There were small gems in it, and the blade looked poisonous. I ripped my eyes from it and looked at Emile.

'I'm guessing this one is yours.' I said, while pointing to the shorter sword. Her eyes lit up.

'The other one is Desmond's, but I personally think that mine is more... elegant, I suppose. But I may just be biased.' Emile said.

'If you want elegance, then this sword is perfect. Well, it's perfect either way. What on earth is that on the blade?' I whispered.

'What do you- oh. It must just be leftovers from the last time my mum used it. She quite likes poison. I'll have to clean it before training starts.' Emile said carelessly. I squinted. It must have been some sort of venom; it had a purple shade, a colour popular among toxins.

My eye caught on another display cabinet, an empty one.

'Who's this one for?' I asked. I already knew the answer.

'You, obviously. Desmond made a new one as soon as he found out we would have company.' Emile said with a soft laugh. I already knew how pleased Nathaniel would be at the progress I was already making.

'You'll have to remind me to thank him. When will I get a sword to put in it?' I pushed. Having a sword forged by the same people who had made the ones I had just seen would no doubt give me an advantage in the war.

'Whenever you want. We were thinking tomorrow, if you're okay with that.' Emile said.

'It's not like I'll have anything else to do.' I said. It would be best to get it as soon as possible, in case I messed up early.

'Well, that's enough of this room; the only interesting thing about it is the display. The rest are just backup swords, bows and arrows, knives and so on. We barely use them, anyway.' Emile said, walking out.

We went to the room next door, then. It looked quite small from the outside, but when we went in it felt like it was the size of the full floor itself.

It was a library, and an inhumanly big one. There were so many books and shelves that I couldn't keep up. It smelled... old. Used. It seemed unusual for it to be in the place where we were learning to fight.

'It's an old room. It's been here for hundreds of years.' Emile explained, running her fingers over the spines of a few books.

'I like it.' I said. And then, I simply walked out without offering an explanation as to why. Libraries gave me bad memories; memories I didn't want to resurface.

Emile came out quickly after. To my relief, she didn't ask about my haste to leave the room. Instead, we went to the room opposite; the room with a sign above the door that read *αίθουσα χορού*. *Ballroom*.

It was even bigger than the library. Every step I took resulted in flurries of echos. It was the most majestic thing I'd ever seen.

My jaw must have dropped, because I was sure my mouth was still agape when Emile spoke.

'If you think this is good, you should see the ballroom back at the castle.'

I looked up. The ceiling stretched for miles. I could've sworn the room had some sort of magical enchantment that made it so captivating.

'Is this an old room, too?' I said.

'No, Maximus. We made it especially for my arrival.' Emile said sarcastically. I rolled my eyes.

'Well, there isn't too much to do in here. Can we go downstairs?' I said.

Emile didn't answer, instead heading back out and down the final flight of stairs.

The first floor had the same layout as the second; two doors on one side and a single one on the other. I looked at the sign on the door by itself; *αρένα Arena*, it read. I swallowed as I stared at it.

'What are those two there?' I said. Emile didn't look interested at all in the other rooms, though.

'Just the living room and kitchen. Boring, really. This is the room we want to be in.' Emile said, gesturing towards the door I couldn't take my eyes off.

'Right.' I said stiffly. Emile went through, waiting for me to follow by the doorway. I took a deep breath and went inside.

It looked nothing like the arena back in Rendo. The walls were clean and white, unlike the bloody stains upon the one's back home. It's floor was cool against my bare feet; smooth and slick from it's latest clean. The actual fighting part of the arena's floor was made from wooden panels; it was the utter opposite of the old arena, but it still gave me the same uneasy feeling in my stomach.

'It's amazing, don't you think?' Emile said. She was leaning on one of the seats, which was made from red velvet. It would have stunned me how calm she was, but I realised I was probably the only warrior who hated arenas of any sort.

'Um… yeah.' I mumbled. I could feel the tension in my muscles as we went into the middle of it.

'I can't wait to fight in here.' Emile said. I cleared my throat and mind before responding, so that my strain wasn't so obvious.

'Have you never fought in an arena before?' I asked silkily. I was surprised I had managed to speak so clearly.

'We don't use them in Kendra; I just fought wherever I could. We have an outdoor one here, too, but it's only for if we can't use this one.'

I figured I would have to get over my fear of the place quicker than I'd thought.

'Oh.' I said simply. I knew that I'd be fine when I was fighting; but for the moment I wasn't fighting, and I felt like crying.

'Right. Well, I don't suppose you care for the living room and the kitchen, so I'll take you to your room, if you want.' Emile said.

'Um, yeah, I'll go to my room.' I said. Emile nodded and we left.

When I came to my bedroom, I was fully expecting it to be the smallest room in the house with a single bed and maybe a bedside cabinet. I was wrong. It was just as big as Desmond's, if not bigger, with a full double bed, a desk and some of the most beautiful painting's I had ever seen.

'I'll leave you, then. Good night.' Emile said, closing the door. I collapsed on my bed, shutting my eyes. I hadn't felt comfort like that since George had let me sleep in his room.

I opened my eyes only to check the clock; it was 1 in the morning. How long had I been passed out for? And why were Emile and Desmond awake so late?

I groaned, rolled onto my side. Somehow, I managed to fall asleep again. At that rate I would never sleep again. I hadn't even changed out of my clothes, although I didn't know if I even had anything else to wear. It was a bit of a mess.

I didn't have a dream. If I did, I didn't remember it.

Or I didn't want to.

⚔ Chapter Three ⚔

I WOKE UP AT six the next morning. The sky was strange in Kendra, I noticed; rather than the soft blue the sun rising normally had, it was a dull pink and orange.

I felt unusual; my head was inexplicably light. Though, that was probably because of how much I had slept recently.

I heaved myself out of the bed with effort and brushed through my hair with my hands while looking through the mirror. Apparently the rest had paid off; my complexion looked better than usual. Although I still had the prominent bags under my eyes. They were likely from genetics, though.

There was an abnormally big wardrobe in the corner of the room. I wasn't expecting for there to be anything in it, but when I opened it I was greeted by items of clothing I didn't even know existed. With a raised eyebrow, I pulled out a grey shirt and baggy jeans; I didn't need to wear any of the training gear until we started, which wasn't today.

I quickly dressed and pulled on some shoes; the only pair I could find were some worn out black boots, but I wasn't too bothered. They looked like they would serve me well during practice, anyway.

When I finished getting ready, I left my room and went downstairs to the first floor. If anyone was awake, that was where they would be. I went into the kitchen first, but it was empty, so I checked the living room to see Desmond sharpening a knife.

'Um- good morning.' I said quietly as I stepped in. Desmond showed no response as I sat beside him at the sofa, his eyes narrowing at the knife.

'Um... hello?' I said, shifting uncomfortably. It seemed he only noticed my presence then, as he risked a small look at me.

'Good morning, Maximus. How are you?' Desmond said. I'd forgotten how kind his voice was, how *gentle* it was.

'Oh, erm, I'm fine, thanks. How- how are you?' It was extremely odd, asking such a question; we never wasted time on small talk at home.

'I'm doing great, thank you. This knife is a bit of a task, but I've missed doing things like this.' Desmond said. I looked a little closer at the dagger; it was purely black, even the blade, and had very small gems in the handle.

'Is it yours?' I questioned.

'Yeah. Do you like it?' Desmond said with an inclined head.

'Well... it is nice, I suppose.' I admitted. Desmond stopped for a moment and turned to face me.

'Do you know how to use a knife in battle?' he asked. I stifled a laugh; of course I did. Nathaniel taught me how to use nearly everything, even things that weren't technically weapons.

'Yeah.' I said. Desmond regarded me for a moment.

'How good are you, then?' he pressed. I sat silently, stiffly; I didn't want to seem overconfident, but I didn't want to seem weak, either.

'It depends on what I'm fighting against.' I said slowly. Desmond looked pleased by that answer.

'If you want, you can have this one.' he said. My eyes widened considerably; I was rarely offered things like that knife. I'd never even had my own dagger before; I always had to use George's.

'Really?' I said in disbelief.

'Yeah, yeah. I don't use these things anymore, so it would be better to give it to someone who's going to appreciate it.' Desmond said.

'I- I would love it. Thank you.' I stammered. I would've thought he was playing a joke on me if he wasn't 60 years old.

'Here, take it. There should be some sheaths in the cabinet next to your bed. And you don't need to thank me, son,'

I took the dagger and made my way back to my room. The name 'son' gave me a queerly euphoric feeling.

Sure enough, there was a range of sheaths and scabbards. I chose a black one, as it matched the knife. At least if I didn't get a sword, I would have the knife to help me.

I went back down to the living room. Desmond was still there, although he was talking to Emile. She was still in her nightgown; if she had been Rendan she would've been shamed for letting Desmond and I see her wearing so little. But, evidently, the Kendrans didn't care much for things like that.

'Ah, Maximus, you're back. We're just saying that I'm going to go make your sword, today.' Desmond said as he saw me. Emile turned around, too, and I felt rather sheepish under both of their eyes.

'Um, thank you. For a lot of things.' I said under my breath. It was a grab for sympathy. It looked like it worked, too.

'Oh, don't worry about it. We're honoured to have you here.' Desmond said kindly. I nodded and went to sit on his other side.

'Desmond, when will training start? I'm desperate to begin.' Emile said. She hadn't even bothered to brush her hair.

'If you're this desperate, we can start tomorrow.' Desmond said with a fake sigh. Emile's face lit up.

'Yes! In the arena, too?' she said. Her voice was high from excitement.

'Yes, Emile, of course we'll be in the arena.' Desmond laughed. I bit the inside of my cheek. That stupid arena was going to be the reason I was caught.

'Oh, I can't wait.' She paused for a count. 'I'm going to the kitchen; I'm hungry.' Emile said suddenly, walking out. Desmond shrugged at me when I shot him a questioning look.

'So, about that sword.'

We went to the weapon room and Desmond pulled out all sorts of materials. I was only there to tell him what I wanted it to look like.

'Do you want the blade to be a different colour?' Desmond asked. I thought about it for a moment.

'Um, I'll just have it normal. Silver.' I said.

'Alright... and what do you want the handle to look like?' Desmond said. I already knew what I wanted.

'Sorry if this is too much, but can it be made from leather with a diamond on a sort of stand thing at the top?' Diamonds weren't worth much in Kendra, but in Rendo even royalty didn't have them. I was going to take advantage of that. 'Could it also have a sort of swirl going out at the bottom of it?'

'It's not too much at all, of course I can do that. Now, go enjoy yourself while I make this. Hunt some animals or something.' Desmond said, practically shoving me out of the door.

I left, the door slamming behind me, and blinked in the harsh light. Emile was leaning on the wall opposite me, her legs crossed and hair tied up in a loose bun. This time, she had bothered to dress properly.

'Hello.' I said, voice appearing surprised. Emile didn't move. She looked a little like a statue; perfectly still and pale as snow.

'That will take until tonight to be ready.' she said after a few beats. I raised an eyebrow.

'And?' I said. If I had said that to the Rendan prince he probably would've had me executed. Emile simply quirked the corner of her mouth up.

'And I suggest you should find something good to do with that time, rather than moping around like the majority of boys your age do.' Emile said. Her face was strung with teasing question; like she was daring me to answer back, daring me to say what I wanted to say.

If I said everything I wanted to say, I would be dead by now.

'What do you propose?' I said steadily. From the look on Emile's face, my response was the correct one.

'I propose we do exactly as Desmond said and go hunting in the woods.' she said.

'You've been listening to our conversation? That isn't very polite to your guest.' I observed.

'Oh, hush. You weren't talking about anything interesting, anyway.' Emile scoffed. There was a pause. 'Well?'

'Well what?'

'Goodness, you're insufferable. Will you accompany me on a ravishing trip to kill some animals?' Emile said. I hadn't thought that she was being serious, but apparently she was.

'Well, I suppose there isn't a reason not to.' I said. Emile's dimples showed through as she pushed herself up from the leaning position on the wall.

'Wonderful! We're using knives, by the way; it makes it so much more challenging.' Emile said.

'I was going to use a knife, anyway.' I responded under my breath as we went to the third floor.

I grabbed my new dagger from my cabinet draw and left, waiting for Emile as patiently as I could. She emerged from her room with a new leather jacket and a change of shoes.

'You took your time, didn't you?' I said. Emile didn't answer; she sprinted off, leaving me to try and follow her.

Emile was quite fast, I had to admit. But not fast enough. I caught up to her within seconds, the wind stinging against my skin. She caught my eye as I stopped myself from going any further in front of her and shot me an impressed glance.

The woods were smaller than I had thought they'd be. Well, I wasn't expecting much, but I had hopes of what they may look like. They did not reach my hopes; although they did reach my assumptions.

'It's not a lot, but it hosts a load of rabbits.' Emile shrugged, unsheathing her knife. It was much more luxurious than my own; keeping with the same golden theme of her sword. I pulled out my own knife, throwing it gently to my left hand.

'You're left handed?' Emile asked, eying the dagger clutched in my palm.

'Yeah.'

Emile's jaw clicked and she made her way into the woods, her tentative footsteps causing barely any sound. I followed, treading lightly.

It was much darker under the trees; the blaring sunlight was barely visible. I shivered. The lack of sun made it quite cold, too.

After walking for about 20 minutes, Emile stopped. I stood beside her and looked around, trying to find what had caught her eye. I found it quick enough.

There was a rabbit. It looked like it might be sleeping, it was so still. I turned to look at Emile; her knife was in her hand, but she didn't look like she was going to use it.

'You do it.' she whispered.

'Really? You sounded awfully excited to come here, and now you're just letting me do it.' I said in a low voice.

'I want to see how good you are with a knife.' Emile said. I gave her a sceptical look before turning back to the rabbit and starting to pace towards it.

'What are you doing?' Emile said. She spoke so loud that we were frozen for a minute. Nothing happened.

'What do you mean? I'm killing this thing, like you told me to.' I said, exasperation laced in my tone.

'You can't sneak up on it; it isn't possible. The creatures have unnaturally good senses.' Emile said, agitated.

'Well, what do you expect me to do, then? Go make friends with it? That'll work much better, won't it?' I said sarcastically.

'Shut up, for heaven's sake. You throw the knife, obviously. Hit it in the stomach or chest.' Oh. That made sense, actually.

The only problem was that I had terrible aim. Nathaniel had always said it would be my downfall; he said a lot of things would be my downfall, actually, but he was serious about that one.

I couldn't throw a good shot to save my life. It was humiliating, really. Still, I took a deep breath and aimed my knife, praying it would hit the aim.

It did. The blade pierced through the animal's fur and past it's flesh, inducing a yelp from the rabbit and a sharp inhale from me.

'That was amazing!' Emile exclaimed, grinning broadly as she ran up to the body.

'Lucky shot.' I said nervously. It was the truth; that would be the only time I ever did that well when throwing.

'Lucky shot or not, it was flawless.' Emile said, pulling my knife from the rabbit and throwing it to me. Luckily, I was better at catching than I was throwing.

I pulled out a handkerchief and wiped the sticky red from the blade before sheathing the dagger again. I looked to see Emile stuffing the rabbit's corpse in her satchel.

'Is that not a bit morbid? Keeping a dead rabbit's body?' I said.

'It's to eat, you idiot.' My eyebrows knitted together.

'Don't you have, like, all of the food you could ever need? Being a princess and all?' Emile shot me a deathly glare.

'Don't you, like, have your own business to mind? I haven't eaten rabbit for ages, because it isn't *formal*, so that's why I'm keeping it. Besides, it would be worse to just leave it to rot.' Emile pointed out.

'Ah.'

We carried on walking for a while, but we couldn't find anything else. Emile looked rather disappointed when I suggested we head back.

'Head back? I haven't had a chance to kill anything yet.' Emile said; she sounded quite crestfallen.

'Well, you did let me take out that rabbit back there. Come back without me tomorrow, or something.' I said tiresomely.

'We have training tomorrow.'

'So?'

Emile bit down on her lip as we left; I felt a little bad, but hardly. I was too focused on my task.

She was starting to grow friendly with me. Well, she seemed to be friendly with anyone, judging from how laid back she'd been ever since meeting me. But we weren't close enough for her to reveal what I needed to know; it was expected, really, considering I'd known her for a day. But I was to move fast, so that would be what I'd do. I needed to be the closest person in her life, her best friend, the one she told everything to. And I needed to get to that stage soon.

It wouldn't be that difficult. We were in a desolate countryside with no one else to talk to, aside from a middle aged, retired trainer. The only mildly strenuous part would be getting her to trust me enough to tell me her secrets. Trust was a sacred thing, even more so in the days of war.

We came back to the house. It looked quite unstable from an outside perspective; what with its three floors and an attic too large for it.

I walked through the doors after Emile, and a warm gust of dusty air greeted me. I coughed lightly as the fine powder infested my nose.

'You get used to it soon enough.' Emile said. My coughs intensified.

'When my lungs are diseased and broken I'm blaming you.' I said when I could speak normally, again. Emile looked rather irritated as she walked to the kitchen. I stood by myself for a moment before going up to my room, the knife heavy in my pocket.

☆✯☆

It was about 9 at night when my sword was done. Emile rushed into my room, her face bright, not bothering to knock.

'Your sword's done.' she said. I stood up from my bed and patted down my hair.

'A knock would prove sufficient, I think.' I said.

'Well, I'm terribly sorry, but you need to see it; it's stunning.' Emile said, already running away. I sighed before following her.

We entered the weapons room to see Desmond standing with his hands behind his back, a grin lighting up his face.

I wanted to vomit, it was so clichè.

'Alright, son?' Desmond said. I wished Nathaniel would call me son, but he would sooner die than show any fatherly affection towards me, even if he had raised me.

'Hi.' I mumbled. I still wasn't used to how open he and Emile were with a complete stranger.

'I assume Emile told you that your sword is done?' Desmond said. I looked at Emile, who was standing next to me. I hadn't realised how close she was.

'Um, yeah.' I said. Desmond gave Emile an accusing look, but it didn't look like he meant it.

'Well, here it is. Mind you, it's a beauty.'

The sword *was* a beauty. I could see that as soon as it was revealed.

It was exactly like how I had imagined it. Somehow, Desmond had captured my thoughts, entrapping them in the weapon. It's shine caught my eye, and I was entranced.

'Do you like it?' Desmond asked, pulling me from my daze. He was staring at me in anticipation.

'It's wonderful.' I breathed, 'Thank you.'

'Oh, don't thank me for this. It was obligatory. I'm sure you'll have plenty more opportunities to thank me in the future.' Desmond said, handing me the sword. My arm brushed against Emile's as I took it, wrapping my fingers around the soft leather of the handle.

I held the blade in my right hand, staring at the sword. It was magnificent. I'd never seen something more intricately made, so filled with care and detail in my life. I was astonished, to say the least.

'No, honestly, thank you so much. Take it; I don't thank people very often.' *Because I never get a reason to.*

Desmond's eyes glittered as he gazed at me, on the border between perplexed and touched.

'You're completely welcome, Maximus.' he said eventually.

'Are you done, yet?' Emile asked, her tone bored. My head snapped up to meet her eyes; they were guarded and hard through the layers of royal blue.

'Um, yeah. Why?' I said.

'I'm really hungry. Can we eat, Des?' I noticed that she'd called him 'Des'; it seemed the pair were closer than I thought.

'Yeah, sure. Here, put the sword in the case.' Desmond said. I hesitantly stepped towards the glass container and clicked it open, tentatively placing the sword on the stand. I shut its door and turned back around, reluctant to put it away already.

'Right. So what are we having to eat?'

☆✯☆

By the time I went back to my room, it was midnight. I changed into some pyjamas that I had found in the wardrobe and climbed into bed. I appreciated, now that I wasn't half asleep, how soft the blanket was against my bruised legs.

I lay sprawled out, facing upwards. I had so much space. I didn't have to worry about accidentally falling off at 4 in the morning; I felt utterly carefree.

But I wasn't. And a small voice in the back of my head was reminding me of it, whispering words, scratching at me, waiting for me to break.

I nearly did. I nearly screamed out in frustration. Yet I managed to restrain myself, keeping my most dangerous knowledge where it couldn't be used against me.

Emile and Desmond were both nice enough; they were easy going and polite, to the point where it was somewhat annoying. It wasn't intolerable, simply irksome.

From a first glance, it would seem effortless for me to get what I wanted. But I had spent all day studying Emile's actions, and all afternoon with Desmond's. They were hiding something. Possibly a lot of things, actually.

I had a rather useful way of catching everything; I was unusually attentive, something deprived from harsh words and even harsher actions. So it proved facile to figure out that they weren't as open as they pretended.

I had asked Desmond about his career; in response he told me that he was past that point in his life and that he wanted to move forwards. It would seem normal if I hadn't been watching as closely as I was. I saw the way his shoulders tensed, the way his hands flexed, the way his eye twitched. The actions were so minute they were scarcely visible, but I saw them all the same.

It wasn't a serious question. More a trick. I wanted to get a response out of him, and I did. It meant that, when the time was right, I could ask whatever I wanted without being worried about him lying to me.

Emile was more of an obstacle. I asked her about a scar just above her collarbone, and she said that it was nothing. Just an old childhood memory. I searched for some change in the way she was sitting, for a clenched jaw, anything, but I didn't find it. Only when I prodded on the topic did I notice how her pupils dilated. It was an obvious dilate, too; they made her eyes so black I could only just see the river of blue peeking from behind it.

I changed the subject hastily after that. I had what I needed. It was enough for one night, unless I wanted a target on my back already.

I blew out a breath of air. I might as well have had my eyes shut, as I couldn't see anything as it was. So I did. I shut my eyes so tightly it produced phosphenes.

When I finally fell asleep about an hour later, it was a restless one. I couldn't stay in the black pit of my mind for longer than 30 minutes without waking up in a cold sweat; I didn't know why. I could not remember my dreams.

I fell asleep for the last time at 6:30, the blanket on the floor and my top damp.

⚔ Chapter Four ⚔

GREY EYES STARED BACK at me. My own grey eyes. George liked to remind me of how unique they were, but it only made me feel like even more of an outcast.

I stared at myself, eyes drooping. I looked like a mess. My skin was sallow and pulled tight in all of the places it shouldn't have been, the purple bruises under my eyes more evident than usual. It was 7:30 in the morning, and I had just gotten out of bed after trying to fall back asleep for half an hour. My previous sleeping episode had drained, and I had never been so fatigued before.

My black locks were a stark contrast to my ashen face. I thought, perhaps, I could pull off being sick and miss the first day of training. I certainly *felt* sick, even if it was just tiredness. And I had an awful headache to add to that.

But the training was a perfect chance to see what I was up against; I knew that the first thing we were doing was fighting Desmond in turn, so I could see how good Emile was.

Just as I stepped away from the mirror, my door swung open and heavy footsteps were coming towards me. I spun around to see no other than Emile herself, armour on and shield at the ready.

'Where's your shield?' she asked. Her features were lighter than usual.

'I don't have one.' I responded. She made a face of annoyance.

'Oh. Right. I forgot about the crash.' Emile shrugged. 'We can pick one up from the weapons room while we're getting our sword; come on, I'm excited!' Emile exclaimed, speeding off. She was oddly energetic, all of the time. It was quite refreshing.

I quickly caught up with her and she slowed down as we entered the weapons room. She had to restrain herself from pulling her sword straight out.

'What shield do you want?' she asked.

'I don't know. A good one.'

'All of them are good.' I shrugged at her as she picked up the closest one, a strikingly silver shield with stripes of gold. She passed it to me softly; it was surprisingly heavy.

'Thanks.'

'You're welcome.'

Emile's hand shot straight out for her sword. It was even more outstanding out of the layers of glass. I marvelled at it for a moment before getting my own.

'Are there helmets in the arena?' I inquired as we started walking down. The word tasted sour on my tongue.

'There should be.' Emile said dismissively. I wasn't that bothered about the helmets really; I had fought without armour many times before.

The moment we arrived at the door the awful, sickening feeling erupted in the pit of my stomach. It was like acid was burning my insides, crawling up my throat and along my tonsils. I restrained myself from gagging.

It only got worse when we went in.

I clenched my fists to try to clear the images from my mind, but they didn't stop coming. Blood pouring from a stranger's mouth. Bones left on the floor, grey and decaying. Small pieces of flesh scattered. Organs. Eyes. Teeth.

I wanted to blind myself.

Shakily, I took a seat on the front row. We had silently decided that Emile would fight first. Desmond wasn't yet there, though, so Emile seemed to be warming up as she pulled the helmet over her head, concealing her icy eyes and golden freckles.

I should've been warming myself up, too. But my knees were too unstable and my breathing ragged.

Desmond entered about ten minutes after us. By then I had calmed enough so my vision wasn't blurred, but I was still having hallucinations. Not even that; they were memories.

He walked up to the centre of the arena, his head armour already on. *How come he gets his own helmet?*

Emile was ready in a flash, her sword facing upwards and her stance that of a warrior. I could almost sense Desmond's grin. But that might have just been because my senses were all on high alert.

They stood mirroring each other, perfectly still. It was almost too much; I almost ran out, out of the house, out of Kendra, as far as I could. But I held myself together, a thin string wrapped loosely around my consciousness.

'You'll play a fair game, I hope?' Desmond said.

'I wouldn't dream otherwise.' Her voice was muffled from under the metal, but it held the same frigid undertone as it always did.

Then it began.

I could barely hear anything through clashing shields and swords colliding. However, I could see perfectly well.

The way Emile fought was... different, to say the least. It looked like she had planned every move ahead of time, her hands working before her mind. She was the epitome of grace.

Wisps of crimson hair fell from under her head armour, slashing the air as she spun around and dodged a blow to her chest. I could imagine the look on her face; her nose scrunched in concentration and her eyes hard and dark. But from her body language, precise and effortless, you would think she wasn't even paying attention. She made the skill look easy, like a child could do it without an issue. It was enchanting.

It seemed Desmond was a good match for her. His own movements weren't as accurate, a consequence from his tiring muscles and old age. But, during the fight, it looked like his age had gone back fifty years, and he was still a teen, living for every moment as his sword swung in calculated hits, aiming for the most vulnerable places.

There was a moment where he came close to slicing open Emile's forearm, but she deflected it just in time. I could feel her raised eyebrows as her moves became more aggressive yet more controlled and delicate at the same time. It was like it fuelled her.

I realised, then, that my breathing was normal, again. I had stopped seeing things. My forehead creased as I blinked and refocused on Emile and Desmond.

It looked like the battle was coming to an end. Desmond was closing in on Emile; it was expected for him to win, anyway. I only hoped she wasn't too prideful.

However, her next move was definitely not expected. It was so complicated that I could hardly keep track of where her limbs were.

She crouched to the floor, so quick it looked like she'd never been there at all, and swiped under Desmond's feet. If he had been paying attention, it wouldn't have affected him. But he stood in shock for a moment, and that moment was long enough for Emile to take her victory.

Her sword collided with Desmond's, causing it to fly off sideways and land on the floor. She raised the tip of the blade and pushed forwards until Desmond was backed against a wall, his hands in the air in defeat and a sword pushed against his adams apple.

I thought she was going to kill him, for a moment. But she dropped her sword and outstretched her hand to shake Desmond's, their skin marked and covered in small cuts.

They both pulled off the helmets. Emile threw hers to me, the grin on her face heartwarming. She looked so proud of herself I nearly congratulated her, but thought against it as I pressed my lips together.

Desmond was smiling too. He was a good loser, which was a remarkable trait. If it were Nathaniel in his situation, Emile would've been dead already. I shivered. It seemed strange to think of them dead; it was strange to think of anyone dead. But these people, so full of life, so warm to the touch… cold and deceased? The image didn't sit right in my head.

'Maximus, you're up!' Desmond said. His voice echoed against the pure walls. I sighed and pulled the helmet over my head; it was rather depressing how easy this was going to be.

Because I had already seen Desmond fight, I knew his weaknesses, his moves, the weak link in his armour. It was a mistake not making me go first.

A rule in Rendo for fighting was that you never let the opposing person see you in battle. I had seen him, and now he was an easy target.

I stepped into the centre, blocking out my surroundings. The arena wasn't so bad now that I had been in it for a while. Yes, it still felt like there was a blockage in my lungs, but I felt okay.

Emile's eyes bore into me as I got myself in position. It was just as natural as I remembered.

My sword was in action before Desmond had a chance to speak.

I toyed with him for maybe 30 seconds, using my shield far too much. He must've seen that I was only messing with him, as he calmed down and his movements became sloppy. I stifled a laugh as I threw my shield to the floor, reveleshing in Desmond's temporarily puzzled stance.

Becoming bored with the prospect of playing around, I finally let myself fall fully into the fight. It must have only been milliseconds when Desmond's sword was in my right hand and he was on the floor with two swords at his chest.

'That was something, kid.' he mumbled as I threw his sword to the side and pulled off my helmet. Desmond did the same, and I saw beads of sweat trailing down his brow. I touched my face. Bone dry.

'Here.' I said, offering a hand. Desmond took it and I pulled him off, brushing down my armour and turning to see a wide-eyed Emile. She looked, metaphorically, like a puppy.

'Are you alright?' I asked. She looked... fascinated. I didn't blame her. I was taken by her, too, even if I wouldn't admit it.

'That was amazing.' Emile breathed. I shrugged, sheepishly. Trying to act humble. My acting was getting better by the hour.

'Thanks. You were, too.' I said politely. Emile wasn't modest as I was.

'Oh, I know. I haven't fought in a while, so I was slightly out of practice, but it was a good fight for getting my muscles warmed up.' Emile said. She looked... happy. She looked better when she was happy, small dimples forming in her cheeks. I found myself smiling back at her.

'Okay, guys, we're having a break until after dinner so I can sort out what we're going to work on.' Desmond said. I coughed lightly and let my smile drop.

'Oh. Well, I'll be in my room if you need me.' I mumbled, my head spinning as I remembered where I was. And the strange look on Desmond's face that filled me with confusion: an unusual emotion.

☆★☆

I was back in the arena at 12:30. Walking in stole my breath, again, but it wasn't as bad as it had been the day before; at least, this time, it was bearable.

Emile and I were up together, then. We weren't using helmets, as they were too heavy to wear for so long, but the rest of our bodies were fully armoured.

Desmond came in front of us; his shield was at the stands, weirdly enough. I spared a glance at Emile, but she wasn't looking back.

'For the first half of this lesson, we're going to work on defence.' he said loudly. My eyebrow shot up; I was good at defence, but it wasn't as much of a thing from birth as it was something I had strained to learn.

'This is to help you, Emile. You're skilled with offence, but when it comes down to you only having a shield to fight with, it might just crumble. I'm not saying it will, as it probably won't, but if you were to come across a particularly skilled warrior and you were in that situation, it could end up bad.' Desmond said. I saw Emile nod out of the corner of my eye; she was better at taking criticism than I thought she would be.

'Maximus; you are skilled with a shield, no doubt, but I can see it isn't as easy as handling a sword is, for you. If I could see that, then a trained eye could definitely spot it. You think too much when you use it; you have to focus on the opposite side, not on what position will work the best in your advantage.' Desmond said. I was slightly startled by how accurate he was, but used to it from

Nathaniel's constant degrading. I could feel Emile's eyes on me as I gave a sharp nod.

'Now, Emile, I want you to put your sword aside. Maximus, you can do the same.' Desmond carried on. Hesitantly, I placed my sword next to Emile's on the nearest seat.

'Emile can go first. Take a seat if you wish, Maximus.'

I sucked in a breath and sat next to the swords.

Emile's freckles had gone quite pasty; you could tell how much she valued her sword during a battle. That weakness would make it easier for me to defeat her when the real war began. If Desmond hadn't fixed it by then.

It wasn't that Emile herself needed fixing; there were just certain flaws that would cause her end. I didn't like to think of it that way, considering I knew I would eventually be the one to make that end. I didn't care for Emile; I just hated taking lives in general. But I forgot any sense of human decency when I was in the battle.

'Focus, Emile. Think. Imagine. You haven't got a sword in this scenario. For example, it might've been snapped in half, or thrown in a lake, or stolen. Whatever it is, you can't get it back.' Desmond said slowly. I watched as Emile swallowed hard. 'What do you do in this situation?'

'You take the enemy's weapon.' The answer came from her faster than light. But she didn't look pleased by it. In fact, she looked grim.

'Correct. You take my sword. But how are you to do that when I'm in possession of both the sword you want and a shield?' Desmond pushed.

'I- I don't know.' Emile mumbled. Her cheeks were tinged pink.

'Exactly. You aren't meant to know. Unless you're some kind of psychopathic genius, you won't be able to make a plan in such little time.' Desmond grinned. The plan I had formed in my mind quickly vanished at the words.

'Well, what am I supposed to do, then?' Emile demanded, frustrated. She looked irked, then, her free hand resting on her hip in an aggravating manner.

'You relax. You need to really feel this shield as if it's a part of you; it's your lifeline, the only way of protecting yourself. Without it, you're dead, and that's the truth. Your main focus is keeping the shield on you at all times; knock my sword from my hand, take me by surprise, do anything that will get a weapon back on your side.'

Emile didn't answer. She was waiting for it to start, waiting for it to be over with, by the looks of it. She wasn't one that took to losing very well, and it seemed like she had already made up her mind about not winning this fight.

Rule number 1, I thought; *never go into a fight thinking you're going to lose.*

Desmond must have seen the doubt lain across her features, too, as he faltered for a moment.

'Another thing; the glass is half full, not half empty.'

He had taken the words from my very mind.

I saw fear flash in Emile's eyes swiftly as Desmond started moving; but it was gone as quick as it came.

She was doing surprisingly well. But, as I had figured would happen, Desmond got the shield out of her hand and cornered her. Emile huffed out in feigned annoyance, but her smile came back after a second. It wasn't too bad of a smile, really.

'You thought about it too much and it frightened yourself. You were acting like Maximus, except for the fact he seemingly has no fear.' Desmond said. That was wrong; I was scared of many things. I didn't waste such a vulnerability on something I was good at.

'Speaking of Maximus, come on up. Emile can take your seat.' Desmond added. I stood up and went towards him, crossing past Emile.

'Okay, then. So, I've picked up, by this point, that you're very attentive. Now, just because you have a hawks eye, doesn't mean your enemy is going to be blind. In fact, they could be even better at your own specialty than you are. You're not as good with a shield, and that's going to be used against you. We need to work on it so it's as easy as breathing.' Desmond said. He was much kinder than Nathaniel ever was.

'The only way to reach perfection is to have a perfect image.' I mumbled. Many times I had a corrupt vision, and many times it had almost caused my end.

'Right. But you can't be perfect. Everyone has flaws, everyone has weaknesses; even you. But to be the best you possibly can be, you have to work with the flaws. Make them work in your favour. Flaws aren't some disease that you have to get rid of; they're a part of you, and the first step to overcoming them is accepting them.' His words were full of a wisdom I couldn't comprehend. 'What would you do if the enemy found your weakness before you had found theirs?'

I spoke before even thinking. 'I would make the weakness invisible; I would conceal it within me until what came out was rage, at myself, at him, at my eyes for not working quick enough, and I would channel it into the fight.'

'That's a good tactic, it is. But weaknesses don't become invisible; I know what you're saying. You would trick them into thinking that the weakness wasn't a weakness. It's smart and if anyone could pull it off, it would be you. But, sometimes, wit doesn't overpower strength. Think about it, this time, and answer again.'

I stood for a few moments. It wasn't often that I had to think about things; most of the time I already had what I needed at the tip of my tongue. But I understood what Desmond was saying, and it wouldn't hurt to learn from an outsider. It would certainly help when going against him.

'I would do as you said, then. I would work with the weakness and make it into something powerful. For example, my shield is my weakness. I would throw away my shield, as I did with you earlier, and take the advantage of surprise while I had it.' I said. The shield trick was an old one of mine, but there would be plenty of times where it wasn't my shield that was my weakness.

'Surprise wouldn't be the only thing you induced. People have weaknesses for a reason; they're afraid of them. They make you feel exposed, weak. But if you use them in the right way, they can become so much more than just another silly liability.' Desmond's eyes flickered over to Emile, who was watching in fascination. 'As lovely as that chat was, I think Emile's feeling left out. Come on up, dear.'

☆✯☆

'What do you think Desmond's weakness is?' Emile asked. We were in the weapons room, putting away our helmets, swords and shields. My head spun around so I was facing her full on.

'What do you mean?' I said cautiously. I was acting stupidly naive on purpose; I didn't have a feasible lie for the question.

'I mean that he was saying all that stuff about *being one with your flaws* and all that, but he had to know that from somewhere, and he never had a tutor. So he must've found out for himself.' she paused, running a hand through her hair. 'So what was it that triggered that? What's *his* weakness?'

I regarded Emile for a moment. She was so outgoing, so boisterous that it seemed ridiculous to share such a secret with her. Especially after only knowing her for two days. Especially after hating her and her people my whole life. Especially because I was there to figure out how to kill her.

But it wasn't my secret; it was Desmond's. And, from what I could gather, they'd known each other for a long time. They weren't secretly on opposite sides, too.

I decided, almost begrudgingly, that it wouldn't hurt anyone if I told her what I knew.

'I think his weakness is a fear of himself.'

Emile looked at me like I was mad. But when she realised I was being serious, it turned to faint bewilderment.

'Desmond? Afraid of himself? For a start, how is that even possible? And, secondly, how do you know that?' Emile rambled.

'Technically, I don't know. Not for sure, anyway. But I can see it in the way he deflates at his reflection from his sword, in the way his face falls every time he beats one of us, in the way he winces at any mention of his past in the army.' There were more things I could add to the list, but if I said everything I could, I'd never finish speaking.

'Why would that show him being afraid of himself, though?' Emile asked curiously.

'I don't think it's necessarily him in general that scares him; it's the idea of what he is. What he's done. What he's become. It's like you said; he didn't have a tutor or anyone who could teach him the art of killing, and we all know that any sane person doesn't enjoy it. He's seen men and women die at his hands, hundreds, if not thousands, of them. That's what scares him.' I said. Emile looked astounded.

'Why is your brain so complex?'

'It isn't. I just look at things from a different perspective.'

Emile didn't remove her gaze from me. I felt like I was under some sort of spotlight. In return, I held eye contact with her for as long as I could, willing for her to look away first. She did, and I nearly gasped in relief.

'Are you going to sleep?' Emile said. I looked at the time. It was only 11:30, but I was still tired from my lack of sleep the night before.

'If I can, yeah.' She didn't ask what I meant by that, much to my relief.

'I'm staying up, so just go up now, if you want.'

I hesitated. I wanted to go to sleep, but it was a perfect chance to get to know her better. The more I knew, the easier it would be to finish the task and leave.

'What are you doing?' I questioned. She raised an eyebrow at my sudden interest.

'I'll just be reading in the library. Why?' Emile said. I considered it for a moment, but eventually decided I was too tired to stay up. Besides, I had training the next day.

'I was just wondering. Good night.' I said, walking away.

'Good night.' Emile called back, her voice soft. I stopped in my tracks and turned around. She was watching me, just as I thought she would be, her eyes glazed over. My breath hitched in my throat.

'Don't let the bedbugs bite.' I whispered.

Then, I was gone.

⚔ Chapter Five ⚔

BEFORE I KNEW IT, February was over, taking winter with it. The flowers had begun to blossom and the woods were filled with dark green grass; spring was truly one of my favourite seasons.

By then we were in some sort of a routine. Training on weekdays, resting on weekends, and barely any spare time. I had been trying to find a way to forge more information, but I was far too exhausted. Luckily for me, Desmond decided that, because we were doing so well, we could spend Fridays off, too.

Emile and I weren't very close. We had a strange friendship; we talked only when it was needed, but at times I could feel her eyes burning into my back. I knew that time was passing quickly, and that I needed to get a move on if I wanted this to be successful.

I mulled all of that over as I picked at my breakfast with a fork, resting my head on my free hand. It was one of those moments when she was close enough for me to hear her heart beating, but with no idea of what to say.

The silence was jarring. I looked up to see her staring at me; she didn't try to act like she wasn't.

'Are you going to eat that?' Emile asked. I clenched my jaw; all she ever thought about was food, for goodness sake.

'I'm not hungry.'

'Neither.'

That's a day I'll remember; Emile Elires doesn't want to stuff her face with junk.

Still, we sat there. I took a sip of my water. She did the same. I was madly trying to come up with something to say, but my antisocialness wasn't working in my favour. So much for Desmond's lessons on *working with your weaknesses*.

'How are you?' I said eventually. It was unnaturally formal, as we'd known each other for over a month now. But it seemed our relationship hadn't made any progress; she was still loud and unashamed while I was still awkward and introverted.

'Awful, actually. I feel like I'm drowning in my own fatigue. How about you?' Emile said.

'I'm fine.'

Silence.

I played with my fingers, absentmindedly, awkwardly; my mind was running a mile a minute, trying to think of what I could say to get her to open up without being too forward. Nothing came. It was exasperating, as I usually had an answer for every situation.

'I expect, as you're so tired, you'll spend your day sleeping?' I said. It was a trick question; no one in their right mind would spend a day off sleeping, especially if it was Emile. She seemed to barely sleep as it was.

'Me? Spend a day sleeping?' she scoffed, face incredulous. 'Have you lost your mind?'

'It was only a question. Don't get so defensive.'

'I'm not.' She was very tiresome, for all she was pretty.

That was another thing about Emile; she was drop-dead gorgeous. I would be foolish to say otherwise; anyone would be. She had a way of looking perfect at any moment, all of the time. George would scold me for thinking such, as she didn't meet the

Rendan beauty standards whatsoever with her flaming hair and amber freckles, but even after that he would admit that she was, in fact, gorgeous. I supposed it might've just been the way she held herself that made her so attractive.

'What will you be doing instead, then?' I said. The remnants of her offence faded; her emotions changed awfully fast. It was confusing at times. One minute she was laughing and jumping around, the next she was sitting against a wall with her head buried into her knees. I didn't understand it.

'I don't know, to be honest. I might have a wander around, outside, as the weather's so nice.' Emile said with a half-hearted shrug. 'What about you? How will you be spending your time?'

'I don't know.' *Why am I so bad at holding conversations?*

'Well, figure it out before the day wastes away.' Emile said sharply. Her voice held a note of authority; it felt like every word was a demand.

There it was again; that awful, awful silence. It was the kind of quiet that you could hear; a buzzing in your ears, so loud you wanted to tell it to shut up, but there wasn't any noise in the first place. It was a suffocating silence, a deafening silence, and it made me want to rip out my eardrums.

'I will.' I said, under my breath, my voice breaking through the hush like it was a layer of thin glass.

'I'm leaving, now. So hurry up and make up your mind. The days pass faster when you aren't paying attention, so stop being so indecisive for once and make a decision.' Emile said, walking out. I sat by myself for a few minutes before walking out of the kitchen and up the stairs.

I aimlessly paced the corridor of the second floor; my eye caught on the library door every few minutes, but I couldn't go in there. But I had felt that way about the arena, and going in had stopped the images all together. Perhaps the library would work in the same way...

My feet were taking me there before I could stop them.

I stood outside of the library door for a moment. It wasn't so bad from the outside.

Slowly, I pushed open the door and stepped in, letting it slam shut behind me.

My heart positively leapt into my mouth.

It was just like the arena, only ten times worse. At least when I was there I could protect myself. Here, I had nothing. Only my extensive mind running itself through every traumatic experience with a library it could find.

I leaned against the wall, squeezing my eyes shut. It didn't work. I could still smell old books, the aroma of burning candles. I coughed at the intensity of it's scent.

My eyes opened involuntarily. At first I was okay. But as soon as I started walking, it came back.

I winced as a certain memory took hold of me. It felt as if I was reliving them. I wanted to leave. But I realised that the only way to be okay with the place was to get over this idiotic fear of it. And I could do that by reliving every single moment my brain could conjure up.

It was simple, really; in the arena, as soon as I had no trauma left to offer, it went away. The process was long and painful, but it was worth it. So surely it would work the same way, there.

I must've been standing against a bookshelf, panting like a dog and trying desperately not to fall to the floor, for at least an hour. By the time I was stable enough to stand on my own, my knees had gone numb from the lack of movement.

I took a long breath of air. And the door swung open.

A fleeting breath of panic overtook me. Hastily, I spun around to face the shelf and pretended to be observing the books, trying to hold off any other memories.

The footsteps I heard were light, hardly audible at all. Desmond wouldn't be so gentle; it was quite clearly Emile. *How is she everywhere?*

I prayed she wouldn't find me, perspiration dripping from my face and my cheeks sunken. My prayers didn't work; they never did, anyway.

'Maximus; why are you in here?' Emile's voice said. I turned to see her walking towards me. *It's none of your business.*

'I'm finding a book.' *Idiot.*

Emile looked at me, almost suspiciously. I had made it quite clear over the past month that I did not read, unlike her. She had an obsession with the library and its contents.

'What kind of book?' she asked. I was expecting her to be excited, but her voice was a monotone. I repressed a frown.

'I'm not bothered. Any I suppose.' I said. Emile didn't move for a moment. But then she came beside me and observed the section I had previously been having a panic attack against, running her slender fingers over the spines of the books. I noticed that her hands were even paler than her face.

'What about this one?' Emile said, pulling one from its place. It looked older than the rest, and the cover was beaten and worn down. She held it so gently, like she was caressing it. I read the cover; *Maiden Tales for Before You Sleep.*

'What's it about?' I asked dumbly.

'Well, it hasn't got a specific topic, really. It's full of short stories.' Emile said wistfully. It was fascinating how much she loved fictional tales.

'Have you read it?' I said. Emile looked at me like I was thick in the head; I felt like it, anyway.

'Of course I have. I wouldn't have suggested it if I hadn't.' Emile said, her stern tone back.

'Every single story?' I said. It looked quite long, even for someone like Emile.

'Would you believe me if I said yes?' Emile said.

'Yeah.'

'Then yes. I have read them all.'

I wasn't that surprised, to be honest. If anything, I would've been shocked if she hadn't read them all.

'Which one's the best? I'll read that one, as I'm not very good at reading and couldn't do it all if I tried.' I said.

'I can't decide which is the best, it isn't up to me. I can only have a favourite.'

'Then tell me your favourite.'

I didn't know what she meant when she said it *wasn't up to her to decide which was the best*. I hadn't thought she'd take it so literally.

'If I had to choose, it would be the 28th story. It's on page 84.' Emile said after deep thought.

'Has it got a name?'

'It doesn't need a name. It's the story that counts.' She was being queerly sentimental.

'What's it about, then?' I asked.

'Oh, stop asking so many questions. It's barely a few pages long, for goodness sake, so just get it read.' Emile said in annoyance. Her temper was very short.

Tenderly, I took the book from Emile's clutch. She left her hands in the same position for a moment before letting them drop to her side. The palms of her hands were filled with cuts and marks; it was unusual, considering she was a princess.

'Are you picking a book, too?' I inquired.

'Never mind what I'm doing; go and have a read of that. I promise you'll like it.' Emile said. I nodded curtly and walked away. I didn't feel as out of breath, anymore, and the images had ceased. After an hour of torment, it seemed only right that they should go away.

There was still that pang in the back of my throat, though. It came every time I felt scared, upset or euphoric. I was guessing this was a moment of fear.

In the corner, there was an area with sofas and bean bags. It looked more modern, but there wasn't a reason it should be. I shook my head and sat on a couch, opening the book to page 84.

It was handwritten. Surely Emile knew how much it was worth; written by a feather quill from, by the state of it, hundreds of years ago. I didn't feel worthy of holding such an artefact.

But I read it. There was a reason that it was Emile's favourite, and that reason lay within it's pages. The reason could help me. I just had to read a singular short story.

I squinted. The scrawl was difficult to make out. It did have a name, after all. I wondered why Emile hadn't wanted to tell me what it was.

The Story of the Girl Who Evaded Death.

I read it over a few times, thinking back to my childhood and trying to remember if I'd ever heard of the name before. It was familiar, that was for sure. But I couldn't recall anything about it. So I divulged into its depths and read on.

Once upon a time, long long ago, lived a girl who went by the name April Meadows. Now, April was a girl of many talents. At the age of seven, she could throw a perfect axe and hit an impossible target, without even an ounce of training. She was especially talented in the way of the sword, as her young hands had a way of holding the weapon as if it were a baby, cradling it's handle in her grip.

Many young women were envious of her countless gifts. They would make plans and plot against Meadows, but anytime they came close to her, their plans failed and they were thrown back into their poor lifestyles. It seemed the teen had no weaknesses.

But, concealed beneath dazzling smiles and charming words, April had a weakness that was eating her from the inside out; a staggering fear of death itself.

Now, it seems strange to be afraid of something so natural, does it not? April tried to tell herself that over and over, but to no avail. She still felt that same pang of fear in her heart at any near death experience.

Meadows wanted to do things with her life, things she couldn't do in only a few decades. She wanted to be remembered. And that wouldn't happen if she was stuck in a grave, rotting and lifeless.

One day, in the month the girl was named after, April felt that pang of fear more strongly than usual. She was in the middle of a forest, with seemingly no way out, and could hear the wild animals in the distance.

Blinded by desperation and distress, April managed to rip out her own heart in her frenzied state, the dark blood staining her hands.

For a moment, she was at a loss. But then she remembered the clock in her pocket, a device filled with the magic of her deceased father. She pushed the clock in place of her heart, experimentally, and it, somehow, worked. April was gasping for air, the organ that held her life clasped in her red hands.

April ran back home, her instincts at their highest, clutching her heart to her shirt. She sprinted to her room and collapsed against the door, tears falling down her face. April entrapped the bane of her existence in a childhood plush toy, not entirely sure of what had happened. What she definitely did not know, however, was that the lack of her source of emotion would strip her of any redeemable features she might've once had.

A year passed in a flash, and April had become so cold and cruel that even her own mother couldn't comprehend what had happened. But, one night, Meadows held the plush toy that held her heart to her chest, gently squeezing it, she was overwhelmed by a rush of guilt. She had to tell her mum what was wrong; she had to tell her the true story.

So, that was exactly what she did. April opened up and revealed her worst secret, speaking until she was as empty as she had been hours before.

But her mother betrayed her. Disgusted by how her daughter had defiled her body and ripped apart her soul, Mrs Meadows seeked the plush toy and ripped it to shreds, destroying April's heart in the process.

And when April died on her knees at the doorway of her room, begging her mother for forgiveness as tears streamed down her pasty cheeks, Mrs Meadows felt no remorse.

See, this wasn't the first time that it had happened. April's father had committed the same thing, using the exact same clock that he himself had charmed to connect to his veins and heart, keeping him alive. He had kept his heart in a chest and thrown away the key, hoping to never experience the thing they called death.

But when Mr Meadows admitted that it was his 300th birthday, when April was only 3 years old, Mrs Meadows couldn't handle the shock. It was against nature's wishes to do such a thing, to live for so long with no sign of age, no sign of ever dying.

She stole the chest and threw it to the bottom of the ocean, watching in horror as water spewed from her husband's mouth and he choked to death in his pleas.

When asked, Mrs Meadows said that April had died from a heart disease inherited from her father. And when she thought about it, she realised it wasn't necessarily a lie.

As soon as I finished, my eyes scanned the room for Emile. She had left. Was I really that slow of a reader?

I looked over the pages again. The story was very… morbid. The whole idea of it was death. It made me worry why Emile liked it so much.

At first I thought *she* might be afraid of death. But it wasn't dying that she feared; I could see it in her eyes. It was losing she was scared of. In fact, she would probably rather be killed than lose in front of people. That made me think that she may fear humiliation, too.

With an exaggerated sigh, I stood up and pushed the old book back to its place on the shelf, it's rough feel staying on my skin after I had let go of it.

I was hit by a wave of vellichor. When I wasn't shaking and unable to breath, the library was curiously comforting.

☆★☆

The next time I saw Emile was the Sunday after. She was in the living room, sprawled out across the sofa, her fiery hair around her head like a halo.

'Hi.' I said. She didn't react; simply opened her eyes and sat up, staring at me with an unknown force. I squirmed a little.

'Hello.' Emile responded. Her voice sounded sleepy; a raspy tinge, I supposed.

'I read that story.' I said.

'What did you think of it?' Emile said. I didn't exactly know how to respond; I hadn't been thinking of my own opinion on it. I was more bothered about hers.

'It was different. Not a bad different; just different.' I said.

'How is it different?' She was very vexatious, sometimes; how was I supposed to know? I wasn't her student.

'The story; it was much darker than anything I've heard. I liked it, though.' I was lying through my teeth. Of course I'd heard of darker things; and I didn't even know if I liked it. I only read it in the first place because she told me to.

'Oh. Well, that's good.' Emile said. I snatched the opportunity as soon as it presented itself to me.

'Why did you tell me to read it?' I said.

'I already told you that. You asked me for my favourite, and I gave you that one.'

'Well, I know that. I was wondering why it's your favourite, really.' I pressed. At first, I thought she was going to shout at me, tell me to get out of her business; it seemed she was thinking of it, from the look on her face. But, suddenly, her features softened and she was speaking.

'I like how it reminds me not to succumb to my desires. If I'm ever having a bad day, or I'm thinking of doing something I'll regret, I reread that and it makes me remember that everything bad, no matter how good it feels, comes to an end. And that the end hurts more than the present.'

Her words were so… intelligent that it felt abnormal hearing them come from a seventeen year old's mouth.

'I don't know what to say.' I responded, quietly. I was right; she wasn't afraid of death. She was quite similar to Desmond. Only, instead of being afraid of herself, she was afraid of what she did.

'Give me some smart words in return, Maximus. You always have a way of making me feel like you're a thousand years old.' Emile said, laughing humorlessly. I couldn't tell if it was a compliment or not.

'I think that you shouldn't feel obliged to enjoy something because of a deeper meaning. Obviously there is always going to be that reason that makes you like it so much, but sometimes oblivion is better than knowing. I would rather appreciate something for the sake of it than because of some part of my subconscious relishing it.' I said. Emile stared at me. I wanted to look away, but I couldn't bring myself to. Her eyes, her dark blue eyes, seemed to have a hold on me.

'How are you so ingenious?' she asked. It was a rhetorical question, but I felt like I was being willed to speak.

'Maybe it isn't me that's smart; maybe all of you just don't look far enough.'

⚔ Chapter Six ⚔

THE SWORD HIT MY blade. I rolled my eyes and hit back, watching as Desmond dodged my blow with ease. We had been fighting nonstop for hours on end, and I had to admit, it was becoming quite tedious.

'You are getting better, you know.' Desmond said breathlessly, throwing his shield in front of his face as my sword swung forwards.

'I didn't know that was possible.' I said mockingly. I could feel his small smile from under his helmet. I could also feel royal blue eyes burning into my back.

'Don't get ahead of yourself, kid.' Desmond said. I was almost offended. To prove a point, I disarmed him, pulling my helmet off my face to show my smug expression when his sword went flying.

'Well done. That's the eighteenth match you've won in a row, now.' Desmond said, shaking my hand.

'Let's make it nineteen.' I said, grinning. I was just about to pull my helmet back on when I heard an unfamiliar noise; one I recognised to be a doorbell ringing.

Desmond frowned. The doorbell shouldn't have been going off; nobody was allowed to be here. As soon as I had arrived, extensive security measures had been placed all around the area, meaning that if anyone was there they had to have proof of identity, proof of relations to any of us, checks for weapons, checks for anything that held threat, and many more things. It seemed like it was a little much just for a visit, so whoever it was must have had an ulterior motive.

'Who is that?' I said. *Oh, yeah, because they're going to know.*

'I don't know.' Desmond responded. He sounded just as puzzled as I was; not very comforting.

I span around to look at Emile. She didn't seem as worried as Desmond and I; in fact, she looked bored.

'Do you know who it is?' I asked. Emile looked disdainfully out of the window.

'If I knew who it was, I would be a lot more excited than this.' she said, crossing her arms.

I turned back to Desmond. His hand was resting loosely on his knife and he was heading for the front door.

The wait for him to come back was intense. I tapped my foot impatiently, my eyes flickering to the clock now and then. After ten minutes had passed, I was about to go and see what was happening, but was stopped by Desmond finally coming back.

'Who is it then?' I asked, quickly. Desmond looked… suspicious, perhaps? He wasn't happy; relieved, maybe, but he looked like he was trying to figure something out, putting pieces together.

'I believe you'll recognise them when you see them.' Desmond said, stepping to the side. In came two people I thought I wouldn't see for at least another year.

'Hello, Maximus.' I dropped my sword; not so much from joy than shock. What joy would I have at seeing a person who used me like an object?

'I- Nathaniel.' I stammered. Nathaniel looked worse than usual; his skin was unnaturally pale, even though he was mixed race, and he looked as if he hadn't slept in weeks. He looked... weak. I could never say that out loud, as he would kill me on the spot, but I could think it all the same.

But there was someone else. Behind Nathaniel, another person entered, and another after that. They stopped there, coming forward so I could see who they were.

'George! What are you-' I cut off, my eyes catching on the girl next to him. She was only 12 years of age, her skin darker than her brother's and eyes a deep brown. I didn't see her much anymore, but I knew who she was.

'Adelaide; I haven't seen you since you were eight.' Four years ago. I hadn't seen my best friend's only sibling for four years.

'Hello.' Adelaide muttered. Her hair was frizzy and unbrushed; I caught Nathaniel throwing her annoyed glances because of it.

'Maximus, the Flint family have informed me that they would like to speak to you alone.' Desmond said, shifting his weight from one foot to another. I didn't move. I didn't want to speak to them alone; I had nothing they would wish to know, and was granted 11 more months as it was. Could they really not wait?

'How about the living room? I'm sure that is a perfectly comfortable place for you to catch up with Maximus.' Desmond said. I saw Nathaniel nod, but stayed planted on the spot. I could positively feel the blood drain from my face.

There was a minute of silence. Nathaniel glared at me and Desmond still looked wary, but I ignored them. It was Emile who finally broke the quiet; in all honesty, I had forgotten she was there.

'We'll leave, then, if Maximus is so adamant on staying.' she said. As soon as George and Adelaide saw her they proceeded to bow and curtsy, Nathaniel following their lead. Emile didn't even acknowledge it, instead trying to look me in the eye. I didn't let her.

'Come, Desmond.' The door slammed and doom washed over me; the arena was soundproof. He could do whatever he wanted to me without anyone finding out. The only aspect that would stop him would be Adelaide, but she was too young and naive to understand.

However, I remembered what I was like at her age and realised she wasn't so different in maturity to me. And, when I looked closer, I saw a faint purple bruise all around her eye. And the way she flinched when someone so much as raised their hand. And the way she cowered before her own father.

I'm going to kill him, one day.

'Take a seat, Maximus.' Nathaniel said, settling in the front row. I pulled a chair up in front of him and sat in it, trying to relax my shoulders. George was at his right, his arm around Adelaide.

'Why are you here?' I said in a low voice.

'What happened to your manners, Maximus? I'm afraid that your time with these thugs has had an impact on you.' Nathaniel responded smoothly, an eyebrow arched.

'Just answer the damn question.' I snapped. It was reckless speaking to him like that, but I was in control in that house. All I needed was one sign he was going to do anything and he was out.

'I'm only here to see how you're doing.' I knew he didn't mean in general; he only cared about the damn task. Of course, I cared about it, too; it was my turning point. It was going to be the thing that made me stand out in a good way, finally. But I wished he actually cared about *me*.

'It's only been a month, Nathaniel. You can't possibly think that I've found what we need in such little time.' I said in outrage.

'Don't get cheeky with me, boy.'

'Stop calling me 'boy' and maybe I'll think about it.'

Nathaniel looked like he wanted to slap me. I wanted to slap him in return, to be fair. But neither of us did. We both knew there would be consequences for our actions.

'Tell me what you know.' Nathaniel said shortly.

'Would you like to specify what it is exactly you wish to be told of?' I questioned.

'Tell me about Desmond. He seems like a threateningly good warrior, with a high level of training. Say anything that I can use against him.' Nathaniel demanded. *Very specific*, I thought bitterly.

'He's a strange one. An open book, yes, but in a strange way. He's afraid of what he has become. He doesn't like killing people, but has done so to hundreds. As you already know, he has experience with war, and will be a more difficult target. But he is easily shocked. Use the element of surprise against him, and he's all yours.' I said. Nathaniel thought over the information for a few moments.

'That's good, for the time you've had. But not enough. As he knows of the horrors of war, surprise won't be as effective on the battlefield. But I can use his guilt against him. Well done.' Nathaniel said.

'What else do you want?' I said. I just wanted him to leave. I didn't want to have to look at his awful, pointed face any longer.

'Tell me about the girl.' Desmond said. I felt a pang; I knew near to nothing about her. Emile was so secretive, so closed up, that the only thing I could think of that was relatively useful was her feeble skills with a shield, but that would be of no use. By the time the war began, she would've learnt all about the art of defence.

'Emile's harder to crack. We are acquaintances, and I know very little about her, but in time I'm sure I'll be able to give you what you want.' I said carefully.

'I don't care if it isn't useful, Maximus, just tell me what you know.' I bit on the inside of my cheek.

'She- she likes to read. And she has a scar above her collarbone that she doesn't like to speak about. And she has a name, in case you haven't noticed. I would appreciate it if you used it.' I said harshly.

'Is that all you can tell me? I know what you're like; you know everything about everyone from a single look. So figure it out. Surely there's something, Maximus.' Nathaniel said. I considered telling him about the defence thing; but if I did I would drown in my guilt. I was the one who would eventually have to kill her. Not him.

'There is nothing.' I said quietly. Nathaniel sighed.

'Very well, then. I will leave you and George to talk. He has been desperate to see you. Adelaide, come.' he said. George stood up.

'Adelaide wants to speak to Maximus, too. She idolises him for his bravery for coming here.' he said. I raised an eyebrow; it wasn't like George to be so forward.

'So you would go against what I say?' Nathaniel asked, voice more surprised than menacing. *Why does he think he's better than us?*

'I would be happy to speak with Adelaide.' I cut in. I could feel George's thankful expression. I chose to ignore it.

'Adelaide, is it true that you want to speak to him?' Nathaniel asked. I saw how wide Adelaide's eyes were and realised she was terrified.

'I- yes.' she said. Nathaniel left, finally, and it felt as if a weight had been lifted off my shoulders.

'He can't hear us?' George whispered. I shook my head. Before I knew it, I was being crushed into an embrace.

'Are you okay?' George asked after he let go of me.

'Yes, yes, I'm doing wonderfully. Well, not in means of the reason I am here in the first place, clearly, but I feel fine.' I said. 'What about you?'

'I'm good. I've missed you, you know. It feels a lot darker without you around.' George said, sitting back down.

'I'm surprised you think it's me who lightens the place. If anyone, I would say it's you.' I said. My gaze flickered to Adelaide. 'Why did you lie about her? She clearly doesn't want to be here.'

'I would like it if you didn't speak about me like I'm not here.' Adelaide said sharply. Her eyes widened, as if she were shocked at the sound of her own voice.

'I would rather her be here than out there alone with my father.' George said. There was the word father, again. I wished he would just say *pater*.

'Has he been hurting you?' I asked. I already knew the answer; the attempts made to cover her injuries were pathetic.

'Well, what do you think?' Adelaide mumbled, her cheeks red. I looked at George; he was desperately trying to conceal his anger.

'And what about you, George? Does he do to you what he does to her?' I said.

'It would be only fair, wouldn't it?' George said dryly.

'I'll kill him. Right now. I'll do it.' I said furiously. I knew that Nathaniel hit George; he had confided in me years before. But George had sworn he had stopped, and it was the only reason I didn't turn down the task. I didn't know if he had lied or if Nathaniel had just gone back to his abusive self. I knew for sure he never stopped with me.

'No, no; you have to wait until the moment is right. Besides, we have other things to talk about.' George said. 'I want to know everything. Adelaide won't tell father a thing; she's grown exceptionally good at keeping secrets. So spill your guts.'

'Where do you want me to start?' I said.

'Tell us about Emile, please! I've never met a princess before; what is she like? Mind you, she's gorgeous.' Adelaide said dreamily. *I know she is.*

'Oh, well, she's very outgoing. Talks a lot. Whenever we speak, she carries the conversation. As I said before, she loves reading and the library. She shared a short story with me a week ago, but it was a bit dark for both of your likings.' I said.

'Tell us more about her! I want to know if she's as lovely as she looks.' Adelaide pushed.

'Um, well, she's stubborn. Really nice and supportive, but doesn't like losing. I think she would rather die than lose. Though, I don't think I should be telling you the good things; if you end up attached it'll be my fault.' I contradicted.

'Maximus is right, Adelaide.' George said. Adelaide looked slightly abashed for a moment, but she was back to asking questions soon enough.

'You said there's a library. Is it big? What does it smell like?'

'Um, yeah, it's really big. Like, the size of this arena big.'

'Maximus.' George said, suddenly. I blinked and nodded my head at him, gesturing for him to carry on speaking. 'You went to the library?'

I remembered then that George knew of my... experiences with libraries. He was the only person I'd ever told about them.

'Yes.' I said quietly. George didn't say anything else about the topic; he had been through as much as I had in that room.

'Wait, since I'm not allowed to know the good things about princess Emile, could you tell me the bad things?'

'Adelaide, if you're so interested in her why don't you just meet her yourself?' George said. 'That is, of course, if you're allowed.'

'Of course she is.' I said with a frown. 'You go, too. Tell Nathaniel I want to speak to him, again, on your way out.'

'Are you sure you want to be with him alone?' George asked.

'I'm sure.' There was a pause.

'Don't do anything foolish Maximus.' George called on his way out. 'And don't grow too attached.'

I didn't have time to ask what he meant; the door was already shut and the arena empty.

Nathaniel entered quickly after. He looked almost eager as he practically ran to the stands, but his eyes were cold and hard. They were always cold and hard.

'Have you remembered something, then?' he asked. I was expecting at least a trace of excitement in his voice; instead there was nothing. It was a monotone, plain and even.

'I have remembered something in a different manner to the one you want.' I said silkily.

'What do you mean?' Nathaniel questioned. I nearly laughed at his feigned innocence.

'You didn't *really* think that you had done a good job of covering Adelaide's black eye, did you?' I said.

'It wasn't supposed to be a good job, I'm afraid; it was supposed to stop people with a less attentive eye from seeing it.'

'So you're finally admitting it? It's funny, you never could do that with George and I. How is he, by the way? I've heard you've gone back to a certain habit involving him.' I said.

'I suggest you don't say anything else.' he said slowly.

'Oh, well that's a shame, because I'm done listening to what you suggest. Do what you want to me; as soon as I get the chance, you're dead.' I snapped. A sharp pain bloomed in my cheek as I realised I'd been slapped.

'Keep on going like this and you'll have another scar among the others on your stomach.' Nathaniel said. I didn't speak any more; I knew he was being truthful from the careful way of his words, from the way his voice did not change in tone or texture or loudness whatsoever. But he did it anyway. And no amount of biting on my tongue could prevent the screams that left my lips.

☆★☆

It turned out that I didn't have the power to kick Nathaniel out as soon as I saw fit; I realised that as I traced the fresh cut that went across my belly button, wincing in pain.

As soon as I had gotten out of the arena, they went back. George knew something was wrong; I could tell in the way he looked at me. But I was in my room before he could ask any questions.

Without thinking, I let my fingers go over the rest of the scars. They felt raw in the new pain. I hadn't been given one of those things for at least a year; they were the worst kind of punishment.

His words rang through my head, torturing my mind. He spoke about George, first; he said that he would kill him, break every bone in his body, carve his name into his skin. He spoke of all the things he'd make George do before, slowly torturing him as he begged for his life, forcing him to do things that George would never dream of doing. All just to kill him.

He didn't say anything about Adelaide. For a while after, I pondered over why that may be, but he was only speaking of people I truly cared about. It sounded awful, but I didn't really care for Adelaide herself; I only really protected her for George.

The person after that was Desmond. *The piece of Kendran scum can choke on his own vomit*, he had hissed. Somehow, Nathaniel had found out about his Domvan parentage, but the racial inequality was strong, and Nathaniel thought it would be humorous to make fun of it.

To be quite clear, it was not humorous.

And then he spoke of Emile. I flinched as I replayed the words in my head, over and over again until they were sound only. Until they were hardly a humming sort of noise in the back of my brain. A whirring. A white noise that refused to quieten.

'I'm going to torture her in ways that you can't even imagine.' he whispered, his voice slithering in and through my ears, penetrating my eardrums.

'You underestimate my imagination, Nathaniel.' I had said flatly, the pain so strong it was numbing itself.

'Oh, I am sure that I don't.' He paused, dragging his nail across the fresh gash searing my skin. 'It's a good thing that I'm going to tell you exactly what I'm going to do with your lovely little princess, then: isn't it?'

Images flooded my head and my neck arched back as I groaned aloud.

The day I kill Nathaniel Flint will be unforgettable.

However, the problem haunting my head was much different to that one.

The problem of how I was going to look Emile in the eye after hearing what I had heard.

⚔ Chapter Seven ⚔

THE FIRST TIME EMILE tried to approach me was two days later. I had been avoiding her, but it came to nothing on a Friday morning when Desmond was sleeping and I was in the living room by myself.

I was playing with my fingers absently, slouched against the comfortable leather of the sofa. I didn't even notice that she had walked in until she sat down beside me. I froze for a moment. The words filled my ears. I couldn't think of her in the same way.

'Good morning, Maximus.' Emile said with a delicate smile. I didn't look at her. I couldn't, even if I tried.

'Hi.' I mumbled. I suddenly felt very light; the weight had shifted over to her slightly. She was so close. More words from his dirty mouth. More evading eye contact.

'So, how are you?' Emile inquired. She was being so formal. I was being so formal. It wasn't right. But every time I heard her voice I felt the pain return in the scar on my stomach, and it reminded me of what he had threatened to do. The urge to kill him was even stronger.

'I'm fine. And you?' My voice cracked. I felt ill.

'I feel wonderful. I was wondering if you could tell me more about Adelaide? She's bright. She has a big future ahead of her, I think.' Emile said with a smile. *Calm down. I can do this. It isn't that hard. You're only speaking to her, for heaven's sake.*

'Oh. Well, she's only twelve years old, but she probably said that.' I stuttered. Every word was a reminder. I had overestimated myself. I couldn't do it.

'Are you alright?' Emile said, worry laced within her tone.

'I- I have a headache. I'm going to my room.'

I could feel her confused stare on me as I rushed off.

☆✫☆

The second time I was approached was merely the day after. She had caught me pacing the corridors of the second floor and thought it would be a good idea to engage in conversation with me. It wasn't a good idea at all.

'Maximus! There you are; I couldn't find you yesterday.' she said. Somehow, she was oblivious to my discomfort.

'Emile. Hello.' I said in return, I had stopped walking at that stage, and was trying not to move on the spot.

'How's your head?' she asked. She sounded so genuinely concerned that I felt a little bad for lying, but it was better than enduring the pain of speaking to her. The memory was too fresh in my mind. Perhaps I could handle it better after a night's sleep.

'It's much better. I- I suspect I was-' I cut off. I wasn't ready. I couldn't face her. I would end up telling her, and then he would kill me, only to carry out the awful deeds. I swallowed the lump in my throat. 'I suspect I was merely dehydrated.'

'Oh, well I'm glad you feel better.' Emile said. 'Was the boy your friend, George? And the man Nathaniel? Desmond mentioned them both before you came, but I must admit, I had forgotten they were Rendan. Their accents were so similar to yours that they could've passed off for Kendran, had they wished.' She laughed gently, but stopped when she saw I wasn't laughing with her.

'Yes, they were.' I said. My voice cracked, again. I was pathetic; if I couldn't handle a few threats, how could I handle a war?

'Oh. Well, are you sure you're okay? I'm sorry if this offends you, but you look terrible.' Emile said. I cleared my throat.

'I- maybe I'm not fully better, after all. I'm going to get a glass of water.'

I didn't know why it was affecting me so much.

☆✹☆

The third time was partly my fault. It was lunchtime on a training day, and Desmond wasn't in the kitchen. I felt slightly better about the situation, but it was still troubling me. If he had said the words so easily, how easy would it be to actually do it?

I swallowed a piece of meat. I didn't know what the meat actually was; I wasn't paying attention to that. My eyes had wandered to Emile, sitting opposite me, her red hair falling in strands in front of her face. It was the first time I could bring myself to look at her for a week, so it made it exceptionally hard to rip my gaze off her.

She looked up and caught my eye. Royal blue on stormy grey. I wanted to look away; the images were painful and revolting. But I couldn't bring myself to.

'Are you talking to me, yet?' She sounded hurt. That hurt me. I wasn't doing it on purpose; I was postponing the inevitable.

'I'm always up for talking to you.' I said. It was a lie. I still wasn't ready, and I knew it, but I couldn't keep on preventing seeing her. If I wanted to complete the task, I would have to get a grip of myself and stop acting like a child.

'Really? You've been avoiding me like the plague!' Emile said, slightly angry. I looked away. She was only going to make it worse.

'Oh, don't flatter yourself.' I said roughly. I knew she was glaring at me, but I had a bigger worry. My mind was filled with the images, intrusively, and I was unable to ward them off. My vision was blurring from the unfairness of it. I hadn't asked to be thrown into that mess. I just wanted to be back in my warm bed, before I had been scarred again, both physically and mentally.

'When you've come to terms with how rude you're being, you can speak to me.' she said promptly. Sharply.

I knew a dismissal when I heard one.

☆★☆

The fourth time was a week later. It was nearing April and I had made no more progress. I couldn't speak to her. Whenever I tried I was swarmed with the images, playing out before me as if they were real, and I would run away, as I ran from all of my problems.

I was in the living room. It felt like a repeat of the first time. Only, this time I was slightly calmer, and slightly more stressed at the same time. It confused me just thinking about it.

This time, she sat on the armchair opposite me. Usually I sat there, but I was lying across the sofa that time, my eyes shut tightly and my breathing fast. I could feel her presence; it made me feel disorientated.

'Are you sleeping?' Emile asked softly. I considered not answering, letting her believe I had drifted off. But my mouth ran itself off.

'No.' I replied. I didn't dare open my eyes. If I did, I would be consumed by the images and words that haunted me. The sound of her voice was enough to alarm my subconscious, but it didn't do anywhere near as much harm.

'Will you at least tell me what I've done wrong?' Emile asked. I wanted to tell her the truth so bad, it was eating me alive. I was known for my honesty, especially when it was brutal, in Rendo; it felt wrong to go against my most identifiable trait. But I couldn't tell her. It would ruin everything.

'You have done nothing.' I said. She let out an exasperated breath.

'If I had done nothing then you would be able to look me in the eye without flinching. Spare me the agony, please! It's exhausting!' Emile declared.

'I can't tell you what is not true.' I said quietly. *But I can. And I will continue to do so.*

'I refuse to speak to you until you can tell the truth.' Emile said adamantly. *If you knew, you would never speak to me again.*

'Then it should be an ease to converse with me, as I have spoken nothing but the truth.' I said.

'I will not talk of this anymore when your eyes are closed and you're speaking to me like I'm your grandmother.' Emile snapped. I heard the patter of her feet and I was alone, yet again.

I wish I knew my grandmother to speak to her like this.

☆✹☆

The fifth time was so short and uneventful I nearly forgot it had happened at all. It was in the kitchen that same afternoon, when Emile had come back from hunting in the woods. For some reason, she enjoyed taking the lives of animals to eat them, even though she was at the expense of all the food she could wish for. It didn't make much sense.

I walked in, testing my emotional strength in a way, seeing if I could speak to her. She turned away from the rabbit she was unpacking. Her hair was tied up in a loose bun, her hunting gear still on. I fought to stay looking at her.

'Before you ask, I have not come to tell the truth. Or whatever it is you think is the truth, anyway.' I said.

'Then leave.' Emile said, curtly. I supposed she was always one for holding grudges. But the images, fresh in my mind, weren't leaving, and it felt only right she should know part of it.

'You- you wouldn't understand. I- I'm sorry. I might not have been entirely truthful with you, but I am deeply sorry.' I said. Her gaze was even and steady.

'I said leave, Maximus.' she repeated, simply. I nodded once and scuttled off like an infant. I felt like an infant. I felt awful. Like an awful infant.

I could not keep my mind away from her for the rest of that day. Not in a good way; in a terrible way. She would kill me if she knew what I knew, and I couldn't cope with feeling so... worried for her.

Worry. An odd feeling. I would not have felt it at all if the threat had been death or violence; she could live with the violence, come to forget it. And as for death; it was only an exit from a useless existence.

However, the threat itself was something much harder to live with. I couldn't live with myself if I let that happen to anyone, not just her. I didn't know why, but the thought of someone having to live out their days, knowing that someone had done that to them, made me feel sick to the stomach.

☆★☆

The sixth and final time was the day after, in the library. I felt like my mind was going to explode, so I went there, seeking a way out. It had been, for about an hour. The curious comfort in the burning candles, the overwhelming vellichor, the old books; it was enough to calm the most anxious of minds.

I was standing between two bookshelves when she came in, straight in the middle of both of them. I didn't move when she strode up to me; I focused on the aroma, trying to push myself away from reality.

Until I was pushed into a bookshelf.

I gasped aloud as her hand came in contact with my chest, spinning me around and shoving me against the structure. Her eyes were full of determination, an unwavering goal. It felt like my feet were glued to the floor. I was too shocked to leave, too shocked to move.

'Good afternoon.' Emile said calmly.

'What are you doing?' I asked, looking down to where her hand was loosely clutching my shirt.

'I'm making sure you don't run away like a baby.' Emile responded, shooting a careless glance towards her hand.

'Could you not have done it in a more civilised way?' I said, partly amazed and partly enraged.

'I have tried to be civil with you for weeks now, and it has come to no avail. Look at what I, a princess of high honour, has had to resort to.' Emile said. It annoyed me how she took nothing seriously.

'What do you want?' I asked, irritably. It came out more cruel than I had hoped, and I immediately regretted it. I was trying to get closer to her, not make her hate me. Luckily, Emile wasn't as sensitive as she acted, and she simply raised an eyebrow at me.

'I just want us to speak like normal people. Come on, Maximus; you don't have to tell me what's bothering you. But you should stop avoiding me; it's really quite lonely when the only person your age doesn't even want to be around you.'

'I never said that I didn't want to be around you.'

'Then stop acting like it!' Emile took a deep breath. 'I'm sorry. I'm not mad at you. Honestly.'

'It's fine.' I said. 'I'm sorry, too. I'm just stressed out. I didn't mean to take it out on you.' It wasn't necessarily a lie.

'Don't feel sorry for feeling stressed. It was just really weird when you were speaking all posh with me. I thought you knew how much I hated it.' Emile said. *I did know. But I didn't care. Because I'm a horrible person. And you shouldn't be speaking to me.*

'I won't do it again.'

Emile gave me a small smile. The pressure of her skin was making my chest burn up. She was holding so effortlessly I could slip away if I wanted. But I stayed. If it kept on going the way it was, progress would most certainly be made.

'Good. If you do, I won't be so forgiving.' Emile warned.

'I'm sorry, but your forgiveness is not worth very much to me, Your Highness.' I joked.

'If you *ever* call me 'Your Highness' again, I might be sick.' Emile laughed. I realised, then, that her laugh wasn't as perfect as I'd convinced myself it was. It was wheezy and consisted of few snorts, but I had made it sound angelic. I frowned internally. How had I not seen that?

It wasn't that I liked her laugh any less. In fact, I liked it better when it's imperfections were out on show, bold and daring. It made me laugh, too; and not at it. With it.

'That wasn't even funny; I don't know why we're laughing.' Emile said, her dark eyes light. I was suddenly submerged by a wave of scent, all from her.

Coffee, smoke, and that smell the earth had after it had finished raining. Petrichor was the word for it. She smelled of coffee, smoke, and petrichor.

'I don't know, either.' I said quietly, after we had stopped giggling. It was strange that her scent was so obscure, considering she was a princess. I would've expected something more expensive, not what I was greeted with. I wasn't complaining, though.

'Well, I'm glad we're on good terms.' Emile stepped back, her hand falling from me. It didn't fall far, though, as it was quickly stretched out towards me. 'Friends?'

I hesitated for only a second before taking her hand and shaking it. I suppose that was the moment our strange relationship became a fragile friendship.

'Before you go to your room; it's my birthday next week. I'll be eighteen.' Emile said. I didn't understand why she was telling me that, but answered all the same.

'I turned eighteen in December.' I paused. 'Which day?'

'Wednesday. The 4th of April.'

'You're lucky; four is a lucky number.' Emile chuckled lightly at my words.

'I suppose it makes me luckier that my birthday is in the 4th month, then?'

'I suppose it does.' There was a beat where silence overcame us. I swallowed. 'I'll be sure to get you a present.' I said, before going to my room.

I lay awake that night. Thinking. Planning. Plotting. Mainly just thinking.

My chest felt cold. I could feel the imprint of her hand, her soft fingers, the papercuts in her skin, the lines etched upon its palm. I placed my own hand there to try and make it warm again, but it didn't work. It was cold inside of me. An icy cold.

Her fragrance was all I could smell. The coffee, the bitter coffee, so painfully pleasant. The petrichor, the earthy petrichor, so queerly soothing. And the smoke. I didn't know how she smelled of smoke, but it was there, and possibly the most distinctive of them all. The smoke, the consuming, but yet awful smoke. The one that kept me up at night.

I could finally say that she was my friend. My second friend ever; George's words rang through my head at that thought. *And don't grow too attached.*

It was not an attachment to be someone's friend when the friendship wasn't real; I would use the friendship to gain trust, information, and then leave Kendra as soon as she revealed what I needed. Besides, how could I ever be attached to someone like her? Arrogant, extroverted, obstinate.

She was the complete opposite of me.

But I still found myself in the situation where I couldn't take my mind off her. Perhaps it was just her valiant gesture; her thrusting me against a shelf was quite preposterous, but it achieved what she wanted it to.

I shouldn't have been happy about that. But I was.

I bit on my lip. It was natural to care for people; a normal human thing. I cared for people before I killed them. I cared for Nathaniel, once upon a time.

But Emile wasn't Nathaniel. It was horrific to even think of comparing the two.

Still, I wouldn't give my own life, my own reputation, to save some silly princess. It was ridiculous to think that I would. No, I had worked far too hard for far too long to give it up.

Her hair flashed before the eyes of my mind. It was darker than the blood that stained my hands. But that made it more beautiful, in an immoral, profane way. She was quite scary, I had to admit. Her fierceness rivalled that of my own, and her indignation was to be feared on a good day.

No. I couldn't let myself think of her like that, I *would* not. After all, the day would come where I had to kill her, and George had a point. I had a knack for getting attached. And I knew that, if there was another way, I would take it. I would take it in a heartbeat.

I groaned and rolled over to my side, squeezing a pillow into my head. It wasn't until I was falling asleep that I realised I had not seen the images since before I had seen her. She'd stopped them.

Somehow, she had stopped them.

⚔ Chapter Eight ⚔

It was Monday the 2nd of April. Two days before Emile's birthday. We had been informed, the previous night, that we would be learning archery in training, today. That wasn't good. My aim was my one fatal fault. Surely they would realise I was, in fact, useless when I proved my lack of skill with a bow and arrow.

I was the final person to get to the clearing in the woods, the place where we would be learning the skill. The bows and arrows were already there, my knife laying in the draw of my bedroom. I felt vulnerable without some sort of weapon that I could actually use, and I didn't like it.

Emile and Desmond were talking when I arrived, the bows scattered across the floor and the targets set and ready. I already knew that it was going to go massively wrong, on my half.

'Maximus, there you are! Can we get started now?' Emile said.

'Alright, alright, get yourselves a bow and a sheath each. They have enough arrows for the lesson in them.' Desmond said. I bit my cheek and grabbed them both, flinging the sheath over my shoulder. I was already starting to panic.

'So, which one of you wants to go first?' Desmond said. I instinctively took a step backwards.

'I will happily do the honour.' Emile said, getting into stance. *Of course she has good aim; she's constantly disappearing to hunt.*

Emile hit the target, a small can, on her first try. I winced when Desmond called me up, looking with disdain at what I had to try and knock over. All of the targets were the same; empty cans. But it was so small I could hardly see it, nevermind hit it. With a sigh, I pulled an arrow from the sheath and squinted.

I didn't hit it. Of course I didn't. I hadn't expected to. The look of disappointment on Desmond's face was dismaying, though.

'I don't have a very good aim.' I mumbled. I could feel the heat crawling up from my neck to my cheeks.

'Don't kick yourself about it, son. We'll work on it.' Desmond said encouragingly. But there was no mistaking the disheartened look in his eyes.

'I don't think aim is something you really 'work on'. It's just one of those things. I don't have to be good at everything.' I said uncomfortably.

'Don't be daft, Maximus.' I looked to my side. I'd nearly forgotten that Emile was there. She didn't look as downcast as Desmond; in fact, she looked amused, if anything.

'I'm not being daft.' I said.

'Yes, you are. I wasn't just born being able to do all of this. I had to learn it. Just because you're naturally talented at one thing, doesn't mean you get the full pack.' Emile said.

'You're making me sound like a brat.'

'You're *acting* like a brat.'

My eyebrows knitted together. I wasn't being that bad; I was simply stating that I didn't think I could learn to have good aim. She was thinking too much about it; although, I couldn't really say anything when it came to that. I always thought too much.

'No I'm not.' I muttered, so quietly she couldn't hear.

'She's right, Maximus. We all know you're extremely gifted when it comes to swords and such, so we're just going to have to teach you how to use this.' Desmond said.

'You say it like I'm not always right.' Emile cut in.

'Well, you can attempt to teach me, but I'm not sure how it'll work out.' I said resentfully. Emile's face broke out into a sly grin.

Her cats grin.

'Trust me; it'll work out beautifully.'

☆✯☆

We spent the rest of that day sword fighting. As soon as I had a spare moment, I snuck a few tools from the weapons room and continued working on Emile's birthday present.

Because we were in the middle of a desolate countryside, I couldn't buy her a gift. So, instead, I was crafting one. It was made from oak wood, the only wood I could find in the woods, and I was carving it into a small sculpture.

I had spent the whole weekend trying to figure out what she would like. I was originally going to carve it into a mug, but it was too boring, too bland, and not enough for a princess. I had to strain to think of something she may like.

It hit me at a random moment. Her birthday was the 4th day of the 4th month; 4 being a number known for being lucky in both Kendra and Rendo. Emile had a fondness for rabbits, even if she did hunt them; and rabbits were also known for their good look.

So, it was official that I was going to carve a rabbit. But it still didn't feel enough; it was still dull, and she wouldn't be impressed.

My idea was rather ingenious; I decided to make a stand, and carve words of Rendan into it. I didn't know which words. I wanted to keep the theme of good luck, but I couldn't think of anything that resembled that. Instead, my mind wandered to Desmond's talks of weakness. Emile's weakness wasn't just defence; it was losing, too. The words sprang to my mind without even thinking; *There's bravery in accepting failure.*

All I had to do now was etch the words. I sat at my desk and pulled out my knife, getting to work. I had hoped to finish it that night and have the next day free.

I had one word left. A single word. I was about to start on it when I was stopped by a knock at my door. I checked the time; it was 12:30. There wasn't a feasible reason for someone to need me so late.

I quickly hid the sculpture and opened the door. Emile was there, looking rather impatient. I noticed she was still wearing her gear from training.

'What's wrong?' I asked.

'Nothing is wrong. I just have a request for you.' Emile said with a shrug. I raised an eyebrow.

'And what is it? The request?' I said.

'I am requesting that you join me for personal archery tutoring.' Emile said smoothly.

'What?'

'Did you not hear me? I said-'

'No, no, I heard you perfectly fine,' I said, rubbing my forehead, 'I mean, why? Can Desmond not teach me?' Emile looked stung.

'Are you implying that Desmond is better at archery than I am? Because, I'll have you know-'

'I'm not saying that, I swear! I just mean, it seems a little over the top; I don't need to have good aim. I can survive not knowing how to use a bow and arrow.' I explained.

'You might not need to, per say, but it doesn't mean you shouldn't. Come on; I'm bored and I spend my free time reading. Do you not want me to do something else? Are you really that bad of a friend?' Emile said, feigning sadness. I didn't answer for a moment.

'Fine. I'll come down in a minute, let me find some shoes.' I said, exhaling deeply. It wasn't out of pity; I was as bored as she was, and an archery lesson didn't seem too awful. If they worked, my most costly weakness would be a strength. It was worth a try.

'I'll be in the clearing at the woods, where we were this afternoon.' Emile said, walking away.

'But isn't it-' The door slammed. She had a thing for dramatic exits.

I pulled up my single pair of boots and left for the woods while shaking my head. It was pitch black outside; I didn't know how Emile was expecting it to work. But still, I came to the clearing, her face only just visible in the moonlight.

'I was beginning to think you weren't going to come.' Emile said.

'I was really quick, I'll have you know. You need to learn the concept of time.' I responded, 'Are the bows and arrows still here?'

'Of course they are. You might have to feel around to find a pair; I did. But, if I'm correct, they should just be by your feet.'

She was right. I found a sheath and bow straight away, preparing to start after. Emile's odour caught me off guard, again. Coffee, smoke and petrichor. The smoke was stronger, for some reason.

'What do you expect me to do? I can't see anything.' I said.

'Oh, please stop complaining. I know what I'm doing. Just get into position; I'm in the track of the cans, so face me.' Emile said. When I finally found her, it was from her eyes. They looked lighter under the dim moon.

'What now, then?' I said, starting to grow frustrated. Surely she was joking; there was no way that whatever she was planning was going to work.

'Close your eyes.' Emile said softly, moving out of the way of the targets. I scowled.

'How is that going to make it any better? I'll be able to see just as much either way.' I scoffed.

'Don't question me; I'm the heir to the throne. You have to do what I say.' Emile said. I reluctantly shut my eyes. Phosphenes danced in my vision.

'Relax your shoulders. And all of your other muscles. I can see how tense you are from a single glance.' Emile said. I tried to do as she said, but it wasn't too effective.

'Just get on with it.' I muttered. Emile huffed in annoyance.

'You already know where the target is; why do you have to see it to carry on knowing? It isn't going to move. So, instead of panicking and convincing yourself that it's in a different place, aim straight forward and stay in that direction.' she said. I was extremely doubtful as I pulled out an arrow and aimed forwards.

'I've already told you that you need to relax. I don't see why you're so tense, anyway.' Emile said.

'I can't help it! You're stressing me out even more so by telling me how obvious it is.' I dropped the bow and let my eyes open. 'This is useless.'

'Stop being so pessimistic, for Hades' sake! Pick up the damn bow; you're eighteen years old, not eight.' I bit on my tongue to stop myself from responding as I crouched down and picked the bow back up.

'I'm not shutting my eyes, again.'

'Yes you are. Do it before I force you.'

I wondered, for a moment, *how* she would force me.

I decided after a moment of thought that I didn't want to find out, and I was back in position quickly enough.

'Calm down. Don't focus on your surroundings; keep your mind on your bow and the target.' Emile said. I tried, but it didn't work. She must have realised that.

'What are you so anxious about?' she asked.

'If I knew that, I don't think I would be anxious at all.' I said. I felt a shift of weight from Emile, and she was behind me all of a sudden.

'Focus on the bow.' she said quietly. I jumped as her hand rested upon my own, guiding my bow to the straight line it had been in before. Coffee. Smoke. Petrichor. I gulped down the lump in my throat.

'And now I simply shoot?' I asked apprehensively. I felt Emile's chest heave against my back as she laughed.

'It's completely cheating if you do it while I'm holding the bow. Besides, you haven't loosened up yet. It isn't that hard, Maximus.' she responded. She was close, too close. I tried to soften my muscles, mainly so she would step away.

'You aren't very good at this, are you?' Emile mumbled.

'I thought we had already established that.' I murmured, my breaths coming in short and ragged huffs. My arms were beginning to ache from being up for so long, my nose stinging from Emile's odour. Coffee. Smoke. Petrichor. I inhaled sharply.

'You're just going to have to try it as you are, now. It barely changes anything, so don't worry.' Emile said, peeling her hand away. I was suddenly a lot colder than I had been a minute ago.

'And I just… let go?' I said.

'Not yet. You mistrust yourself; if it's going to hit the aim, you have to have a positive mindset.' Emile said. My mind jumped to our first training lesson, when Emile had been forced into a battle where she was guaranteed a loss. *Rule number 1,* I had thought, *never go into a fight thinking you're going to lose.* The same rule applied to this; if I thought I was going to miss, I surely would. But if I thought I would hit, then the chances were already higher.

'Okay. When I'm ready, I just shoot, right?' I queried.

'As soon as you're prepared, go for it.'

I didn't feel prepared at all. In fact, the only thing I was prepared for was humiliation when I missed by miles. *Remember rule 1.* There was as much chance of me hitting as there was missing, what with my eyes shut and basing my direction off trust. It wasn't too positive of a mindset, but it was a start.

Rule number 2, I thought, *always go with your gut instinct.*

My gut instinct at that very moment was telling me to shoot.

It felt like time slowed as soon as I let the arrow leave the bow. My eyes snapped open, trying to see where it was going. When it became clear I wasn't adjusted to the night, I used my ears to detect it.

There was a small crack, and then a sound of leaves being trampled. Emile was already running up to the can to see what had happened.

I stood perfectly still as I waited for her to return. She did, her hands behind her back and a grin lighting up her face. It was the second time I'd seen her cats grin within a few hours.

'Well? Did your little trick work?' I said. Emile removed her hands and placed them where I could see, the can clasped in one of them. There was an arrow pierced through the middle of it. I didn't believe it. Somehow, I had hit the target more effectively blind than I had with sight.

'No way.' I breathed.

'I told you that it would work!' Emile exclaimed. I felt the corner of my mouth twitch at her excitement and I had to remind myself that she wasn't my real friend; that it was just a decoy to get closer to her. I restrained the smile threatening to break free.

'I'm sorry I ever doubted you.' I said, my head inclined. I was leaning toward her, I realised, quickly taking a small step back. Emile stared at me blankly for a moment before regaining herself by quickly clearing her throat.

I pretended not to hear the increase in her heartbeat.

'As you should be! I'm a trustworthy person, thank you very much!'

I couldn't help it. The smile broke loose.

☆★☆

On the day of Emile's birthday, I woke up at 7:30. Desmond had offered to let us take the day off training, but Emile was adamant on still doing it, so he had instead made it so we only had a half day.=

I'd finished carving the last word the night before; Emile and I had agreed to do archery on Monday nights only, so we had time off, as well.

I was only waiting for Desmond to come in, now. We didn't have a cake or anything big to celebrate with, so he had done the same as me and made a gift. He had made a small dagger, one filled with sapphires and diamonds and emeralds. I had to admit, it was stunning.

I self consciously grabbed my rabbit sculpture, pacing my room as I waited for him to hurry up and get me. By the time the clock hit 7:40, I was starting to get annoyed.

Just as I was about to go looking for him, my door swung open and in came a rather untidy looking Desmond.

'Took your time, didn't you?' I said.

'Sorry. I slept in. Come on, she'll be downstairs in about 5 minutes.' Desmond replied. We went to the living room and kind of just sat there, waiting for Emile to enter.

Desmond's calculations were exactly correct; after 5 minutes had passed, she came in, her hair in a low ponytail and purple bruises prominent under her eyes.

'Happy birthday!' Desmond yelled with a grin, handing over the dagger. For a 50 year old, he had the tendencies to act like a child.

'Oh, you really shouldn't have! Thank you, Desmond, it's lovely.' Emile gushed, admiring the knife. Her eyes flickered over to me and I cleared my throat awkwardly.

'Um, happy birthday.' I said. Emile turned around to face me and I held out the rabbit. For a split second, I thought she hated it. I thought she was going to deny it, tell me that it was awful, everything along those lines. But her eyes brightened and she grabbed the rabbit, her bottom lip sucked between her teeth.

'You made this for me?' Emile murmured.

'Well, yeah; that's what friends do, isn't it? They do things for each other?' I said. I caught her lips tilting up.

'I suppose it is. But you didn't have to do so much, Maximus; it's so intricately made, so detailed...' Emile trailed off. I followed her line of sight to see she had found the sentence.

'There's bravery in accepting failure,' I quoted, 'I couldn't think of anything else, so I hope that's okay.' I scanned her features for signs of irritation, vexation, offence, anything; but she was unreadable. An empty page in her open book.

'No, it's more than okay. Honestly, thank you.' she whispered. I looked at Desmond; he was staring at me, frowning.

What? I mouthed. He blinked, momentarily stunned, before pulling himself together.

How did you know it? The failure thing? Desmond mouthed back. I'd forgotten that he was quite attentive, too; he wasn't as good as I was, obviously, but he was good enough to realise that much.

The same way that you know, I'm guessing.

Desmond just pressed his lips together and looked away. A flash of worry had passed over his face; it was so vague, so brief, that I nearly didn't see it. I realised he must be concerned that I knew his weakness; he was good at hiding it, yes, but not good enough. I didn't tell him that, though; the knowledge would come in useful during the war.

'So, what are we going to do this morning?' I said.

'What do you mean?' Emile asked absently. She was still focused on the small rabbit, her eyes still empty. I was confused as to how she tuned out her emotions so quickly; it was difficult for even me to do that.

'Well, it *is* your birthday, so we should do something to celebrate it.' I clarified.

'Maximus is right; why don't we bake a cake or cookies or brownies or something, I don't know, you can choose, Emile.' Desmond said.

'I do not want to celebrate it. There isn't that much to celebrate, anyway; I'm just one more year older. And I'm an adult, technically. I don't want to celebrate that.' Emile said, her voice suddenly cold, 'I'll see you both this afternoon.'

She walked away, the rabbit clutched to her chest and the dagger pressed against her leg. I shared a puzzled look with Desmond.

'Ignore her. She's always like that; her mood swings are normal. You'll get used to it.' he said, also leaving.

I did not think that mood swings were the problem. There was something else, something that I wanted to know. And once I got the itch to find something out, I wouldn't stop until I knew.

⚔ Chapter Nine ⚔

THE NEED TO KNOW what had caused Emile's detachment became so insatiable that I found myself up at 2 in the morning, staring at my wall and trying to find answers. It wasn't just a one time thing, either; it was every night, like a roaring wave I couldn't tame. It was exhausting.

At first, I tried to ask her. But she denied the change in her tone, and said that I was simply hearing things. It was insulting that she thought I was so stupid as to believe her.

Afterwards, I tried bringing up how she was an adult. I searched for hints in her expressions, but she did what she had done that morning of her birthday; she closed herself off and put on the front.

I was at a complete loss. The reason behind it could help me, and I knew it; but whatever it was, she clearly wasn't going to tell me so easily. It was utterly frustrating.

And that was what led me to being awake at 1 in the morning for the fifth night in a row, coffee at my desk and my eyes stinging from the lack of sleep.

I stared at the clock until I was forced into blinking. Another minute passed. I wasn't going to be sleeping anytime soon.

After another few minutes passed, I decided to go downstairs. I was about to go into the kitchen and refill my coffee when I saw the light was on in the living room. Curious, I pushed the door open slightly and peeked inside.

Emile was in there, sitting slouched on the sofa with her head in her hands. *Of course it's her. It's always her. How is she everywhere?*

I took a single step away from the door. It was creepy and weird to be watching her, and I was many things, but they didn't fall under my radar. Unfortunately, in my haste, I dropped the mug and it smashed against the wooden panels, creating a deafening smash.

I flinched. Why did I have to be so clumsy? It was ironic, really; the one time I don't want to be seen is the exact time I make myself more visible than ever.

Emile rushed out and into the corridor, a knife in her hand and her eyes wide. She let out a breath when she saw it was only me.

'Maximus, what in Zeus's name are you doing?' Emile asked, following my eyes to the pieces of mug on the floor.

'I was just going to refill my coffee and I dropped the cup.' I said truthfully. It felt good to be honest.

'What are you doing drinking coffee at one in the morning? Why are you even up at one in the morning?' Emile said.

'I could ask you the same question.' I shot back, eyes narrowing. Emile exhaled in annoyance.

'Well, it would make sense to clean up this before questioning each other, so get on with it.' Emile said, crouching down and starting to gather the fragments. I faltered before doing the same, wincing when a rather sharp piece cut my finger.

After we had disposed of the shards Emile went back to the living room. I stood in the doorway for a moment before following her in, letting the door shut behind me.

I sat at the armchair and Emile sprawled across the sofa. How she was so comfortable all of the time baffled me.

'So, why are you awake so late?' I inquired.

'I couldn't sleep. What about you?'

'The same reason.'

There was a long and unsteady silence. The tension in the air was so thick I was choking on it. That wasn't the only thing choking me. Coffee. Smoke. Petrichor. Why did I ever drink coffee when it practically radiated off Emile?

'Are you tired now?' Emile asked.

'I'm wide awake.' I hesitated, 'Are *you* tired?' Emile chuckled.

'I haven't felt tired for ages.' she confessed. *And I suppose that's because of your adulthood.*

'Me too.' Suddenly, the smell of smoke was so much stronger. It wasn't just a smell. It was in front of my face, coming from Emile. I looked closer; the light coming from the lamp was feeble and I was struggling to see her face properly. I finally focused on her and was surprised to see a cigarette pressed between her lips, emitting a soft flame.

'You smoke?' I said. There was quiet and then another dark grey cloud came my way.

'Yeah. Have you not noticed?' It was quite obvious now that I knew, actually. The black marks on the walls. The random ashtrays. The scent of smoke. I didn't know how I hadn't already figured it out.

'Clearly not. Why do you do it?' I said.

'I don't know. Because I want to. I like how it feels, I guess.' Emile said. I was mute for a moment. When I spoke, I didn't even know what I was saying.

'Can I have one? A cigarette?' I knew what Emile's face was doing even when I couldn't see it; she was scrunching up her nose and regarding me, looking for any sign of sarcasm.

'Yeah. Yeah, come and get one. There's a lighter on the table.' Emile said. I stood up and took one, lighting it's end and pushing it between my teeth. I sucked in gently and was consumed by the ashy, rotten taste that filled my mouth. It was painfully pleasant. I tried to blow out gently, but I ended up coughing anyway.

When the flames died, I stuffed the cigarette in the ashtray at the table and sat back down. My throat felt raw and my chest heavy. I welcomed the ache almost gladly.

'Tell me about you.' Emile said, a hint of a smile across her mouth. Her voice was... sincere. Genuine; I didn't hear the tone often.

'What?' I said. I recoiled internally; why did I always have to sound so cruel?

'You heard what I said. I barely know you and you barely know me. Tell me about you and I'll tell you about me. It's not that weird if you think about the fact that we're smoking at half one in the morning.' Emile said.

'Yeah, well... what do you want to know?' I said.

'I don't know. Give me a random fact. What's your middle name, if you have one?'

'Um, Invictus. Maximus Invictus Blare.' It felt strange saying my middle name, as I hadn't used it for so long.

'Invictus... That's a Rendan word, isn't it? I don't know what it means: just that it's Rendan.'

'Yeah. It means invincible. I'm not sure why my parents thought-' I cut off at the mention of my parents, 'What's your middle name?'

I felt Emile eying me suspiciously. I'd made a mistake there; I'd slipped up on my words. I'd gotten emotional, even if it wasn't very strong. I vowed not to let it happen again.

'Elizabeth. It's after my grandma.' Emile said.

'So your full name is Emile Elizabeth Elires? Was it made with three *e*'s on purpose?' I said.

'My mum probably thought it made me sound more elegant.'

'There's another *e*.'

Emile laughed. I laughed, too. Perhaps it was just the sound of her laugh that triggered me, but it was a real, authentic laugh either way.

'Here we go again, laughing at things that aren't even funny.' Emile said. We calmed down after a few minutes, and the living room was plunged into quiet again. So quiet, you could hear a pin drop.

'Tell me about George.' Emile said unexpectedly.

'What do you want to know about him?' I asked cautiously.

'Anything. You seem close to him, so tell me about him.' Emile shrugged.

'Oh. Um. Well he's... he's very loud. Quite similar to you in that aspect, actually. He always knows how to brighten your day, even if you don't even know yourself,' I hesitated, 'But he's also one of the strongest people I know. Not physically; no, he can barely carry his own weight. When it comes to what he's been through, he's stronger than many, because he keeps on going when he wants to give up. He's inspirational, really.'

I made out Emile's face in the dusk; I wasn't sure, but I thought she was looking at me. Whatever she was doing, it had caused her to clench her jaw and lean forward in her seat. I let myself gaze to where I thought her eyes to be. There was a soft light coming from them, royal blue lighting a small area. I wondered if my own eyes were doing the same thing. Even if they were, it wouldn't have the same majestic feel; grey doesn't come close to royal blue.

'How long have you known him?' Emile questioned, curiosity laced in her tone.

'Since I was 4.' It didn't sound right saying it out loud. If I could say how long it *felt* like I'd known him, I'd say my full life. After all, I could barely remember anything from my life before.

'He's Rendan, isn't he?' Emile said slowly.

'Well, yes, he is, but I don't see why it matters at all right now. I'm technically Rendan, too, by upbringing, but neither you or Desmond ever even acknowledge that.' I said defensively.

'No, I was only asking. I didn't mean to offend you. If all Rendans are like him and you then I would like to know who started this damn war.' Emile confessed.

'Will it be a surprise if I say most of them are the opposite of us?'

'No, it won't be.'

I felt a pang. My own country was known for being merciless, and I was fine with that, but some of the people in it were actually good people. It was just a few bad people that had stereotyped the rest of us.

'Okay, so I know plenty about George, now: what about Adelaide? She was awfully kind.' Emile said.

'Well, um, I don't see her much, as she spends most of her time with her *mater* in the suburban areas but you're right; she is very kind. Too kind, really; people take advantage of her easily. Of course, George never lets them actually hurt her, but she trusts too easily.' It was odd talking so openly about the family that had brought me up.

'You call your mother *mater*?' Emile said.

'I don't have one. But if I did, yes. I would call her *mater*.' I didn't like speaking of her.

'Oh. Well, Adelaide seems just as lovely as I had presumed she would be. This isn't meant to be rude, but how old is she?'

'Twelve.' She was so young to be involved in everything. The Flint family didn't deserve people like her and George. Emile didn't speak for a few moments.

'And what of Nathaniel? He's a weird one, I'll say, but you know more than I do, so take it away.' Emile said.

'His... his eyes are always so hard, and he's so cold. Physically and mentally. I get chills just from shaking his hand. He's a good warrior, I must say, as he is the one who taught me everything I know. But he's hard to read, and I pride myself on reading people.' I said.

'Can you read me, then?' Emile sounded like she was joking, but there was a hint of interest, too.

'You're different. I can read you sometimes, but other times I have no idea what you're thinking. It's frustrating.' I admitted.

'Good. I try to make it so that you don't know what I'm thinking.' Emile said.

'I figured.'

Coffee. Smoke. Petrichor. I coughed gently at the intensity of it.

'Well, it feels only fair to tell you about my parents, now. That is, if you want me to?' Emile said.

'Yeah. I would like to know about you.' I mumbled.

'Well, my mum used to be a farmer, before she married my dad. She has dark blonde hair; I got the ginger from my dad, unluckily'

'I don't see why that is unlucky.' I said. Of course I saw it; it was an omen of bad luck as it was, not to mention the temper that came with it. But Emile didn't feel like a 'bad omen'; it was simply an old wives tale, a superstition.

'I suppose you already know about the omen thing, so I'll say something else to back it up. The colour is unnatural and the beauty standard is brown hair, dull and plain. Any normal person in society with red hair is viewed as sinful and an outcast; the only reason I'm not is because it's the hair colour from the royal bloodline.' Emile explained.

'I like your hair.' I regretted saying it as soon as I did. What kind of teenager went around telling their friends that they liked their hair? I slapped myself internally.

'I like your hair too, Maximus.' Emile said, voice tentative.

'Oh- um, thank you.' I paused, 'Tell me more about your parents. I interrupted you before; sorry about that, by the way.'

'No, it's fine. My dad is always trying to make huge romantic gestures to my mum, but she's too stubborn to take them. I know she loves him, really, but, like I said; she's a stubborn person. They're lucky that they love each other, really.' Emile said, the last sentence coming off quite bitterly.

'How is that?' I asked.

'Well, my dad was meant to have an arranged marriage, but because he's a boy he didn't end up doing it. If I don't have a husband by the time I'm at least twenty five I'll have to be married to one of the princes in a different country, but I don't want that. I don't like the prospect of marriage at all, really.' Emile said.

'Well, *have* you got anyone back home that you would consider marrying?' It was a simple question. Curiosity. But it felt like something else. I pushed the unknown feeling away and pressed my hands together.

'No.'

Once again, it was just a simple answer. Honesty. And, still, that unknown feeling pushed into my stomach, along my spine, down my neck bone.

I shivered.

'So… what's your favourite colour?' I said. Emile stared at me.

'How've we gone from marriage and actual serious things to our favourite colours?' she said.

'I don't know. Mine's white.'

'That's so boring.' Emile was quiet. 'My favourite colour is yellow.'

'Why?'

'How are you going to ask why I like colour?' Emile demanded. She sighed, suddenly, 'I'm sorry. I suppose it's just… a happy colour. It's pleasing to look at. Why is white *your* favourite colour?'

'I don't know. It's like I said about that story: I don't *want* to know why I like it so much.'

I heard Emile yawn. I checked the time to see that it was 2:30 in the morning. I rubbed my eyes.

'Are you tired?' I inquired.

'I can't tell. I could probably fall asleep if I let myself.' Emile said. I could tell from her voice that she *was* tired; it was thick with sleep.

'You can go to your room if you want. I won't be offended; my pride is better than that.'

'No, it's fine. I don't know how you're still wide awake, though.' Emile said.

'I've had about a litre of coffee today.'

'Oh.'

We didn't speak for a few minutes. I focused on Emile's breathing, sharp and attentive; until it wasn't. It slowed, and I found my feet taking me over to check on her. She was fast asleep.

I chewed on my lip and sat back in the armchair. Now that I thought about it, my eyelids *were* drooping. I considered going back to my room, but then Emile would be left alone in the living room. I knew she could handle being by herself, but I still didn't want to go without telling her.

I curled up into a ball and rested my head under my hand on the armrest, letting myself slip away into a dreamless sleep. I didn't notice, but it was one of the best rests I had had since being back in Rendo; even with the draft of the open window brushing against my bare arms.

☆✮☆

'Maximus- Maximus! Wake up!' I jumped awake, Desmond towering over me.

'Where am I?' I asked with wide eyes, looking around quickly. *Oh. The living room. So, then...*

'Where's Emile?' I added on an afterthought.

'I woke her up before you. She's in the arena already. Why were you both sleeping in here?' Desmond said suspiciously.

'We were talking and we fell asleep. I swear it's the truth; ask her if you don't believe me.' I said.

'I believe you, it's fine. Go get your armour and sword, we'll be waiting for you.' I nodded hastily and ran out.

As I rummaged through my wardrobe for my armour, only one thing was on my mind. Well, not really my mind; more my nose. The smell of coffee, smoke and petrichor. It was starting to get a bit repetitive.

Yet, it was different every time. One day the coffee would be sweet and barely there, and the next it was infesting me, bitter and strong. The same thing happened with the smoke, although I now knew that that was based on cigarettes.

The petrichor seemed to be the only part of her scent that wasn't affected by what she did. The earthy smell was something we didn't experience much in Rendo; the lack of grass made it difficult for rain to fall on it.

Then, there was still the matter of her eyes. Her intense, piercing eyes. The glow that came from them in the dark, the way they held my gaze and made it impossible to look away. Yet, they were so icy, so cold; behind the dazzling layers was the real, raw emotions.

I blew out a breath and pulled on my tunic. I'd spoken a lot the night before, and nearly given away secrets about myself that even George didn't know. I couldn't let it happen again.

But her eyes... *snap out of it, you moron. Do I really need to make another rule?*

I couldn't get my mind off of her. It was infuriating.

Fine. Rule number 3; don't get attached.

✕ Chapter Ten ✕

'MAXIMUS, HOW HAVE YOU been?' I turned to see Desmond leaning against the frame of my bedroom door.

'I saw you half an hour ago; can you not tell how I am?' I said irritably.

'I don't only mean just now, Maxims: I mean in general. And can I not speak to my student as a friend, sometimes?'

'Sorry, sorry, I've just been stressed out lately.' I sighed. Desmond came and sat at the edge of my bed, shutting the door as he came through.

'Why don't you tell me about it?' he said.

'I don't… I don't think you'd understand.' I mumbled. My head was pounding and my pulse whirring in my ears; I felt like pitching myself out of the window.

'You do not have to talk about it if you don't want; it would probably help, though.' Desmond said.

'I don't want to talk.' I said quickly. Too quickly. Desmond eyed me for a moment.

'You should try the library. It always calms me down when I'm stressed.' he said eventually. I remembered the burning candles, the vellichor, the old books; it seemed that smell was one of the most comforting senses.

'I will. Thanks.'

I rushed off to the library, falling over my own feet on the way. As soon as I stepped in, the noise in my ears died down and I could hear myself think, again.

Recently, the task had been weighing me down. I couldn't sleep at night, and not because of a resentment towards an 18th birthday; because I was 2 months in with barely any progress and only a new found love for scents.

I leaned against a bookshelf, my knees collapsing from underneath me as I slid to the floor.

'Why does everything have to be so complicated?' I whispered. If I didn't get a move on, the war would be doomed and going to Kendra would be a fruitless effort.

The night in the living room was the perfect opportunity to find something out, but instead I'd wasted it talking about sentimental nonsense. Nevermind the war being doomed; I was doomed.

My eye caught on something; an old journal, laying on the coffee table by the sofas. I pulled myself to my feet and walked over, my footsteps light against the ancient carpets.

It was frayed at the edges and ripped up in awkward places, faint writing scrawled on the front. I squinted to make out what it said; *The journal of Emile Elizabeth Elires.*

My heart leapt into my throat. If it really was her journal, then all I had to do was skim it for the most important parts. I opened it to the first page; *1st of January, 0065.* 5 years ago. She must've had it for a long time, then.

I flicked through the pages until I came to an entry from 3 months ago, the day of my birthday. It was also the day she found out that I was to train here with her. I plunged into its depths.

7th of December, 0069
I've been in this damn countryside for an age now. Lucky me, it turns out I'm not going to be alone for long. A boy called Maximus Blare is coming to train here with me, and not only is he a complete stranger, he's Rendan. Desmond has been trying to say that the reason for him coming is 'perfectly feasible' but how am I supposed to trust him if I don't know the reason myself? I mean, I wouldn't kill for some company, but I would prefer for it to be someone I actually know, rather than some foreign weirdo. Anyway, I wrote a letter to mum the other week, and Desmond said that it should've arrived 4 days ago, but she still hasn't answered. I don't know whether to be worried or offended. I tried to ask...

I turned over the page. By the looks of it, the rest of that entry was about the letter to her mum, and it seemed like it was just full of sappy rubbish. I found the page of my first day here and continued reading.

16th February, 0070
The Rendan isn't so bad, after all. He's rather quiet, something that could be difficult to deal with, but I'm sure he'll warm up to me soon enough. After all, not only am I a princess, but I'm known for my charm. He's alright, though, really. He's different; not in a cliche, quirky way: when he lets himself go, he isn't too bad. Enough of him, anyway. Desmond figured out that I'm afraid of heights; it's utterly humiliating. The only reason he knows is because I turned down the offer to go up the ladder to the loft, in fear of accidentally falling off. He then went on to question me about how I formed the fear, how strong it is, if it affects me in combat and so on. It was tiring. Sometimes I wish that I was just... normal, rather than the warrior princess that the

whole of my country is depending on. I think I'm going to sleep now; I have some ideas for getting the boy to open up to me.

Emile? Afraid of heights? In my head it sounded preposterous, but it made sense when I actually thought about it. Every hero had a weakness, even if it was just a silly phobia. I turned the page to our first training lesson.

18th February, 0070

And now the stranger knows about my inability to effectively defend myself; fabulous! I'm starting to seriously reconsider whether or not I actually like him. But he is a really good sword fighter. I suppose it makes up for his antisocialness in a way. Still, while his weakness is that he's a little bit dodgy with a shield, mine is... that! Unlucky for him, it isn't my actual weakness, and it'll be sorted out soon enough. For now, my mum finally responded to my letter so I need to write back. I don't know what I'm to say; all she said was that her and dad are okay and that he is still in Hevalio 'helping the poor'. She's blind, I swear down; he's having an affair, or about 50, behind her back and she doesn't even realise it. Poor? In Hevalio? She must be on drugs or something; they're only the richest country in the world. Honestly, I don't understand love. Or my parents. Mainly just my mum, though.

I frowned and flipped to the start of March. Perhaps her parents had something to do with how good she was at hiding her emotions.

5th March, 0070

Maximus wanted to read a book, today, I told him to read The Story of the Girl Who Evaded Death, but I don't think I should've. The story is really personal to me, and I don't know what was going through my mind when I suggested it. All I could think about was his scent. Oh, I haven't mentioned his scent yet; it's like heaven to my nostrils! That looks really weird. Anyway, he smells of strawberries, mints and roses. It's like what I want to smell like; sweet and appetising. Not in that way! He's just a friend. Or, at least, he's the closest I've ever had to a friend.

So there was another reason behind her love for the short story; I would have to figure that out. I turned over to the day after Desmond visited.

12th March, 0070
There's something off about Nathaniel and his kids; I can feel it. Maximus has been avoiding me all day today, reckons he has a headache. I don't believe him. Something happened in that arena and I'm going to find out what it was. He can't even look me in the eye! Oh, I miss his eyes already. Did I ever say that they're grey? I've never met someone with grey eyes before; perhaps that's why I like his so much. Whatever the reason is, it doesn't matter if he can't hold eye contact without grimacing and running off. It's utterly ridiculous.

I hadn't thought of how my meltdown after the incident in the arena had affected Emile.

4th April, 0070
So, I'm an adult now. Only a few more years before I'm tracked down and killed. Yay. I suppose, though, that if they kidnap me, I might be able to see Evania again. I miss her so much. I don't want to think about what's been happening to her. Tomorrow it will've been 4 years since I last saw her. I can't think about it without gagging.

I didn't hesitate to turn to a page 4 years before, near to the front of the book.

5th April, 0066

Evania has gone missing. I don't know what to do. Mum has assured me that there are teams searching for her all across the country and that she can't have gone far, but I'm not sure. It's nightfall now, and we've had no news. I think she might be in a different country. I haven't cried at all; my throat feels so tight that I can barely breathe. Oh, my head hurts terribly. I might just sleep it off. For all I know, she could be found by tomorrow.

6th April, 0066

I've never been so scared in my whole life. We got a letter this morning, addressed to me. I don't want to copy it up exactly, but I'm going to leave the letter in the pocket in the back of this. It basically said how as soon as I was an adult and they had the means to get their hands on me, they would. And no, I have no idea who they are. I only know that they took Evania and that, if they don't get me, I'll never see her again. My head hurts, again. I can feel my pulse in my throat. I'm going to have to figure something out, though; I can't let them get away with this. I have to find Evania, and I don't care how long it takes.

That was it. That was all I needed. But my fingers were working faster than my mind. My eyes were on the day of our first archery lesson, and I don't know why. However, I understood more as I allowed myself to read the entry.

2nd April, 0070

Today was rather eventful. Maximus and I have started learning archery with Desmond, and he's useless at it. So I taught him in the middle of the night. Oh, it sounds ridiculous reading it from the paper, but it truly felt like a good idea in the moment! He hit the target, though, so I must've done something right. But, if I'm honest, all I was really focused on was how he smells. That sounds so bad; I've already mentioned his scent, haven't I? Well, I'm going to do it again. He smells of strawberries, mints and roses. It's lovely. I need to stop thinking that; it's plain weird.

I slammed the journal shut and quickly went back to the bookshelf, shoving a book off it to make it seem as if I'd simply dropped it to cover up the noise from the journal. Someone had come in and it didn't matter who it was; either way, I'd be doomed.

'What was that? And who's in here?' It was Emile's voice. *Yes, because in the universe's eyes it would be simply preposterous to bump into Desmond, wouldn't it?*

'It was me. Um, Maximus. I dropped a book.' I called back. Emile came around the corner; she had dressed properly that day. She was wearing a summer dress with frills and flower patterns, her hair tied up in a loose bun. She looked completely different to how she smelled.

'How did you manage to do that?' Emile asked, crouching down and picking up the book with soft fingers. I looked away when she stood back up and brushed down the skirt of her dress. 'Well?'

'I don't know. It just slipped from my grip.' I said. Emile sighed and skimmed over the blurb of the book.

'I don't think I've read this book here. Remember the title for me, will you? It's called *The Tales of Two Heroes*.' Emile said, slipping it back into its place on the bookshelf.

'Is it a true story?'

'I don't know. I haven't read it.' Emile said, looking at me like I was stupid. I felt stupid. 'You're madly clumsy, you know?'

'I've been told this many times before.' I said.

'Why are you in here? I already know that it isn't to read.' Emile demanded.

'Desmond said I should.'

'He said you should... go to the library? Not to read?' I shrugged with one shoulder.

'Don't ask me. I can't read minds.' I said with a shrug. I paused, Emile, do you think that I could write a letter to George?'

I had gotten the idea from her journal. Emile had written letters to her *mater*, so it seemed only right that I got to write to George. Besides, I wanted to know what was happening back at home.

'Well, yeah, you could write one, but getting it there might be difficult. George lives in Rendo and we're in Kendra, so anything going there is suspicious as it is. I'd have to ask Desmond to tweak about a little in the mailing system before you send it off.' Emile said.

'Oh. I hadn't thought of that.' And now I felt bad for making Desmond have to do more work. Great. 'It doesn't matter-'

'No, Desmond will be only happy to help. Don't stress out over a piece of paper. Just write it out and then give it to him, he'll sort it out for you.' Emile said reassuringly, 'And, no, he won't read it.'

We were silent for a minute.

'Why are you in here, then?' I said suddenly.

'What do you mean? To read, of course.' Emile scoffed. However, I didn't miss the pink tinge colouring her cheeks.

'Yeah? You should try do something else, for once. Go to the great outdoors.' I said, waiting for a reaction. Her eyes flickered towards her journal at the table. *And there it is.*

'Emile? What are you looking at?' I asked. Emile's eyes widened before she composed herself, tightening her bun.

'I don't know what you're talking about. Besides, I go to the woods all of the time; that's outdoors.' Emile said stubbornly. It didn't seem like she was going to say anything about her journal; I'd have to wait until the time was right.

'That certainly doesn't count. You go there to kill bunnies; not exactly enjoying the outdoors, is it?' I said, an eyebrow raised.

'*I* enjoy it. Besides, what is there to enjoy about cold and wet grass? I'd much prefer to procrastinate in my room.' Emile said silkily.

'Now that I think about it, I haven't even seen your room. What's so good about it that you'd rather sit there doing nothing than spend time with me?' I wasn't being serious, obviously; my ego wasn't *that* inflated. But Emile seemed to believe my act, as she rolled her eyes at my feigned conceit.

'Don't flatter yourself, darling. My own presence is much more enjoyable compared to yours.' she said dryly.

'Darling? Perhaps I should start calling you something like that, love.' I said. I internally cringed at my words; normally I was awful at flirting, always stuttering and getting all flustered. It was a wonder I hadn't spoken a wrong sentence yet.

Emile scrutinised me. She looked mildly taken aback, if not slightly impressed. After a few minutes of observation, she leaned against the bookshelf behind her and crossed her arms.

'Tell me, then, if you know so much; what's so wonderful about the *great outdoors*?' Emile said. I couldn't tell if she was being genuine or not. Either way, I had to keep the conversation going somehow.

'I would tell you, but it would be such a better experience if you found out for yourself.' A plan was already forming.

'Come on, Maximus, you can't say that. I won't *want* to see it if I'm not reassured in one way or the other.' Emile said. I exhaled exaggeratedly and copied off her body language, folding my arms over my chest and crossing over my ankles. I could've sworn she bit on the inside of her cheek.

'Then I think we should make a deal.' I declared.

'Oh really? What's this deal, then?' Emile said.

'I'll give you a single aspect. Only one. You aren't allowed to bribe me any more. And, in return, I'll take you to the single aspect.' I said. I saw something light in Emile's eyes; maybe amusement, maybe something else entirely.

'That doesn't seem so bad.'

'Flowers. Flowers are one of the most beautiful things the outdoors has to offer.' Emile considered it for a moment.

'I suppose that doesn't seem so bad.'

'Then we have a deal?'

'We have a deal.' We shook hands in a laughably solemn manner and I flashed her a rare and wide smile. *I can't wait to read the journal entry about this.*

'Tomorrow, exactly half an hour after training. Don't be late.' I stalked off, finally letting the red fill my face.

I hated flirting.

Remember rule number 3; no attachments.

☆✯☆

I had been mentally preparing myself every second I had free. At some point I would slip up; surely she knew by now that I was *not* the type to call people 'love' and take them to see flowers. I grimaced.

It had been twenty nine minutes. In one more, she would be outside of my door, probably looking her best, eyes sharp and icy. I didn't have the set up for stuff like that.

But the information I had was too important to let go of. I had to dig deeper, search for her reactions. As soon as I had what I needed, I could go back to my old awkward manner. It was only about an hour or so; I could survive. I had to be confident. Bring back that fake ego.

There were a few knocks at my door. I jumped and patted down my hair, staring myself down in the mirror. I wasn't dressed up properly; I was only wearing a pair of jeans and a plain shirt. I couldn't help thinking that it would be better if I trained...

'Hi? Are you in there?' Emile shouted impatiently. I swallowed nervously before opening the door, straightening my posture as I did.

Luckily, Emile was dressed casually too. If she had come wearing a dress again, I would've been humiliated already. Or she would be humiliated by *my* humiliation. They both sounded just as terrible as each other.

'So, are you going to take me to see these flowers?' Emile said. I cleared my throat.

'I would be delighted.' I said, already walking out. *Chivalry, Maximus. Wait for her.* I stood still and silent as Emile came up to me, her lips pressed together.

As we came to the front door, I halted, holding out an arm. Emile took it before shooting me a questioning look.

'Shut your eyes.' I said. Emile opened her mouth to speak but apparently thought against it, squeezing her eyes shut and fiddling with her fingers. I guided her to the area where a flower garden lay, filled with daisies and lilies and sunflowers. I turned to my right to see a lone red rose, the colour dark as blood. *He smells of strawberries, mints and roses.* Hesitantly, I plucked it from the soil, accidentally pricking my thumb, and tapped on Emile's shoulder with my free hand. Her eyes opened, falling on the rose.

I handed it to her, waiting for a reaction; I was granted with a very small one, a quick change of breathing. I resisted a frown and she composed herself within seconds.

'Well, take it all in then. Perhaps the sight of nature's beauty will stop you from being such a hermit.' I said. Emile's mouth twitched and she pushed the rose into the hem of her shirt, looking at the flowers. Her eyes were empty, again. It was still beyond me how she managed to cover up her emotions so quickly.

'Well? What do you think?' I said. Emile ran her fingertips along the petals of an ambrosia, her bottom lip sucked under her teeth in thought.

'I suppose the outdoors isn't too terrible.' she mumbled.

'So, would you care to do it again?' Emile turned to look at me, giving me a small smile.

'If it makes you happy, of course I would.'

Rule number 3. Remember rule number 3.

⚔ Chapter Eleven ⚔

'MAXIMUS, I HAVE A proposition.' Emile said suddenly. I looked down. While I had been climbing a tree, Emile had been ranting about how 'improper' and 'irresponsible' it was of me. It was pretty rich, coming from the girl who insisted on being informal.

'I'm listening.' I said.

'I think we should duel.' Emile said firmly. *Well, I wasn't necessarily expecting that.*

'With our swords?' I asked carefully. If I duelled her and won, it would ruin her pride so much she wouldn't speak to me again. Her fear of failure stood for that. And if she won, word would get to Nathaniel, and the task would be over. If she could only not be so overconfident, I wouldn't constantly be in bother.

'What else would we duel with? I'll tell Desmond tomorrow. Unless you're too scared.' Emile said slyly. I couldn't turn it down; she would think I was weak and, once again, Nathaniel would find out. I dreaded to think of what he'd do to me if I was seen as weak.

'Scared? Of you?I'd be more scared of a fly.' I said. It was a wonder she hadn't picked up on my mild panic from the flurry of my tone.

'Well, I'm sick of sitting here and watching you walk all over a tree. If you fall to your death I'll get the blame, and I'm pretty sure a criminal record of murder to my own teammate would give me an awful stain. Have fun flouncing about in the leaves without me. And don't forget to be prepared for our duel tomorrow.' Emile said before walking away.

'Tomorrow? But…' I trailed off. Emile was a good sword fighter, there was no doubt about it. But against me she had no chance. Perhaps if we had been fist fighting, or literally anything other than this, she'd best me, but swords were my speciality. I hadn't lost a duel in my entire life.

I jumped from the branch and brushed the dirt off me. I didn't know how I was going to get out of this mess. I could only hope that, when I won, Emile would get over her pride and stay my friend. Because that was all I needed to complete the task; for her to be my friend.

I ran to catch up with Emile, slowing to a stop by the front door of the house, where she was standing.

'Waiting for me?' I said.

'Don't get too ahead of yourself.' Emile said, grinning only just, opening the door and walking in, making a point not to hold it open for me. Her mood swings were rather tiresome.

'So, what do you want to do?' I asked. Maybe I could convince her to call off our duel; it was a recipe for disaster.

'Nothing with you, I hope.' she mumbled, her voice hardly audible.

'Why do you get like this? One minute you're all happy and nice and now you're acting like I'm your worst enemy.' I said, trying to keep calm. It was harder than I thought, considering one of my only friends kept on switching up on me. Honestly, when I thought about it from that perspective, killing her seemed exciting.

'Calm down! I'm just kidding. Sorry.' Emile said. I couldn't even tell if she meant it or not, from the way she'd shut off her emotions yet again. I had to push away the part of myself threatening to murder her with my bare hands. *Great. Now I'm adopting her ridiculous mood swings. Good going, Maximus!*

'It's fine. But if you're going to act like that all of the time, how am I supposed to know when you're being real?' *Simple, actually, considering I'm never 'being real'.*

'I mean, I could say the same for you, couldn't I? It's like you change personalities every day! How am I to trust you when I don't know who you really are?' *Another simple answer; you don't trust me. Possibly the biggest mistake you could make. On your half, anyway. Quite helpful on mine.*

'What do you mean?' I said, feigning sincerity. Normally I didn't have to fake those sorts of things around her, but she was being so different lately that I had to.

'One day you're charming and polite, but the next you're clumsy and hostile. One day you're kind and happy, the next you're distant and short-tempered. One day you're-'

'Okay I get it! You don't know who the real me is. But you can't say much; recently I don't even recognise you!' I exclaimed in frustration. Real frustration, that time.

'You might get it but I don't! Come on! Why don't you just be you, instead of all these weird alter-egos? I've been myself since the first day I met you, and you can't return it.' Emile sounded so genuinely hurt that I nearly felt bad for her. Nearly being the key word.

'Fine! I'll *be myself*! But when you don't like what you see, don't come running back and asking for the old me!'

I stormed off. It was a guilt trip, a ploy for sympathy. Emile would run back to me as I had told her not to do either way. If it wasn't out of the good of her heart, it was out of stubbornness and not being told what to do.

My mind went to the duel the next day. I hoped she would call it off; surely she would see how 'enraged' I was and know she had no chance of winning... surely she would...

Stop kidding yourself. Both of us know that she'll never get over her pride.

Sometimes that little voice in the back of my head was really annoying.

Yeah, well, at least I tried.

I collapsed on my bed. I was a little bit stumped. It would make sense for me to admit defeat in our duel, if we had one, and stay friends with Emile. Surely Nathaniel would understand.

But there was a chance he wouldn't. A rather large chance. I squeezed my eyes shut so hard they stung. *Well, tomorrow's going to be eventful.*

☆★☆

I entered the arena before Emile, for once. Desmond didn't rip his eyes off me as I walked up to him, my knuckles white from how firm my grip was on my sword.

'Maximus.' Desmond said. I ticked my jaw awkwardly as I waited for Emile to come in.

'Emile told me of her plans.' Desmond added. I nodded meekly.

'So, are we going to duel?' I asked. My voice sounded strangely small; very unlike my usual tone.

'I don't see why you shouldn't.' Desmond said slowly. My heart dropped to my stomach.

'Great.' I said. Desmond pressed his lips together, as if deep in though. It didn't really matter. I would have to lose; there wasn't another option. But I knew that as soon as we started, I would forget about that. *Rule number 4; remember to be logical in battle.*

Emile came in about 5 minutes later. She looked tired, her cheekbones prominent and skin paler than usual. Her lips were bloody and sore, as if she had been chewing them non-stop. I realised if my words had had as much of an effect as I wanted them to, there was a good chance she *had* been chewing them to bits.

'Look, Maximus, I'm sorry-'

'Get ready.' I said, cutting her off. She looked... ashamed, perhaps. Still, her sword was out and she was in a stance quick enough.

'Are you sure you want to do this?' Desmond asked. I rolled my eyes and positioned my own sword.

'I wouldn't have asked if I didn't want to do it.' Emile said. She sounded as exhausted as she looked.

'And I wouldn't have accepted if I didn't want to do it.' I said sharply.

'Well... okay then.' Desmond sat down at the stands, 'Then you can begin.'

Emile was faster than I had been expecting. She pounced at me, her movements graceful yet dangerous at the same time. I returned just as much force, trying to keep it as even as possible. If I wanted to make this fight work, I needed a plan, and to make a plan I needed time.

I was almost cornered. I could see the beginnings of a smirk forming on Emile's lips. *Rule number 4. Come on, Maximus, keep it together.*

I moved quicker, pushing myself away from the wall. I could hear her heart beating, feel her pulse thumping. I swallowed; if I killed her I would never be forgiven and my cover would be blown. I had to focus.

'You aren't too bad, are you?' Emile said. I was surprised that she wasn't out of breath. Although I couldn't say much; I didn't have a drop of sweat on me.

'I could say the same for you.' I said. She was against a wall, her movements slower and less precise. *Weakness; doesn't fight as well in close proximity.*

'Can you forgive me? I never meant to hurt your feelings.' Emile said. We were back in the middle of the arena, our swords echoing against the clean walls.

'I would have forgiven you anyway. Don't get too upset, love.' I said. The flirting had been working so well before that it felt almost natural, now. Emile's face brightened; a small mistake on her behalf. She stopped moving for a split-second, but it was long enough for my own sword to find a place in her skin. It ripped through her arm, blood pouring out.

My eyes widened. *Damn it, Maximus; is it really so hard to keep in control for a single fight?*

Emile winced but carried on fighting, her actions more fierce than before.

'Sorry.' I muttered.

'Why would you be sorry?' Emile's voice was more strained, now; I couldn't win. It would ruin everything.

'For slicing your arm open, obviously.' I said. Emile chuckled lightly, taking a blow to my thigh. I dodged it easily, but had to admit that it was a good move.

'We're duelling, Maximus. One of us was bound to get injured.' Emile said. That was unlike her; her fear of failure normally stopped her from saying things like that.

'Oh.' was all I managed to say.

It came to a point where it felt like we were going to kill each other. Emile managed to hit my collarbone, only centimetres away from my throat. I stifled a gasp and quickened my movements; that was the closest anyone had ever come to killing me. And I had actually been trying to ward her off.

I didn't have a plan. I was close to cornering her, again, and I still didn't have a plan. I risked a quick glance towards Desmond; his face was focused and scrunched up. I desperately tried to make eye contact, but he barely noticed. He was too busy watching our swords.

I sighed and turned back, dodging a blow from Emile.

'It's really irritating how you always dodge me. I hope that the collarbone scars to remind you that I *did* hit you.' Emile said.

'I could say the same for your arm.' My sword found her skin once again. It was her other arm, this time, her forearm.

'I am so sorry.' I apologised. Emile flinched as she moved her sword, but was filled with a new determination. She managed, once again, to hit me, slicing my thigh. *Damm. She's good.*

'That's enough!'

I jumped and whipped around. Desmond had stood up and his face held the expression of... worry, perhaps. I didn't blame him. There was blood everywhere.

'Maximus, Emile, we're going to my room to get you both bandaged up.' Desmond said, walking away. I limped after him, my thigh stinging when I put pressure on it. Emile looked just as pained. Her arms were limp and her sword had been left back in the arena. It was a wonder we hadn't both died from blood loss.

I sat next to Emile at the edge of Desmond's bed, holding a hand against my thigh. Emile was simply staring at the blood on her hands

'Are you okay?' I asked. Emile jumped, resulting in a grimace, most likely because of her injuries.

'Yeah, yeah, I'm fine.' Emile said. I gave a small nod before turning back to Desmond. He had rubbing alcohol and bandages as he came forward, his face unreadable.

'I don't know what you two were thinking. You could've died! You could still die! These are deep!' Desmond said in exasperation.

'Desmond, we're really sorry. Honest. I didn't think that we would actually-' Emile cut herself off when alcohol was poured into the wound on her left arm, biting on her cheek. I was surprised she didn't cry out in shock.

'It doesn't matter if you're sorry. What's done is done, and there isn't any going back now.' Desmond said quietly. Emile wasn't paying attention; her eyes were on me.

'Maximus, your leg.' she said. I looked down; there was blood everywhere, clumping up against the cut that bore the liquid. I hadn't realised how much it hurt. I cursed out loud, trying to apply pressure to it.

'Here, put some of this in it.' Desmond said, throwing me the rubbing alcohol, 'I'll have a look at it after I've done up Emile's bandages.'

I caught the bottle and wasted no time on pouring some in my gash, swearing again at the harsh sting that it produced.

'Language, Max.' Emile said. My head whipped around to face her; her eyes were almost shut in concentration.

'Did you just call me Max?' I said. Emile forced her eyes open, returning my gaze.

'Maximus is too long. I don't have the energy to say your full name, so I'll say Max.' Emile faltered, 'If that's okay with you.'

'No, no, of course it's okay.' I said quickly. Emile smiled, but it disappeared hastily, her cheeks going hollow again.

As soon as Emile was bandaged up, Desmond came over to me and wrapped another bandage around my thigh. He rubbed some of the alcohol into the cut on my collarbone; that was left open, as it was only small.

'Right. Duels are officially banned.' Desmond said after he was finished.

'Yeah. Figured you'd say that.' Emile muttered. I frowned; surely she didn't want to duel again? After what had just happened? We'd nearly died!

'Emile, I shouldn't have let it happen in the first place. Now your arms are all weak and I dread to think how long it will take before you're able to properly fight again.' Desmond said.

'I know, I do, but it's just... you, my mum, my dad, even my sister before... you're always so protective of me. I'm an adult now, and I can make my own choices. You don't have to watch out for me forever, you know.' Emile said. I noticed the change in her voice after the mention of her sister. I was sure Evania was her name. I'd have to ask Emile about her and see if she'd tell me anything.

'Emile. Calm down. You know it's only for your own good.' Desmond said, a warning tone in his voice.

'I'm sick of hearing that! *Oh, it's for your own good, Emile, don't do what you want to do for your own good, stay at home for your own-*'

'Emile!'

She didn't stay to listen to what Desmond wanted to say. She rushed out, her hair fluttering behind her and her arms slack. I sat silently for a moment before following her, shooting Desmond an apologetic look.

I wasn't expecting where she went. Emile ran straight into the ballroom, a place I hadn't seen since my first day here. I stopped outside of it's door, my fingers wrapped around the handle. I opened the door and stepped in, letting it slam behind me.

At first, I couldn't find Emile. But when I looked closer I realised it was because she wasn't standing. She was curled up in a ball against a wall, her head buried into her knees. It was strange seeing her so vulnerable. I didn't like it.

'Emile?' I said under my breath. My voice echoed against the walls. A chill ran down my spine.

'Please leave me alone.' she said. I stood still for a moment before going and sitting next to her, awkwardly arranging my legs. I groaned as I accidentally hit my thigh.

'I said to go away.' Emile said, looking up. Her eyes were rimmed with red and her lips were dry and ripped. I didn't move.

'It looks like you would do better with someone here with you.' I said. I didn't know why I cared; it might've been the sight of someone so strong and happy looking so miserable and helpless. Whatever it was, I didn't want to leave.

'Get lost!' Emile said, shoving me. It didn't work. It only resulted in tears falling down her face.

I was at a loss for what to do. There was a crying girl to my right and I was supposed to comfort her. That was what a good person would do in that situation. But I had no experience with things like that; back in Rendo if you were seen crying you were told to suck it up or get over it. Clearly Emile wasn't used to such treatment.

'I- you can- you can talk about it, if you want.' I said. I felt that was the wrong thing to say, as Emile responded by shaking her head violently.

I thought about how George reacted to Adelaide crying the last time I had seen her in Rendo. He usually gave her one of his famous bear hugs and said kind words, words that tasted like toxin in my mouth. But, by the looks of it, there wouldn't be another way. I took a deep breath and welcomed the toxin with open arms.

'I- you're an amazing person, you know. Don't look at me like that. I'm being serious. You always know how to make me laugh and smile and I suppose it must make you feel horrible knowing I can't do the same in return. It makes me feel horrible, too.' I stopped speaking when Emile caught my eye, her royal blue irises cool yet fiery.

'You're making me smile right now.' she whispered thickly. My eyes trailed down to her lips and, sure enough, they were pulled into a reserved but genuine smile. Although they were sore and cracked, they still held a light pink tinge. I looked back up into her pupils.

'I should try being nice more often, shouldn't I?' I said with an awkward laugh.

'Mhm.' Emile hiccoughed. A wave of discomfort overcame me. She was full blown crying again, her head buried in her hands.

So the kind words hadn't worked. I didn't like being so inexperienced with something; normally I always knew how to make something work. However, words had never been my strong point; I always seemed to run out of things to say.

Then don't use words.

That was it. It made sense; people always said that actions spoke louder than words. All I had to do was give her a simple hug… the thought made me feel sick. Such intimacy was unusual for me. But not only would it stop her from sniffling and making a mess, it would surely bring her closer to me. With an internally pained expression, I tentatively placed a hand on Emile's shoulder.

She looked up. Her face was sunken and tear stained. I moved my hand around to the back of her shoulder, doing the same with my other hand, and pulled her in.

I felt the falter in her breath as her chest pressed against mine. Emile's head rested softly against my shoulder, the pressure so light I could barely feel it at all.

I was so close to her. My heart skipped a beat.

Rule number 3! No attachment!

But she was soaking my shirt and crying like she'd never cried before and I couldn't help but forget about Rendo and the task and stupid rules for a short amount of time.

⚔ Chapter Twelve ⚔

I DREAMED THAT NATHANIEL was dead. He was lying in a coffin, his eyes wide and unblinking, and his face as pale as always. When I reached out a hand and touched his skin, I wasn't surprised at the icy cold. He had always been like that.

As if the contact had woken him, Nathaniel blinked. I jumped and stumbled back, watching in horror as he sat up, his soulless eyes staring at me.

'You didn't really think I was dead, did you?' Nathaniel hissed. I felt a lump form in my throat.

'I- you- what-' I stammered, edging away. Nathaniel's face broke out into a haunting smile and he crawled out of the coffin, his limbs tangled and bending in all of the wrong ways. I was scared to the point that I couldn't look away, no matter how hard I tried.

'Honestly, Maximus, you're more stupid than I'd thought.' Nathaniel said in a low voice. I shuddered. What was wrong with him?

'What's going on?' I whispered shakily. He crept towards me, his eyes wild and focused on me directly. I tried to step back but I bumped into a wall; I already knew I was doomed.

'Now, I'll finally kill you.' Nathaniel said. I was frozen in fear, my feet planted to the floor. He was advancing on me, and fast. I felt around my belt for my sword, but it wasn't there. Of course it wasn't there. That was just my luck.

Nathaniel had a dagger clutched in his mangled hand and I had no way to defend myself. I squeezed my eyes shut. The edge of the blade was pressing against my skin. It was about to tear through and take the life from me. I held my breath and pushed away my racing thoughts.

My eyes shot open.

I felt my forehead. It was slick with sweat and burning up. But I didn't know why, and it frustrated me beyond comprehension. I couldn't remember the dream; I never remembered my dreams.

The sound of cries and metal clashing startled me up. Unless Emile and Desmond had decided to fight to the death, which was unlikely, there was no reason for such noises to be produced.

I ran to my window and opened the curtains. What I saw was most unexpected.

It wasn't just Desmond and Emile outside. There were about 20 other armoured people, the Rendan symbol standing out in the middle of their chests.

That was the moment I felt it for the first time; that strange feeling in the back of my throat. There wasn't a way to describe it. It itched at my flesh, waiting to burst out. It was like the beginning of a scream. If it was a colour, it would be the colour blue. But not because it was sad. It was a mixture of everything; happy, sad, excited, you name it. It was that at its strongest point. And it was in me right now.

I didn't bother with my armour. I stuffed my dagger in the sheath in my belt and rushed to the weapons room, grabbing my sword. As soon as I stepped outside, the feeling left. I was engulfed in the battle without even being a part of it.

The first thing I did was find Desmond and Emile. It was easy enough; they were the only warriors without the Rendan symbol. I scanned to see if they needed any help, but it looked like they were handling it just fine. I turned around to find my own fight.

There were about 5 of the Rendans about to advance on Emile. But she wasn't ready for that; she was already fighting three people at once. And doing very well, actually.

I sprinted towards and in front of them, reveleshing in their shocked expressions.

'Maximus?' one said. I shrugged.

'That is my name. I don't know yours, I'm afraid. So I'll have to kill you. How unfortunate.' I said, bringing my sword to the side of his stomach. While the stranger had been speaking, I had been searching their armour for a place I could hit and cause fatal damage.

Blood spurted out and splashed on my bare face. I wiped my lips in disgust before raising my eyebrows at the other 4 warriors.

'Well? What are you waiting for? Fight me, you idiots.'

If I could see their faces, I knew they would be full of terror.

In Rendo I was one of the most famous people, from the moment I killed a man at 12 years old. Hundreds of people came against me, and I bested every single one. Rumour had it that being the cause of so many deaths had made me remorseless, inhuman, a monster. It was quite insulting, really.

The first person was down within seconds. They had been rather obvious about the weak link in their armour, clutching his chest as soon as the victim before him had fallen. He put up a… well, it would be polite to say he put up a good fight, but he didn't. He put up an awful fight. So, after his awful fight, which lasted a total of 3 seconds, he was lying lifeless beside his friend.

Then, I was bombarded with the other three people. They must've gotten out of their trance, as they were surprisingly courageous as they came up to me. It was not their lucky day. They were all dead in less than a minute.

I turned to check up on Emile, again. The three people she had previously been fighting were on the floor. But there was no blood. She hadn't killed them. She'd only knocked them out.

My eyes caught on a dark figure behind her. He wasn't wearing a helmet and I recognised him as one of Nathaniel's cousins. *So it must've been Nathaniel who organised this. But why?*

The figure had his sword raised and was about to strike. I bolted over and disarmed him, using the moment of shock to slice off his head. Emile whipped around and let out a small scream.

'Hey, calm down, it's just me.' I said hastily. Emile's eyes were wide and her hands were shaking. I gently touched the place on her armour where her injuries were; they stuck against her skin. They were bleeding, again. *She* was bleeding. Surely that wasn't good.

'Why are they not dead? Did you knock out anyone else?' I asked quickly. I had to dispose of those people before tending to Emile.

'I- yeah, 2 others. I- I'll take you to them. I couldn't- I couldn't kill them. I'm sorry.' Emile stammered. I realised then that she'd never actually taken a life. I bit down on my lip.

'Right. You have to help me, here. How many unconscious people do you think you could hold?' I said.

'Um, I don't think about that sort of thing often. 2? Maybe 3.' Emile said uncertainly.

'2 is great. Go get those other people, I'll get these. Take them into the arena.' I said. Emile nodded and hurried away, still trembling.

I looked down at the people at my feet. Before throwing them over my shoulders, I looked over to Desmond; he only had one person left to fight and he was doing a good job of it.

My gaze fell on the scattered bodies. With a sharp inhale, I picked up two of the people and tossed them on top of each other on my right shoulder, using my left shoulder for the other person.

'Ow.' I muttered before walking as quickly as I could towards the arena, my limp still apparent. It had been a week and both mine and Emile's wounds hadn't fully healed. Apparently they were more severe than I had anticipated.

As soon as I entered the room, I dropped the people on the floor and collapsed against a wall, breathing heavily. Emile entered about a minute after, placing them next to the other three before standing still as a statue.

'We have to tie them up.' I said. I saw Emile's chest heave.

'What, like keep them hostage? Maximus, I-'

'What happened to Max?' I cut in. I didn't show it, but for once in my life, I was genuinely hurt. And I didn't know why.

'Max, Maximus, it doesn't matter! I'm standing in the same room as 5 people who want to kill me and you're fine! How are you fine? Why are you okay with this?' Emile stopped for a breath of air, 'I'm not even bothered about that. Not really. I know that I could take all of them on at once and win. I'm more bothered about the fact that I'm going to have to kill them. I don't want to kill people! I'm not a murderer, Max!'

I let out a breath I hadn't realised I'd been holding. She'd called me Max. She wasn't mad at me.

'Calm down, okay? Go in the corridor while I tie them up, if it puts you at ease. We can't talk about this right now. These people are going to wake up soon and they can't be like that when they do. I'm sorry. Truly.'

I wasn't sorry. I didn't know the meaning of the word.

'Do you have rope?' Emile asked. I looked around. There was a draw in the corner. I went over and pulled it open to see scissors, cellotape, string and... rope.

'Yep. All the rope I could possibly wish for.' I said, pulling out as much of it as I could and throwing it over to the bodies.

'Oh. Ok. Good. I'll be- I'll be outside.'

Clearly she was quite shaken.

I walked up to the people and stared at their faces; each had a bruise forming in some spot of their forehead from where Emile had struck them. I picked up some rope and tied it around the wrists and legs of the first person, a woman I knew to be George's aunt, Fae Flint.

She was generally a cruel person, with pointed features and greasy black hair. George and I had never liked her. She took pleasure in watching people's deaths, encouraging the predator and revelling in the prey's pain. All in all, she came off as a sociopathic sadist.

I stuck some tape over her mouth and went to do the same to the next person, a young boy called Darius. I hadn't seen him much, but there was a time when he came to watch one of my battles, and I could distinctly remember the way colour drained from his face when the opposite side's warrior bled out. I hadn't taken him the type to battle the most prestigious warriors from both Kendra and Rendo.

The next person was a man who I didn't recognise. I quickly felt around for a tag around his neck, as Rendans normally had one that showed their name. Strangely, there wasn't one. I frowned and moved on to the next person.

She was a woman who went by the name Luna, and was known around Rendo for being both the most ruthless and the kindest. She was only my age, and we had grown quite good friends over the years. It felt wrong to tie her up like this.

The last person was a girl in her early teens, her name being Anastasia. It was quite confusing, as I knew her to be a servant of the royal family, a quiet girl full of witty remarks and knowledge beyond her years. I was sure she was only around 13 years old. On the contrary, I also knew her to be an exile of Kendra, a once widely known girl turned slave. Sometimes I would wonder why, but most of the time I brushed it off.

I didn't know if these people knew about my task. I could only hope that Nathaniel had let them know to not mention my past. I scanned the hostages carefully. Nothing sharp, no weapons, nothing to help them escape. Good. That was good. I spun around and marched out, keeping the door open slightly.

Emile was gnawing at her fingernails, slumped against the wall opposite the door. Her hair was a tangled mess and her normally visible eye bags looked as if they were swelling.

'You did good out there.' I said. 'Do you know what Desmond is doing?'

'He's getting rid of the bodies.' Emile said, her voice breaking. I resisted a groan; she was very sensitive for a girl destined to be Kendra's greatest warrior.

'Ok.' I said awkwardly. Why was I so awkward? I really needed to learn how to be socially comfortable.

'Did you recognise the people in there?' Emile asked. I didn't answer for a moment. I knew she was hoping I would say no. But surely she knew better than that...

'All of them except one.' I responded smoothly. I looked for a reaction, but I couldn't find one.

'Were they- who are they?' Emile said. She was starting to get on my nerves, now; sure, she was allowed to be frightened. It was her first time witnessing murder firsthand. But it was getting to the point where it was extremely tiresome.

'I don't know them very well.' I lied. If I told her the truth it would put her in an even worse state, and I didn't have enough energy to deal with that.

'Did you fight without armour?' Emile asked. I looked down at myself.

'Yeah. I guess I did.' I said dismissively. The corner of Emile's mouth twitched up.

'You're really good at sword fighting. It's a shame you have the worst aim I've ever witnessed.' she said. The small smile became a grin and I was grinning back, for some reason. Maybe it was because she'd given me her cat's grin; I saw it so rarely it was strangely euphoric when I did.

'Maximus, Emile!' We turned to my left to see Desmond running up, covered in blood. I raised an eyebrow.

'Have either of you been injured?' he asked. I was about to shake my head, but my mind went back to Emile's arms.

'Emile's cuts were reopened, I think. Aside from that we're fine. What about you?' I said.

'I'm ok. Right, I'm checking you too Maximus. Are the people in there securely tied up?'

'How did you know about them?'

'I saw Emile knocking them out.' He was nearly as attentive as I was. I didn't know whether to be impressed or worried.

'If they manage to get out they're either geniuses or just have superhuman strength.' I said. Desmond nodded curtly.

'Right. Come on then. We're going to sort out Emile, check out your thigh and then we'll wake up those motherfu-'

'Desmond!' Emile cut in. I resisted the urge to roll my eyes at her and her touchiness when it came to swearing.

Ridiculously ironic, considering she was a princess.

'Right. Ok. Let's go.' Desmond said. He looked stressed. It wasn't very often I saw Desmond like that; he was always such a calm and collected person, always finding the good in things. I pushed it away and went up to his room.

My thigh was perfectly fine, the bandage clean and purely white. Emile's arms, on the other hand, were most certainly not fine. Blood ran all the way down to her wrists, clumping at her curves and crevices. It was a shock that she hadn't bled herself dry.

After Emile had been tended to, we went back down to the arena, the people there still unconscious.

'I'm guessing you know them, so you can choose which one we kill first.' Desmond said.

'Do you mean talk to?' Emile put in. She looked better now, her features lighter and eyes soft.

'We'll do both. Wake him up. I don't know that one.' I said, pointing at the man without a name. Desmond nodded and pulled out some smelling salts, pressing them under his nostrils.

When his eyes opened, I nearly recoiled in my disturbance.

There was blood gathered in the bottom of them, and instead of a coloured iris it was purely black. I looked at Emile; she showed no sign of shock. *No wonder she's acting so weird, if she did that.*

'Emile, what did you do to him?' I said in a low voice. The man was screaming in pain, rubbing at his eyes furiously.

'I knocked his eyes with the handle of my sword.' she shrugged. I was in the middle of being concerned and proud.

'How are we supposed to get information from him now?' I hissed.

'You don't need to speak to him! There are loads of other people!' Emile protested.

'I want to know who he is, though!' I exclaimed.

'Just because you want to, doesn't mean you need to.' Emile countered. I let myself stare at the man, again; Desmond had calmed him down slightly, and he was no longer screeching at the top of his lungs.

'Just kill him.' I said, 'Put the poor thing out of his misery.'

Desmond wasted no time in doing exactly that. He pulled his dagger from his belt-sheath and pushed it straight through his heart, killing him immediately.

'Who now?' Desmond asked.

'The girl with the brown hair. She's my friend; I'm sure she'll tell us something.' I said.

'She's your *friend*?' Emile said in disbelief.

'She's really quite nice when you get to know her.' I responded. Emile rolled her eyes.

'I suppose it's a shame we're going to kill her, then.' she said.

'I suppose it is.' I said dryly. Luna's eyes shot open and she scanned the atmosphere, making a face when she found me.

'You can take the tape off her mouth.' I said. Nathaniel nodded and ripped it off, ignoring the glare he received.

'Maximus, sweetie, could you do me a quick favour and take off these blasted ropes?' Luna said with a tilted head.

'I'm afraid I can't. I'm on a tight schedule.' I said, smiling sarcastically. It seemed Luna must've known about the task, considering she hadn't asked a single question.

'What's your name?' Desmond asked. Luna batted her eyelashes in feigned innocence.

'Luna Partayne.' Luna said, sugar coating her voice.

'What are you doing here? What do you want from us?' Desmond pushed.

'Calm down, my lovely, I've only just recovered from being so kindly knocked out.' Luna said, fixating her gaze on Emile.

'Ignore her.' I mumbled. Emile rolled her eyes.

'I'm not sure if you're aware, *my lovely*, but you're the one who's come to kill me.' she snapped.

'Next time just kill me, darling; you look weak now.' Luna said silkily. She was doing as I usually did, although she wasn't being as secretive about it.

'I'll kill you right now, if that's what you want.' Emile shot back, fury laced in her voice.

'Go for it. I bet you won't-'

She was cut off by a knife piercing her chest. I gaped at Emile for a moment; I supposed she wasn't so bothered about killing people, after all.

'Why did you do that?' I demanded. Emile shrugged half-heartedly.

'She was asking for it.'

It seemed I had a long day ahead of me.

⚔ Chapter Thirteen ⚔

THE HARDEST PERSON TO kill was Darius. From the moment he opened his eyes and his muscles clenched in fear, I knew he was the same person that I had seen all those years ago. Just a boy, desperate to prove himself through all of the lies and terror. Just a boy that I had to murder in cold blood.

'Darius.' I said when he woke up. I'd already taken the tape from his lips, but it didn't look like he wanted to speak, anyway.

'I'm guessing you're called Darius, then. Tell me this before one of us impulsively kills you; why are you here?' Emile said.

'Emile, calm down.' I said quietly.

'I- I- I'm not- I don't know.' Darius whispered. His hair was sticking to his forehead and his cheeks were flushed red.

'Hey, hey, it's okay. We won't hurt you.' I said. I ignored the look Emile and Desmond gave me.

'I just wanted to- I don't want to kill people. I don't know why I'm here. Why did I do this? Oh gods.' Darius breathed shakily.

'Can we please kill him? He can't go back to Rendo anyway and he isn't going to tell us anything.' Emile said impatiently.

'Give it a bit more time.' I said. Emile huffed out a breath and crossed her arms.

'Ok then, Darius, who do you work for?'

The strange, blue feeling erupted in my throat again and I struggled to swallow it away.

'I can't tell you.' Darius murmured.

'Then what can you tell us?' Desmond questioned. Darius's eyes were wild and bloodshot as he looked around in fear.

'It doesn't matter. I'm going to die either way, aren't I?' he said miserably.

'Well, you did just try and kill a princess, son. Ever heard of treason?' Desmond said, smiling humorlessly.

'I'm sorry.' Darius said.

'Can I kill him, now?' Emile said. I glared at her as she widened her eyes innocently.

'Since when were you a bloodthirsty psychopath?' I said.

'I'm not. He tried to kill me so I have every right to return the favour.' Emile said promptly.

'If anyone's killing him it's me.' I said harshly. Emile rolled her eyes carelessly.

'And you're saying that your word is better than that of a princess's?' she asked sweetly.

'I'm saying that I want to make his death as quick and painless as possible. Something you certainly won't be doing while you're in this mindset.'

'If you two don't shut up I'm going to kill him myself.' Desmond cut in. I bit on my tongue and walked up to Darius, crouching down to his level. I felt awful, but I had to kill him. It was only right. Technically speaking, it was me who had brought him into the mess, and it was up to me to get him back out of it. Even if it was by killing him.

'I'm sorry.' I whispered before bringing the sword to his chest. Darius choked for a few moments, his face tense with fear. But then he spoke.

'George.'

After that, he went silent. Nobody else had heard what he had said; I wished that I hadn't heard it. He was trying to tell me something, and I didn't want to know what it was.

'Who are we waking up now?' Desmond inquired. I forced myself to look away from Darius's bleeding corpse and focus on the last alive hostages, walking back to Emile and Desmond.

'The one with black hair. I want her death to be especially painful.'

☆✯☆

I had a sticky body pressed against me and I had to admit, it was rather uncomfortable. Emile must've felt the same way, as her face had gone a tinge green. To add to the prospect of holding a dead person, all I could smell was iron and vomit. I restrained a gag as we left the house.

'This is vile.' Emile said. It was our final round of disposing of the Rendans, and even I felt quite grim. I could kill people with ease, but handling their cold, rotting remnants was a whole other thing.

'Well, it isn't necessarily pleasant.' I muttered. It was Emile's fault that she was doing it instead of Desmond anyway, though, so she had no right to complain. It was her who insisted on coming out with me, the stubborn idiot.

'I can't believe you made me do the one with greasy hair. Not only is there dead-people juice all over my shirt, there's grease.' Emile said.

'I would rather take out the bodies of people I actually liked than trust them with you. No offence meant.' I said shortly.

'That's rich coming from the person who killed them.' Emile shot back. I pressed my lips together into a thin line; she was insufferably annoying, sometimes.

'I'm going to kill *you* in a minute.' I said.

'It was a joke. Besides, I'm too fabulous to be killed.' Emile said airily. *I wouldn't count on it.*

'Mhm.' I murmured. If only she knew what was waiting for her; I was sure she wouldn't be talking about how fabulous she was if she did.

'As soon as this whole war thing is over I'm snapping my sword in half.' Emile declared.

'Why on earth would you do that?' I asked.

'Because not everyone enjoys murdering people, Max. I'm pretty sure that's just you.'

'How do you know that I enjoy it?'

'I saw you this morning. You were merciless. Didn't even give the opposing side a chance.' She had a point there.

'Am I meant to give them a chance?' I questioned. Emile didn't answer; she was too good. The type of people like her never got far in wars; I knew that from the stories Nathaniel told me simply to frighten me.

'You weren't talking about giving people chances when killing those hostages.' I countered.

'That was different. They'd already had their chance. And I actually gave them one, unlike you.' It baffled me that she was even going to war in the first place.

We stopped at the fire pit and threw in the two bodies, wiping our hands against our trousers. Emile turned to leave but I grabbed her wrist, accidentally pulling her close. So close, so close that I could feel her breath mingling with mine. So close that the smell of death had left, to be replaced with her familiar fragrance. The fragrance of coffee, smoke and petrichor.

'We live in a world full of savages. If you give the wrong person a chance, they'll kill you. You look out for yourself and nobody else, no matter the consequences. To destroy yourself out of compassion would be giving in to the temptation of goodness, and you can't afford to be good when you're surrounded by brutes and barbarians.' I said in a low voice. Emile's royal blue eyes were alight with a blazing fire, burning my soul as she stared at me unwaveringly.

'Did it ever occur to you that most people would rather die than live surrounded by sadists like the ones you speak of?' she said. I felt a sting at her words; if only she knew who I really was.

'I suppose you're a part of those people?'

'You already know the answer to that.' My grip on her skin tightened for a moment, embracing it's sticky warmth as the fire raged on beside it like a blanket.

'Then you're deranged.'

I let go and stalked off, a sudden cold taking over the palm of my hand. I shivered and pushed it into the pocket of my jacket.

Emile followed me but didn't bother to catch up, her steps staying the same pace as mine as she stayed a distance. Desmond must have sensed something, as his eyes raked over me in confusion when we re-entered the arena, my hair windswept and my cheeks pink.

'We have one more person to wake up.' Emile stated, finally coming in line beside me.

'I saved her for last because she's an exile from Kendra. I thought you both might know her.' I said. Anastasia was the last hostage, her hair as white as snow and stained with blood.

'What's her name?' Emile asked.

'Anastasia Ivene.'

Desmond spun around and stared at me, his eyes wide. *Well, I'm guessing that means that they do know her.*

'Ivene? As in Ivene the duke?' Emile said. *So now little Anastasia who George used to babysit is the daughter of a duke. What else could possibly happen?*

'She isn't the one who killed those twins, is she?' Desmond said. *Fantastic. Utterly fantastic.*

'What? She's only thirteen, not to mention that she was exiled at seven; you're trying to tell me that Anastasia killed two people at the age of seven? I don't believe it. She wouldn't hurt a fly!' I rambled.

'It's definitely her. I can remember Ivene himself referring to her as Ana, and that's simply Anastasia shortened.' Desmond said.

'She won't even remember us.' Emile said in wonder. I was still in shock from the new information.

'Right, can we just wake her up? I'm feeling a bit overwhelmed right now.' I said.

'That isn't going to help in the slightest.' Emile pointed out. I felt a very sudden urge to stab her instead of Anastasia.

'Leave him be, Emile, we have to wake her up anyway.' Desmond chided, going up to Anastasia.

As soon as she woke I knew that what they said was true; I could see it in her eyes. The hidden depth of cruelty and menace, one I could barely fathom. It was disturbing to see it on a thirteen year old.

'Well, isn't this a surprise.' Anastasia said sarcastically. Even her voice sounded different, now. The malice wasn't as hard to uncover once I knew it was there.

'Lovely seeing you, Ana. Long time no see, eh?' Emile said.

'Well, I never. The princess of Kendra. It's an honour, really. If I wasn't tied up I would curtsy right now.' Anastasia said, 'And I see Desmond is here, too. I haven't seen you since you escorted me to being a slave for the past six years of my life.'

'You killed two infants.'

'Five, actually, if you count the ones that were never found out.'

By some miracle, she was crazier than I was. Well. Not really a miracle, considering I was fairly crazy myself.

'How could I have missed you, Maximus! Oh, you were good to me, unlike these two. Both you and George.' Anastasia said, her eyes falling on me. I couldn't judge her for the murders. I had done the same sort of things at that age, if not younger. It wasn't my place to hold a grudge for that.

'How are George and Adelaide?' I questioned. I figured I may as well ask it while I had the chance.

'I don't know about George; he spends his time locked up in his room like the moody little git he is nowadays. I'm guessing it's because he hasn't seen you in so long, Maximus. Adelaide, on the other hand, is doing great; I'll make sure to mention that you asked.' Anastasia

'You won't go back to be able to mention it.' Emile said curtly.

'Why so hostile, princess? Aren't I just the baby who you bought dolls for all of those years ago?' Anastasia queried, batting her eyelashes. It was quite strange; I didn't understand the logic behind eyelash batting. It just made her look ridiculous.

'For a start, you ripped the dolls up. For a second, you've come here to try and kill me, have you not?' Emile said.

'Oh, yes. From what I've heard, your sister was much easier to get rid of.'

I could practically feel Emile's heart as it began to race, threatening to burst out of her chest. *Well, I guess I'll find out about that whole ordeal faster than I had anticipated.*

'You're with the people who took Evania?' Emile said. Her voice was smoother than her breath, which was beginning to grow shaky and quick.

'Did I not just say that?' Anastasia said.

'Is she ok? What did you do to her? Is she-' Emile cut off and cleared her throat awkwardly.

'I would answer those if one, I knew, and two, she was actually alive.' The words hit Emile like a sword in her stomach.

She recoiled, her eyes flickering and her lip sucked under her teeth. I let myself look at her, watching in faint interest and concern as she clenched her fists and inhaled heavily.

'Surely you knew. I mean, she's been missing for five years, now. You can't have thought that she was still alive.' Anastasia said.

'Shut up before I kill you on the spot.' Emile mumbled. Anastasia raised her eyebrows and gave way to a small smirk.

'We were here to do the same thing to you. It didn't work, clearly; somehow the mere three of you managed to beat twenty of the best warriors we have.' she continued.

'How are *you* one of their best warriors? Your technique is insulting.' I said, an eyebrow lifted.

'Just because you're perfect, Maximus, doesn't mean we all are.' Anastasia snapped.

'Look, why don't we all just calm down and speak like normal, mature people would.' Desmond put in.

'Look who finally decides to speak.' Anastasia said.

'How do you expect we speak 'normally' and 'maturely' when we've just been told that her organisation killed Emile's sister?' I said.

'Well, obviously, but- how did you know about Evania?'

'Because we've just been told! I already said that!'

Desmond was now starting to infuriate me just as much as Emile usually did. Well. He wasn't *that* irritating, I reasoned: just very, very close.

'Oh. Right. Well, now that we know why you're all here, who do you work for?' Desmond asked.

'It isn't just a specific person. The Vayne family; they live in Hevalio, if you want to track them down.' Anastasia said. I recognised the country *Hevalio* from Emile's journal; she had said that they were one of the richest countries. So why was the Vayne family using Rendan scum to do their dirty work? And clearly Nathaniel had to be involved, too; I could tell that much from the people who had come. What was he planning? What were *they* planning?

'Why is a family from somewhere like that using people like you?' Desmond said, speaking my mind for me.

'Don't ask me. I just do as I'm told.' Anastasia shrugged. I turned to Emile, sick of looking at Anastasia's smug expression. Emile herself didn't look as fazed as I thought she would be. Saying that, she had already grieved for Evania. 5 years had passed; she'd gone through the mourning and the pain. Even if she had hoped that her sister was alive, some part of her would've known that she wasn't coming back.

'Are you alright?' I said, speaking quietly so only she could hear me over Desmond and Anastasia's bickering.

'Me? I'm fine. Honestly. We have more pressing matters to deal with over my feelings. Besides, I've already been too emotional today. I need to get a grip, really.' Emile said silkily.

'Oh. Well, as long as you're ok, I suppose.' I responded. Emile laughed lightly.

'Don't get all sentimental, darling. I'm sure we have worse to come.' she said softly. I nodded and looked back at the other two, who both seemed like they were going to murder each other.

'You can't kill me.' I heard Anastasia say. It was laughable how confident she sounded.

'Why is that?' Emile cut in.

'If you do, I'm almost certain this special war of yours will be starting a lot earlier. And, considering Maximus can't make a good throw or so to save his life, you probably need more time to train.' Anastasia said.

'Sweetheart, we just killed nineteen people. I think we'll be fine.' Emile said, looking at Anastasia incredulously.

'Then you, Maximus. You can't kill me because of George and Nathaniel, and I suppose Adelaide too, although you rarely see her.' Anastasia said. My gaze intensified.

'What do you mean?' I said slowly.

'I thought you wouldn't have heard. Your dear Nathaniel has taken me in, and Adelaide and I have grown rather close. Kill me and she'll never forgive you. Do you know what that means? Neither will George. Because we all know he would pick his biological sister over his unbiological brother.' Anastasia said.

That day was only getting worse and worse.

'You're trying to blackmail me, now?' I said in disbelief, 'You do realise that I could kill you and make it look like an accident, right? Besides, it isn't like anyone's going to find your body.'

'You can try, but everyone knows that I'm here. If I don't return they'll simply have to assume I'm dead.' I was starting to think that I hated a literal child.

'Desmond, write a letter to my parents.' Emile said suddenly. I raised an eyebrow.

'What do you want me to say in it?' Desmond said.

'Explain the situation and tell them to come here as quickly as possible. Until then, Ana can stay in the cells underground.' Emile said.

'There are cells here?' I said.

'Yeah, and we're going there right now, Ana.'

Soon enough it was only Desmond and I in the room. Just as he was about to leave, an idea passed over me.

'Wait, Desmond!' I called, running up to him. He stopped and spun around.

'What is it, Maximus?' Desmond asked tiredly.

'Could I write a letter to George, too?' I had been meaning to do so for a while by then, anyway. I might as well have done it when another letter was being written.

'Go ahead.'

I nodded and bolted off to my room, a million words racing through my mind. I had so much to say and only a parchment of paper to say it on.

Now, I thought as I sat at my desk, *where to begin?*

Dear George,

boy, do I have news for you. Before I get into any of that, I have to ask; is Anastasia really living with you? She'd better not be in my room. Anyway, if she is, I thought you might like to know the reason she was exiled in the first place. She killed five people; five! At the age of seven! Surely you must see that she's even worse than I am.

So, now that that's out of the way, how have you been? It's been weird not being able to go and speak to you whenever I please. On the plus side, I don't have to listen to your annoying voice anymore. That was a joke! Don't kill me!

Speaking of killing me, I've been told that if I murder Anastasia you'll do just that. Now, I don't want to do so; she's only a child, after all. But she came here with the intention of sabotaging the task, and she would've killed me herself had she been given the opportunity, so I'm really not sure what to do.

How has Adelaide been, by the way? I hear she's quite fond of our brand new serial killer friend.

Why on earth has Nathaniel let this happen? I don't know what to do, George. Seriously. For once in my life, I don't know what to do.

So, basically, the main question is this; am I allowed to kill Anastasia without losing you and Adelaide? Because if not I'll send her straight back to Rendo, I promise.

Now that that's out of the way, I thought you would like to know that I've been learning archery. Turns out that my aim isn't as terrible as we had always said it was, although I have to give Emile most of the credit. She's been teaching me, and it's actually working, somehow. Who would've thought; an orphaned Rendan being taught archery, of all things, by the Kendran princess. If you had told me about all of this a year ago, I wouldn't of believed you.

I'm sure you know about Evania now, right? I've realised that I never mentioned Emile's fear of failure. Well, I'm pretty sure her sister's disappearance has something to do with it. Here's my theory; after Evania went missing, Emile couldn't forgive herself for not being able to protect her only sister and thought of it as somewhat a failure. Therefore, it would induce a fear of that exact thing, as Evania's abduction most likely was a tipping point in her life. And now she's let the phobia spiral out of hand, making it the way it is now.

Of course, that might not be the actual case. But from what I've gathered, it's something like that. Desmond was on stepping stones around the topic when it was brought up today. Mind you, that

Anastasia is nothing but trouble; I don't know why Adelaide would want to be friends with someone like her. Well, saying that, we aren't much different, are we? And you're my closest friend. I really need to stop being so judgemental; it brings down my character.

I have so much more to say, but this piece of paper is too small to fit my words. Write back to me as soon as you get this.

Sincerely,
Maximus Invictus Blare

⚔ Chapter Fourteen ⚔

THE RESPONDING LETTERS FROM both George and Emile's parents came about a week later. Anastasia had become quite restless by that stage, spending her time banging on the bars of her cell and screaming unintelligible insults. When it got out of hand and neither Emile nor Desmond could settle her, I was finally sent down, seeing the old cells for the first time.

As soon as I took the last step down stairs I previously hadn't even known were there, I was overwhelmed by an awful smell. There wasn't a way to properly describe it; the scent of mould and rot was a good start, though.

It was as if there was a decaying body down there, but I knew that that was only my imagination playing tricks on me. It was just an old prison. I could surely go without vomiting.

I ended up pinching my nose with my fingers to get rid of the smell.

'If you're here to tell me that I'm disturbing you upstairs again, I think you should know that I couldn't care less.' Anastasia said as soon as my footsteps echoed off the old walls. Her voice sounded thin; as if it would break at any moment. That wasn't like her. To break. Sure, I didn't know her very well, but from the small load of information I had, I could tell that she didn't give up easily.

'Um, no, I'm not here to say that.' Technically, I was, but she clearly didn't want to hear that.

'Maximus? Well, it's pleasant to be blessed with a different voice.' Anastasia said sarcastically. I walked up to her cell and peeked through, stifling a gasp at the sight of her face. It was streaked with blood and dirt, her usually light blonde locks mangled and dark.

'Are you- are you alright?' I inquired carefully. The last thing I wanted was for her to get even more mad at me; I probably deserved it, but it didn't mean I wanted it.

'Oh, yes, I'm at the prime of my life sitting in the dark of this crumbling old cell.' Anastasia snapped.

'Yeah, um, well you did bring it upon yourself. You should know better than anyone that there's always a price for what you do.' I said awkwardly.

'I didn't choose to walk into my death bed! I chose to walk away from it!' Anastasia exclaimed. My eyebrows knitted together; whatever that meant, it didn't sound very appealing.

'What are you talking about?' I asked slowly. Anastasia laughed; it wasn't a laugh like that of Emile's, where her stomach clenched from it's intensity and her eyes scrunched up. No, it held a dark undertone, full of anger and injustice.

'I thought that you should have realised by now. We both know that dearest Nathaniel isn't the little spot of sunshine that he's made out to be.' Anastasia said. My eyes narrowed involuntarily.

'What has he done?'

'Wouldn't you like to know.'

I bit down on my tongue in a desperate attempt to not start yelling at her about how she needed to take things seriously for once in her life. I had gone there to calm her, not to infuriate her even more.

'Look, I really need to know if he's done something, ok? Remember what he used to do to George and I when you stayed over? I can sort it out. You need to trust me.' I said. Anastasia was silent for a few moments; I could hear her mind racing. When she eventually spoke, her voice was quiet and thick.

'He said that if I didn't come here he would-' she cut off, the visible skin on her face flushing red.

'What? He would do what?' I thought that I knew what she was going to say. I didn't. She completely caught me by surprise.

'He said he would tell the government something, ok?' Anastasia said. It sounded ridiculous when she said it; there wasn't much that the Rendan government actually cared about. But I looked closer and I could see the glossy coat over her green eyes, tears threatening to spill over her eyelashes.

'You can tell me, you know; I've grown quite accustomed to keeping secrets during my time here.' I said tentatively. It felt strange being so kind, but I needed to know what had managed to get a near psychopath in such a state.

'You don't understand. I want to tell you- I want to tell the whole world. But I can't.' Anastasia said under her breath. I chewed on my lip; it didn't look like she was going to tell me anything.

'Look, I won't bother you about this ok? Just don't make as much of a racket.' I said. I could hear a faint call of Desmond yelling for me, 'And I have to go. I'll come back. I promise.'

With that, I ran up the stairs and back to the corridor of the first floor, coming to a halt in front of Desmond and Emile. I brushed down my shirt and waited for them to speak.

'A letter addressed to you is here.' Desmond said, handing me an envelope. I flipped it over and picked up on the neat handwriting on it's back.

'This must be from George. Did your parents respond, too, Emile?' I said.

'Yeah. They said they can't come for three weeks.' Emile said forlornly. My mouth fell agape.

'Three weeks? We have to deal with Anastasia for three weeks?' Just because I was being nice to her before, it didn't make her any less of a nuisance.

'That depends on what your friend has to say on the matter.' Desmond said, watching me expectantly. I looked down at the letter; I would've preferred to open it in my room, but it wasn't the end of the world. I ripped it open and divulged myself in his words.

Dear Maximus,

it's nice to finally hear from you, considering it seems you must've simply forgotten that I exist. No, it's not that big of a deal; I've missed seeing you whenever I please, too.

Surprisingly, I'm not doing too bad. Of course, it's been quite awful over the past months, but I'm getting used to it. I barely see Adelaide anymore; she spends all of her time with my newest housemate, Anastasia. And no, she isn't in your room.

I'm not sure about the whole thing for killing her. Obviously it would be better if you did; for you and I alike. But I agree with Anastasia in the sense that Adelaide wouldn't forgive you if you did. She's the only friend she's ever had, and it would most likely break her heart if she were to die at your hands.

If you need to do it, I am by no means stopping you. I'm aware of why she went there, now, and it's frankly disgusting. I told Adelaide about how she's a bad influence and all, but she doesn't seem to care. In fact, she told me that I was starting to sound like my father when I chided her for the second time! I was agonised! Your theory of Emile is quite interesting. It makes sense, though; I only know about Evania now that you've told me, but I did a little research and everything you wrote lines up perfectly. I think that you're onto something here. You have to update me on it as much as possible.

How are you, too, by the way? By the sounds of it, it doesn't seem like you're doing terribly. Of course, I know that Emile is extremely kind from when I met her before, so surely she must have a factor in this, if you understand what I'm trying to say. But please remember what I said before; don't get attached.

I look forward to reading your response.

Kindest regards,
George Flint

I came to the end of the letter and immediately stuffed it in my pocket; Desmond and Emile could never read it. My whole cover would be blown if they did.

'Well? What does it say? Can we get rid of miss loudmouth downstairs?' Emile asked eagerly.

'See, it's a little unclear at the minute. He said I should only do it if I need to.' I said.

'I think we should. She keeps on giving me the details of every murder she's ever committed.' Emile shuddered, 'And she's rather descriptive, too.'

'Has she threatened to do anything to any of us?' I said. Silence was my response. 'Then we'll keep her alive until Emile's parents arrive, and they can judge it.'

'That sounds fair to me.' Desmond said. I shot him a small smile. Emile, however, was most certainly not smiling.

'My parents will just set her back to Rendo! Come on, Desmond, you know what they're like. My mum cares too much and my dad will do anything she says.' she said.

'If the Queen thinks that she should be set free then I will not be the one to argue with her.' Desmond said.

'I second that.' I put in. Emile groaned and rolled her eyes.

'You're a pair of wusses. Honestly, when we send a criminal back to civilization you two can take the blame.' she said before sauntering off.

Desmond and I shared a sceptical look. I had come to the conclusion that Emile had absolutely no filter whatsoever. She said what she wanted when she wanted.

'I should probably write back to George.' I said uncomfortably. I was having one of those days where my usual awkward manner had returned.

'Go for it, son.' Desmond said, his lips pulling upwards slightly. He looked worn out; I couldn't blame him. After being retired for years, he was required to train not only one teenager, but two. And he had to deal with stuff like Anastasia and Emile and I nearly killing each other in a duel that never should've happened in the first place.

I nodded sharply and walked off to my room, the weight of George's letter suddenly heavy in my pocket. Darius's last words had come to my mind for some unknown reason, and now I couldn't stop thinking about it. *George.* His voice had been so shaky yet so firm. I had to ask George what the meaning of that was.

Dear George,

              I'm doing great, actually. We've decided to let the Kendran King and Queen decide Anastasia's fate. Don't worry too much, though; Emile has said that the Queen is very forgiving.

I have to ask you something, and I'm not sure of the extent of how serious it is. Before Darius died, his last words were your name, and he said it directly to me. I have no idea why, though. I would appreciate it if you elaborated on that.

Anastasia seems to be under the impression that if she hadn't come here Nathaniel was going to reveal some secret of hers to the Rendan government. Can you write a list of the things that might be considered serious, as I can't remember the majority of them myself. Or, if it's easier, you could simply find out what Anastasia's secret is. I'm sure that Adelaide will know, if they're as close as they claim.

I don't see why you keep telling me to 'not get too attached'. If by that you mean Emile, you're mistaken. She's nothing but an obstacle for me, and I'm going to eventually kill her when the time is right. If I truly cared for her you would've known by now.

However, that gives me an idea. If I manage to make her attached to me, it will be easier to kill her, as she wouldn't be able to bring herself to fight back. But I might not even have to do that; she has a habit for showing mercy to her enemies, as she did with every single person she merely knocked out yesterday. I personally think it's ridiculous, but *it could work to my advantage.*

I don't want to bore you, so I'll finish up here and let you carry on your day. Be quick in responding, please, as I have only 3 weeks until Emile's parents visit.

Sincerely,
Maximus Invictus Blare

I threw my feather pen across the desk and grabbed an envelope, gently placing the paper in it stamping the address on the back. I realised that the colour of the stamp was a startling blue; it really felt as if the universe was trying to tell me something. The colour blue was making a lot of appearances lately, from the colour of Emile's eyes to the colour of the feeling I got in my throat.

I sighed nonchalantly. If I wanted to win the war, I needed to get a hold of myself; why on earth were Emile's eyes the first thing that came to my mind when I thought of the colour blue? I didn't think of George's eyes everytime I saw the colour brown, so why should blue be any different?

If it was possible, I would've kicked myself. Why did I have to insist on constantly being an absolute, dim-witted moron? She was an annoying, self-absorbed fool, and I didn't need to waste my time thinking about her *eyes*. Of all things, it had to be her eyes, didn't it? Why couldn't I instead focus on her irksome personality… even if it wasn't really all that irksome.

She had a way of making everything feel better than it was. She found out that her sister was dead, and brushed it off within minutes. She killed a person for the first time, and put it down to anger and revenge.

But then there was her scent. Coffee, smoke and petrichor. It seemed to have made a home amongst my nose.

She was too headstrong; the complete opposite of me. I couldn't let myself feel anything for her. A dull numbness would be better than whatever it was that was making my head throb.

To add to that, she was my enemy! I had to kill her, one day! She was on the opposing side, and I couldn't like her. No. I couldn't feel anything for her. I had to focus on the numbness.

Even if I knew, somewhere in my heart, that my country wasn't as innocent as it was made out to be.

I shuddered and recited the rules internally to try and take my mind off the subject. *Rule number 1; never go into a fight thinking you're going to lose.*

Rule number 2; always go with your gut instinct.

Rule number 3; no attachments

Rule number 4; remember to be logical in battle.

Rule number 3 ran through me in an unsettling manner, tracing it's fingers against my ribcage and sending chills running down my spine. Why did I have to be like that? Why did I always end up thinking things like that?

Rule number 5; never forget who your enemy is.

☆★☆

By the time George finally wrote back, it was only a day before the Kendran King and Queen were due to arrive. I didn't blame him, really; I had asked him quite a lot. But my excitement at the arrival of his letter drowned out any blame I might have felt as I ran to my room and ripped open the envelope eagerly, reading so quickly it felt like my eyes were on fire.

Dear Maximus,

I'm sorry for taking so long to answer, I've been trying my best to find out Anastasia's secret. Unfortunately, Adelaide wasn't willing to uncover anything, so I took up finding a list of the most important rules and restrictions. I'll write it out below.

- To harm, murder or kidnap any member of the royal family is considered treason, and the penalty is death.
- To harm, murder or kidnap any member of high authority, such as a member of parliament, is given a death penalty.
- Anyone who is helping a native Domvan stay here is given 20 years in jail.
- Any native Domvan staying here is given life in jail, if not the death penalty.
- Any person who is caught participating in inappropriate activities with a person of the

same sex is given up to 50 years in jail, if not death penalty.

In conclusion, the laws are messed up and Rendo is still living like they're from 100 years ago.

The most likely things are that she is either helping a Domvan in Rendo, has killed a parliament person or my father has caught her with a girl. They're all likely, so you'll have to do a bit of digging to find it out. Update me when you know what it is.

Adelaide told me to tell you that if you kill Anastasia she won't forgive you, but she won't murder you until you've won the war. I suppose it's better than what we were originally expecting. Don't write back to me until you have some more information on Anastasia. When you think you've figured it out tell me, and I can get confirmation from either father or Adelaide. Whoever cooperates the best.

As for the thing with young Darius, I honestly have no clue. I haven't spoken to him in awhile, so it was probably just my father trying to get inside of your head. Carry on doing well, and don't keep lying to yourself about the attachment thing. Trust me, it's better to be honest.

Best regards,

George Flint

    Well, he was one to talk about being honest, wasn't he? He'd told more lies than I could count, only to reprimand me on being truthful. Honestly.

    On the other hand, I had been rewarded with some rather useful information. Out of the three things that George had said were the most likely, I could take away the one of killing a member of parliament. She wouldn't do it for the mere reason that Nathaniel wouldn't have bothered trying to cover that up for her: meaning if she had done it, she would've already been executed.

    That left the remaining two options being either helping a Domvan refugee or being caught with a girl.

    I didn't understand both of those rules. The country of Domva was struggling with poverty and terrorists at the moment, so it seemed only right to let them stay in Rendo. I didn't see why they would want to, considering it's racial prejudices and pathetic homophobia, but it was better than being there. It wasn't like they were hurting anyone because of their race, for goodness sake.

The same thing went for people liking people of the same gender. We were all the same; why did one small difference have to equal a much larger one? It was utterly senseless.

But Anastasia could wait; the King and Queen could not.

☆★☆

Emile's parents didn't come until midday, after we'd eaten our dinner. For a short amount of time, we were under the impression that they weren't going to turn up at all.

'They're never normally late. My dad hates being tardy.' Emile had said anxiously, her eyes turned down.

'Calm down; they're probably on their way now. Your dad might hate being tardy, but I know for a fact that he hates breaking promises even more, and he promised he'd come today.' Desmond had responded reassuringly. I wasn't as sure as he was; he might've known the Kendran King better than I did, but if I knew anything at all it was that people changed. A longing to keep promises could fade quicker than the light of day did at sunset.

When they did eventually knock at the door, Emile was practically dancing around in excitement. She gave Desmond and I the small gift of her cat's grin, staring expectantly at Desmond as he let in her parents.

'Emile, darling, I've missed you so much!' the Queen exclaimed, grabbing Emile and squeezing her tightly. I felt a pang of jealousy; my own *mater* hadn't been alive for long enough for me to remember hugging her like that.

'Hi, mum.' Emile gasped, struggling for air as she was finally let go. Her *pater*, the King, looked out of place. He smiled at her but said no welcoming words, no embrace, not even a simple touch of her shoulder. It felt uneasily like the way I felt about my own *pater*. And I hated him, even if he was dead.

'It's good to see you.' Desmond said stiffly. I realised, then, that I probably should have bowed. But it was too late to do that by then, so I stood awkwardly and waited to be told what to do.

'And you, too. Now, what is it that was so urgent we needed to come here?' the King said hastily. It seemed he was in quite the hurry to leave.

'Right. Um, it's probably better if Maximus here explains it. He knows better than us.' Desmond said. I felt my cheeks flush as everyone's attention turned to me. Without knowing it, my eyes found Emile's electric blue ones, seeking comfort in their warm depths. I almost forgot that I was supposed to speak before a small cough from the King snapped me out of my trance.

'Um, hi.' I mumbled. While the King's cold pupils didn't move from me, the Queen's face broke out into a smile. I felt myself relax, slightly.

'So you're Maximus- well, it's a pleasure to meet you. Please, tell us what the matter is, if you don't mind.' the Queen said kindly. I nodded reluctantly, picking apart the pieces of the situation I could say in a millisecond.

'As you must know, we were attacked by the same people who stole Princess Evania. I'm sorry for your loss, by the way.' Perhaps if I were nicer than I usually was, they would like me better, 'Anyway, one young girl, an exiled daughter of the Duke of Ivene, thinks that we shouldn't kill her as my friends, and basically family, back in Rendo are unnaturally close with her.'

'Then we should let her go!' the Queen said immediately. I wondered, briefly, if she was fit to be a Queen in her strangely forgiving state.

'Now, we need to think about this-' the King started.

'No, we do not.' the Queen said, cutting him off. 'I know the girl that they're talking about. Young Anastasia. She can change, I know it. Trust me.' I realised, then, that I had forgotten her name. I knew that the King was called King Septimus, a name that sounded very close to serpent. I knew I probably shouldn't judge him upon first meetings, but it was rather difficult not to.

It took quite a bit of strain to remember her name; I eventually did, though. Queen Acela. Strangely enough, I was positive that her name was of Rendan origins, meaning *flower from the ash tree*. I brushed it off with an air of unease.

'Well, if we're going to let the Ivene heir free, Emile is going to be coming back to the palace for this weekend.' King Septimus said firmly. I saw Emile's eyes widen.

'What? Dad, I-'

'I don't want to hear it! You will be in the safety of the palace until we're sure that Ivene is back in Rendo.' King Septimus said harshly, 'Go and pack your belongings.'

I thought Emile was going to refuse for a moment. But she simply bit on the inside of her cheek and strode off, her head held high. I supposed that pride *was* her strong point.

'Septimus, I don't think this is necessary.' Queen Acela said cautiously. Her husband dismissed her with a wave of his hand; she almost looked offended.

'This is my judgement, and I say she comes back with us for a few days. She can come back here on Monday; see, it's only 3 days. I think Desmond and Maximus here can survive for a single weekend.' King Septimus said. He was being extremely cruel to me, considering I was known for my ruthless brutality when it came to getting rid of people I didn't need.

I especially didn't need someone with a name as ugly as his.

'Right. Yeah. I'll just say goodbye, then.' I muttered, walking up to Emile's room. I knocked at the door and waited, tapping my feet impatiently against the wood of the corridor.

She finally came out about 10 minutes later, a suitcase in hand and her eyes hard and dark. It was nearly frightening to see her like that.

The door slammed shut behind her before I had a chance to see what her room looked like; I did wonder why she was allowed in mine but I wasn't in hers.

'Um, your parents seem nice.' I said, stumbling over my words. The corner of Emile's mouth twitched up and her eyes softened.

'Yeah, sure they are. I mean, my mum's really nice, but my dad's a little hostile with strangers. He'll warm up to you.' she said. I nodded a little too quickly, the silence hanging over us like a veil.

'So, erm… enjoy yourself? I don't know what I'm supposed to say. I never say goodbye to people. They just… go.' The blunt reality of my words stung.

'Don't get so sentimental. Just make sure that, by the time I'm back, Ana's back in Rendo.' Emile said.

'Right. Yes. I will.' I said awkwardly. Just as I was starting to walk away, her voice forced me to turn back around.

'Don't have too much fun while I'm gone.' Emile called. I pressed my lips together to fight off a smile.

'Fun? Without Emile Elizabeth Elires? That surely must be a crime.' I said. Her scent lingered, even though I was across the hall from her. The smoke was at its prime; she must've been smoking in her room. I didn't want to say anything about the habit, but it was starting to worry me.

'It is. So don't commit it.' Emile warned jokingly. I could feel my eyes sparkling.

'Are you not the very person who told me, and I quote, to not be afraid to disagree with you? Surely that must go for this, too?' I said. Emile shook her head at me, but I could see the way her features had lightened.

'How on earth do you remember that?' she asked incredulously.

'It's insulting to question my ways.' I paused. 'I just have a really good memory.'

Emile laughed quietly but it carried through, echoing off the walls beside us. They suddenly seemed a lot narrower.

'I'm only gone for a weekend. You'll be fine.' she said. I let a smirk replace what once was a blooming smile.

'And who says I want you to come back so early?' I said innocently. Emile rolled her eyes.

'Goodbye, Maximus.'

'Goodbye, Emile.'

The scent of smoke stayed with me long after she had boarded the carriage and left.

⚔ Chapter Fifteen ⚔

WE ARRANGED A BOAT to take Anastasia back to Rendo for the morning after Emile had left at 8:30am. However, I still had unfinished business with her. That is why I woke up at 6:00am on the very day she was due to be shipped away and snuck into the old dungeons, my eyes dry from sleep and my hair still unbrushed.

The quiet down there was enough to put off a man who had seen deaths of thousands; that wasn't even mentioning the stench. It felt like, since the last time I'd been there, it had somehow gotten even worse. Maybe there actually was a body decomposing in the place. Whatever it was, I didn't necessarily need to know. Or want to.

As I stepped off the stairs, I could've sworn I saw a rat scurry across the landing in the dim light. I blinked at the spot where I presumed I had seen it before walking away, deciding it was just my mind playing tricks on me.

'You again? I thought that I was leaving today. Came to kill me after all?' I would've thought the voice was just a hallucination if I hadn't seen the strands of Anastasia's hair hanging out of her cell. I went up to it before jumping back, startled by how close she was to the bars. Her full face was pressed against them, causing it to look rather frightening.

'No, I'm not here to kill you. I just want to have a conversation.' I said smoothly. In her head that probably sounded like I was implying torture; good. If she suspected the worst, my investigation wouldn't seem so bad.

'Get on with it, then. I don't have all day.' Anastasia stopped and broke out into a laugh; in fact, no, it sounded more like a cackle, as cliche as the word is. But her voice was so high and... different to what it was before that it felt suitable.

'Is there a reason you're laughing?' I said. She couldn't respond for a moment; by the time she had eventually calmed down, 5 minutes had passed.

'Oh, no, I just think it's quite amusing that I can say that I don't have all day and actually mean it.' Perhaps she had gone mad after all.

'Right, well, that's great and all, but I'm being serious here.' I heard a sigh come from her mouth before a sound of slumping.

'As I said before; get on with it.' Anastasia said.

'Yes. Alright. I will.' I stopped to clear my throat, 'So, if I remember correctly you're here because Nathaniel knows a secret about you, yes? And that it involves him telling the government of Rendo if you didn't cooperate? No need to answer. I already know the answers. Well, I've done some research and it's come to my attention that there are only 2 possible options for what your secret could be.'

I could feel Anastasia stiffen as I paused and waited for her reaction to my revelation.

'Keep on speaking, then.' she finally muttered. I nodded and wasted no time in getting back on track.

'Either you have a Domvan refugee friend back there, or Nathaniel has caught you with a girl. Would you care to tell me which it is?' I said. If someone could have a heart attack because of what they'd heard, I was sure that was happening to Anastasia that very minute.

'How did you figure it out?' she whispered, her voice cracking.

'The point is that I didn't. I need you to finish the puzzle for me, if you don't mind.'

I was very doubtful of Anastasia actually telling me what I wanted to know. But I had to at least try and get it out of her; even if she didn't say it directly, something in her body language might tell me the right option.

'Are you stupid? This must be easier than getting me to even tell you about it. And let me tell you, I only said it because I was sleep deprived and living in pitch black, half out of my mind.' Anastasia sounded more normal now, as if she's been shocked back to humanity.

'I'm afraid it really isn't as easy as you make it out to be.' I said, restraining myself from yelling at her. She deserved it. But then I'd probably wake up Desmond.

'Figure it out yourself. Just think about it really hard and it won't be that difficult.' Anastasia said, turning away. She wasn't going to say anything else; that was clear. So, with a deep exhale, I went up to my room and sat at my desk, mulling over what she had said.

By the time the clock hit 8:20, I was still stumped. Although, in my defence, I had nearly fallen asleep multiple times, meaning I technically only thought about it for about ten minutes, if that.

It hit me in a wave. I started considering her personality, and it dawned on me; Anastasia was generally an awful person. She didn't care for anyone except for herself.

And Adelaide.

Would a person as cruel as her really think to help out someone who might as well be blacklisted? The short answer is no, definitely not. And if that was the case, Nathaniel wouldn't have used it as a threat; he would've killed the Domvan and shunned Anastasia.

But Adelaide was his daughter. As horrible as he was, he wouldn't sentence his own child to death.

I didn't know how it hadn't occurred to me before. In George's letter, he had implied that Adelaide did, in fact, know about Anastasia's secret, but wouldn't share it with the person she was closest to in the whole world. The reason being it wasn't just Anastasia's secret; it was hers, too.

I quickly checked the time. It was 8:29. If I ran fast enough, I would be able to see Anastasia.

So I did exactly that. I dashed down the stairs and out of the front door, not slowing once as I made way for the western river.

I thought it was too late; I thought that the boat was gone and I was going to have to live knowing what I now did about Anastasia when she didn't even know that I knew. But it wasn't gone; I could see Anastasia's silhouette, tall and lean, as I went even faster, desperate to see her.

'Anastasia!' I yelled. She turned and her eyes locked on mine. I came to a stop, panting for breath and clutching my knees.

'Did you really just run all of that way?' Anastasia asked.

'I figured it out.' I said quickly, evading her question. Anastasia's cheeks went a light pink as she glanced around.

'I suppose you hate me, then?' she said, a miserable undertone overwhelming her voice.

'What? No, of course I don't.' I said, frowning. I thought, then, that I saw Anastasia smile; a real, genuine smile. But it was gone as fast as it appeared.

'Right. Well, don't tell anyone. Adelaide said that she would kill me if anyone found out about her.' Anastasia's eyes widened, 'Wait, I-'

'I figured that out, too. And don't worry. I wouldn't dream of telling a soul.' I said, cutting through her.

'Oh. You're better than I thought.' Anastasia said.

'Thanks. I guess.' I said, my eyebrows furrowing slightly.

Anastasia turned towards the boat; there was a faint call of her name coming from it.

'I'm going to go now.' Anastasia declared. 'Goodbye.'

'Goodbye.'

So now I know that my best friend's sister is a secret criminal... good for her, I suppose.

☆✷☆

I walked down the corridor of the third floor, running my fingertips along the wall. I was completely and utterly bored out of my mind. It was a regular occurrence, when I thought about it; boredom wasn't new to me. But still, as I paced, my mind whirring, I wanted to take the thing inside of me causing it and squash it until it was little but a stain.

I came to the bathroom for possibly the 20th time. *I could have a shower... no, I had one yesterday. And the day before. And the day before that, too. If anything I should stop showering as much.*

With an annoyed huff of breath, I started down the stairs, my legs aching from walking for so long.

On the second floor, I came to a stop outside the library. I could smell candles from outside, slipping through the cracks in the door. I was tempted to go in, but stopped myself. I was a little tired of the library, really; I went there more than I was in my room.

I made my way to the first floor, my steps now echoing as my shoes hit the hard, wooden floor. *I could go down to the dungeons.*

Why on earth would I want to do that? Maybe I'm cracking up from being in Kendra for such a prolonged time period.

The door to the living room was open, slightly; I squinted so I could see through it. Desmond was in there, sipping at a cup, probably of coffee as he sat at the armchair. *I could go and sit with Desmond.*

I stood silently for a moment. *Yeah. That's probably the best idea.*

The small crack in the barely open door became a full opening and I stepped in, letting it shut fully behind me.

'Is it ok if I sit in here?' I said. Desmond placed his coffee at the table and shot me a smile; it felt authentic, fake. But even so, his eyes were warm and kindly in special sort of way. It was difficult to explain, but no one had the same feeling as he did.

'Of course it is, you don't need to ask.' Desmond said, beckoning me in. I sat at the sofa, my shoulders far too tense, and tried my hardest not to grimace; it felt unnecessarily awkward, that day. But it was probably just me. I was awkward with nearly everyone, George being an exception. I supposed that Emile could be classed as one too, but only just. The only reason I wasn't constantly uncomfortable out of my mind with her was because she always knew what to talk about.

'So, um… how are you?' I said.

'The same as I always am. What about you?' I wondered what he meant by *the same as I always am*. It could've meant a range of things, but it would only be weird if I asked which one he was referring to.

'Um, great. I'm doing great.' I responded. Tranquility lay it's blanket over us for a few minutes. I could see Desmond struggling to say what was on the tip of his tongue, so I stayed quiet while waiting for his internal battle to come to an end.

'I- I've noticed that- I've noticed something.' Desmond said eventually. I raised an eyebrow.

'Could you elaborate on that?' I said curiously.

'It's about- It's about Emile.' he said. My raised eyebrow shot even higher. Why would he talk to me about her? I'd only met the pair a few months beforehand. Could he not have said whatever it was he wanted to say to her parents?

'Do go on.' I said. Desmond nodded a little too fast, coughing clumsily.

'I think that she- she doesn't normally open up to people. She hasn't opened up to me; I know that for sure.' Desmond laughed humorlessly. I bit on my lip; where on earth was he going with this?

'You- you know things. It sounds weird, but you're like some genius. It's kind of creepy. But what I'm trying to say is that you can read her like an open book; I've seen it. You can read anyone like an open book, really. Look, the point is that she lets you do it.' Desmond stopped, waiting for my reaction.

'I don't understand what you're trying to say.' I did understand. I understand perfectly.

'Come on, Maximus, you've seen how quickly she shuts off her emotions. Normally she's like that all of the time. But, in the past few weeks, she's left her emotions where anyone can see them. I asked you how you found out about her fear of failure because I knew she wouldn't have told you. I only knew because her mum told me. But you read her, and you read her because she let you.' Desmond said. I swallowed.

'I know that. But I don't see what the point of telling me this is.' I said, lying through my teeth.

'Yes, you do.' Desmond said simply.

'This hasn't- I- you don't know what you're talking about.' I said. It came out sounding harsher than I had intended.

'That's the thing; I know exactly what I'm talking about. You might be smart, but that doesn't make you wise. And by the way, I'm not trying to say that I'm wise in any way whatsoever.' Desmond said.

'Then what are you trying to say? Go on, tell me if you're so sure.' I demanded. Desmond sighed.

'I see the way the storm in your eyes calms at the sight of her. I see the way your pupils dilate in the slightest when you hear her voice. I hear the way your breathing escalates when she smiles that stupid, too big smile. I hear the way your voice cracks when she makes contact with you.' Desmond said calmly.

I think that was my breaking point.

'I'm done talking about this.' I said, storming off and back to my room. My head hurt too much to listen to him rambling about this ridiculous, cliched stuff. Everything he said was a falsehood; I was convinced of it. I would never succumb to small shows of weakness like that.

I had to admit, what he said about Emile sounded true. There were flickers of uncertainty that lit her features whenever she let her emotions show, but I normally just brushed it off. I didn't have the time to bother with her feelings when I was going to kill her anyway, so why would a small show of discomfort bother me?

Well, it did now. I couldn't stop thinking. Of course, nobody can simply not think; the idea was preposterous. But I wished that I could just shut off my brain, sometimes.

Why. Are. You. Like. This?
I wish I knew.
WHY. ARE. YOU. LIKE. THIS?
I DON'T KNOW!

I wanted to scream. I did scream. I pushed a pillow to my face to muffle it and screamed until my lungs were empty and my throat was hoarse.

I wasn't really bothered about what Desmond had said; I was bothered about what it had triggered inside of me. It reminded me of everything I had fought so hard to get rid of.

There were certain feelings I felt to be below me. Things such as sadness, despair, hope.

It seemed that the stupid place had brought every single one upon me.

I was torn. I think that I must've realised that my home, Rendo, wasn't the place I thought it was. I still loved it; it was my whole life. But this place, Kendra, was so much more accepting, kind, welcoming. It wasn't a country of war. No. We had brought this to them.

Yet, I still had a strange hatred for the innocent Kendra that burned in the pit of my stomach, a flame that would not be put out. I couldn't accept that it was better than my country. So I didn't. After a long time of punching my bed frame until it broke and smashing up my room, I sat at my desk and started writing a letter. I would write to George; he always made me feel better. Besides, I had to tell him about Anastasia too, although I couldn't mention Adelaide. George wouldn't tell anyone; I knew that from my years in the Flint household, and the secrets that lay with it.

Dear George,

I figured it out. I can't tell you what it is, since it really isn't my secret to tell, and I know that if I were in Anastasia's situation I would kill her for telling anyone about it.

I hope you don't resent me for it. If you really wish to know, you could ask her yourself: I've been assured rather implicitly that she is actually quite fond of you, George.

On a different note, you really must stop with the whole attachments thing. I think you'll find that one of my, so far, 5 rules include no attachments. Here, I'll copy them out for you.

1) Never go into a fight thinking you're going to lose.
2) Always trust your gut feeling.
3) NO ATTACHMENTS.
4) Remember to be logical in battle.
5) Never forget who your enemy is.

There! I made a whole rule about not forming attachments; do you really think I'm going to ignore it? Besides, you should know better than anyone that I have a thing for pushing people away. I've done it to you for as long as I've known you.

So, in conclusion, we did what we needed to do and I made my point very clear. I'm the most honest person ever! I couldn't possibly lie to myself!

Write back to me.

Sincerely,

Maximus Invictus Blare

I threw my pen away and didn't bother putting the letter in an envelope; I could send it off the next day. For now, I wanted to sleep.

My dreams were empty. That time, they actually were. Instead of the usual nightmares that I forgot the next day, I was haunted by darkness and smells.

The smells of coffee, smoke and petrichor.

I was haunted by electrifying eyes. Royal blue eyes.

I was haunted by a hair the same colour as the flame inside me. Fiery and dark.

But, worst of all, I was haunted by a smile. A smile that reminded me too much of a cat, a smile that tugged at the corners of my mouth and made my throat run dry, that made the warm blood running through my veins go icy'

I woke up the next day with a headache and a sweaty forehead.

But the sweat wasn't cold and it wasn't sticky or awful. It was the type of sweat that felt… nice, as strange as it sounded.

I blinked once before collapsing back down.

The weekend was over as quickly as it had come.

⚔ Chapter Sixteen ⚔

SOON ENOUGH I COULD see the carriage which Emile sat in riding over the horizon, it's golden walls glinting in the sunlight. For some reason, I thought it was fit to wait for her by the front door of the house. It might've been Desmind's words; they had unnerved me heavily And when I felt like that I always ended up doing things I shouldn't do.

Emile stepped out quite eagerly, nearly running up to the door. Desmond came out just as she had nearly reached us, his face sagging more than usual.

'Emile, it's wonderful to see you again.' he said, smiling a reserved sort of smile. He always seemed so tired; a lot of my time was spent wondering what was wrong with him.

'Hello! It's great to see you, too!' Her voice hit me like a wave. It's regal undertones hadn't been much of a miss, but there was something that caught me off guard in the sound of her speaking, causing me to cough rather awkwardly in an attempt to clear my mind.

'Um, hi.' I mumbled, my cheeks flaring up. I could feel her cats grin, even with my eyes planted on the ground.

'You look a state, Max; what on earth is wrong?' Emile asked. *You.*

Desmond. Anastasia. Adelaide. George. Nathaniel. Me. Everyone. Everything.

'Nothing. I'm fine, see?' I forced the colour from my cheeks and smiled, my face already aching from the motion.

'Last time you said that when looking like this you didn't speak to me for, what, a month?'

'That was different.'

'I don't see how.'

But you wouldn't, would you? Because you only see what you want to see, what you choose to see, just like everybody else.

'You can't see what I don't show you.' Emile's eyebrow raised, the corner of her mouth twitching upwards yet again.

'What I do see is that you're still as witty and clever as always.' she responded silkily.

'I'm not witty. Or clever. I do the opposite of you, though; I look for the things that aren't visible.' I said. It sounded harsh, but I supposed that didn't matter; maybe she would realise that she could never be friends with someone like me, someone as awful and vile as me. The resentment I had for myself that was buried deep in my bones was rising again, moving through my bloodstream and drowning me from the inside-out. I would've given anything to get rid of it, but the only thing I could do was accept it.

'That makes you both, then. Besides, what normal person would ever say something like that? I know I wouldn't.' Emile retorted.

'Are you really arguing with me about whether or not I'm smart?' I saw a look pass over her face; a brief flash of hurt. *Good*, I thought bitterly, *hurry up and leave me. Please. Do yourself the favour and stop me from finishing this task before I kill myself in the process.*

But the hurt was gone as soon as it had come.

'Is that you admitting that I'm right?' Emile asked. I wanted to say no; I wanted to carry on making my point, as ridiculous as it may be to her ears. But I was too exhausted, too confused, too everything. I didn't have the time, nor energy, to bicker like a married couple.

'Yes. If it pleases you.' I said before walking off and back into the house, my head pounding and my eyelids heavy.

'What's wrong with him?' I heard Emile ask.

'I don't know.' Desmond responded before I was out of earshot. But I heard the flicker of uncertainty in his voice; he knew something. That wasn't good. Even if it was only the knowledge of the effect of his words, it wasn't good at all. *Rule number 5; remember who your enemy is.*

It seemed I would be referring to that rule a lot more.

☆★☆

'Right. We have some new rules that I'm going to enforce.' Desmond said on Monday the next week. I had felt the curiosity rising off Emile; I didn't feel much about the announcement. I had already sensed that some things were going to change; it had only been a matter of time.

'Go on, then.' Emile said, faint interest laced within her words.

'For a start, we're going to be working longer and harder every day. Lunch breaks will only be if we need them.' Desmond said.

'Ok, that isn't so bad.' Emile said slowly. There was a silence and I quickly realised they were waiting for my input.

'Oh, um, yeah, what she said.' I stammered. I hadn't been paying attention; I'd already guessed what was going to happen.

'Right. Well, we're starting back up with archery again. It will be one week of swords, then a week of archery, and so on in that sort of pattern.' Desmond said.

'Is that it?' Emile said.

'The point isn't a set amount of rules, Emile. It's that we're going to work harder and longer, all day everyday.' He paused, 'Except for weekends and Fridays. We still need breaks.'

'I get all of that, but why?' Emile said incredulously.

'Have you forgotten about the attack? If that were to happen again, with more people and stronger warriors, we'd be doomed. We need to train for this sort of stuff, Emile, and that means you need to work until you're falling asleep standing.' Desmond snapped. I flinched slightly at the tone of his voice, hiding it hastily. I didn't hide it hastily enough. Emile gave me a confused look, asking a silent question with her eyes; *are you okay?*

No. I'm not okay.

'Are we starting today?' I asked, trying to clear the tension. But there was a small crack in my voice that only caused more perplexed glances. By that stage, Emile had noticed that something was up.

'Maximus? Are you-'

'I'm fine. Can we please just get started?'

She nodded and brushed it off, but I could see the determination to figure out what had caused me, the unflinching Maximus, to do exactly that; flinch.

Stupid, stubborn girl. You'll never learn, will you?

Her answer hung in the air as if she had actually spoken; *to learn is to give up, and you know that I will never succumb to that. I will only learn what I choose to learn.*

I bit down on my lip. Even when she wasn't saying anything, what I thought she would've said irked me.

Just like how you see. You only see what you want to see.

I let my gaze fall on her. She was fighting in the middle of the arena with Desmond, a simple warm up. But her helmet wasn't on and I could read everything, taking her vulnerability as a moment to find out what I wanted to know.

It was written over her face as plain as day. *I will find out. I don't care how long it takes, or how hard it is. I always find out; I never miss.*

My heart jumped. *If you really think it will be so simple, you're mistaken. Don't make the mistake.*

But the voice was gone. Silenced by my fear.

Stupid, stubborn boy.

☆✭☆

That night, I felt more tense than usual on the walk to the clearing in the woods. Emile and I had decided that we would carry on with the archery during the night, as they had been helping me a lot. Well. It was more of Emile's decision than mine. That was probably the reason I was so nervous on the way there.

The first thing I noticed when I got there was the light. There were about four lamps with candles in them, lighting up a small square. Next to two opposite lamps were chairs, small and light ones.

The second thing I noticed was that there were no bows, no arrows, no targets. What kind of archery lesson didn't have any of those?

And the third thing I noticed was a hand on my wrist, pushing me onto a chair, and the overwhelming scent of coffee, smoke and petrichor.

'What's going on?' I said cautiously. Emile had sat at the chair opposite me, her royal blue eyes dancing in the light of the flames.

'We're going to have a little chat.' she responded smoothly.
I always find out; I never miss.
I swallowed hard.

'About what?' I said. Emile laughed softly, the breeze carrying her voice and breaking it apart, breaking it down, down to every last piece. I wanted to do the same.

'It would ruin the whole prospect if I told you, wouldn't it?' Emile said, her eyes now glinting.

'Then what do you want to know?' I asked. My patience was wearing thin, yet it was thickening by the minute. I could feel myself being consumed by her, by her arrogance and petulance, by her eyes, her eyes, her stupid eyes. I inhaled sharply and sat back on my seat, as if I thought it might help.

'I want to know about you. Not your friends, not the people who made you; how you made yourself.' Emile said, her voice soft. I eyed her, half curious and half suspicious.

'Ask me a question, then. Go on.' I said, forcing aggravation into my tone. It didn't fool Emile, who merely raised an eyebrow.

'I'm not going to ask you anything. I want you to tell me.' she said.

'How do you expect me to say the right thing, then?' I said. Our chairs suddenly felt closer.

'There is no right thing. Say what you think of.' Emile said. I stared at her for a minute, watching the quiet anticipation as it filled her expression and threatened to spill out. *It would spill out like a waterfall*, I thought, *blue and steady, soft and dangerous, clear and hiding it's true depths.*

'I think you overestimate me.' I said carefully. Stalling. Biding my time. Would she really want to know the me that hid under my skin? I didn't think so. Would she like him? No. Nobody who knew ever had. Nobody but George, and he hadn't written to me for weeks. Perhaps he didn't like the me I wanted to be after all.

'Elaborate.' Emile said. It wasn't a question; she was demanding my answer, her hair blending with the soft fire.

'I- I don't know what to say, Emile. You ask me these questions and expect me to know the answers. Well I- even if I did, they wouldn't be the ones you were looking for.' I said. Emile's eyes were unreadable; I could only watch them as they flickered over me. I didn't squirm under her gaze, as I usually did with everybody else. I fought to ignore the blue that had grown in my throat and fidgeted with my fingers. It would be better to pretend to be okay.

'Who are you, Max? Really. Answer it properly. Who are you?' Emile said. Only Emile would be able to think of a question that was out of my reach, too far for even my fingertips to graze.

'I'm a boy with a sword. Nothing more, nothing less.' I said harshly. What gave her the right to go messing around in my personal life? She was out of *her* reach, nevermind mine.

'But that isn't you. You're a boy, yes, but the sword? It only contributes to making you. Without it, you're still you, just a different version.' Emile said. She was being very calm for the situation she was in.

If you want this so bad, take it. Don't even flinch. Look me in the eyes and take it, like everybody else has had to do.

The skin on my face felt a lot tighter when I spoke.

'I'm a killer. I was made to be a killer. You can deny it all you like, say it's merely a "contributing factor", but I know otherwise. Who would I be if I hadn't become this person? I would be nobody. Nothing. But that never would have happened, would it? I was always destined to be this way. A killer, ruthless and merciless, cold and unflinching. Whichever you prefer, really. They all make sense.' The words tumbled out of me before I had time to process them. I wasn't as angry as I was making out; I just wanted to be seen. Properly seen.

But you only ever see what you want to see.

Emile was silent. Then, she stood up, picked up her chair and moved it forwards until we were suffocatingly close, and her knees bound in between mine in a sort of pattern. My left leg, then hers, then my right leg, and then hers again. I tried to stop my eyes from widening.

'You're a killer, yes; I'm not going to deny it to make you feel better.' She watched for my reaction. I showed none in response. 'But that doesn't define you. Think about it, Max. You are everything and nothing, nobody and everybody, everyone and no one. What are you? *Who* are you?'

I didn't want to speak; I knew my voice would tremble and the blue would only grow. But there was something that inspired me. I opened my mouth and let the words form on my tongue before letting them out, as if they were animals to be tamed. Animals that could never be tamed.

You are everything. 'I'm the stars, my visibility, my everything, defined by the decisions of others.'

You are nothing. 'I'm the fish, small and unheard, my voice unable and my only ability only useful when others need it.'

You are nobody. 'I'm death itself, taking those who do me wrong and leaving those who wish me well.'

You are everybody. 'I'm disease, infecting the people who aren't careful enough, and doing the same to the people who are careful too much.'

You are everyone. 'I'm a current, I'm never the same as I once was, always changing, always adapting.'

You are no one.

My voice stopped. It was the easiest answer of all, but the hardest to share with someone else. Her bare ankles pushed into mine and I could feel my skin burning up, scalding.

You are no one.

Am I, though? I am me. That's not no one. It isn't much, and it certainly isn't enough, but it's still someone.

You are no one. 'I'm a blank book, my pages erasing themselves and rewriting it the way I've sculpted it, not the way it is.'

It was so vague. Surely she wouldn't see what I meant; but, somehow, she did, and her kind eyes hardened as she bit on the inside of her cheek. I let my arms unfold and my fingertips dance on my kneecaps, fidgeting to pass time. Her fingers brushed mine and there was static in the air. I was breathing in electricity. My breath hitched and my fingers stopped moving, coming to a halt as they lay only just touching hers. Enough to drive lightning bolts up my veins, through my blood, but not enough to cause an electric shock.

Don't pity my past. Pity my present. Pity my future. Pity anything but my past. For your own sake and mine.

'Who did this to you?' she asked. It didn't matter, really; I was always going to end up like that. I couldn't change the past. I could only change my future.

'It doesn't matter.' I said. *Does it, though? Or are you just lying to yourself, like you always do?*

'Then...' Emile hesitated, cutting herself off.

'Just say it. I'm not going to lash out at you.' I said. I was beginning to grow tired; actually tired. Not of her. She was always presenting me with something new; how could I ever be tired of her?

'What did they do to you?' Emile said, barely whispering. I would tell her, if she really wanted to know. But that would be sick and twisted; Emile wasn't like that. She was curious beyond her years, yes, but even she wouldn't want to know that.

But curiosity killed the cat, didn't it?

'You wouldn't care to know.'

Wrong words, Maximus. Why must you always be difficult?

'I care about you and I care about your past.'

Wrong words, Emile. Why must you always be difficult?

'Care about me and leave my past alone. Don't go messing around with things you don't understand.' I snapped. She didn't falter, though. Her patience was running higher than usual, today.

'You're past is also you. If I'm going to know you, I need to know you properly. You can't avoid it forever, Max. You'll have to tell me someday.' Emile said.

I realised, then, how cold it was. The icy air had tinged my face, and I felt numb. Emile was shivering, goosebumps erupting all over her bare arms. I wondered what to do in a situation like that; I couldn't go back to the house. Not only would she not let me, but I didn't want to. For some odd reason.

I looked at my own arms, covered in a soft cloth. I thought about it for a moment. I really wished, at times like that, that I had more experience with social interactions.

My mind traced back, finding what George would have done; he had always been much more outright than I had been. When Luna had been cold, he would give her his jacket. As soon as we arrived back home he always encouraged me to do the same. I never did, of course; I didn't have the confidence for that. But when Emile's eyes caught mine, I felt a surge of something new burst inside of me.

'Are you cold?' I said. I expected her to say she was going inside, or maybe just leave; it surprised me when she didn't. I supposed we both enjoyed the painful pleasure of the wind at night.

'Yes.' Emile said simply. I sat still for a minute. Then, I pulled my jumper over my head, my skin writhing at the sudden exposure.

'You can wear this, if you want.' I said carefully. Emile looked at my outstretched hands, their redness hidden under the material. Slowly, she reached for it and plucked the jumper from me, pulling it on.

'Thank you.' Emile said quietly. I nodded, my movements jerky. I was so cold I could barely breathe. A chill ran through me and I let my fingertips rest again. Hers were back quickly, restless, as if they were yearning for my contact.

'Do you know what time it is?' I asked. Emile pulled up the sleeve of the jumper slightly and looked at a watch wrapped around her wrist before, once again, letting her hand brush mine. I felt tingles all over.

'1:30.' Emile responded. I paused.

'We should probably go to sleep, then.' I said, my voice low.

'Yeah.' Emile said. Neither of us moved. The time ticked on as we sat in silence, the tension so thick it felt like I was choking. I coughed lightly and pressed our legs together tighter, trying to warm myself up even in the slightest..

'Do you want your jumper back?' Emile inquired, already taking it off. She was too generous, too eager to be kind. She shouldn't have been so nice towards me, not when I was planning what I was.

'No! I mean, no, keep it.' I said. Emile scrutinised me before letting it fall back into place, slumping on the chair.

'Are you tired?' she said. I was about to say yes when I was overwhelmed by the scent of coffee. I could've sat there surrounded by the fragrance all night, and I would never have fallen asleep.

'No.' I said, 'Are you?'

'No.'

We were engulfed in silence once again. The moon shone down on Emile and she looked… frail. Fragile. Like she would break if I so much as moved us. I refrained from pressing a finger to her arm, seeing if she really did break, and bit down on my lip. *What is going on with me today?*

'Do you want to go back inside? You're trembling.' Emile said.

I looked down at myself; sure enough, small quivers were reverberating off me.

'I'm just cold.' I said, my eyes trailing back up.

'That isn't much better.'

But still, we didn't move. It went on like that until Emile finally forced herself to leave, taking me with her. I couldn't sleep at all. I realised she still had my jumper, the only one that I had from Rendo. I hesitated outside of her door the next day when I went to retrieve it.

Let her keep it, I thought. And I did. She kept the jumper and I kept the memory.

✕ Chapter Seventeen ✕

ONE WEEK LATER, GEORGE finally wrote back. I had wasted no time in grabbing the letter and running off to my bedroom with it, eager to finally hear from back home.

What I hadn't noticed, however, was that the handwriting on the envelope did not belong to my friend. It belonged to someone I knew, yes, but not anyone who I would wish it to be. I didn't think to check that, though, when ripping it open and devouring its contents.

Dear Maximus,

in case you have not noticed, this isn't George who is writing to you. But I urge you to carry on reading and hear me out.

If you write to us again, I will hold Adelaide, Anastasia and George hostage where you'll never find them. I'll torture them until they've forgotten their own name, give them hope, and then kill Adelaide in front of Anastasia and George. Instead of murdering them on the spot, I'll let them live with the guilt for a few months.

We all know how good of a person dear George is. That is why I'll then kill Anastasia, still in front of him. Would you like to know what I will do next?

I will take you from your precious Emile and your precious Desmond and force him to torture you, saying that if he doesn't I'll kill you instead. Then I'll kill darling Emile and Desmond while you have to watch, and it should surely prove where your loyalties lie.

All of this, and much more, will happen if you fail to carry out this task. I've trusted you- I've trusted an arrogant, petulant moron to fulfil something that even I could barely do. If you don't stop worrying yourself with the princesses feelings and keeping in touch with George, I will take everything you hold dear and destroy it. Do not doubt me.

For now, I trust that you will be okay. If I hear of you again I will be coming straight there to take you away and kill the two idiots you call your friends. As I said before; do not write back.

From,

Nathaniel Maligno Flint

My heart was pounding in my face. At first I thought it was a joke; some silly prank that George was playing on me. But his mind, his kind heart, could never allow him to think up, or write, things like that. Besides; there was no denying that the signature at the bottom belonged to Nathaniel.

I ripped the paper up and threw it in the bin. Why did I even bother trying to keep him happy? He always came back, his mood worse than ever, no matter what I did to please him. I couldn't wait for the day I could finally be rid of him, the inhuman sadist.

Stay calm. Don't do anything rash.

I ran out of my room, past both Desmond and Emile, ignored their puzzled gazes and found myself in the ballroom. No one would think to look of me there, and I needed time to process.

Nathaniel had seemingly read all of the letters, meaning that if it came to it, he had evidence of me confiding in the entire situation of Anastasia and Evania and things I had intended for George only.

Was I hyperventilating? I wasn't sure. I was barely in my own body anymore. I didn't even notice when the door swung open, nor when footsteps advanced towards me. My eyes were fixated on the floor and I was pacing nervously, my head pounding.

'Max?' I jumped. Looking up, I saw Emile had walked in, her face full of concern. *Here's your perfect opportunity to pity my present, love.*

'Are you okay?' Emile asked slowly. I refrained from laughing aloud. *Do I look like I'm okay?*

'Why do you care?' I said roughly. My voice sounded hoarse and raspy, the ache in my throat unavoidable. Something else that was unavoidable was the mixture of hurt and anger that flashed over Emile's face.

'Because you're my friend.' Emile said cautiously, as if she was afraid I would lash out at her. I felt a pang of guilt, but the rush of frustration drowned it out.

'If you were truly my friend, you would leave me alone.' I snapped, turning away from her. My senses were overloaded. I could smell something else radiating off her; a tinge of salt, and a strange metal like scent. I ignored it and focused on facing the wall so far away from me.

Just as I had suspected she would, Emile took a wary step forward, gently laying her fingertips on my shoulder. I shivered at the contact and took another step away. It didn't phase her, though; Emile came back in front of me, her face set with determination. I hadn't wanted to kill her so much until that day; what did she not understand? I was clearly not in the right state of mind. If I hurt her, it would be her own fault, not mine.

'Can you please leave me alone?' I said. Emile scanned me, her royal blue eyes taking me in.

'I'm afraid I can't. As I said before; you're my friend. I care for you. And there's clearly something wrong.'

Ignore my past. Pity my present. But most of all, dread my future.

'There's nothing wrong. Now leave.' I said. Emile didn't falter, taking a step back as I took a step forward. I hadn't meant to do it; but I was so angry that my feet were moving themselves.

'Why are you here, then? In the one place you've only been to twice? Don't lie to me. I can see right through you.'

I'm like a stained glass window. You only see what I want you to see, and you deceive yourself into thinking that it is true. You see the picture, but you don't see what's behind it.

'I said leave.' I repeated. My feet moved forwards again. Emile's moved backwards again.

'And I said no.' Emile responded. If I could, I would've killed her there and then. Instead, I took another step forward. I didn't know what I was doing, and neither did she, by the looks of it. I was out of my head but I couldn't stop.

'Was it the letter? From your friend, George?' It was insulting for him to be perceived as so little to me.

'He might as well be my brother.' I corrected, evading the question. That time, it seemed Emile actually got a glimpse through the glass.

'It was, wasn't it? What did it say? What has caused you to be like… this?' She gestured at me. I didn't see the problem; this was how I usually was. It had only changed since I'd gone to Kendra. Stupid Kendra. I never should've gone in the first place.

My feet took me forward again.

'You act like you're all strong and clever,' Emile said, her voice breaking as she stepped back, 'but you aren't as much as you make out to be. You hide in your room and you pretend that nothing is wrong, but you have no idea what to do with yourself, really.'

'Shut up.' I said quietly. We were nearing the wall now. Three more steps and we'd be at it. My heart picked up speed.

'Oh, yes, you know that I'm right.' Emile continued, her eyes hard and wide, 'But you're in denial. You don't know who you are, do you? It was all nonsense. I should have known that you were lying. You're nothing but an awful, rotten liar-'

'I said shut up!'

Oh, I knew she was messing with me, trying to make me admit to something.

But she was just so good at it.

I had made a mistake. But she had been there, so close, her back pressed against the wall, and it hadn't been only my feet that were moving themselves. My hand found itself in the space of the wall just under her jaw, and I couldn't breathe. I thought my heart was going to burst out of my skin.

Emile looked like she was going to melt, her fiery hair in a sort of halo around her head. I could see the rise and fall of her chest, abrupt and quick; I wondered if this sort of thing always had that kind of impact on people. It certainly did on me.

My mouth opened before closing again; I felt like the fish I had described to her only 7 days ago. Gaping and unable to move. I should've stepped back, let her leave. But I only had one hand on the wall. If she wanted to, she could've easily slipped away. She didn't. She stood staring at me, her eyes dark and cheeks sucked in.

'Don't go meddling where you aren't welcome.' I said. It had meant to be cruel, perhaps to force her to leave, but it was hardly a whisper. I didn't trust myself to raise the tone any higher. I knew my voice would betray me and break if I did.

'Just because you aren't welcoming me, it doesn't mean that everybody else won't.' Emile responded, her own words barely audible, but her breath hot in my face as they left her lips, all the same. My breath caught. She was inches away from me. All it would take was a mere movement of my head, and we would be touching.

'Don't flatter yourself.' I whispered. My eyes trailed to where my hand lay; I could feel the warmth of her skin, millimetres away from my own. Her soft jawline, her curved collarbone, the scar she never spoke about, her golden neck. She was golden. All in all. Glowing and golden. Like a sunray, or maybe the sun itself. She was just golden.

'Then speak to me.' Emile said under her breath. I let my gaze travel further down to see her hands, clasping the wall near her hips as if she was going to fall. And her hands, so golden, so glowing, seemed to feel my stare, as their grip loosened and her breaths suddenly came quicker and heavier, so much so I could hear them.

'You ask of me the one thing I cannot do.' I mumbled. It wasn't true; I never spoke the truth anymore. Something I had once prided myself on had become my biggest downfall. I was an ocean of lies, showing myself to the clearings that had not been infected by my falseness. I had infected Emile the moment I saw her. And now she was infecting me, with something else, something new. Something I did not like at all.

'How am I to trust you if you don't trust me?' Emile asked. There wasn't an answer that I could give. I did something I would never have normally done, next. I took my hand from the wall and pressed it to Emile's jaw, her faint pulse speeding under my grip. I swallowed hard and forced myself to look away from her eyes, as they seemed to have puddled under my gaze. All she had to do was take a step to the side. I waited for the move, but it never came.

'Don't trust me, then.' I said eventually. My fingertips danced over her skin, the warmth radiating from it. Emile's cheeks had a pink tint, a contrast to it's usual ashen tone.

I let my fingers splay out, pressing tentatively into the heated skin of her cheeks, my own hands boiling at the contact. I felt like she was devouring me with her eyes, melting me to nothing as I stood, her eyes soft, so soft, so soft that I could read everything that was going through her mind in them.

Everything was a blur, and I never wanted my sight to clear again.

'I trust you.' Emile said quietly, her voice hardly a breath. 'I trust you impossibly. Improbably. Irreversibly.'

My throat tightened at her words, my organs constricting.

I let my hand fall to the side of her neck, cradling it with the hands of a murderer, the hands of a thief, the hands of a liar. My thumb pressed into the base of her throat, bobbing as she swallowed hard.

'You don't understand the weight of words.' I said in a muted tone, the words falling like hexagons as they struggled to land on a surface, as they struggled to stay away from the corners, from the edges, as they struggled to balance their weight. Their weight. The weight of the words.

'Do I not?' Emile said, voice much too breathy, much too shaky.

I looked into her eyes and my brain just about collapsed.

I had memorised every small sign of her emotion, engrained each tell of her lies into my head, imprinted the repeated words of her uncertainty into my heart.

Emile was about as unreadable as a book in a foreign language.

She was difficult at first, but I got the hang of her. I got used to her, to the way her eyes could never watch the same spot, the way she picked at the dry skin on her lips every few minutes, the way she picked at scabs and flinched when they bled.

Emile was a story that I wanted to know. A story that I always wanted more of, a story that I would stay up late to read, a story that I would search and search just to find another glimpse at it for.

Her always moving eyes stilled on mine.

I swallowed, taking a single strand of her hair in my fingers, running them through it.

The breath she was taking halted, and she stopped breathing all together.

'You should trust me too, Maximus.' Emile mumbled, almost slurring as she spoke. 'I don't know as little about you as you seem to think I do.'

Her words sent me reeling into my normal headspace with a long shudder. It was fuzzy, dizzying, and I could barely process what I was doing. Her skin was hot in my hand, her knees pressing into mine. I restrained a gasp.

Coffee. Smoke. Petrichor.

I pulled my hand away and my skin flushed icy cold.

Emile stood frozen for a moment, staring unblinkingly as I took an uncertain step away. I left before she could say anything, my neck

scarlet red and my head whirring.

What were you thinking?

I wasn't.

That isn't good enough.

I hit my leg in frustration, accidentally slamming my bedroom door behind me.

Rich coming from the voice without a body.

How had I gone from hyperventilating to whatever that was?

All that means is I don't have the weight of existence, unlike you.

Surely that hadn't been me; I would never do something that rash. I would never do that at all.

And yet you've still managed to end up stuck with me, an awkward, blood thirsty mortal.

If I could, I would have killed someone, then. I didn't have the time for a rendezvous such as that. My path was a straight line; I couldn't let myself be let astray by clearings in the darkness.

And, yet, you went through one of those clearings, didn't you? You only just found your way back out again. Do you want to know why?

Can you not just leave me alone?

It's because you wanted to see what was in the unknown. You can brag about how strong and malicious you are all you like, but your curiosity will always get the better of you.

I said to leave me alone.

And not just that-

LEAVE ME ALONE!

I wondered what Emile thought of it. She hadn't left; she could have. There was a space to her side where she could have simply slipped away, without saying a word. But she'd stayed. I couldn't tell if that was better or worse.

This is where you need to blank out your emotions. You might think it's better, but it isn't. It's much worse. Think about it, Maximus.

Finally being helpful, are you?

Think about it.

I did. I thought long and hard. I thought until there was nothing else left to think. I eventually came to the conclusion that it would have been better if she, or I, had walked away, but I could make use out of the situation it put me in.

Rule number 6; listen to your head, not your heart.

⚔ Chapter Eighteen ⚔

MANY DAYS PASSED, BUT we didn't speak. I saw Emile during training and we still did archery lessons, but aside from that we didn't make any contact whatsoever. I thought that, perhaps, she was angry at me. *I* was angry at me, nevermind her. I had apparently forgotten that we had been arguing that day; it was, in fact, Desmond who finally reminded me.

We had been in the kitchen, cutting up meat or something like that; I couldn't properly remember. I had stopped, my head pounding, and rested my face in my hands. I didn't know why I did it. It was one of those moments; I had them often. I always had. They were small periods of time where the whole world fell away, and I had nothing to grasp onto that would keep me sane. It was like an explosion. It took away my breath, made my eyes water and my heart pound. I sometimes thought that maybe there was just something wrong with me; it wasn't the only strange symptom that I had. But when I told George, he simply laughed and said 'The only thing that's wrong with you is the fact that you're an undiagnosed psychopath.' I had laughed along, although I didn't really want to.

But apparently Desmond noticed my small portion of weakness. It was as if he sensed it. The moment my knife cluttered against the table and I had buried myself away, he was over, gently prying my fingers from my skin and looking at me with faint confusion.

'What's wrong?' he asked, his voice a soft blanket. I clung to it and heaved myself back, my forehead slick with the sweat from something I had only imagined.

'Nothing. Nothing. I'm fine.' I said. But I didn't sound like how I usually did, the strange force that normally compelled people to listen gone. Now it was compelling people to leave, to leave the weak boy to fend for himself. *Weak, weak, weak.*

'If I hear you say that one more time, I might just have to kill you with my bare hands,' Desmond said lightheartedly. His expression changed rapidly when he saw my attempted smile had become something that resembled a grimace.

'Come on, Maximus, you have to tell someone. This, whatever it is, is eating you from the inside out. Speak to me.' Desmond said tentatively. I wanted to. Oh, how I wanted to. I nearly did.

Weak, weak, weak, the ever changing voice inside of my head sung. I looked away from Desmond's kindly face and dug my fingernails into the palm of my hand.

'Stop worrying about me. I can handle myself.' I said.

'I have done that for long enough. You look awful to begin with; look, you're bleeding!' Desmond ran his thumb over a cut that ran over my eye.

'It's a scar, I've had it for years. It must have just reopened, caught on something.' I said, stepping away from his thumb. I didn't like people touching my scars. If they were to be the part of me that never changed, they were going to stay mine, and only mine.

'Right. Well, that's past the point. Even if it isn't me you tell, you have to tell someone.' Desmond said. *You don't know me.* My internal thoughts paused for a moment. *I don't even know me.*

'Who do you suggest?' I said wearily.

'I suggest the only other person here in this house with us.'

My breath hitched and I looked away.

'I'm afraid I can't do that.' I muttered.

'And why not?'

'I can't tell you.'

'It seems to me like you're avoiding telling anyone anything right now.'

'And how would you feel if I said you weren't wrong?"

Desmond didn't respond. He chewed down on his bottom lip, eyes seeking out mine. My throat felt tight with unease.

'Has something happened between you and Emile?' he asked quietly. I took a step back impulsively.

'What? Why would you think that?' I blubbered, my tone higher than normal.

'Don't lie to me, Maximus. I know you care for her, and she cares for you, too. Speak to her. Apologise. Please.' Desmond said. I looked away, heart thrumming in my ears.

'Do you- do you know where she is?' I asked under my breath. I could practically hear his smile.

'Try the ballroom.'

'Thank you.'

I almost ran off, tripping over my own feet as I stumbled up the stairs. My breaths were sharp, inconsistent; I wanted to speak to her, I realised. I really wanted to speak to her, to see her, to look at her without feeling as though the weight of all my actions was being piled upon my shoulders.

So do it.

The doors to the ballroom seemed a lot more intimidating that day. My hand lingered over the doorknob for a moment.

Do. It.

The door swung open and I stepped inside, letting it slam behind me. The sound was loud in such a large space.

'Emile?' I called. Silence. 'Emile?'

'Maximus?' Her voice was quiet, soft; she stepped out of the shadows, eyes wandering over me. She looked... tired. Her skin was sunken and her hair unbrushed, but not in the big, electrifying way it normally was. It looked thin, fragile. I swallowed and made my way towards her, until we were but two steps away from one another.

'I just- I wanted to- I just needed to say that I'm sorry.' I spat out. I'd always hated apologising; I supposed I hated admitting I was wrong.

'Why would you be sorry?' Emile asked.

'Why would I not be?'

Silence stretched between us. I pressed my lips together, waiting and waiting and waiting.

'I'm sorry, too.' she eventually whispered. I let out a breath of relief.

'It's okay.' I said.

'I just-' Emile cut herself off, fiddling with her fingers. I took a step forward, prying her hands apart gently; I didn't let go of them after, though. Her skin was hot, clammy- relieving. Proof that both she and I were alive. She looked down at our fingers, intertwined. My stomach was flipping over in itself.

'Speak to me.' I breathed.

'I have a better idea.'

One of her hands untangled from mine, trailing up my side, stopping at my neck. I could practically feel my pupils dilating.

'And what is your idea?'

'Dance with me.'

It wasn't a question; it was a demand. My arm, limp at my side, slowly brought itself up to Emiles waist, clutching the fabric of her dress as if I were about to fall over. Her grip on my neck was gentle, but it caused an explosion inside of me all the same.

'Where's the music?' I whispered. Emile pulled me closer, until our stomachs were almost touching.

'Listen to the music of the whirring in your ears and the pounding of your heart.'

At that, my heart pounded just a little bit faster.

My ears whirred just a little bit louder.

I took a step, and then another, and then another, her movements following flawlessly, the rough feel of her skin against mine keeping me conscious, keeping me alive.

I spun her out and she came back in, full body pressing against me. I took a step back, before pulling her back in, hands clasping by her hips. Emile grabbed my shoulders, the force knocking me backwards.

'Excited there?' I mumbled.

Emile rolled her eyes at me and I felt myself grinning back at her.

I was out of my own body, but I was brought back at the impact of my back hitting a wall. Emile's hands weren't on my shoulders anymore; they were trailing down my chest, leaving sparks running through me.

Gently, I took my own hands from her hips, pressing one against her hand and letting the other curl at her cheek.

I swore quietly as she pressed the palm of her hand against my chest, my heart thumping against it, other hand twisting around mine, now against my shoulder.

Emile pulled her mouth to my ear, her breath hot.

'Now who's excited?'

I brought a finger to her lip in a sort of shushing motion; her lips were chapped but moist, as if she was both nervous and ecstatic at the same time. I knew exactly how she felt, as I dragged my finger down and let my hand fall to my side.

'Emile, you… you're…' I trailed off, unable to find the right words as I curled a coil of her hair in between two of my fingers. 'You are everything. Everything and nothing, all at once.'

I didn't say anything else. I simply slipped away, head spinning and eyes wide.

☆★☆

My first kiss was with a girl from my childhood. I could hardly remember much about her, aside from the fact that Nathaniel had been mortified once he'd figured out about her.

Her name was Rosalin. I called her Rose. The sun was hot and I was merely 13, sitting on a swing as my friend Rose pushed me. A wholesome scene to imagine, I'm sure.

We were there, just children, enjoying the summer together while we still could. Swinging on a swing.

Suddenly, the swing stopped. I looked up, eyes meeting hers; she was close, knees pressed onto mine.

And then she kissed me.

It was awkward at first, a mixture of clattering teeth and accidental bites, but soon we fell into a rhythm, a smooth rhythm, one that was interrupted as we broke apart laughing and dancing and talking and… well, and laughing even more.

But we were caught, by none other than Nathaniel himself, and Rosalin was executed while I stayed in the shadows. Nathaniel could never kill off his best fighter; it just wouldn't make sense.

Instead he killed the girl he'd deemed as useless.

I'd made a mistake letting myself get so close to Emile.

Letting myself get so attached.

I knew what happened when I engaged like that with the enemy; the image of it played out in my nightmares, the image of a girl barely a teen being hung because of my stupid mistakes. Only the Gods knew what Nathaniel would do if he found out about mine and Emile's…

Interactions.

She was my friend. For the time being. Even if Nathaniel did find out, even if I somehow stayed with her, the truth would come out and she'd never forgive me. I wouldn't blame her, either. What I was doing was the highest level of betrayal, and I knew it.

Thinking about it made me hate myself even more.

I was a bad person. An extremely bad person. Gods, I killed people regularly, just to prove a point. I'd let Rosalin die over myself in a heartbeat again, if it meant going to Kendra and learning so much about myself and my own stupid country still.

I needed to talk about this to someone. I couldn't talk to George anymore, I couldn't talk to Desmond, oh no, for sure not Desmond.

And although she was the cause of my problems, Emile was still the person I went to to solve them.

☆★☆

'Emile? Are you here?'

I was rapping at the door of her room tirelessly, pausing only to breathe.

'If you are, please open the-'

'Max?'

The door swung open and there she was. I exhaled deeply, although my eyes were stinging and I felt sick to the stomach. Even on the verge of tears, she made me feel okay.

'Can I talk to you please?' I whispered.

'Have you been crying?' Emile said with a frown.

'Please. I need to talk to you.'

Emile stood there for a moment. Then, she stepped out of her room and the door shut behind her.

'We can go to your room, or somewhere else, if you want.' she said quietly. I nodded, making my way towards my bedroom. Emile followed, closing the door as we went in.

'Are you okay?' she asked. I couldn't speak. My throat was closing in on itself.

'I don't- I-'

'Maximus, calm down, look at me.'

Her hands were on my face and I still couldn't breathe, but her eyes, her dark, deep eyes, they latched onto me and made my heart beat a little bit faster.

'Hey, breathe. Breathe. It's alright, it's okay…'

I squeezed my eyes shut.

And I positively broke down.

My knees failed me and I collapsed in a heap on the floor, Emile's hands being replaced with my own as I tried to muffle my sobs.

'I can't- I don't- I can't do this.' I spluttered. Emile was on the floor in front of me, her fingers tight around my wrists. 'I'm so alone I can't breathe.'

'You aren't alone, Maximus. You'll never be alone for as long as I'm here.'

'You think that now, but soon you won't.'

'Don't be ridiculous. I- I care about you. More than you know. Tell me what it is that's making you feel like this.'

'I- I can't tell you. I want to so bad. I want to tell you. But I can't.' I whispered, voice breaking. Emile pulled my hands from my face, clasping them as if she was afraid I'd run away.

'Listen to me, Max. You're not alone. You have me. And Desmond. And that stupid oaf George that you call your friend. Speak to me, please, I want to be here for you.'

'I don't want- I don't want to talk about it.'

'Then why did you come to me?'

'I don't want to talk about it; I just want to talk to you.'

I stared at her, my gaze not breaking. I saw everything. I saw the lump in her throat as it moved down, the faint pulse in her jaw as it's pace quickened, the way her eyelashes fluttered with every blink, the way her lips were slightly parted, always.

'And what would you talk to me about?'

'Would it be so preposterous to suggest I would only talk about you while talking to you?'

'Many would, indeed, think that to be preposterous.' Emile's voice was barely a whisper. 'But I don't think that.'

'Oh?'

Emile paused; I watched carefully, cautiously, as her skin pulsated, as her mouth opened, as words formed.

'I suppose I would speak about you, also.' she said. The tears on my face had dried, now; I was starstruck, completely and utterly beguiled by the eyes of a princess I was supposed to despise.

'And what would you say about me?' I asked; teasing, some might call it. I call it curiosity.

Curiosity killed the cat, Maximus.

It's a good thing I'm not the cat here, I suppose.

As if on cue, Emile's face broke out into her grin, her lovely cat's grin, the one I've been looking to see ever since I first saw it.

'The better question would be to ask what I would not say about you.' she said. I could feel my own smile burning in the back of my throat, bubbling like a potion a child might make.

'Would you not like to know what I would say about you?'

'If you insist on telling me, I won't say no.'

'You're like an eclipse.' I said. Once I started saying it, I couldn't stop. 'An explosion. A volcano eruption, a flurry of birds on a hot summer day. You're alive. You're more alive than I could ever be. You're so here, so alive, so... so much, that it hurts me, sometimes. But... I'm lucky, I am, that at least for now, I have you as a... as a friend.'

I think we both looked away as I spat out the word friend.

'I don't purposely hurt you.' she said quietly. 'You know that, right?'

You have no idea why you hurt me. You don't want to know. But you will, soon, and there's nothing I can do about it.

'Yeah.' I said, voice trembling. 'Of course.'

☆★☆

That night was another restless one. I had no sleep. Oh, no- there was too much to think about, too much to worry about.

Too much to plot.

I'd been planning my 'great betrayal' for some time by then. Gods, it was going to be a show for the ages; Nathaniel and George would burst through the door, coming to my sides, and I would smirk as I explained what I had done. What *we* had done.

'How could you?' Emile would say, tears filling in her eyes. In my defence, I didn't know her when I played out this little scene in my head, and I imagined her to be as a stereotypical princess would. Emotional, a 'damsel in distress'. In fact, she was actually quite the opposite.

'This is war, Your Highness- I did what had to be done.' I would say gleefully.

'You're a dirty liar, and you'll pay for what you've done to me. For what you've done to Desmond.' Emile would spit.

However, I would laugh aloud, my cackles filling the high walls and roofs.

'Oh, but I'm afraid this is a book in which the bad guy wins.'
Then the scene would cut. I hadn't planned it past that.
Now, thinking of what awaited me, I didn't want to go through with my big betrayal. I didn't want to be a traitor.

I couldn't stop thinking about what Emile had said.

'I don't purposely hurt you. You know that, right?'

The words made me feel sick.

The whole incident was making me realise how much of an awful person I was.

But you're an awful person that's falling for a princess. You can't be so bad if you can feel this strongly, can you?

Stop it. Stop it. I'm not falling for her. I just... like her. A lot.

You like her enough to see her in the stars.

I see George in the stars, sometimes. I see Nathaniel in the stars, and I don't even like him at all.

It isn't in the same way, and you know it.

I turned over to my other side, exhaling shakily. Could it be possible that the great Maximus Invictus Blare was falling for a princess?

No.

No.

I didn't fall for Rosalin, and I kissed her; I hadn't even kissed Emile. Gods, we'd hardly hugged twice.

Did you replay every conversation you ever had with Rosalin in your head at nights when you couldn't sleep? Did you memorise every shade of every splotch of colour that made up her eyes? Did just her scent drive you crazy? Did her touch make your skin go hot?

...

Do not compare what you and Rosalin had to what you and Emile currently have.

The hardest part of feeling that way for someone was admitting it to myself, apparently. I pushed my face into my pillows and clenched my fists until it drew blood. The last thing I thought of before falling asleep was an eclipse. An explosion.

A royal blue sea.

⚔ Chapter Nineteen ⚔

FRIDAY'S WERE ALWAYS THE worst days. Well, I say that as if they were torturous; they weren't *that* terrible, I suppose. Just the worst of days.

George used to love Fridays; they were his day off, just like it was my day off in Kendra. In Rendo I loved no days; there were no days off. Just hour after hour after week after month of endless, painful, labour.

However, I would have much preferred to spend my Fridays in the arena than wandering around the house aimlessly. I was much too used to spending all my time working; perhaps it was a good thing. It would certainly be beneficial in the war.

It was a Friday, surprisingly. I clambered out of bed at around 11am, just to fall straight back down as I reached the living room. I groaned and stretched out, burying my face in a pillow. I was far too tired to even function.

'Max? What on earth are you doing?' It was Emile's voice, softer than the blanket in my bedroom. Gods, I wished I had that blanket in the living room.

'Sleeping. Leave me be.' I grumbled, shutting my eyes tightly.

'Oh, get up you lazy lump of no good.' Emile snapped. I rolled onto my side, pushing myself up to rest on my hand.

'Hi.' I said sleepily.

'Hey.' Emile said, an eyebrow cocked.

'You got any plans for today?' I asked. Emile shrugged, perching gently on the edge of the armchair.

'Not any that I can think of. You?'

'I'm planning to spend my day sleeping, actually.'

'That's a terrible plan.'

'It seems quite appealing to me.'

'Still a terrible plan.' My eyebrows rose, and I pushed myself to sit up properly.

'And have you got a better idea?' I asked slowly.

'When you put it that way, sleeping doesn't seem all too bad.' Emile said with a small smile.

'I mean, we could always talk.' I suggested.

'About?'

You, I thought. *Always you.*

'You choose.' I said, averting my eyes. Sometimes I found it hard to look her in the eye; other times, I wanted to devour her with only my sight, to suck her all in and keep her to myself like the selfish person I was.

'How about the war?'

I blinked, looking back up. *Of all the topics you could have picked, this is the one you choose. How ironic.*

'I can talk about that if you can.' I said. Lying once again. My tongue was an endless sea of lies at this point.

'Do you think the Rendans- do you think they could win?' she whispered.

I considered what I should say.

Lying again would be the best option. But, it didn't have to be a direct lie; just an aversion of the truth would do.

'With the two of us fighting for the Kendrans?' I stretched my face into a painfully forced smile. 'I doubt it.'

'But what if they have someone better than us?' Emile pushed. I tried not to laugh out of spite.

Oh, the Rendans have the best they possibly could have, darling. They have me.

'They won't.' I assured her. 'Not to sound self absorbed or anything, but do you really think anyones going to be more skilled than the two of us? Nathaniel said I'm the best he's seen in his entire life, and he knows Rendo inside out.'

'What if something happens during the war? What if I die? What if Desmond dies? What if-' Emile cut herself off. 'What if you die?'

'You won't die. I won't let you.' I said.

How many more lies until it becomes too much, Maximus?

'You can't say that so surely. Anything could happen. You can't just predict the future, Max.' She looked at her knees. 'I'm afraid. I'm really afraid.'

I felt a pang in my chest.

You'll be even more afraid when you find out about the monster you've been living with for months now.

'Don't be afraid.' I said quietly. 'If anyone hurts you, if anyone dares try and touch you, I'll make all their worst fears dance before them, like a bonfire. I'll always be there for you.'

You let her believe that; it'll only hurt her more when she finds out.

'The same goes for you, then.' Emile said after a moment of silence. 'I've been thinking about this damn war my entire life, and it never seems to get any better. I wish I knew why it started; maybe then I wouldn't be so scared of it.'

'I wish that too, sometimes.' I mumbled. 'The people who missed out on it in the 10 years it's taken to get to this stage are abnormally lucky. Imagine the relief; knowing that you wouldn't be a part of it, a part of the biggest terror to rein upon the two countries.'

'But imagine the guilt.' Emile put in. 'Their children, their grandchildren, they have to fight instead. How could they die peacefully knowing what awaits the future of their family? It would haunt me in the afterlife; the pain of not knowing. The guilt of not being there.'

The guilt I feel right now is a mighty rival to that.

'Do your parents feel that guilt?' I asked. Emile thought it over for a few counts.

'They try to act strong, for me, but sometimes their facade fades. In the nights that they argue, when I'm sent to my room, I can tell how much they wish I wasn't the one risking my life for our country.'

'You're lucky that they care for you so much.'

'I know I am.' Emile agreed.

'I can't say the same for my parents.' I laughed. If I didn't laugh I would cry about it, so it seemed like joking was the best way to go.

'Do you want to… talk about them?' Emile asked hesitantly.

Normally, the answer would be no. But when I was with Emile, the only thing I could think of was how I wanted her to know everything. Even the stuff I'd told nobody else before.

'My mum died during childbirth, so I can't say much bad about her. I have no idea what type of person she was. Hopefully I didn't get the whole bloodthirst thing from her.' I said.

'What about your dad?' Emile inquired.

Do you really want to go there? Do you really want to talk about that?

If it's with her, yeah. I do.

'He probably blamed me for her death in some sort of weird and twisted way. All I know is he sold me to…' I had to make some adjustments to fit my previous story, then. 'He sold me to the Rendan army as a kid. I say they kidnapped me, but only because it hurts less than the truth.'

'Dirty Rendans.' Emile snapped. 'Buying a damn kid. If they don't lose this war then karma isn't real.'

I swallowed hard. She was right, and I knew it; Kendra deserved to win. They really did. But that would never happen with me fighting for the Rendans. It was painful, but it was true,

'Yeah.' I murmured.

'It's alright, now, though. You have Desmond, and me, and that's all you need for now. We're going to win this war and get your bloody revenge on those pigs.'

'I'm glad my sob story enticed such confidence in you.'

'Shut your mouth.'

I laughed, relishing as she tried not to. With every smile I caused from her, my heart melted a little more.

'Hey, do you want to see something?' Emile asked suddenly.

'That depends. What is it?'

'It's a secret. But trust me, you'll love it.'

'If it's you I'm trusting, I'm all aboard. Show me.'

☆🌟☆

She took me through the dungeons, to the end. At first, I thought I was going to look at something in there; but then Emile pressed something and a wall opened like it was a door.

'Woah.' I whispered. Emile grinned, stepping inside. I went in after her, the wall reclosing itself when I was in. 'What is this?'

'Desmond showed me it. It's like a secret room, I guess.' Emile walked over to a violin in the corner, running her fingertips over it tentatively. 'Originally, it was built to be a bomb shelter, a safe space, a hiding spot, you know? But as the years have progressed and Kendra's become a safer place, it was made into this. A nice, comfortable little hideaway.' She paused. 'But, I suppose now that we're on the brink of war this room is more than likely going to go back to its original use, so we might as well make the most of it while we can.'

'Is that a piano?' I whispered.

'What else would it be?'

I bit down on my lip; I used to play the piano in all of my free minutes back in Rendo. I'd missed it so much.

'If you'd shown me this a few months earlier I would have kissed you on the spot.' I said, mesmerised.

'Because of the piano?'

'Because of the piano.'

'You'll have to play something on it for me sometime.' Emile smiled. I looked over to her, ripping my eyes from the organ.

'Do you play the violin?' I asked.

'Yeah. I do. How did you guess?'

'I mean, an obvious sign would be the way you're looking at it. But your hands, also. They have the same feel as a violinists.'

'I'm taking that as a compliment.'

'Good. It is one.'

Emile's lip quirked up. She picked up the instrument, running her fingertips down one of the strings.

'Would you like to hear a song, then?' she asked with a raised eyebrow. I bit my lip.

'Is that even a question? Play away.'

Her fingers were restless upon the violin. They moved quickly, elegantly, gracefully, but with some urgent sense of need. It felt raw, it sounded raw, it was raw. Raw and real.

Art is a form of expression. Music is a form of art. That's how most people look at it. However, the part that people neglect is the expression part.

When people think of expression, they don't really think about it. They don't properly think about it. You can have expressions, you can express how you feel, so and so, and that's all they think they need to know.

But is it really?

The dictionary definition of expression is 'the process of making known one's thoughts or feelings'. When people call art a form of expression, they don't stop to think about what thoughts and what feelings are being put out there. Expression is a vulnerability. Art, music; it's a way to make expression feel a bit less vulnerable.

I look at art properly.

I listen to music properly.

I look for the feelings behind just pencil and paper.

I listen to the thoughts behind what may seem to be just useless sounds.

When I listened to Emile play, I felt a form of recognition. At certain points in the melody, it was louder, harder, faster… quieter, softer, slower. Her music vibrated with emotion, full and there, physically enchanting.

The song came to an end, eventually.

'So. How was I?' Emile asked, her face radiant.

Perfect. Somehow you always are.

'It was amazing.' I whispered. 'Play me something else- play me… a lullaby. Play me a lullaby.'

'A lullaby? That's an odd request.'

'Just do it.'

She did.

But all I could think about was the lies I was telling. The lie I was living. The lies I would carry on telling.

I suppose some might say I was listening to a lullaby of lies.

☆★☆

We must have stayed in that room for hours. When we finally emerged, giggling and high on happiness, the sun was on the verge of setting.

'Ever really watched a Kendran sunset?' Emile asked.

'Now that I think about it, no, I haven't.'

'Gods, I can't imagine! Come on, I have to watch it with you now.'

She grabbed my hand, probably without thinking, and ran out of the house, dragging me after her.

It felt as if my skin was on fire.

'Where are we going?' I yelled. The breeze was fresh against my cheeks, after being underground for a full day.

'The first place I find where we can properly see the sky.' Emile responded.

Fair enough.

When she stopped, it was in a small clearing in a place I hadn't yet explored. Flowers and weeds danced with each other in the soft wind, as if they were friends, meant to grow next to one another.

'Look at it, Maximus, before it fully sets.' Emile said. I did look at it; I stared at it, even, a dark blue that rivalled Emile's eyes.

I glanced at her. She was already looking at me when I did.

'Hi.' she whispered.

'Hi.' I whispered back.

She was still holding my hand; it was starting to sweat now, from the heat of her body.

Body warmth comes from closeness; I'm sure you can get closer than that.

I looked back up at the sky, edging closer and closer and closer, until our shoulders bumped together. I could feel her gaze burning into me, but I didn't dare meet it. I watched the clouds, instead, tinged pink and orange from the sunlight.

'Want to know a fun fact?' I asked.

'Of course.'

'Your eyes burn brighter than the sun ever will.'

I regretted it as soon as I said it, but there was no going back. I wasn't a wizard, or a sorcerer, much to George's disappointment. I was just a human, just a boy, and I made mistakes.

So why did that not feel like a mistake?

'Would you like to know a fun fact in return?' Emile breathed. I finally let myself look at her; she was staring at me fiercely, as if the world would end if she dared look away.

'Tell me.' I said.

'Every minute spent with you means more to me than an eternity.'

My heart skipped a beat.

'It's cold.' I mumbled. It wasn't.

'Yes. It is.' Emile responded breathlessly.

'We could go back…' I trailed off.

'Do you want to go back?' she asked. *Yes. Yes. I want to go back to my bed and dream of blood and murder and winning wars.*

'I'd rather stay here with you.' I hesitated. 'Even if it's just another eternity of a minute.'

Emile smiled, and my face felt bright.

'Then I suppose I'll stay out here with you, also.' she said.

'That would be nice.'

'You say it as if I'm lying.'

'I've grown rather accustomed to lies, actually.'

My eyes widened after I said it. *Wrong move, Maximus, you dense idiot. Why would you say that? Now she'll question you and you'll have to leave and it'll ruin everything and-*

'I wouldn't lie to you.' Emile said. I shut my eyes; it was too painful to look at her, then.

'I wouldn't lie to you, either.'

Ironic, really, that my proclamation against lying was, in fact, a lie itself.

'You're afraid.' Emile said. My eyes snapped open. 'Why are you afraid?'

'I'm not afraid.' I protested.

'You said you wouldn't lie to me. So stop lying.'

My breath hitched. Emile turned around to face me forwards, her body inches away from mine. She looked up at me, apparently unaffected by the fact that I could feel her breath on my face.

'Do you really want to know why I'm afraid?' I asked. She simply nodded. I took a few steps forwards, letting her step backwards, until we hit a tree. One hand against the bark, the other grabbing the side of Emile's neck, it was as if I'd lost any sense of myself.

'Tell me, Maximus. I want to know.'

'Why should I tell you?'

'Tell me.'

'Make me.'

I felt the pulse quicken in her neck, underneath my fingers. I tightened my grip slightly and let my body push against hers; it was almost as close as I could possibly get, but it wasn't close enough. It would never be close enough.

Emile's hands were on my hips, pulling me closer, still, before I had time to breathe, and her nose was touching mine. My nose was full of coffee and petrichor and smoke. Her breaths were hot and heavy, her pulse sharp and fast, but somehow her voice remained calm.

'Tell me, Maximus.' she whispered.

'This is why I'm afraid.' I breathed out. 'I'm afraid of the way you make me feel. I'm afraid of the way you make me lose control, the way you make me forget everything I am, everything I've done, everything I'm destined to become. I'm afraid that I'm not enough to even be near you, Emile. I'm so afraid. Because I'm not a good person, and you are, you're so, so, terribly good that my chest aches just to look at your eyes, and I try to forget the flutter in my chest but it just keeps on fluttering and I feel sick and ridiculous and so, so afraid. It's stupid, I know, but I'm so afraid that you're going to get sick of me and leave, I'm so afraid that it haunts my dreams and my nightmares, I'm so afraid that sometimes I just sit and cry because I'm not good enough for you and we both know it. I'm terrified of this, of you, of us, but I can't stop thinking about you and it kills me. It's killing me. It's killing me so much, slowly, and all at once, quickly, but as if I'll never just die. You make me feel everything. You make me happy and sad and ecstatic and numb and confused and stressed but most of all you make me afraid. You make me afraid.'

'You're more than good enough. If anything, you're too good. I can't lie, either; you make me just as afraid as that, you make me feel all of that, also. But you make me feel alive.'

'I want to be the reason you live. Not the reason you survive, not the reason you force yourself to keep on going: the reason you really, truly *live*.'

'You already are.'

☆★☆

I did not go straight to sleep when I went back to my room.

I shut the door and slid down with my back against it, face hot in my hands, heart soaring uncontrollably.

Did I really just say all of that?

Yes, I did. Oh my Gods I did.

She'd told me I was the reason she lived.

That only made my guilt even stronger as it weighed down on me like a ton of bricks.

I was her reason for living.

What did that mean she would do when she found out?

What did that mean she would do when the inevitable came upon us?

I should have listened to George, and I knew it. I was young and stupid and reckless; we were both young and stupid and reckless.

But we were the type of reckless that people read about in books.

The type of stupid that people dreamt about.

The type of young that teenagers strove to be.

I wanted to be with her all the time. I wanted to listen to her talk about her interests, I wanted to hear every song she could play, I wanted to watch her face light up at my words, I wanted to be the reason she was afraid, just like she was the reason I was afraid.

It was destined to end in tragedy.

So why was I finding it so hard to cut off?

My reputation as Maximus the merciless would not last long at that rate; not when I was letting my feelings get in the way of my job.

That was… unless…

My job there was to find her plans, and her weaknesses.

Now that I was getting even closer to her, it surely wouldn't be so difficult to figure out what she and Desmond were planning for the war.

And her weakness was the one thing Nathaniel would never have expected; me.

A new plan was hatching.

A new plot was forming.

I could make her fall in love with me. I could make her fall in love so hard that she couldn't think straight around me.

And then, when we went to war, when our battle came, she wouldn't be able to kill me.

But I would be able to kill her.

It seemed it was time for a new rule.

Rule number 7; take your mistakes and use them.

⚔ Chapter Twenty ⚔

I QUICKLY DEVELOPED QUITE an obsession with the room through the dungeons. When I properly examined the secret door that led into it, I realised that the mechanics behind it weren't all that complex. Impressive at first glance, yes, but a little disappointing when you know how it works.

The floors were made out of hard stone, the walls some sort of wood that I didn't recognise; whatever wood it was, I had decided it was bulletproof from it's texture, although I wasn't sure of the need for bulletproof walls when the room was underground.

And then there was the piano. Oh, how I'd missed it. At first I was slightly stiff with the way I played my keys, but it only took me a few tunes to fall back into my own rhythm. Piano, music, art, expression; it was a way to make the world around me disappear, to put me in a place where only I could go.

It was quite refreshing, actually,

Autumn had since dawned upon us; it was nearing October, and the wind was no longer soft. It was harsher, more brutal, in a way that made your skin burn.

I loved autumn almost as much as I loved winter.

It was one of those days where stepping outside just made you want to shut your eyes and sigh, small smiles filling your face. I did that, the sighing, the squeezing my eyes shut so tightly that phosphenes danced in my vision. I didn't smile. There wasn't much to smile about, really.

My feelings for Emile were more confusing than anything else. I wanted to touch her, to look at her, to do all of that, but I desperately wanted to hate her too. In a way, it only made me hate myself. I'd let myself grow attached to her; there was no one to blame but me.

If anyone ever needed proof against me being a psychopath, it was right there, written plain and clear in just the way I looked at that stupid girl.

I was barely outside for a few minutes. I went back into the house, the house I was starting to love as if it were my own, making way to the living room.

Unluckily for me, both Desmond and Emile were in there, talking to one another in hushed tones. I leaned against the door frame, suspicion rising in the pit of my stomach.

'Hi.' I said. My voice seemed much too loud in the quiet room. Desmond jumped slightly, patting down his hair as he turned to look at me with wide eyes. Emile wasn't as fased; she just looked annoyed.

'Hello, Maximus. I was just about to come looking for you, actually. How are you?' Desmond said with a smile.

'What were you talking about, just there?' I asked, ignoring what Desmond had said.

'Oh, I would love to tell you!' Emile said enthusiastically. Too enthusiastically. I narrowed my eyes, taking a seat at the armchair..

'Emile-' Desmond started.

'Don't you think he deserves to make the choice himself, Desmond?' Emile cut in with an accusatory tone.

'War isn't about choices.'

'Oh, well it's a great thing we aren't at war yet, isn't it?'

'It's too dangerous, we need him.'

'Well that's up for him to decide isn't-'

'Can you both shut up?' I snapped. The two of them turned to look at me at the same time. 'Stop talking about me as if I'm not right here for a start, please and thank you.'

'Sorry.' Desmond mumbled.

'And stop keeping secrets from me, for the gods sakes. Just tell me, alright? I highly doubt it's going to be that bad.' I said tiresomely.

'You say that now.' Emile said sarcastically.

'Emile has a point in what she was saying. You deserve to make your own decision about this.' Desmond's face was creased with lines of worry. *Perhaps it is really that bad.*

'Why don't you tell me what it is, and I'll make the choice you both want me to make so terribly.' I said, trying not to cause an outburst.

'I have a job for you and Emile.' Desmond said.

'Elaborate.'

'A group of Rendans have been spotted past the border.' he began, leaning forwards slightly. 'They're in the sacred forest. Now, if it was a group of peaceful Rendans, it might not have been such a big deal that we would need you and Emile. But not only are there around thirty of them, they're trained sword fighters, good ones, too. We've dispersed multiple people of the Kendran army to try to break up the group and get rid of them, but they're scarily good. That's why we need you two.'

I looked at Emile, as if by default. She looked worried. If what I was thinking was right, it would be just us two against thirty trained fighters; the odds of us winning, and surviving, were very unlikely.

'Now that you've told me, I see Desmond's point.' I mumbled, a small frown forming. A plan was hatching in my mind. 'I can't exactly say no to that; it could ruin Kendra's chances of winning the war. Usually, the chances of us winning such an unbalanced battle would be impossible, improbable.' I paused, watching their expressions carefully. 'But we're the best of the best, Emile. I could fight any member of those Rendans with my eyes shut. With you? We can do it. Hopefully.'

'Maximus is right.' Desmond said. 'I wouldn't have asked you two to go if I didn't think you could survive. You're both key to this war, and we can't win it without you. Think of this like a prologue, showing you what's to come.'

'Is that you saying yes, Max?' Emile asked, eyes boring into me. *No,* I thought, *because if I say yes, it's final, that I'll have to go somewhere with you, alone, and I don't know what I'll do if I'm fully alone with you, Emile.*

'Give me two days,' I said, standing up. 'And I'll have an answer, then.'

☆✶☆

I spent that night tossing and turning.

There were multiple reasons as to why I shouldn't go.

1) I would be killing off people from my own country, people I probably knew.

2) I would be alone, with Emile.

3) It was dangerous. Extremely dangerous.

4) What would the consequences be when I went back home? Nathaniel would be furious. More than furious, he would be raging.

I didn't want to know what he would do to me at that level of anger.

But... if I didn't go, they wouldn't forgive me. Desmond and Emile, I mean. I would be the cause of their downfall.

And if they didn't forgive me, neither would Nathaniel, because the task would be over.

It was a conundrum.

Just go, for goodness sake, Maximus. Imagine what you could find out while you're there. When you get back... Nathaniel will understand, he has to.

But what if he doesn't?

Does it really matter? You're going to kill him when the time's right anyway, are you not?

What will he do to me before that, though?

The worst he can do is kill you, and he wouldn't kill his best fighter before the war.

It isn't death that I'm afraid of.

I had heard the screams of children and adults, women and men, rich and poor alike when they were left alone with Nathaniel. I knew what he'd done to George. I knew what he'd done to Adelaide.

I knew much too well what he had done to me.

And I knew much too well what he would do to Emile if I wasn't the first to kill her.

I'd rather betray her than let him hurt her the way I knew he would.

Does it not give you peace of mind knowing that he's already done that to you? You could handle it then, you can handle it again.

I don't want to handle it again.

You don't always get what you want.

I can't handle it again. Please. You don't understand.

I knew Nathaniel like nobody else did. He'd shared his darkest secrets with me in the midst of the night, confiding in me like a friend after causing my screams for help.

The only advantage to what he had done to me was that I knew everything and anything. I knew his weaknesses, his strengths, the stuff he did when he was alone.

Oh, boo hoo, poor you. I went through it too, remember. I am you. I feel everything you do, but a million times worse.

You're the most revolting part of me.

The last time it had happened was exactly a week before I left for Kendra. The memory was still fresh in my head.

'I'm just preparing you.' Nathaniel had said after, his words slurred, lying starfished next to me. 'You never know what that Kendran scum could do to you.'

I was numb, arranged like a stiff, wooden board, hands clenched at my sides, eyes squeezed shut.

He stripped me of everything.

I didn't even have any dignity around him.

What about Emile?

What about her?

The stuff you could get out of her while you're alone... it's an opportunity you can't afford to miss.

Information means nothing when I feel this way about her.

I know exactly how you feel about her. But you're going to have to get over it, aren't you? You can't let your feelings get in the way of this. What happened to rule number 3? Rule number 6?

I can't help it.

She's falling for you, Maximus. Love makes you crazy. She'll tell you everything, anything you want, if you only ask.

Yeah? Well maybe I'm falling for her, too!

I sat up sharply. It had been quite a struggle admitting that, even just to myself.

You think I don't know that? Sometimes you have to choose what's right over your stupid love life.

But what if this isn't right? It certainly doesn't feel like it.

If you let yourself fall for her, if you choose her, what would Nathaniel do to her? He wouldn't waste his time on you; he would go straight to her, straight to where it would hurt you the most. And then he'd ruin you, and you know it. You're saving her by doing this.

There's got to be a different way. Maybe... maybe I can save her during the war, and go to her when it's finished...

Do you really think she'll forgive you after what you've been doing? This is the only way.

What if I could bring her to the Rendans?

They would never want her. She's the heir to the throne of the country we're facing in this war. Besides, what makes you think you could ever make the princess of Kendra fight for Rendo?

What if-

Don't even think about it. I won't let you think that.

Surely there's something I can do.

There's nothing. The sooner you realise, the better.

I chewed on my tongue. My head throbbed. I was so tired, so exhausted, but I couldn't sleep. My brain was whirring. I had the answer to everything, every problem, every battle, every argument, every war; the answer to everything but this.

Fine. I'll go. But when I do what I already know I will, you'll have nobody to blame but yourself.

Don't tell them yet. Make them think this is a hard decision for you; make them feel bad, guilty. Then, when you do go, Emile will have no choice but to tell you. She'll think she owes you.

Your advice is terrible. But I suppose I have no other choice.

Choice was a term I was not used to. I'd never had the privilege of it, the privilege of my own free will.

It took me at least another hour to fall asleep after that.

Oh, but then, I dreamt.

And how I dreamt.

☆★☆

Emile was in front of me. She looked… scared. Her hair was darker than usual, sticking to her forehead. I looked at her hands. They were shaking.

'Maximus?' she whispered.

'Emile? What's wrong?' I asked, almost urgently.

'How could you?' Emile murmured. *'HOW COULD YOU?'*

I flinched as she yelled, taking a wary step back. I realised, then, that she was tied up, rope securing her to some sort of pole. I looked around, taking in the atmosphere; we were in the basement of Nathaniel's manor. Why were we there? *How* were we there?

'What are you talking about?' I said, forcing calm into my voice. Emile, on the other hand, was the opposite of calm. Her eyes were bright with anger, wild, blood crusted around her mouth, nose, ears, eyes…

Why was she bleeding so much?

'I trusted you.' she said shakily. 'I trusted you with everything. This is how you repay me? You deserve nothing. You are nothing.'

'Why are you bleeding? Who did this?'

'I would tell you, if I still trusted you. Think about it really hard, Maximus.'

I didn't have to think to know.

'What did he do?' I whispered. Emile stayed quiet. 'I said what did he do?'

Why I was shouting, I didn't know. But Emile stood her ground, royal blue eyes blazing furiously.

'He did nothing to me that he said he hadn't done to you.' she snapped. My heart dropped to my stomach.

'No. No, no, no… you're lying. Stop it. Why would he do that? I've done everything he asked, I've been everything he wanted me to be… what more could he want?' I spluttered, my throat closing up.

'Oh, yes, you've been perfect. You fooled me. But… if only you hadn't fallen in love with me.'

I blinked. My heart had melted at hearing what he'd done to her; but hearing her say that only hardened it again.

'You can't say much. I see the way you look at me. I hear the way your heartbeat quickens when I speak.' I said.

'Imagine what we could have had. A shame you chose a sadistic, murdering rapist over me.' Emile snarled.

'It isn't like that.'

'No? Then what is it like?'

'I was trying to save you from this! I thought… I thought that if I killed you first, that if he did it to me instead, he would leave you alone… I can't… I don't…'

'Maybe you should've tried harder, then. But well done, I suppose. Your plan worked. Kendra stands no chance of winning the war now that they've lost Desmond and I.'

'Desmond? What- what happened to Desmond?'

'You don't know?'

I didn't say anything. The guilt was enormous. I could barely breathe. Emile laughed, almost manically, throwing her head back.

'Your darling George killed him. You should have seen the look on his face! I can tell that the Flint heir had never killed a person before that, my goodness. He threw up straight after, crying all over his little sister's top.'

'No… no, George would never…' I cut myself off, rubbing my brow in frustration. 'Desmond's dead? No, I don't…'

'You don't believe me? You should. It's all your fault, remember?'

'Shut up.'

'I'm not wrong. It's all you-'

'I said shut up!'

My eyes snapped open. I was sweating, but I was in my room in the Kendran countryside, and I was awake and okay and Desmond wasn't dead and Emile was alright and-

'Maximus? What on earth is wrong?' Desmond burst through the door, Emile coming in after him.

'I- what?' I stammered.

'You were shouting at someone to shut up you daftie; what's happened?' Emile said. I blinked.

'Nothing. Bad dream, that's all. I'll go back to sleep now. Goodnight.'

Yeah. A bad dream. One that's destined to become real life.

⚔ Chapter Twenty One ⚔

I WOKE UP LATE the next day. Even then, I was still tired. Perhaps I was just mentally tired; there was no chance I could be physically tired.

I almost fell down the stairs as my vision blurred. I was so exhausted, so drained; I wasn't sure if I could handle looking both Emile and Desmond in the eye.

Some people say that dreams are warnings of the future. Warnings aren't visions; they aren't set in stone. They can be moulded, changed. I would change the future if I had to, if it would prevent that from happening. I would do near enough to anything to prevent it.

'Good morning, Maximus.' Desmond said cheerfully as I went into the living room. I collapsed onto the sofa, head spinning.

'Morning, Desmond.' I mumbled. I'd never been so dizzy in my entire life.

'How are you feeling?' Desmond asked. I blew out a heavy breath.

'I feel fine. You?' I said. He simply raised an eyebrow, apparently not convinced.

'I'm alright.' he said. 'Have you been thinking about the task?'

'Yeah.'

'And?'

I hesitated a moment. 'I want to go- I do. But... it's just so dangerous... I don't know if I'm willing to risk it.'

'Emile has said that if you decide to not go, she'll still be going by herself.'

Oh, if there was ever going to be anything to wake me from the dead, it would have been those words.

'What? Surely you can't let her do that.' I said, laughing nervously.

'She's an adult, Maximus. If she wants to do it, I legally have no way of stopping her.'

'But- surely she wouldn't-' I couldn't finish my sentence. Why would she risk her life like that? It made no sense. She was too alive, too happy, too...

Too stubborn.

Of course she would still go. Who was I kidding?

'I don't want to force you into doing something you don't want to do,' Desmond paused. 'But I know that you wouldn't let her go into such an uneven battle alone.'

'I don't-' I stopped. *Drag it on a bit more. Make it seem difficult. Make him feel guilty.* 'You aren't forcing me. I just- I want to make sure we both live.' I averted my gaze, staring at my knees.

'You're both the best sword fighters I've ever met; if I was going to pick anyone to do this, out of all the people in the world, it would be the both of you, in a heartbeat.' Desmond said quietly. 'You'll make the Rendan's wish that they'd never bothered with Kendra in the first place.'

Ouch. That one stung.

'It's just risky.' I mumbled. *Ha. Sure it is. So risky. Like I couldn't beat all thirty of them by myself when I was 13 years old.*

'If you haven't decided what you're going to do by tomorrow night,

Emile's going to have to just go by herself.' Desmond said. I saw the guilt flash across his face. *Small wins make large victories.*

'I'll know by then.' I mumbled, trying to force tension into my tone. It worked, I thought. Apparently I was a better actor than I had previously imagined.

'See me as soon as you've decided.' Desmond said.

I stood, making way to leave.

'Don't worry. I will.'

☆★☆

I found Emile pacing the library; her hair was straight. It was the first time I'd seen it straight, or even properly done. I let my eyes trail all over her as she ran her fingertips down the spine of a book. She was wearing a long dress, rose gold, the skirt of it dancing in the light breeze. My gaze latched on to her hands, one gripping the book, the other stroking it. Her fingers were slender but calloused, the veins in her hands prominent. My line of sight travelled up, stopping at her lips. They were slightly parted, until her bottom lip was sucked under her teeth.

I could watch her for hours and not get bored.

'Hi.' I said finally. My voice felt too loud in such a quiet place. Emile looked up swiftly, eyes catching on mine

'Maximus.' Emile said simply. She removed her stare from me only to put away the book, but not before looking back at me. The few feet we were from one another felt like miles.

'How are you?' I asked, clearing my throat awkwardly.

'I'm fabulous. You?' Emile said. Her voice sounded like a warning; her eyes were colder than usual. Cut off. I felt a pang in my throat.

'I'm okay.' I paused, looking down, and then back up. 'You look... nice.'

'Well, I thought that if this was going to be one of my last days before going and risking my life, I would make a bit of an effort.' She raised an eyebrow. 'But since I only look 'nice' it seems I might as well have not bothered.'

My eyes widened. 'No- I- that isn't what I meant.' I said. *Stupid, stupid Maximus. Why do you even care if you hurt her feelings? You'll be hurting more than that soon enough.*

'Oh? Then what did you mean?' Emile asked, feigning innocence as the corner of her mouth quirked up.

'You look stunning.' I said, a little too quickly. My cheeks het up, but Emile looked pleased, if a little surprised.

'Tell me something I don't know.' she said with a smirk.

'I'll take it back if that's how you feel.'

'Oh, no, you can do that, but now I know that you think so.' Emile laughed slightly. 'I suppose you look rather pretty today, too, in your own rumpled way.'

I swallowed.

You look rather pretty today, too.

'I'm flattered.' I said, in an attempt to be sarcastic. It didn't seem to work. My voice cracked, and I could hardly bring myself to blink; I could see on Emile's face that she felt the same way.

'Have you thought about the task?' Emile said. I let out a hard breath. I was sick of thinking about that damn task.

'Desmond told me what you were planning on doing.' I said tightly. Emile's eyes hardened once again; just as they were softening, too.

'And what am I planning on doing?' Her voice was frigid, icy. It sent shivers running through my bones.

'Going alone. Facing thirty fighters, *alone*.' I watched her face for any show of emotion; she looked emotionless, if anything.

Numb, perhaps.

'And what do you expect me to do? Sit around while the Rendans tear my country apart?' She was walking towards me, until she was right in my face. Emile was scarily intimidating when she wanted to be. 'Oh, no, but you'd be just fine doing that, wouldn't you?'

'That isn't true. You have no idea what's going through my head.'

'Oh? Is that so? Then why don't you tell me?'

'I can't let you go there alone. It's too dangerous.' My fingers latched around her wrist; her skin was red hot. Emile barely flinched at my harsh and sudden contact. She just wrinkled her nose at me.

'Then come with me.' she spat.

'What happened to me making my own choice?'

'That was before the damn Rendans killed my aunt and uncle!' Emile cried out.

'What? I didn't know. You can't blame me for that.'

'Why are you so afraid to come? I know that you aren't scared of the battle. Hell, you could best the lot of them and more with your eyes closed.' Emile pulled me closer, until our noses were almost touching. There was some sort of malicious gleam in her eye. 'Is it still me that you're afraid of?'

'Shut up.'

'Why are you so scared of me? Of this? Of... of us, for the Gods' sakes! It's a couple days that you'll be alone with me, Maximus, it isn't the end of the Goddamned world!'

I released my grip on her, stepping backwards.

'You don't understand.' I said harshly.

I'm done pretending to be nice just to satisfy you.

'You're right, Max, I don't understand. Why don't you just tell me?' She sounded exasperated. Hurt, maybe.

Aw. What a shame. You'll have to survive without knowing every single thing inside of my head, won't you?

'You'll never understand. How could I expect a princess to understand it, anyway?' I said. 'No, you're so accustomed to getting everything you want handed to you on a plate that you don't stop to think about the fact that I never got that, Emile! I don't get things handed to me on a plate! I've lived my life in solitary, in a cruel and unforgiving solitary!. You don't understand me, just like I don't understand you. How does it feel? To be even with someone for once in your life? To not be superior and better in every single way?'

'We both know that you're far better than me at nearly everything, Maximus. Don't you dare play the victim here.'

She tried to put on a strong facade, but I knew that my words had gotten to her. They'd crawled under her skin, through her blood and her veins and her bones, consistent, haunting, tormenting. The manipulated becomes the manipulator, some might say. I supposed that statement was quite true, as a small smirk spread across my lips.

'Why not play a part when I'm so terribly good at acting?'

I strode off, slamming the door behind me before Emile could get in another word.

☆★☆

I was under the impression I may have made a minor mistake in the way that I had spoken to Emile.

Minor? You'll be bloody lucky if she tells you anything, now.

What did you want me to do? I can't help myself. When my tongue starts running itself, it just doesn't stop.

Oh, I can tell that much you damn idiot. If you two don't make up in the time it takes before you leave for the forest, you're going to be royally screwed. Just a heads up.

You act as if I don't already know that.

You don't know most of the stuff that I tell you, somehow.

Lies.

I knew I was still going to go to the forest; it was inevitable, now. If there was going to be any way to make it up to Emile, then it would be that.

Speak to Desmond about it. Let him run you through the entirety of the task, tell him of how terrible you feel for hurting Emile like so. He'll tell you to speak to her. And then, while you're speaking to her, while you're professing your sincerest apologies, tell her that you're going to go with her. She'll be overjoyed, and she'll surely forgive you.

How do you know that all of that will happen in the exact way you imagine it to?

I just do. Trust me.

Easier said than done.

I checked the time. 7pm. I still had time to speak to Desmond; talking to Emile again, on the other hand, would probably have to wait until tomorrow.

My feet took me downstairs, into the living room. He was there, unsurprisingly; it was a shock to ever see Desmond not in the living room or his bedroom on a day off.

He looked up sharply. I wasn't sure why, but I could feel tears prickling in the corners of my eyes. I blinked them away harshly, gently shutting the door.

'Can we talk?' I whispered. My voice trembled, for some reason. I cleared my throat awkwardly.

'Of course we can. Come, sit here.'

I sat on the sofa opposite him, not daring to let our eyes meet. I could imagine the look of worry on his face; I didn't need to actually see it.

'What's happened?' Desmond asked. I shut my eyes.

'Can I ask you a question?' I said.

'Ask away.'

'Do you think that... do you think that a person truly terrible, to the core of their morals and their basic sense of humanity, could ever be enough for someone so... so good?' My voice was a slither of a whisper.

'Is this about Emile?'

I didn't answer. I pressed my lips together into a thin, white line, as if that would ward away the urge to cry.

'Maximus, look at me.'

I did. His face was so genuine, so- so kind, it just made me want to cry even more. Was I really so much of a terrible person that I could bring myself to hurt someone so loving, someone who was more of a father to me than Nathaniel and my real *pater* ever were?

'You are good enough. You might not believe me, and that's fine, but you are good enough. You're more than enough for her. I don't know what's happened to make you think this, and I'm not sure if I want to know, but hell are you good enough. If you trust anyone's word on that, trust mine. I see the way she looks at you when you aren't watching. I see the way she smiles every time you best me in a fight.' Desmond said quietly.

'I feel like I'm drowning in my own guilt.' I choked out. I realised, later, that it was an awfully insensitive thing to say to a man who had seen the horrors of war itself, but Desmond was nothing but comforting, understanding, all of the time. I saw his eyes flash with sympathy. He knew how it felt to hear the voices of those he had killed; I could see it in his eyes everytime I mentioned death. If there was ever going to be any I could confide in with that sort of stuff, it was always going to be him.

'Tell me about it.' Desmond said, almost too kindly. 'Talk to me, Maximus.'

'I- I'm eighteen years old, and I've already killed more people than I can count. Hundreds of thousands of innocent people, people I stripped of their lives. I can't- and now, now I'm going to war, where I'm only going to kill more and more and more because goddamn it I made such a reputation for myself back in Rendo, and I regret it so much that it kills me, even though I know it wasn't my fault, it was *his* fault for making me do it and for making me be the better version of him and for hurting me so much so so much that now I can't even sleep because-'

'Who is he?' Desmond cut in. His voice was hard, cruel. I bit down on my lip. I'd made yet again another mistake, in letting myself get so caught up in such a stupid rant.

'I can't tell you.' I said under my breath.

'Why not?'

'I just- I just can't, alright?'

I was crying at that point, my head buried in my hands. My sobs seemed to shake the entirety of the house with the force that they came through me, leaving my body weak and trembling. I was vulnerable once more. I hated being vulnerable.

However, if anything good came from Nathaniel's harsh words and cutting insults, it was that I knew how to change a face in a matter of seconds.

'I've veered off the topic of why I originally came to you.' I said, wiping my eyes gently, my voice smooth as glass. I could see the surprise in Desmond's features at my sudden mood change; but, really, my mood hadn't changed at all. It was just the way I presented myself that had.

'I'm afraid I don't think we even touched upon what seems to be the reason you came to me.' Desmond said. Not accusatory; just honestly.

'I came to speak about the task.' Desmond looked more interested, now; I could tell by the way his eyebrow quirked and he leaned forwards slightly in his seat.

'I'm listening.'

'I want to know everything that's going to happen during it, to your knowledge. The entire plan. How we get there, how long we'll be there, how long it takes, everything.' I paused. 'If you want me to go so desperately, you'll tell me.'

It was the move of a manipulator, but the manipulated becomes the manipulator, as they say.

'I can do that.' Desmond said slowly. 'But why will this convince you to go?'

'That doesn't matter. Just- just tell me.'

'If it'll make you go, of course I will.' Desmond said with a small smile. 'You'll wake as the sun is rising, near enough to 6 in the morning. The journey there will be around 2 days long, perhaps even longer. I'm not sure exactly. You'll be travelling by both train and horseback.'

'Horseback? How long will that be for?'

'Only a few miles. The last train stops a good bit before Sancire, and Emile couldn't possibly enter on foot. It would be improper.'

'It's funny you talk of properness while sending us off to the most uneven battle of possibly the century.'

'It's a last resort.'

'And I am guessing Sancire is the city of the sacred forest?'

'Yes, yes it is. Why?'

'It's a fitting name, that's all.'

'Care to elaborate?'

'In my first language, Rendan, sancire means sacred.'

'Ah.'

There was a strange feeling of danger rising in the pit of my stomach; not a fear of danger around me. Not a fear at all, really. Perhaps the fear of myself becoming the danger. Either way, something was off, and it was obvious in the way I snapped my responses, obvious in the way my patience was wearing thin for near to no reason.

My nerves were on edge.

'What happens when we enter Sancire?' I asked, pushing, pressing, prodding. I was determined to know everything and anything.

'You will be worn out from the days of travel, so there is a small hotel at the edge of the forest you can stay in. The owners there have a room reserved for any time you may come. Just tell them your surnames and they'll know who you are.'

'And what of this hotel? Is there anything I need to know about it?'

'Nothing much. Your room is on the top floor, although I must warn you, it is rather small.'

'Rather small? What do you mean by that?'

There was some sort of a gleam in Desmond's eyes as he opened his mouth to speak again. 'You will be sharing your room with Emile, as the rest of the rooms have been reserved for other guests. It's a double bed, don't worry. I wouldn't have you share a single bed.'

My stomach flipped. I forced calm into my facial features as I realised how intently Desmond was reading them.

Sharing a bed.

Well then.

'I assume we'll only be spending one night there then, yes?' I said, voice slick. Perhaps with worry. Perhaps with excitement.

It did not matter. Either was bad.

'Yes. Only one night.'

Oh, but so much could happen in only one night.

'The next day. What are we doing the next day?' I was distracted, now. Being alone with her seemed bad enough as it was. Alone in a hotel room, in the same room, the same bed; that was a step too far.

'You'll start heading into the forest, then; you're going to have to pack a bag with extra clothes and camping utensils, as it's likely you'll have to set up a camp on your way throughout the forest.'

'And then we fight.'

'And then you fight.'

I was more concerned about Emile and I than I was about the battle ahead.

'Does Emile know all of this?'

'Everything. She wants to prove herself to her parents, prove that she's capable of leading this war.' Desmond paused, eyes raking all over me. 'I suggest you speak to her about it, if you're still undecided about whether or not to go.'

'I will. I- I'll go now.' I whispered, almost tripping over as I stood. 'Where is she?'

'Try the arena.'

'The arena? Why is she there?'

'I am not the one you should be asking this. Now, go, go and see her for goodness sake Maximus!'

I nodded once, sharply, and fled, across the corridor, to the double doors of the arena.

I did not hesitate.

'Emile!'

My voice echoed almost alarmingly, but the door slamming was even louder. I saw her almost immediately. She had her sword in her hand, swinging it around as if it was a dance, her feet springing lightly. Her hair was cradling her face, fiery as it was. Like always, her movements were elegant, flawless, even.

Completely and utterly bewitching.

Yet, she stopped, dropping her sword and turning to let her gaze meet mine.

'Maximus.' she said in response. Her voice was quiet, but it still reverberated off the high walls.

'I am so sorry.' I said, cautiously stepping down the stairs and into the middle portion of the arena. 2 feet distance felt like nothing when she looked so hurt, but so relieved at the same time.

'Don't be sorry. It was my fault. I shouldn't be pressuring you to come. I didn't think you'd respond so harshly, that was all. But I cannot say much, for I would have done the same thing.' Her voice shook, perhaps with nerves.

'No, I- I've spoken to Desmond, about the task. I know how much it means to you.' I said. I looked away for the next part. 'You know that I would do near enough to anything to make you happy, right?'

'What are you trying to say?'

'I'll come with you.' I looked back up, and saw her face lift, her eyes brighten. 'I'll help you prove yourself and whatnot.'

'Oh my gods, thank you thank you thank you!'

My train of thoughts was cut off as she ran at me, arms wrapping around my neck in a positively crushing hug. The force pushed me off my feet and we both stumbled backwards, her on top of me.

It was one of those moments where I stopped thinking about Nathaniel and the war and the betrayal, one of those moments where I could only see her, her cat's grin, the intensity of her dark eyes.

I was painfully aware of her body pressing against mine. Of the brush of skin when her arm came against my neck, of her hands pressed against the floor at the sides of my head, tangling in my hair, her breath in my face, hot and suffocating.

'Hi.' I mumbled. I could see the beginnings of a smirk forming on her lips. Her lips, which were far too close to mine.

'You okay?' she asked, almost teasingly. My hands twitched. One of them snagged her wrist, and I flipped her over, so I was on top, and it was my hands tangling in her hair, and my breath hot in her face.

'Great, actually.' I breathed.

After lying in a tense silence for a few minutes, I pushed myself off her, laying instead on my back beside her.

Her hand clasped mine.

And even though my conscience was screaming at me, I held hers back.

⚔ Chapter Twenty Two ⚔

I HARDLY SLEPT THE night before. My brain was whirring, running itself through all of the endless opportunities that were awaiting me.

What if it's all for nothing? What if you die out there?

Are you mad? I'm not going to die, of course I'm not. I could take out the lot of them by myself if I wanted.

What if Emile dies?

Emile isn't going to die. I won't let it happen.

What if you die protecting her?

I'm not stupid for the Gods sakes! You act as if I'm unable to protect both her and myself without trouble, when you know I can.

I am only preparing you for what they may do to you.

Flashbacks.

'I'm only preparing you. You never know what that Kendran scum could do to you.'

I would much prefer it if you stopped preparing me, then.

Oh, but what if the war begins while you are there? How on earth are you supposed to go through with your great betrayal?

I highly doubt they'll start the war with both me and the Kendran princess off the radar.

What about that hotel? Goodness knows what could happen then.

Oh my Gods, will you shut up?

I rolled over onto my stomach, holding my hands at my ears as if it would silence the voice inside of my head. Sometimes I thought I was going mad. Technically, I was speaking to myself.

But what form of madness could give such good advice? The voice would whisper, and I'd be able to hear the grin in it's words.

Tonight there was no grin; only stony words and cutting remarks.

When I eventually fell asleep, I dreamt of a world other than the one I lived in. A world where my love wasn't limited to the approval of one man.

☆✯☆

'The sun is rising, Maximus. Wake up!'

I woke with a start, blinking hazily as my eyes adjusted to the light. Desmond was leaning over me, his face a picture of accusation.

'Already?' I asked wearily, pushing myself up. Desmond simply rolled his eyes, already turning to leave.

'Get washed, dressed, and grab your stuff. You're leaving in 40 minutes.'

'40 minutes? But-'

I didn't have time to finish my sentence. The door had been slammed and I was left with only the breeze it emitted, alone again. I groaned, forcing myself out of my bed and to my wardrobe.

'It's too early in the morning for me to be doing this.' I grumbled to myself, pulling out a plain top and some joggers. I quickly changed, combed through my hair and pulled on a jacket, making my way to the bathroom with my duffel bag on my shoulder.

Emile was doing the same as I; she, instead, had a backpack slung over her back, her head over the sink as she washed the face wash from her skin. She looked up and gave me a small smile.

'Excited?' she asked, grabbing a towel and drying herself.

'That's one word for it.' I mumbled. She laughed a little.

'See you downstairs, *amor*.'

I blinked after her in faint surprise. She'd just- she'd just called me *love*, in Rendan, in my own language. I stared at the space of where she had been for a few moments before finally bringing myself to get washed.

Both Emile and Desmond were waiting for me by the door. I could see the worry in Desmond, as he tapped the ball of his foot against the wooden floor, as his eyes flickered to the clock continuously. His gaze latched on me, and he positively exhaled in relief.

'There you are! Right, come on, we have to leave.' he said urgently, opening the door for us. 'Come on, then, we haven't got all day!'

Emile and I rushed out, not bothering to wait for Desmond as he locked the door.

'How nervous are you on a scale of one through ten?' Emile whispered.

'For what part? The fighting or the being with you?'

I hadn't meant to say it, but that didn't mean I regretted it. I caught her eyes, watching as her pupils pulsated.

'When you put it that way, I'm much more curious about the scale of being with me.'

'A solid nine out of ten.'

I looked away, then, coming to a halt to wait for Desmond. He came up to us with a smile, but not before speeding ahead.

'Hurry, kids!' he called back. Emile and I exchanged looks.

'Hypocrite.' Emile muttered. I tried not to laugh.

It only took around ten minutes of walking to reach the border of the countryside. The lines of Kendran guards and soldiers were rather intimidating, I had to admit. But we were let straight through, straight to a large train directly in front of us.

'Right, you get off when everyone else does. Then, you go straight to the train lined up after it. There are five trains altogether. Once you've gotten off the fifth train, find the stables and take a horse each. Emile, you'll know the way to Sancire from there.'

I know my way from here, nevermind from that close.' she said bitterly.

'You can sleep on train two and train four. We have Kendran guards located in those trains, so they can wake you when it's time to leave. Have you got any questions?'

'How long will we be riding horseback for?'

'Only an hour or two, if that. Now, go on, onto the train.' Desmond said. Emile hesitated, though, pulling him into an embrace. I saw the shock flash across his face, but he melted into it. I realised, then, that Desmond was as much of a second father to Emile as he was to me.

'Goodbye, Des!' Emile yelled back, disappearing in the train.

'Maximus. You'll do great. I believe in you.' Desmond said gently, holding out his hand. I took it, shaking it almost too hard.

'Thank you. For everything. Nothing I could ever do would repay you in the lengths that you have gone to for me.' I said. My guilt was an ocean; deep, black, and a place where you certainly don't want to be lost.

'You don't need to thank me. Go on, go and join Emile.'

I nodded, waving my goodbyes.

I found Emile almost immediately. She had taken one of the seats that were arranged like a table. I sat opposite her, throwing my bag on the chair beside me.

'What is your nervous scale now?' she asked. I watched her for a moment. I watched the tentative throb in her jaw, the stray strands of hair that tangled in her face, in her mouth.

'Probably a ten. Yours?'

'I'm not nervous.' she said with a grin. A cat's grin. 'My scale would be a two out of ten.'

'If not nervous then what are you?'

'Free.'

I raised an eyebrow. Not sceptically; just curiously.

'Oh? Care to explain that one?'

'Do you have any idea how long I've been trapped in that damn house for? Way over a year, now. I've missed my country, you know? I've missed wandering the streets of the cities in a country I could call my own. I've missed the people and the atmosphere and the scenery and the shops and- and even the language, for Gods' sake.'

'What language do the Kendran's speak?' I asked suddenly.

'Αυτό εδώ.' Emile said. *This one.* It was called Graecus in Rendo. Luckily for Emile, I was fluent in nearly every language.

'Είναι τόσο?' *Is that so?*

Her face split into a grin.

'How do you know so many languages?' she asked. I shrugged.

'I was taught them to prepare me for anything. The only languages I haven't had the pleasure of learning are the ancient ones, but nobody uses those anymore, so I'm not too worried.'

'Out of all the languages you know, what is your favourite?'

'Rendan. Forever. The words sound like- like poetry, no matter what you're saying. It's hauntingly beautiful. I-'

I was cut off as the train started moving with a jolt. I swallowed, and it seemed Emile did the same.

'Finally leaving, eh?' I muttered.

'Finally leaving.' Emile confirmed, pushing her hair behind her ears. She looked fresh, happier than I'd ever seen her before.

I watched her as her eyes flickered to the window, staring out wistfully. I wondered what she was thinking.

'Penny for your thoughts?' I said. Emile didn't flinch.

'I doubt you have a penny on you.' she said. She wasn't necessarily wrong...

'I'll give you one of my thoughts in return for one of yours.'

Emile looked now, her interest sparked.

'I can do that. But only if I choose what you're telling me.'

'It isn't really a thought then, though, is it?'

'Maybe I don't want to exchange thoughts. Maybe I want to do

something else.'

I was leaning forwards, my fingers laced together as I rested my chin on them.

'And what do you have in mind?' I asked slowly.

Emile's face split into a grin, one full of mischief.

'There's a game that the children of the palace play, to pass time when they're bored. 21 questions. We'll make it 20, though, because my version is different. The question you ask, you also have to provide an answer to it. You down?'

'So I ask a question, then you, until we get to 20? Any questions I like?'

'Yeah, obviously. Now, are you down?'

'Of course I am. You can ask first, if you like.'

'I was going to ask first anyway.' Emile was leaning forward in the exact same way I was, her body almost mirroring mine. I could've sworn I'd once heard George say how that was a sign of affection…

'Question one: have you ever been in love?' Emile asked. I tilted my head at her as I thought.

'I don't think so.' I said eventually, although doubt creeped into my voice. Emile arched an eyebrow, as if urging me to carry on speaking. 'I've liked people, certainly, but I'm not even sure that I understand what love is.' I said, chewing on my lip.

'How is that?' Emile asked, eyes glittering. My head inclined even further.

'That's an extra question, your majesty; I think not.' I paused. 'Wait, do I need to address you like that now that we're out of the house and the countryside?'

Emile laughed slightly.

'I could make you if I wanted to, but what's the fun in that? The guards know that you're a companion of mine, so don't worry about it.' she said.

'Am I though? A companion?' I said.

'You- you're the closest friend I have.'

'Are you sure that I'm just your closest friend?'

I was being overly confident, I was stepping out of my comfort zone; it was unnatural for me, and Emile knew it. But it was not unnatural for her.

'Oh? Then what do you suppose we are?' she said, the corner of her mouth lifting upwards.

'Perhaps we're best friends.'

'Or perhaps we're even more, still.'

Her gaze was piercing. It dug holes into my soul, left me fragile and gasping for air.

'I don't think that this language has a name for what we are.' I mumbled. I was stumbling into dangerous topics, uncharted territory. But still, I was stumbling, falling, and I could not seem to catch my balance.

'I don't think that any language has a name for what we are.;'

She was closer than she had ever been before. I let my eyes trail down to her lips, parted, poised as if they were waiting to meet mine. I swallowed hard.

But then the train window flew open and we jumped apart, looking at it with mild panic.

'What on earth?' Emile gasped, holding a hand to her heart. I burst out into laughter, and so did she.

☆★☆

When we boarded the second train, I briefly remembered Desmond telling us to sleep on it. I couldn't even if I tried. The eyes of the Kendran guards were burning into me, and I was much too afraid to fall into the vulnerability of sleep in front of them.

Emile took the window seat, and I sat next to her. There was almost no space to breathe. I could feel our arms touching, the soft hairs on them brushing against the hairs on mine.

'Are you tired?' Emile asked. I risked a glance at her; she was staring at me, shamelessly.

'No, not really.' I'd had a fair share of caffeine; there was not going to be any chance of me sleeping on that train. I would have to wait until the fourth one. 'Are you?'

'I'm completely shattered.'

'Go to sleep, then. If you don't now you'll have to wait until the fourth train.'

'I was planning on it.'

A few minutes passed, before I felt something rest on my shoulder. I looked down at it cautiously, only to be greeted with flaming red hair and the sound of gentle snores.

My shoulder felt hot at her contact, and my head was screaming at me to push her off. But I didn't. Of course I didn't. Did anyone really think I would have?

☆ ★ ☆

Before I knew it, a day had passed, and the sun was rising through the window of the third train.

'It's been nearly 24 hours moving, I think I might just be sick.' I said, rubbing my forehead. Emile laughed.

'What, do you get travel sickness or something?'

'Usually, no, but after this long? I'm not ashamed to say that I do feel rather travel sick.'

'Fair enough.'

'We still have another day yet.'

'Please, don't remind me.'

'I want to die.'

'Good thing we're on our way to the battlefield, isn't it?'

I rolled my eyes, slumping in the chair. It was much more uncomfortable than the other two had been, made out of metal, and not even separated as they are in buses. It went sideways, with a pole and space for walking in front of it. I felt as if I was going to slip down the damned chair at any given moment.

'I'm so thirsty.' I groaned, my head falling back.

'Did you not bring any drink aside from coffee?'

'I hadn't thought to.'

'Here, you can have one of my bottles of water.'

'How much water do you have?'

'You don't even want to know.'

I grabbed the water thankfully, taking a large gulp of it. I drank about half of it in one go.

'Gods, you really are thirsty.'

'I'm dehydrated.' I said defensively. 'In my entire lifetime my mouth has never felt as dry as this.'

'Well keep drinking then.' Emile said with a raised eyebrow. I rolled my eyes and took another swig.

'When I get back to the house from this entire charade, I'm going to get so drunk that I forget my own name.' Emile said wistfully.

'Mind if I join you?'

'Not at all.'

☆✭☆

I ended up falling asleep as soon as I sat on the fourth train. Or, as soon as I lay down, I should say. It was another one of those chairs where there was a table separating them, so Emile took one side and I threw my bag into the other, collapsing with my head nestled in it. I could've sworn I heard a gentle laugh as I was drifting off. It didn't matter. I was much too tired to care.

It was one of those sleeps where I was so deep in I didn't have a dream, whatsoever. One of those pitch black sleeps.

I was awoken to a finger on my shoulder and a face in my face. I blinked, opening my eyes groggily, and being greeted with an explosion of royal blue.

'Hey.' I mumbled, instinctively pulling back a little. Emile only grinned, slumping back on her chair.

'We're stopping in about 10 minutes, so I thought that I'd give you some time to wake up properly.

'How long were we on this train for?' I asked, pulling my bag over my shoulder and settling into the corner seat, directly opposite from her.

'Hmmm, I'm not sure exactly, but this has for sure been the longest yet.'

'So I had a good nap?'

'Oh, I think I see a spot of spit in the corner of your mouth, still.'

'Shut up.' I rolled my eyes as the corners of my mouth pulled up. Emile pressed her lips together. There was a gleam in her eye. One I couldn't quite place.

'Did you not sleep?' I said.

'Nah, I had a few cups of coffee. Don't think I'll be sleeping till that hotel now.' Emile said with a small laugh. Ah. I'd almost forgotten about the hotel. Key word being almost.

'I'm not sure I'll even sleep then, considering how much caffeine I'm about to inhale.' I said with a raised brow.

'Oh? And what will you be doing instead of sleeping?'

My breath hitched.

'I suppose I'll be thinking of that then, and not now, as now I'm thinking about the fact that the train is stopping and we need to get off.' I said, hastily veering off the topic as I jumped to my feet, speeding off to the train door.

'You alright?' Emile called, running to catch up with me.

'I'm alright.'

'Are you sure?'

'I'm sure.'

'You don't look sure.'

'I might not look it, but I sure am.'

'You can tell me.'

I stopped, turning around to face her fully. 'Can we please just get on this train before you start interrogating me?' I said in exasperation.

'Sure, but only if you're sure.'

'What? You know what, bye, I'm done talking to you.'

'Oh, but no, you couldn't!' Emile made her voice as high as possible, feigning mortification. I suppressed a laugh and boarded the next train, my cheeks flushed and my neck burning red.

☆★☆

That train was a blur of coffee, blankets and overly nice attendants. It had gotten to a point where Emile was convinced one was flirting with me.

'Flirting with me? Why on earth would she flirt with me?'

'Well, you're mysterious, handsome, and you're with the princess of Kendra; hell, I'd flirt with you if you weren't Maximus Invictus Blare.' she teased, although I saw something pass over her features in the last part.

'You think I'm handsome?' I said with a smirk. Emile wasn't fazed; she only raised her brows.

'Yes, since I'm neither blind nor a fool. It isn't so deep to admit that you're good looking when you clearly are.' she said, matter-of-a-factly.

'You have no idea the leverage that you have just given me.'

'Oh, shut your mouth. I wasn't meaning to inflate your ego- you asked why someone would flirt with you, and I told you the exact reason why.'

'Well, I suppose you could be a little more exact if you-'

'It is impossible to have one normal conversation with you, isn't it?'

'You could say that.'

That train was the quickest we'd been on. It felt almost as if we were on and then off. As the fifth and final train reversed in front of us, Emile stared, the both of us standing frozen, silently, for a moment.

'We should probably go find those stables.'

'Why so eager, Maximus?'

'I would prefer to be in a safe city before the sun sets, if that isn't too much of a bother for you.'

'Not a bother at all.' Emile winked and then hurried off, leaving me to follow her.

The stables were much more extravagant than I had been expecting. Of course, I didn't think it would be like the dumps they used for horses in Rendo, but I also didn't think it would be so… big. And clean. I certainly didn't think it would be so clean.

'Take any horse you want.' Emile stopped at a large black one, a smile spreading across her lips. 'Except Oak over here. Oak's mine.'

'The horses have names?'

'Nope. Just this one.'

'That's shameless favouritism.'

'And? I don't care.'

I chuckled, letting my eyes run over the rest of them. I caught on one with ginger hair, and a blonde sort of mane. It was big, much bigger than the rest of them, but it looked sort of… friendly. Welcoming.

'Is that ginger one a boy or a girl?' I asked.

'She isn't ginger, she's a shade of blonde… or brown. Not sure, actually. But yeah she's a girl.'

'I want her.'

'Then go get her out and we'll set off.'

'Sure you know the way?'

'Is that even a question?'

Judging from the dreary grey of the sky and damp coolness of the air, I was guessing it was mid afternoon. Meaning we had plenty of time to get to Sancire before the sunset.

Meaning that in a few hours, I would be in the same room and the same bed as the person I really should not have been trusted with so closely.

'How long approximately do you think this is going to take us?' I asked.

'An hour? Not that long, at this speed.'

'Good. I can't handle being on the move for too much longer.'

'At least you aren't on a train.'

'I'd rather that than a bare horseback.'

Emile was right. The horse journey flew by, and soon enough, we were in the stables at the border of Sancire. The sky was dark. It felt much more endearing now that we were actually there.

'You ready?' she whispered.

'Ready as I'll ever be.'

⚔ Chapter Twenty Three ⚔

THE STREETS OF SANCIRE were beautiful. I'd never admit it out loud, of course, but they truly were.

Lanterns lit the unused alleys, and there were people, happy people, laughing around every corner I turned. It felt odd to see people so content when there was a bloodbath in the forest their city was named after. Not even odd; just plainly morbid.

The hotel did not look like one a princess would be staying in. I figured that was the whole point; we did not want the wrong people finding out about our lodgings.

By the time we'd finally gotten to our room the moon was high and it was deep within the night.

The room was somehow even smaller than I'd imagined. Perhaps it was just my mind playing tricks, but that double bed did not look large enough to be a double bed.

'I'm going to go get changed in the bathroom.' Emile said, grabbing her nightdress and rushing off. I collapsed on the bed. Already I was on the verge of running away, and we hadn't been there for 3 minutes.

This is a disaster, I thought miserably, pulling myself to my feet to rummage through my bag for a change of clothes. I found some

grey joggers and a white top, and waited patiently for Emile to come out.

When she did, I almost passed out.

And it was not because of the fact I nearly got whiplash from how fast the door opened.

It wasn't that I'd never seen her in a nightdress before. It was that I'd never realised quite how flimsy and small and thin it was. It was that I was going to be sleeping right next to her when she was wearing that. I didn't think I would be able to bear it.

'I'm- I'm also going to change.' I said with a small smile. I slammed the bathroom door shut behind me and slid down against it, eyes wide. Oh, I already knew that Emile was sitting out there smirking at my reaction. The too clever prat knew everything.

I got changed as slowly as possible, throwing my clothes on the radiator next to Emile's before hesitantly walking back out to a candlelit room. Not in a romantic way; there wasn't any electricity, and it was dark, so apparently Emile had lit the candle to bring us light.

'Are you tired?' I asked, standing awkwardly at the door of the bathroom. Emile was on my right, legs crossed over her, eyes dancing in the light of the flame.

'I suppose I'm slightly tired.' she said, blowing out the candle. With a swallow, I climbed into the bed, staring at the ceiling as my eyes adjusted to the dark.

'Maximus.' Emile whispered.

'Yes?'

'Look at me.'

I stayed silent, still.

'I said look at me. Look at me.'

My eyes flittered to the side, meeting hers. A jolt ran through my bones. I could feel my hands sweating.

She was an explosion, even in the dark. Her eyes still stood out, shining, glittering. I let my sight travel them, every vein, every burst of colour.

'Is this why you were afraid?' she mumbled. I wanted to get up, to sleep in the bathtub, to sleep on the floor, just to get up, to get out. But I was frozen in my place.

Her fingertips grazed mine, trailing gently up my inner arm, stopping at my shoulder.

'Say something.' she breathed. She started to pull away her hand, but I grabbed it, letting it push against my skin.

'Don't move.' I murmured. I felt drunk, high. Whatever I was, it didn't matter. Her skin, her sweat ridden, ridiculously hot skin was on mine, and we were lying in the same bed, and I could feel her breath on my face, and I didn't want it to stop.

'Why are you afraid of this?' she asked.

'You don't want to know the answer to that question.'

'I want you, though, Maximus.' she blurted out. 'I want everything about you. Please. Just let me in. Don't push me away again, please, I'm not asking for much. I want you and I know you want me too. Say it. Admit it. Give me this one thing, if nothing else. Let me hear you say it.'

'I want you. I want you more than I've ever wanted anything.'

'Then have me! I'm here, I'm waiting, but I won't wait forever. It's now or never, Maximus, please. I'm begging.'

I let go of her hand, standing up.

'I need some fresh air.' I said curtly, rushing out of the room and to the corridor. I collapsed against a wall, burying my hands in my hair.

I want you, and I know you want me too.

I want everything about you.

It's now or never, Maximus, please.
I'm begging.

My heart was breaking with every small confession she made, with every small confession I made.

'Maximus?'

She was there, holding the door open, her hair dishevelled and her dress rode slightly up her thighs. Her lips were slightly parted, eyes hurt. I inhaled sharply.

And then I started walking.

I wasn't thinking.

Of course I wasn't thinking. What good was that?

She saw me as I was coming, eyelids widening.

I didn't care. I didn't care, I didn't care, I didn't care.

She was there and I was there and what more did I need?

'Maximus-'

My lips crashed onto hers, the force pushing her backwards as my hands grabbed the sides of her face.

My lips crashed onto hers and the world exploded.

We were in the room, and I scrambled with the door, slamming it shut and pushing her against it. Her fingers were on my neck, and my neck was so hot, so hot I could feel the sweat, but I couldn't stop, not once I'd started.

I wanted everything all at once.

She wanted everything all at once.

I could feel my face sweating everywhere, beads of it bundling in the crevices of my features. My hands were restless. They went from her face to her hair to her shoulders and her waist, until there was nowhere else left to touch.

Emile did not falter in her own movement.

I took both of her hands in my right one and pulled them up and over her head, pushing them against the door. My other hand stayed at the side of her neck, gripping it both roughly and gently at the same time.

I could feel every part of her lips; every crack, every dint, every patch of dryness.

I hadn't realised how hungry I had been.

I'd been starving cold until I kissed Emile Elizabeth Elires.

I had never quite understood that blue feeling in my throat: but now, as the blue exploded, as it filled my body and my soul until I was being crushed by the pressure, I understood it fully.

I struggled to breathe, unable to pull away and unable to snatch any oxygen when she dared to.

'Are you-' Emile cut off, inhaling sharply as I let my lips press against her jaw, trailing down her neck. I had kissed every freckle on her face, every patch of skin I could find. 'Are you still afraid?'

'Terrified.' I mumbled into her collarbone, kissing the scar there, kissing the scar she would never speak to me about. 'But I'm sure that you are too, now, are you not?'

I felt her chest push out as she exhaled deeply.

Then her hands were on my face, pulling me up and pressing her lips against mine hungrily. Wildly.

'Of course I am.' she whispered.

She pushed us off the door, pushed us away and away and away and everything inside of me coiled and curled and shrunk, just to expand all over again, blossoming and swelling and blooming.

I was uncontrollable.

But it was expected.

I had stopped myself for so long, and I had finally given up to the temptation of... whatever that could be classed. And, yet, I had never felt more sure. Everything I did felt right, like even if I messed up in massive amounts the moment would not be ruined.

Oh, and if there was ever going to be a time where I had to choose my favourite moment, the moment that made me as I truly was, it would be that one without a second thought.

How can you accurately describe such a thing?

It was the type of moments that poems sung about.

True, I supposed, but not true enough,

It was the type of moment that romantics dreamt of.

Once again, true, but it didn't quite live up to it.

Hold on. I think I have it.

It was the type of moment that made villains wish to be heroes.

Hmm…

That one felt right.

⚔ Chapter Twenty Four ⚔

IT WAS AN EXTREMELY big mistake. I knew that when I did it, I knew it while I slept, I knew it when my fingers were interlocked with hers.

The only problem was that, for some reason, I didn't care.

I woke up early the next morning. My head throbbed. Perhaps I had been drunk; I'd certainly felt it. Besides, that would've explained why the hell I'd done it in the first place.

But I sat up and my gaze found her, watched her breaths come and go lightly with her hair wild and her lips parched, and I knew that I'd do it all again.

Well done, Maximus. Now you really are the largest idiot in the entire world.

I kissed her.

Oh, well nev-

I kissed her. She kissed me back. Oh, Gods, oh my Gods, I kissed her!

This is not a matter to be excited about.

I can't believe it. I can't- oh my Gods.

What are you going to do when Nathaniel comes for you?

Let's keep our eye on the prize here; I kissed her. I'll worry about

Nathaniel when we get back to the house, but I feel like right now I deserve to be overly excited about this.

Whatever you say.

I gently stood up, making sure not to wake her as I found some new clothes and ran to the bathroom. I pulled them on, looking at myself in the mirror once I was dressed.

My lips were swollen and my cheeks were tinged pink, my hair a complete mess.

But for all that I looked completely atrocious, I looked happy. I *felt* happy.

I left the bathroom, and came face to face with an already dressed Emile.

'Hi.' I said, blinking.

'Hey.' Emile said, opening the curtains. 'So.'

'So.'

'Do you regret it?' Emile blurted out. My brow creased slightly. I could see the look of mild panic on her face.

'What?'

'I- do you regret it? Because I really need to know, because I don't regret it, but you might, and I don't want to be an idiot and-'

'I don't regret it.'

Emile hesitated. Her look was burning me.

'You don't?' she said quietly.

'I don't.' I confirmed, my lips quirking up slightly. She let her face relax as a cat's grin crossed over her features.

'That's good.'

'It's great.'

'Fabulous.'

'Fantastic.'

Emile cleared her throat. 'So, um, what's the plan for today?'

'Well, we have breakfast, start making our way through the forest until it gets dark, set up camp and sleep.'

'Oh my Gods. We have to walk for a full day?'

'We'll stop to eat dinner, obviously.'

'This is going to be tortuous.'

I laughed softly.

'So, I'm guessing you know all the good breakfast places?' I asked, slinging my bag over my shoulder. Emile's eyes sparkled.

'Oh, you can count on it.'

I ordered pancakes for myself; Emile had said they were the best thing on the menu, and I really had no other choice than to trust her. So then, obviously, she ordered the same, face lit with glee as the meals were set in front of her.

'I haven't had these from this place in years.' she proclaimed, grabbing a fork.

I took my own fork and ate my own, but really I was only focused on her.

Once we finished eating, we set off immediately.

It wasn't too hard to find the entrance to the forest. Considering the roads were cut off by humongous signs and slightly threatening tape just before it, I'd say it was fairly straightforward.

'Hi, could we come through to the forest, please?' Emile said with a smile to one of the men guarding it. He looked at us warily.

'Who are you and why are you here?' he asked.

'Oh, right, this is Maximus Invictus Blare, my... my companion, and I'm Emile Elizabeth Elires. I'm sure Desmond Axel has told you about us coming?'

The man blinked in slight shock. 'Oh, I- I'm terribly sorry for stopping you, Your Highness, please, come straight on through.'

Emile winked at me and smiled at the man, sliding past him. I followed with a smile of my own, only to be returned with a rather cruel look.

'Did you see the dirty look he gave me?' I muttered. Emile laughed aloud.

'Oh, well I hope he didn't hurt your honour too much.' she said teasingly. I shoved her gently, letting my hands linger for a moment. She swallowed and I dropped them back to my sides.

'So, do you know the way?' I asked.

'The way? I'm afraid we don't exactly have a way. Whichever trail we follow, it leads to the centre either way. Obviously we'll cut off the path when it hits night to set up camp, but aside from that we just follow the stone, I suppose.'

'At least we aren't raking through trees and mud.'

'When you put it that way, this day doesn't sound too awful after all.'

The sunlight was positively golden as it found its way through gaps in the forest's roof; the lighting was beautiful. I watched it bounce off Emile's face, and watched as her hair glistened in it. Sweat dripped off her jaw in the scalding heat. I felt the odd desire to wipe away the droplets with my fingertips, just so I could see her reaction at the proximity.

I was surprisingly aloof. My legs were desperate to walk faster, my heart beating strangely faster than usual. However, after perhaps an hour of walking my pleasant mood had decreased significantly.

'When do we get a break?' I asked, slouching. My feet were dragging against the floor behind me. I felt like throwing up.

'Gods you're grumpy, aren't you? What happened to you skipping around and throwing flowers in the air, hm?' Emile said with a smirk.

'Shut up, I did not throw flowers in the air.' I retorted, rolling my eyes. 'Do you know the time? I'm desperate to eat.'

'You're desperate to stop walking. Don't lie to me.'

'It isn't necessarily a lie to you if I'm also lying to myself.'

'It's eleven am. You still have at least another hour of walking.'

I groaned exaggeratedly, making sure to slump my back a little more to add effect.

'Half an hour.'

'Fifty minutes.'

'Forty.'

'Forty-five.'

I grinned, stopping in my tracks and spinning to the side with an arm outstretched. 'You have yourself a deal, Miss Elires.'

She grudgingly shook my hand. 'Never call me that again.'

Emile was true to her word. After exactly forty five minutes we stopped, going off the path a little to sit on the grass and eat a bite of food.

'What do you have?' I asked, happily chewing on my sandwich. Emile raised an eyebrow.

'I have a sausage roll. It's very nice. Have you had one before?'

'You did not just say that sausage rolls are nice. They're absolutely horrifying.'

'Oh my Gods, how dare you insult them like that!'

'How dare you defend them!'

She clasped her hand over her mouth, as if it would hide the fact she'd burst into laughter. I could tell from the muffled sounds that escaped through the cracks between her fingers, from the creases in her cheeks and the way her eyes lit up.

I looked away and bit my lip, preventing a smile from coming across me, also. After a few moments, we were silent. I'd accidentally put my hand on the floor, the one which I was holding my sandwich in. *Well that's ruined now,* I thought mournfully. I let my eyes flick back up to her. She was staring at me unblinkingly.

'Are you finished eating?' I asked. The tension was clogging up my airway.

'Yeah, yeah.' Emile said with a small cough.

'Then let's start back up with our legendary walk.'

The time actually flew by once we'd started again. Soon enough, the sun was set and the moonlight was shining dimly through the leaves, leaving us practically in the dark.

'Can we set up here?' I asked. Emile shook her head, apparently looking for something.

'Just a little bit further... here! Here it is!' she exclaimed, jumping up and down and running towards the nearest tree in excitement. 'When I was younger me and my father used to camp out in this forest, and it was always here. There used to be a bunch of squirrels here, too. We named them and everything.' Emile laughed quietly.

'I would love to hear all about these squirrels after setting up this tent.' I said, throwing my bag on the floor. 'Was it you or me who had the tent?'

'Me. You have the sleeping bags.'

'Ah, yes, that would be right.'

We quickly set up the tent and threw in our bags. I let Emile put down the sleeping bags as I put up a fire and sat by it, letting myself warm up.

'Hi.' Emile said, her voice in my ear. I jumped, my head snapping to the side.

'Hey.' I stammered. Emile stood up straight and sat herself next to me, arranged deftly on her knees.

'The sleeping bags sorted?'

'Yep.'

'Good. I can't wait to sleep.'

'Neither. But I need warmth first.'

I didn't respond, watching the flames grow and decrease, as if they were dancing, almost. Mine and Emile's thighs were touching. I gulped, keeping my hands tightly on my legs.

'So. The squirrels. How many were there?' I asked.

'Oh, right, yeah. Um, I think there were 10, maybe 11.' Emile said with a blink. She pushed herself to her feet, taking a few steps away.

I followed until I was right at her back.

'What were their names?' I questioned. Emile crossed her arms over, rubbing them slowly.

'One was called... Nutmeg. Or Meg.' she said. I took a step closer, and another, until I was so close that my breaths ruffled her hair.

'Um... another... another was called...' I ran my fingertips up the sides of her arms and back down, watching as the hairs stood on end. 'Rosie. Another was called Rosie.'

'Rosie sounds familiar.' I mumbled into her ear, resting my chin on her shoulder. I heard Emile inhale sharply.

'There was-' she cut herself off with a shiver as I gently pressed my lips to her jaw. 'There was one called- called- Flo?'

I liked making her flustered.

'Mhm.' I murmured, dragging my lips down from her jawline to the side of her neck before pulling them off her skin, my breath lingering.

'I don't... Rory... I think.' Emile was breathless. I could tell just from the way she rushed through her sentences, through the way she hesitated, the way she was forgetting the names of the squirrels that were clearly so special to her.

'That's four.' I whispered, pulling my head from her right shoulder to her left shoulder, letting my nose run across the back of her neck.

'Only four?' she asked. 'I could've sworn...'

She stopped, turning to look at me. I could see the red tinge in her cheeks. She took her hand and ran her fingertips down my face. I shut my eyes.

I vaguely felt her take a step away, and a step around to face me fully, but not before gripping my jaw firmly with her right hand.

I didn't dare open my eyes as she grabbed my left hand with her left hand, as she came up so close to me, as I felt a breadth of a kiss grace me…

And then she disappeared and the air went suddenly cold.

My eyes shot open.

Actually, no, she hadn't disappeared. She was behind me, her arms wrapping around my waist as she pushed her lips into the small of my back.

I felt my heart race. I didn't dare say a word. I wondered if that was how Emile had felt when I'd done practically the same to her.

My hands gripped hers and I spun myself around.

The corners of Emile's mouth quirked upwards, and I couldn't help but smile myself.

Slowly, so slowly, she pressed her lips onto mine, her hands tugging at my hair. My lips stretched into a smile against hers.

For a moment that should have felt so wrong, it felt awfully right.

I already knew what the consequences of Nathaniel finding out about those specific details about that specific trip.

He won't find out, I thought desperately in the midst of the night as I was curled up in a sleeping bag, although it was more to convince myself than the damned voice in my head.

But I knew that there was a very high possibility that he would. Somehow, Nathaniel always found out. I couldn't have any secrets in that household; nobody could.

Yet, every single time that I dared to let myself conjure up one of the many tortures he could inflict upon me, I wasn't afraid. In fact, the only thing I could think about was the Kendran princess herself.

It was mainly my head screaming in every different emotion. Mainly fear.

Even if I did find a way to get back to her after that stupid betrayal, the more stupid part would be to think she would ever forgive me.

I'd forgive her for doing this to me. Hell, I'd forgive her for doing anything and everything to me.

That's because you're a lovesick idiot, Maximus.

What, and she isn't?

She has a duty. She's the heir to a throne. She's been brought up knowing how to deal with situations like this one.

Don't let Nathaniel know you think so lowly of him.

Shut up.

Did I even want to fight for Rendo anymore?

I didn't think I'd be able to bear it. The Gods knew that I would have to be the one to kill her, and the Gods also knew that I could never bring myself to do that. And Kendra... it was just so good in comparison to Rendo. It frankly hurt how good it was.

I knew that Rendo was in the wrong. I knew that the Kendrans deserved to win that war.

But they would never win with me fighting for the Rendans, no matter how good of people they were.

I rolled over, unable to fall asleep.

You'll regret it when you're falling asleep on the battlefield tomorrow.

I know, I know. I just have a lot on my mind.

When I eventually fell asleep, it was restless.

And my dreams were haunted by my unconquerable feelings for a certain redheaded princess.

⚔ Chapter Twenty Five ⚔

'MAXIMUS, WAKE UP YOU lazy swine for goodness sake, Maximus, I-'

'Holy hell.' I muttered, rubbing my eyes and groggily sitting up. Emile jumped to her feet, already suited up in her armour. 'What time is it?'

'Quarter to seven.'

'What? You've woken me at six in the morning? Are you mental?' I collapsed back again, pulling the sleeping bag over my face.

'Hurry and get dressed, we have a big day ahead of us.' Emile said, completely ignoring what I had said.

'Make me some coffee, will you?' I called out.

'You don't have to ask me twice.'

I lay down for another minute or so, giving my head time to clear up. Then, I forced myself to stand, pulling out my armour and quickly changing.

I'd brought my larger sheath, the one that connected to my belt. It had an area for two daggers and my sword. I wrapped it around me and put in my weapons, grabbing a shield and leaving the tent.

'So, once we've beaten the hell out of those morons we come back to camp, right?'

'Right. Unless anyone's injured. That's why I have this little button installed into my thumb; I press it and ambulances come.'

'Good thing that nobody's going to get injured then, isn't it?'

Emile didn't look as sure as I was. She handed me my coffee in a

travelling mug, deftly sipping at her own.

'How are you feeling?' I asked. Emile's eyes were on the floor.

'A little nervous. I think we'll do fine, though. How about you?'

'Not nervous at all. I know we'll do great.' It was meant to sound encouraging, but Emile didn't look any different. 'Are you alright?'

'I'm fine.'

There was silence. A light breeze came upon us, rustling with my skin and blood and bones, sending breaths of shivers running rampage down my back.

Emile was a spectacular fighter; everyone around her could tell just from the way her gaze held hard. But she was afraid. Much more afraid than she ought to be, considering her talent.

'So. Thirty swordfighers. Split it in half, I'll take 15 and you take 15, hm?'

'Sounds like a plan.'

'I'll watch your back to make sure no one's sneaking up behind you if you watch mine.'

'I thought that was a given.'

I smiled slightly, my eyes raking across her. She was shivering, but not from the cold.

'Still up for getting so drunk you forget your own name when we get back?'

'*If* we get back I'd be glad to, if you're still up to join me.' Emile responded. I noticed how she changed the when to if.

'Oh, of course I am. I'll need it after this little trip.' I said, gulping down the last of my coffee. 'When should we leave?'

'Hold up, I need to warm up. And finish my coffee.'

'Warm up? How are you going to warm up?'

'Do you not warm up?'

'I- no, I just get on with it.'

Emile looked appalled. 'Gods, I can't believe that. I've never once met someone who doesn't warm up. Do you not know how many injuries you could get because of that?'

'I haven't gotten too many so far. In fact, it's safe to say you were the first to injure me.'

'Oh, stop it. I'm off to warm up now, so you can either sort out these dishes or watch me.'

'I'll take the latter, thanks.'

I sat on the floor as she whipped out her sword, slowly moving her arms and legs, as if in some sort of dance routine. Her eyes shut as the speed increased, until her movements were practically a blur. It was sort of entrancing. I couldn't look away.

After about 10 minutes, she walked over to me, extending a hand and helping me to my feet.

'Done. We can leave now.'

I only nodded my head, quickly checking I had all my weapons. They were there, just as I knew they were. I wasn't exactly sure why I'd felt the need to check. I mentally shrugged, following Emile out back to the trail.

'So, how long of a walk do we have left for the centre, then?' I asked quietly.

'I'd say thirty to fifty minutes, perhaps.'

It felt a lot more real once we were less than an hour from it.

'Right.' I mumbled, inhaling sharply. 'Let's set off, then.'

Emile stayed silent, already walking. I followed in her steps, making sure I didn't trail behind.

The entirety of the walk was uncomfortably quiet. Of course, neither of us would've spoken even if we wanted to. Our minds were on something else.

Something much bigger than a bit of awkward tranquillity.

I knew we wouldn't lose; I'd faced much more difficult things in my life. See, it wasn't myself that I was worried about. It was her.

I hadn't quite realised how dangerous her fear of failure could be for us. It was clearly distracting her already, and we weren't even at the battle, yet. I didn't want to seem like a twat, but if she carried on so pessimistically, something was bound to happen. And not something good, either.

I was scared for her. Scared of what might happen to her. I knew she could shut off her emotions in the time it took for me to blink, but something seemed off that day. It was disconcerting.

It wasn't as hot as it had been the day before. Sure, the sun was radiant, coming down in luminous strokes as it hit off Emile's already fiery hair, but at least it wasn't suffocatingly warm.

As we ventured deeper into the forest, the sounds we had before frequently heard grew quieter and quieter, until they vanished completely. There was no sign of life, not even a rustle in the trees. The breeze had disappeared. It was so still, so unnatural, that I felt myself shiver.

'It isn't normally like this.' Emile whispered. Her voice was low, but in the hush of the forest, it felt awfully loud.

'What?' I said under my breath.

'There are- there are normally birds, waterfalls, too big bugs that cause me to run around myself in circles. Life. There's normally life.'

I saw the fear in her face. My own face fell slack at her tight expression.

'We're going to fix it.' I promised. 'You can trust me.'

She could not trust me, actually. But how else was I going to be rid of that scarily terrified face she was pulling?'

'I do. Trust you, I mean. I do trust you.' Emile said, looking at the floor as her steps quickened.

Oh, I really wish you didn't trust me.

After about 25 minutes of walking, I realised that Emile wasn't the only one who was quite literally petrified. Cold sweat dripped from my brow, pooling unpleasantly at my collarbones. My fingers felt hot. I was unconsciously chewing on the inside of my cheek, clicking my jaw every now and then.

The sun was almost invisible at that point. It was so dark that I couldn't even see my own shadow. I couldn't see any shadows. They'd been swallowed by an unconquerable void of black.

Another five minutes passed.

And another.

And another.

And just before another could come by me, I had a hand pressed against my chest and a finger at my lips. I looked at Emile. *Shhhh,* she mouthed hastily.

We were behind a bunch of trees. I didn't dare look past them, but Emile did. She quickly pressed her back against one of the trunks after peeking around, face pale.

'I'm guessing that means we're here, then.' There was no amusement in my voice, which was only a notch above the breadth of a whisper. Emile nodded once, slowly, cautiously. As if she thought we were being watched.

I looked around the tree myself. Sure enough, there they were.

A gang of bulky men, all of them practically identical. Dark hair, tan skin, no armour. *No armour,* The idiots weren't prepared. They were standing around each other, laughing boisterously, their swords hanging lazily by their hips. I almost laughed myself. This was what everyone was so afraid of? They were drunken morons, for Gods' sake.

'They aren't prepared.' I whispered urgently. I saw relief flash over Emile's face.

'How are we going to do this?' she asked quietly.

'We aren't going to storm in.' I said, my eyes narrowing as I thought. Thinking, planning, plotting. 'They're blackout drunk. It'll give us an advantage. However, I've fought like how I normally do even more drunk than the whole of them out together before, so don't get too excited about that.'

'Noted.'

'They'll realise who we are as soon as they see us. We have to be fast. Faster than usual. Like, being chased by a serial killer fast. Are you okay with that?'

'Did you not watch my warmup this morning?'

'That's a yes, then. Basically, we get it done as quickly as possible. They don't have armour on, either, which is good. It means we don't have to waste time looking for the weak parts in the metal covering them. Just- just make sure you actually kill them. No chances, this time.'

'No chances. Got it.'

Emile already looked breathless, but not out of fear. She seemed almost excited. I found that quite amusing.

'Have you got anything to add?' I asked.

She shrugged. 'Don't die?'

I nearly smiled. 'Great advice. With that being said, let's do this.'

Neither of us moved. We both knew that I had something else to say. I cleared my throat, the sound of rambling men catching me off guard.

'In case something happens-' I cut off, averting my gaze. 'I want you to know this in case I don't get another chance to tell you.

I- even if I act like it, just know that I will never regret meeting you. You- you're the best thing that happened to me. You make me think I can explode the world. You make me think I can drain the seas and oceans, just with the force of the shivers that run through me every time we touch. I-' I stopped myself, looking at her. 'Just don't forget about me, yeah?'

'This makes it sound like you're going to die.'

'I'm not going to die.'

'Then why are you telling me this?'

Because I know that you'll never listen to it if I tell you after I've done what I'm going to do so soon. I know that this is the only opportunity I'll ever have to tell you this.

'Just felt like the right time to say it.' I croaked, my throat dry and closing in on itself. Emile didn't speak for a moment or two.

'When you look at me, I feel euphoric. Everything around us blurs and it's just us, staring and staring and staring, as if everyone could die right there and then and it would be okay, because I would have you.' She coughed. 'Are we ready to do this?'

'I'm as ready as I'll ever be. Are you?'

'The same goes for me.'

'You sure?'

'I'm sure. Are you sure?'

'I'm pretty sure.'

I took a deep breath, positioning myself. 'On the count of three.' I whisper. 'One... two...'

'Three.' Emile finished.

We're already moving when she speaks.

We slipped into the shadows, crawling forwards like wild animals, closer and closer, until we were each a step away from the circle these men that come from my own home country have formed.

My eyes caught on hers.

I took a few gentle steps forward, my footsteps eerily silent.

Our first kill was simultaneous. Peaceful, almost. I used a dagger, shoving it into the left of their back. I felt it scorch his heart. Then I stepped away, slipping into the shadows once more, as the two men fell to the floor, vivid red blood pooling around them.

I watched the emotions flash over the rest of their faces.

First, it was fear. Then, confusion. Confusion melted into anger and anger melted into fear once again, and then their emotions were shut off. I knew an invitation when I saw one.

I stepped out, sword in hand, a grin on my face.

'Hey, boys. Missed me?'

And then everything is chaos.

I was right when I said they'd still be good fighters, as drunk as they were. However, as well as their arms were working, their feet and legs did not comply half as well, and they were a stumbling mess, eyes glazed over with haze.

They must have thought of it as some sort of joke. They weren't taking it half as seriously as they should've. Emile knew it. I knew it.

The ghosts of their dead friends probably knew it.

After about three more kills, there was a circle around me. One of the men stepped out. I recognised him…

'Maximus.'

My eyes widened.

'By the gods, if it isn't the Rendan prince himself.' I laughed, running a hand through my hair.

'I don't want to kill you, Maximus. We both know Nathaniel wouldn't react very well to that. Stay with me here, and I can get you sent home straight away. Leave the princess. Your job was to kill her anyway, was it not?'

I looked over at Emile. She was fighting off a number of men, her face the picture of concentration. I felt a pang of guilt.

'My job isn't to kill her. Not yet, anyway.' I mumbled.

'Maximus-'

'So. Have you gotten any worse at sword fighting in the time I've been away? It didn't seem possible the last time I saw you.'

I jabbed out at him. He deflected it just a moment before it hit him. I smirked.

'Hm. You seem better.'

'I don't want to hurt you.'

'That's great, then, because we both know that you won't.' I said mockingly.

And then the fight was in action.

I had to admit, his royal highness wasn't all too terrible. He was hesitant to properly rein down on me, because only the Gods knew what Nathaniel would do to him if it came down to my death. But eventually he realised he was going to end up dead himself if he didn't fight back with all his will, because I could feel the tension of the battle build up, the speed quicken, the light in his eyes darken.

He was doing well with his hands, for the most of it.

His biggest mistake was trying to use his stupidly unstable feet.

Of course, I wasn't exactly going easy on him. I knew I could kill him in a snap of my fingers if I really wanted. I just wasn't too keen on committing treason.

As it turned out, I didn't even need to try. He did half the job for me.

The prince of Rendo took his foot, which was practically shaking, by the way, and shot it around, as if trying to latch it around my ankle and pull me down. Instinctively, I jumped up, and he fell to the floor with a thud. In a split second I'd shoved my sword through his throat with so much force that blood splattered all over my face.

I wiped my mouth, nose wrinkling as my tastebuds were overwhelmed by a metallic taste.

'Well, who's next, then?'

I went through the rest of the men easily. In fact, I accidentally beheaded one of them whilst fighting another.

'Sorry, what was his name?' I asked the man I was previously fighting. 'I like to know the names of all the people I've killed.'

The man was caught off guard, and I took off his head during that time, too.

'There. Go and see your friend.' I said to his pale and lifeless body as it slumped to the floor.

Once I'd finished off the men surrounding me, I looked at Emile.

She was cornered, but still fighting hard. I watched her carefully, not wanting to ruin her chances of fighting them. She was the princess, after all.

It didn't happen until the final two fighters. As she was preoccupied with one, another came up behind her. I saw it all in slow motion. The slight raise of his sword. The hunger in his eyes.

I ran forwards, faster than I'd thought possible, and stabbed the man through his chest.

It seemed, however, that for all I'd run extremely fast, it had not been fast enough.

I looked at my stomach. I watched as the fabric of my shirt stained a dark, soulless red.

I almost gagged as I staggered forwards, away from Emile, away from the dying man who had just slashed me.

How he had managed to hit the weak part of my armour accidentally did not occur to me. I fell to my knees, clutching my top, desperately trying to push pressure onto the wound with my weak and trembling hands.

It was a different pain to the one I felt when Nathaniel hurt me. It was merciless, snatching my breath, messing with my head.

I faintly heard Emile call my name.

'I- I'm here.' I said as loudly as I could. Emile was already there, grabbing my face and forcing me to look at her. She was stark white with fear. I swallowed, trying to make my eyes focus.

'It's okay. It's okay. I pressed the button. Help is coming. Just- just stay awake, okay? Don't fall asleep. Don't you dare fall asleep.' 'Talk to me.' I mumbled. Everything was spinning. There were two Emile's, and four royal blue eyes.

'How did it happen? C'mon, Maximus, you're too good of a fighter for this to have happened, explain it to me.' Emile said desperately. Her voice was fading away.

'It- it was- you. I was saving you.' I stammered.

'Why would you do that?'

Because I love you.

But everything had already gone black.

⚔ Chapter Twenty Six ⚔

⚔ Chapter Twenty Seven ⚔

I'm drowning.
Sinking.
Skimming the floor of the ocean.

'Swim to shore!' cries a far off voice.
'Resurface!'

But I never learnt how to swim.

I do not resurface.

⚔ Chapter Twenty Eight ⚔

HER ROYAL HIGHNESS, PRINCESS Emile Elizabeth Elires of Kendra was not a stranger to fear. In fact, she had come to consider the emotion as quite a friend of hers, in a sort of way.

She was very afraid when the declarations of a future war were made ten years ago.

She was very afraid when her sister was kidnapped.

She was very afraid when being sent to that damned countryside.

She was constantly afraid while in that same damned countryside.

But when Maximus came, she was no longer afraid. It was as if every thought of lurking danger and demons in the night had been sucked away by that one stupid boy.

Oh, but if he wasn't anything but perfect.

His eyes were that exact shade of grey that Emile had always thought to be terribly dull, but sparkling and alive, with golden freckles spread among their colour.

His hair curled where it wasn't supposed to, flicking up in all the places it should have stayed flat, a shade of black so dark it was like a hole. Emile had always wanted to run her hands through it, from the first she set eyes on him.

He had this way of speaking to her that always made her feel so much less alone. It was as if this one person, this single boy, made up for a country of people that had never really cared about her.

And his smile.

Gods, if his smile wasn't the only thing keeping her going.

At first, it was rare she ever saw it. He was as solemn as a fighter was expected to be, uptight and harsh.

But from the first time she watched his lips split into that crookedly perfect grin, she knew she would go to the ends of the earth just to see it again.

The first time she felt afraid after meeting him was when he stopped speaking to her. It was after that Nathaniel visited.

She never found out why it had caused Maximus to be so hostile.

All she knew was how badly it hurt her.

And how badly it scared her.

She hadn't been properly afraid until that job. That- that stupid mission, the one with the ridiculously unbalanced fight. Even during the battle itself, she wasn't really scared.

So when she saw the blood pour from a gash in the only person she'd ever wanted's stomach, she knew that it was the greatest fear she would feel in her life.

The fear was short lived, though.

As soon as the words left his lips all she felt was guilt.

Horrible, soul wrenching guilt.

It- it was- you. I was saving you.

Emile didn't think she would ever forgive herself if Maximus Invictus Blare died saving her.

She pressed the button in her thumb straight away, as if it would cure him on the spot, as if it would make it all go away.

As soon as he fell unconscious, the helicopter was there, a man jumping out and running towards her.

'What the hell? How did this happen? He's the best fighter Desmond's ever met, for Gods' sake.' the man hissed, hauling Maximus onto the hospital bed as soon as he was presented with it. He turned to Emile. 'Tell me. Please. Just for clarification.'

Emile's tongue felt numb. Heavy. Like a brick in her mouth.

'Me. He was saving me.'

She saw the pity on the man's face. *I don't want your pity,* she thought angrily. *Just save him! Is it really so much to ask for?*

The man nodded and made way towards the helicopter. She knew she was supposed to follow. But, for a moment, she stood still, staring at the spot where Maximus's blood soaked the mud.

She kicked at it blindly, screaming every swear she could conjure.

After, she let a single tear fall from her eye.

Then she made her way to the helicopter, face straight.

There would be time for crying later.

☆★☆

Desmond burst into the hospital a day later.

'Emile?' he called. Emile looked up from the floor, jumping to her feet.

'Desmond!'

She leapt at him, his arms crushing her into him. Emile's eyes were watery and red, getting Desmond's top wet with the remnants of her tears. He didn't seem to care. He held her tightly, as if they would never hug again.

'Is he okay?' Desmond asked hastily. He looked shaken, scared. Very scared. Emile supposed Desmond also thought of fear as a friend. Fear was gaining popularity quite fast.

'He's still unconscious. They- they said he's lost a lot of blood. Almost too much.'

Desmond picked up on the tweak in Emile's words immediately.

'Almost?'

She nearly smiled. Her lips tugged up, and Desmond breathed out heavily in relief.

'Oh my Gods.' he said, leaning against a door. He seemed exhausted, Emile noticed.

'At least we completed the task.' she mumbled. Desmond shook his head in disbelief.

'I don't care about the stupid task, you absolute daftie. I care about the two of you.'

'I care about you, too.' Emile said.

Desmond took her in, her unbrushed hair and her torn clothes, the fact that she hadn't washed in what felt like months.

'How are you?' he asked.

'Scared.' Emile responded.

'I know how you feel about him. I know how much you feel about him.' Desmond paused, thinking over his words. 'Did he tell you that he feels the same?'

Emile's cheeks flushed.

Desmond only smiled.

'I don't know what I'll do if he- if he… if-'

'You don't have to say it.' Desmond said quietly. 'It's going to be just fine. You don't think Maximus would be the type to let himself die from a battle, do you?'

Emile laughed. 'When you put it that way, I suppose not.'

'If it's okay with you, could you tell me how it happened?'

And there it was again. That white hot guilt, scorching her insides, melting her to nothing. If Maximus died, she really would be nothing. She didn't like to think about that.

'He was saving me.' she mumbled, shutting her eyes so tightly her vision was set alight.

'It isn't your fault.' Desmond said immediately.

'Of course it isn't.' Emile said faintly, but she didn't really mean it. Her heart felt like it had disappeared. She felt empty with the feeling of never ending guilt.

'Open your eyes, Emile.'

She stayed still, eyes still shut. She could feel the sting of tears in them

'Emile. Look at me.'

Reluctantly, she did, a droplet falling over her eyelash. They were already wet, her face already stained and raw.

'You can't let this eat at you. He did it because he cares about you. A lot. A hell of a lot.'

'He wasn't thinki-'

'That's exactly my point.' Desmond stopped for a second, shutting his own eyes. 'Only someone completely and utterly in love would ever do something so insane without thinking.'

Emile's breath hitched, stopping halfway in her throat.

'He doesn't love me.' she said shakily, trying to force some sort of surety into her voice. 'He- he likes me, sure, but he doesn't love me.

'Why are you so doubtful?' Desmond asked. 'He may as well have just killed himself for you. Do you really think he would do that if he doesn't love you?'

Suddenly Emile felt extremely small.

'Stop it.' she whispered, biting down on her tongue.

'I've seen the way he looks at you. It's as if you're his very own Goddess, like you're a ray of the sun itself, like he would do anything in the world if only it meant you were happy even in the smallest amount. He loves you, Emile. He loves you, even if he doesn't know it.'

Emile knew he was right. She just didn't feel ready to face the fact that there was someone in the world who truly loved her.

That the one person in the world she was life-shatteringly in love with could ever feel the same way.

'I know. I know, I know, I know. The God's know that I do. Hell, I love him with every inch of me. I love him so much that I feel like if he dies, if he dies from this, I'll just dissolve. And not even from the pain of him dying. From the fact that if I hadn't needed saving, that if I had been just a little bit better at what I was doing, he would be fine. We would be fine. And happy and okay and fine. I wish I could take it back. I wish it was okay. I wish we'd never came on this stupid task.'

Emile buried her face in her hands, her sobs shaking her entire body. She had once said that fear was a friend of hers. It seemed it wasn't simply just a friend; it was the closest friend she had. The only friend she had.

'Hey, hey, it's alright.'

She felt warm arms wrap around her shoulders as she carried on crying. Her hands made fists as she tried blindly to push Desmond away, until it became weak hits, which then became giving up. Emile collapsed into him, her legs almost giving way as she fell into him.

'I'm here.' he whispered. Emile could hear the pain in his voice. She knew how much he hated seeing her like that. It was only making her feel even more guilty knowing that yet again another person was hurting because of her.

But it was okay, she supposed. At least neither of them were dead.

Yet.

☆★☆

The day after, Maximus was able to function by himself. He wasn't awake. No, he wasn't going to wake up for at least a week. But he was going to go home.

Emile didn't actually think he considered the house as a home. She knew that she definitely didn't. But she didn't have the heart or energy to tell the doctors that. She just wanted to sleep in a proper bed, instead of hospital seats.

Of course, she was indescribably happy when she heard that he was okay. That he was going to be okay. But she was so tired that she could barely react. She smiled and nodded her head, trying her hardest not to collapse.

It took a day's journey to get back on the emergency helicopters. She felt a bit of resentment knowing that they could have gotten there so quickly, but she wasn't going to complain. Not when she'd just found out that a damn miracle had happened, that the boy she loved wasn't going to die for her after all.

It sounded incredibly vain when put like that.

She was too exhausted to care.

As soon as they got back to the house, Emile fell into her lovely, lovely bed and fell into a deep sleep.

She dreamt of blood and battle and dying lovers.

☆★☆

When Emile woke up, she was sweaty and trembling. For a moment she didn't know where she was. But it took one quick look around to realise she was in the house, the house, the one she both hated and loved more than anything at the same time.

She fell back down.

And then sat back up.

Maximus, she thought.

And within seconds she was in his room, staring at him, hand clasping his.

She watched the soft rise and fall in his chest.

She took the fingertips of her other hand to his neck, feeling his pulse thump against her skin.

She felt his face, his lips, his eyelids, hand cupping his cheek in a sort of final position.

She lowered her forehead to meet his, eyes shut.

She pulled back and pressed a kiss to his knuckles.

He looked as dead as she had dreamt he did.

'Maximus.' she whispered, trying not to cry again. 'Please wake up soon. I miss your voice. I miss your smile. I miss everything about you. Please wake up soon. Please. I feel so lonely without you.' Emile let go of his hand, almost walking away. But then, she brushed his hair away, and pressed her lips to his ear.

'I love you.'

It was only a breath, so quiet that he could have only heard it in his dreams, and so Emile finally walked away, feeling a sense of accomplishment knowing that she had said those three words.

Maximus did not wake up soon.

He was still asleep five days later.

And that was when they started to worry.

'What if he's in a coma?' Emile suggested. Her cheeks were sallow and sunken, hair framing the new narrowness of her face.

'He can't be. The doctors would have told us.' Desmond said, biting his fingernails.

'What if- what if he's contracted some other disease? Like pneumonia? Or what if he- he has an infection, in the slash? Like sepsis? It could be bad, Desmond, and we're just sitting around letting it happen.' Emile rambled.

'He isn't ill, Emile. He's recovering. Give him a few more days and then he'll wake up and it'll all be back to normal. You have to trust me, dear, please. I can't do this when you're even more stressed out than I am.' Desmond said.

'Trust you? You're the one who sent us on that stupid task in the first place!' Emile shouted. 'You insisted it would be fine, and look at where we are now! I wish I hadn't trusted you! If we'd just stayed here, where we were alright, then none of this would have happened, and we wouldn't be arguing over this!'

'What, so it's my fault now?' Desmond said incredulously.

'Did you ignore everything I've said the past week? I know that this whole Max thing is my fault, but you can't expect me to trust you so readily after you were so quick to send the two of us into… *that*. Do you have any idea how scary it was? Grown men, older than Maximus and I put together, each about 6 feet tall, and fifteen of them all coming on to me at once. Hell, if that's what it's like at war, then I don't want to go.'

'Do not let that ruin your conception of war. We have an army. You'll be more protected than you've ever been.'

'By that you mean I'll be more protected by them than I was by Maximus?'

Desmond didn't say anything.

'He nearly died, Desmond! And not because he was obliged to, because he wanted to! I'm sorry if I feel safer with somebody who wants to protect me over people that have to!'

Sometimes Emile really hated being a princess.

'They don't protect you because they have to, Emile, of course they want to.' Desmond said desperately.

'Are you saying that if you didn't know me and you were forced to come and fight in a deadly war, *for me*, and forced to protect *me*, a person you didn't even know, with your life, you would want to do it?'

'Emile-'

'I wouldn't want to. I'm admitting it. I wouldn't want to risk my own life and hundreds of other people's lives just for one silly royal's life. It's absurd, and you know it.' Emile shut her eyes, taking in a shaky breath. 'If he hasn't woken up in another two weeks, we're taking him back to the hospital.'

And she stormed out, her flying around her face like some sort of a halo.

☆★☆

Another day passed. Maximus did not wake.

Emile sat by his bed for twenty four hours, crying, singing, speaking. She thought she was going insane, at one point.

Three more days passed and her small light of hope was growing dim. He still had a pulse, a vibrant heartbeat. His skin was warm to the touch, and he still sweat under the sunlight.

Emile did everything she could to distract herself from the worry.

From the fear.

From the guilt.

A week passed.

He seemed as deep in his slumber as ever.

Emile saw the way Desmond avoided looking her in the eye, as if he couldn't bring himself to even look at the girl he'd watched over for sixteen years.

Two days before the second week came, Emile had lost all hope whatsoever. She did not dare leave his room. She paced and she plotted and she stared and stared and stared, but he was unflinching. At one point she stuck her face out of the window, desperate for a breath of fresh air after being confined in the same stuffy room for so long.

One day before.

Even Desmond felt as if there was no point in trying.

Emile peeled Maximus's shirt up from the bottom, looking at the stitches over his stomach. But, it wasn't the only scar she saw. There was a variety of smaller ones, clearly old and healed, all over his belly.

She gasped and dropped his top, stumbling backwards.

But then, she stepped forward again.

Would she want that reaction from Maximus if he ever saw her scars?

No. Of course she wouldn't.

So her hand found his once again, and she fought off the urge to cry.

Exactly two hours and fifty seven minutes later, Maximus woke up.

⚔ Chapter Twenty Nine ⚔

WHEN I FIRST WOKE up, I had forgotten everything. The battle, the camping, the hotel, the horses, the trains. Everything before that, too. The only thing I could remember was a dark dark blue, haunting a long and inescapable dream.

You can imagine my surprise when I was faced with the exact shade of blue in front of my face when I opened my eyes.

I sat up sharply, eyelids stuck open wide, only to be greeted by a searing pain in my lower abdomen. I cried out and grappled at it. My head was throbbing. I could hear my pulse pounding in my ears.

'Maximus, Maximus, calm down, please, stop it.'

I froze, letting my eyes latch on the figure before me.

A girl.

With sparkling blue eyes.

Fiery red hair.

And a face stained with tears.

I felt my heart drop as I remembered.

And when I say I remembered, I mean I remembered everything.

'This wasn't supposed to happen.' I mumble, looking around wildly, ignoring the fact that it felt as if my brain was going to implode.

'Calm down, Maximus. You're healing.' Emile pleaded, her hands soft on my face. I flinched and she let them drop, her expression the picture of hurt.

'I shouldn't need to be healed. He- how did I get hit? How did I- I was so stupid- so, so stupid...' I trailed off. It was awfully embarrassing. To know someone had gotten a hit on the untouchable. It felt almost unreal. Like some sort of fever dream.

'You were saving me. I'm sorry. I'm so sorry.' Emile hiccoughed, her breaths uneven. I felt a surge of guilt. I hadn't meant to hurt her. I was only confused...

Through the pain, I brought up my hand to her hair, running my fingers through it, giving it a small tug as I smiled at her.

'Don't be sorry. I would do it again in a heartbeat if it meant saving you. Besides, I'm alive, aren't I?' I teased. Emile swallowed, letting her fingers wrap around my wrist tightly.

'It should be me stuck in a stupid bed. Not you.' she whispered.

'I'm okay. Don't think like that.'

'I feel so terrible.'

I didn't respond for a moment. 'How long will it be until I can fight again?'

'Four to six weeks.'

'I'll give it five.'

'Fair enough.'

I hesitated. 'Visit me every day for these five weeks. Stay with me. And I suppose I may forgive you.' I said slowly, my lips quirking up at the corners.

'Of course I'll visit.' Emile promised, rubbing her thumb up and down on my skin. I shivered at the friction.

'How long did I sleep for?' I asked.

'Nearly three weeks.'

I blinked in shock. 'Three weeks? What? I don't- what-'

'You were just recovering. It's okay.' Emile murmured, her eyes shutting. I could see the bags under them, prominent and purple, almost like bruises.

'You're exhausted.' I noted, my voice accusing.

'I've been watching over you.'

'Well, I'll be fine, now. Get Desmond in to watch me and rest for a bit. For me.' I said. Emile paused, and then nodded, going to stand.

'Before you go, a question.' I said. She turned around, looking expectantly. 'How well can you speak Rendan?'

'I know how to say hi, love and bye. That's it.'

'Just the name type of love?'

'Yeah.'

I paused.

'*Te amo*.' I said, my voice tentative, scared, almost. I saw the confusion on Emile's face.

'What does that mean?' she asked.

'Don't ponder on it too much. Just go get Desmond.'

She narrowed her eyes suspiciously but nodded and left, the door shutting behind her.

I sighed slightly.

I had to say it then and there.

Knowing what she'd gone through whilst I'd just slept.

I'd admitted it aloud.

The moment I admitted it to her would be completely different.

I wanted that moment to be so much more than a sickly, injured boy professing his love to a sleep-deprived, unwashed girl.

In Rendan, *te amo* meant *I love you.*

☆★☆

'Oh my Gods, Maximus!'

Desmond's embrace did a number on my already sore stomach. I jerked backwards, hands flying to the injury. His eyes widened.

'I am so sorry, I didn't mean to-'

'Don't worry about it.' I croaked with a half-hearted grin. 'I'm okay. Give me five weeks and I'll be back to normal, promise.'

Desmond's eyes were light with joy. I felt like there was a hole in my stomach; not literally, of course. Technically, there was a hole there, now. But it was sort of emotional. I was such a bad person. Gods. I felt like I was drowning in my guilt.

'You've spoken to Emile, then?' he said slowly. I nodded. 'She was really worried about you.'

'I know. She said.'

'She cares about you, Maximus. A hell of a lot.'

'I care about her too.'

'You aren't getting it.' Desmond groaned. I blinked.

'What is there to get?' I asked incredulously, pushing myself to sit up a little more.

'Just don't hurt her, okay?'

My heart swelled, but not in a good way. In that horrible way that bruises and cuts and such swell when you play with them too much, in that awful red, raw and painful way.

'I won't.' I said. My voice was smoother than I had expected it to be. There was an awkward silence for a few moments. 'So, when can I go and walk around a bit?' I asked when it became too much.

'A week, I'd say. Just a small walk around the house, though. You don't want to wear yourself out.'

'I feel so weak.'

'You are anything but weak, Maximus.'

His gaze was so intensely terrifying that I had to look away. 'Can I admit something to you?' I said.

'Of course.'

'You know how people say they would die for the person they love?'

'Yes.'

'I'm the opposite. I would live for them.'

'Elaborate.' I could hear the gentle curiosity in his voice. The quiet knowing.

'Everyone knows that it's more painful to be the one living through the grief whilst the one you're completely and irrevocably in love with is... dead. I wouldn't want that. I wouldn't want them to go through that never ending pain. It sounds selfish, but if it was between me or them dying, I would choose them. So I would be the one who had to live through the grief, so they didn't have to feel the pain. I've seen it, now. I've realised the lengths I'd go to not only to protect them from death, but to protect them from life.'

It was an extremely obvious confession. But I felt so small and so vulnerable already; I might as well finish it off.

I let my eyes catch on Desmond's. He knew who I was talking about. I could see that it hurt him, that my words hurt him, even if he tried to hide it.

'Are you sure I'm the one you should be telling this to?' he asked quietly.

'What do you mean?'

I could see his reluctance when he spoke again.

'I mean that there's a girl in the bedroom just across from yours who's had to live through the experience of you nearly dying, and feel as if it's her fault. There's a girl who's gone through everything you've just described to me. And believe me when I tell you she is as completely and irrevocably in love with you as you are her.'

My breath hitched.

'Don't lie to make me feel better.' I whispered.

'When have I ever lied to you, Maximus?'

I wanted to cry. It was an impossible situation.

'Can you leave me for a little bit, please?' I asked shakily. Desmond nodded, leaving without question, the door slamming shut behind me. I flinched. It shook the entire room.

I had no escape.

I'd fallen in love with the one person I was supposed to hate like no other.

And not just that.

I'd let her fall back.

I was so stuck. It hurt.

I'd never considered myself claustrophobic. Not in a physical sense, anyway. It was like the hole in my stomach; more emotional than that.

Imaginary walls were closing in around me.

I couldn't breathe within the proximity.

I wanted to scream.

How was it that Maximus Invictus Blare had been beaten by simple matters of the heart?

My first name meant the greatest.

My middle name meant unconquered.

I was the definition of a warrior; brought up with unnecessarily strict training, horrendous diets and horrific punishments.

And yet when it came to that one girl, I was completely and utterly conquered.

I was crying before I knew it, hands pulling at my hair.

If there was a way out, I would've figured it out by then.

Clearly there wasn't.

☆★☆

Emile was back the next day, shaking at my shoulders to wake me. My nostrils smelled it before my eyes saw it.

'Please tell me that I'm smelling pancakes.' I mumbled, rubbing my eyes and yawning. Well, not just pancakes. The smoke was rather strong, also, I supposed.

'You're smelling pancakes!' she exclaimed excitedly, pushing them onto my lap in a tray. I grinned, staring at her.

'Breakfast in bed, eh? That's a little fancy for a peasant like me, I'm afraid.' I joked. Emile shoved my arm playfully.
'Shut up. I have an apple for myself, before you ask. You need sugar and proper food, Desmond said, since you've only been consuming liquids he had to force down you for nearly a month.'

She was sitting next to my legs on the edge of the bed. I moved along so she had more space, crossing her legs over and biting down on her apple happily. She was too happy for me to bear. I took a piece of my pancake and ate it, positively melting as it entered my mouth.

'Gods, this is amazing. These are the best pancakes I've ever eaten in my entire life.' I said, not wasting any more time talking as I dug in.

The pancakes were finished in about 10 minutes.

I let Emile put her apple core on my tray and I pushed it to my bedside table, fully looking at her.

'You look… rested.' I said, choosing my words carefully. Her skin was bright and golden, lips soft and reddened from the apple. I tried not to look at them too much.

'I mean, I suppose I could say the same for you, considering the nap you've just recently had.' Emile laughed. I was hardly paying attention. She must have noticed, as she nudged up closer, watching me closely.

'You look ethereal.' I mumbled. I wasn't thinking. I just wanted to talk to her, to be near her, to touch her; I wanted her.

'Maximus?' she said, almost confused. I let her cup my face with her hand, shutting my eyes.

'Stop talking.' I whispered.

'I-'

I pressed my lips to hers, slowly, so slowly. I craved her touch. I craved her. Everything about her.

When I pulled away, it was only to say a few words.

'Just let me forget for a few moments.'

She pulled me back in.

It was slower than before. I was savouring it, the sickly sweetness of the taste of her tongue, the way her lips seemed to mould into mine perfectly every time they touched, the way my brain melted at every small jolt she made, at every trembling breath, at every skip of her pulse.

The word 'lyrical' is typically considered a form of dance. But, the definition of the actual word is 'beautiful expression of emotions'. I couldn't be lyrical in the way I spoke of her, in the way I spoke to her. So instead I was lyrical in the way my lips moved against hers, in the way my hands held her, in the way I pushed against her until we couldn't be any closer.

She tore her lips from mine, swollen and even redder than before, and shut her eyes tightly.

'Are you okay?' I asked.

'I missed you. While you were asleep.' She laughed humorlessly. 'I really, really missed you.'

I watched her, let her open her eyes again, staring at me as she waited for my response.

'Prove it.' I said.

She smiled with one half of her mouth.

And then the smiling mouth was back on mine and I was exhilarated.

I didn't know until I was about 16 that there was a word that described expressing with gestures rather than words. I suppose it's sort of like how I'd said about the way I was lyrical with Emile.

Gesticulate. That was the word.

It didn't sound exactly… elegant. Or even nice, for that.

But I guessed the meaning made it worth it.

Her stomach pressed against mine and I ignored the pain that shot up me. In fact, I welcomed it. It was reminding me that everything the two of us had gone through was real. That we were real. I was so doubtful of myself, of us, that even reminders such as that were nice, in a way.

Her hand ran down my new scar tentatively.

I think that was the moment when I realised something very important.

My stomach was vulnerable.

Much more vulnerable than any other part of my body.

She hadn't seen my scars that night in the hotel, but that was because of the dark we were shrouded in.

She must have looked at my stomach while I was sleeping.

Oh, for Gods-

'Wait, wait.' I said, pulling away. Emile looked at me curiously.

'What's wrong?' she asked. I swallowed. I wasn't sure on how exactly to phrase the next bit.

'You know when I was… asleep?' I began.

'Yes, I do, actually.'

'Did you ever, like… check my scar? You know?'

'Of course I did. Why do you ask?' And then, she realised. Her eyes widened and she scrambled back slightly. 'Oh, Gods, I'm sorry, I shouldn't have, it wasn't my place, I-'

'Stop it, Emile.' I said, softly pulling her back. 'You saw them. Didn't you?'

She gulped. 'If we're talking about the, um, the rest of the scars there, then yes, I did see them.'

I tried to stay calm, as impossible as it felt.

'Why didn't you say anything?' I forced, pressing my lips together after. I didn't want to know what she thought they were off.

'I don't know. I didn't want to intrude.'

Actually, I did want to know what she thought they were off.

'So, what did you think? When you saw them?'

'I- I didn't think anything. I know you think I'm lying, but I didn't. I don't like to assume. So I let myself forget about them.'

'Why would you do that?'

'I knew that you'd tell me in your own time.'

I sucked in a breath. I really wished I didn't feel the need to tell her about them, now.

'I'll tell you now.' I paused. 'If that's what you want.'

'You don't have to tell me anything you don't want to, but… it might get a weight off your shoulders telling me. And you know you can trust me. I just- I think if you're going to tell anyone at all, it should be me.'

I bit down on my bottom lip, clasping my hands together so hard that my fingernails drew blood.

She made a good point.

So I started talking.

I didn't specify that it was Nathaniel who had done it; it didn't make much difference. She probably knew. I could tell in her eyes, in the way their blue darkened as I spoke about it. I told her about the scars, about the glinting knife as it created a sick piece of art in my skin. I told her about the nights in unknown beds with breeze rushing through my hair, the open windows my only escape. And I told her about everything that came in between that.

'There was one time that I fought back, kind of.' I said quietly. Her fingers were interlaced within mine, thumb rubbing my wrist gently. 'He said he was going to hold me under the water of the lake until my face went blue and I passed out. Just to psych me out. I hadn't believed him, laughing a little. So he grabbed my legs and threw me over his shoulder, setting out for the lake to do exactly what he'd said. But I- I bit him, and he let go in the shock so I ran back and locked myself in my-' I nearly mentioned George, there. '-in my friend's room.'

I hesitated then.

'I think you get the gist of it, by now.' I mumbled awkwardly, rubbing the back of my neck with my spare hand.

'I want you to say everything you think you need to, Maximus. Don't stop because you feel you need to.' she said.

I was silent for a moment.

And then I carried on talking.

'It wasn't just physical stuff.' I explained, running my fingers through my hair. 'Verbal, too. Gods, he was the most manipulative man I've ever met. He would- he would beat me down and down, again and again, calling out my worth and my ability and my- and even my looks. It was all *no wonder you spend your time killing people: you think that I'm sick? Oh, well, take a look at yourself, Maximus. If I'm a psychopath, I'm not the only one here that is.*"

I cut myself off, staring at the space between us on the bed.

'I think your scars are beautiful.' Emile said. Her voice was like velvet. I looked up at her. Then, slowly, so slowly, she leant forward, pressing her lips to just under my eye. I blinked in confusion. 'That one is for sure.' she said. My fingers jumped to my face, dancing over the scar that had just been kissed by the girl I loved.

Then she moved down slightly, kissing just above my top lip.

'That one, too.'

After that it was the scars littering my neck.

She pulled up my shirt, pulled it over my head.

My chest.

And then my stomach.

I shut my eyes as she got there, feeling her move across every single one as if it were some kind of connect the dots puzzle, her lips dragging from scar to scar.

'I won't do this one, seeing as it's all bandaged up.' She paused, fingers running over the new bandage. 'But I think it's the most beautiful of all of them.'

'Oh?' I was feeling quite overwhelmed. 'And why is that?'

'The other ones will only remind you of all of those terrible experiences you've just told me of in the years to come. This one, though; it will remind you of me. Of what you did to save me. I would say it makes you sort of a hero.' Emile smiled. I supposed it wasn't the time to say that if anything, I was much more of a villain.

'You're going to make me think of it as beautiful too, when you're putting it like that.' I whispered.

'Good. I want you to see yourself in the way that you are.'

'Myself? That's a lot more vague than just my scars.'

'Oh, shut up.'

'What if I told you there was a scar you couldn't see, a rather invisible one, spread out over the full of my mouth? Would you kiss me there, then?'

'Do you really think I need a scar to-'

I cut her off by enfolding her lips within mine, my hand tightening on hers.

Late that night, when I lay alone stranded to my bed, I thought.

I could write a book just from my thoughts.

In fact, I practically did. In my solitude, I pulled out a notebook and a pen and wrote down every thought I had, until I thought my wrist would go black and fall off.

My brain is singing gently to me. Soft lullabies, to the innocent ears of an innocent bystander. But when you stop, when you listen to the lyrics, it doesn't as much feel like a soft lullaby anymore.

Perhaps I am going insane.

Perhaps I am schizophrenic.

Perhaps it is everyone around me who is insane and schizophrenic, and it is only me hearing these things because the rest of the world is convinced they are too unnatural, too unreal, to be considered as true.

There is a word for what I am. Nefarious, I believe it is. It means to be wicked, villainous, despicable. Now, I wouldn't say that I'm necessarily despicable; both Desmond and Emile like me very much, as of right now. But they don't know what I've done. What I'm doing. What I'm going to do.

Sometimes I have thoughts about hurting myself.

I have never physically harmed myself.

I have never taken a blade, I have never cut it through my skin, I have never bled from my own self inflicted injuries.

I don't really need to do any of that. That little voice that torments me day and night in the back of my head, singing lullabies, making me insane, it does the harm well enough for me.

I am a pluviophile, I have realised.

I find peace in the rain.

⚔ Chapter Thirty ⚔

THE HEALING WAS NOT quite so difficult once I could stand again, I found. The first day I built up the courage to try and walk, Emile had been so overjoyed that she kissed me hard, so hard my lip bled, right in front of Desmond. I could practically feel him squirming. That only enticed me to kiss her back even harder.

One night, later on, at perhaps 1am, Desmond was asleep. Well, of course he was. I should have been. But I couldn't. I paced my room, lamp on, before collapsing onto my bed and starfishing on it miserably.

The door creaked open and I warily looked up.

'Saw the light was on.' Emile said, her cheeks flushed slightly. 'Could you come to the library with me? I don't feel like going alone.'

That was another thing. After that task, we never went places by ourselves in the midst of the night, when Desmond wasn't there. I would always say yes when she asked; I didn't have the heart to say anything other than it.

'Of course I'll come.' I said gently, hoisting myself up and pulling on a jacket. I still hadn't changed from my clothes; I was too afraid to check on the scar. It had been particularly sore that day. The house was cold later on. Not in a literal way; eerie, I supposed. It had been ever since that day in the forest.

The physical scar of it wasn't the most painful part. I had many scars; another one wasn't exactly a massive burden. It was just the memory, really, that I was never going to get rid of.

But then again, the same could be said for that.

I had plenty of bad memories. What was one more to add to the growing list of trauma?

We entered the library and I went to sit at the armchair, letting Emile browse as I picked at the cotton of my jacket. It was quite a nice armchair, actually. Extremely big, I had to admit, but enough to fit me and my long limbs, I supposed.

I didn't realise Emile was in front of me. But, sure enough, I looked up and there she was. I blinked, but aside from that showed no sense of surprise.

'Find any good books?' I asked. Emile shrugged.

'Nah. I just wanted to get out of my room.' she confessed, rubbing her arms. I saw her shiver.

'It's cold.' I said slowly. She just nodded. 'We could go to my room, if you don't want to go to yours.'

'I'd like that.'

She'd never admit it, but the task had shaken her up more than she'd thought it would. It had left its own scar in her, deep in her mind, etched into the lines of her brain.

Emile got herself comfortable where I usually lay, sitting with her legs crossed. I raised an eyebrow and sat opposite on my knees.

'How long do you think we have left until the war starts?' Emile asked, quietly. I bit my lip. *Not long at all.*

'How about we think about something else, rather than that?' I said, desperate not to discuss the upcoming war.

'Oh yeah? What do you have in mind?'

I took her chin in my hand and held her lips to mine for a few moments, as roughly as I dared.

'A few things.'

I had never in my life been so happy than in those few months the two of us spent like that, so free, like the weight of the world had finally been lifted from my shoulders.

But my happiness was short-lived.

I felt the change as soon as it came.

The change in question?

Nathaniel.

⚔ Chapter Thirty One ⚔

I LEARNT THE DIFFERENCE between the words lonely and alone.

To be lonely is to, although having all of the friends in the world, be faced with the consistent *feeling* of having nobody.

To be alone is to physically have nobody.

One of my largest mistakes was saying I was alone when really I was just lonely. I only felt as though I was alone. I had George and Emile and Desmond and even Adelaide, really. Occasionally it felt as though I could even have Anastasia.

Once I was fully healed enough to fight again, Desmond was shocked to see that I had not lost any of my skills during my time on bedrest.

Emile was not.

I caught her eye and she gave me a small grin, clearly proud.

I felt very... validated, was it? Validation from Emile was the type I wanted most.

It was late in the year. I knew that soon I was going to be ripped away from this small family I had found, from these people that I had somehow grown to care for like nobody else. It wasn't just Emile I was attached to. It was Desmond, also. He was like a father to me. Much more of one than Nathaniel had ever been.

I had almost convinced myself that Nathaniel would not come back for me. It was stupid to think like that; no sane man would leave the best sword fighter in probably the world in the hands of his enemy.

So I'm not sure why it hit me so hard when there was a knock at our door on a chilly, November day, when the snow was already falling and the air was frosty but fresh.

'Who the hell could that be?' Desmond muttered, already going to answer. My heart dropped. *Oh, no, no, no, no, no-*

'I'll get it.' I said hastily, rushing out of the arena.

I could feel my pulse pounding.

Gods dammit.

I'd done my task. Why was I so upset?

I don't want to leave her. For God's sake.

I didn't exactly have a choice in the matter, though, did I?

And, hell, if I thought this was going to hurt me, it was going to hurt Emile and Desmond a good load more.

I slowly opened the door.

'Maximus.'

His voice sent chills down my spine.

'Nathaniel.' I forced out. He inspected me, a sour look on his face. As if he'd just eaten a lemon.

'It's time. Have you done what I asked of you?' he asked. I considered saying I needed a few more months, but the look on his face said that I would never get away with that.

'Yeah. Yeah, it's done.' I paused. 'So, how are we doing this?'

'Just follow my lead.'

I didn't want to do anything he said. But I was too afraid not to. So I followed him through to the arena.

Emile and Desmond went silent as we came into the room. My face was flushed with guilt. I wanted to cry. I looked at Desmond, first, and I could tell that he already knew. His face was fully closed off, lips pressed together tightly.

Then I looked at Emile, at the faint confusion etched into her perfect features.

I'll never get to kiss you again.

I'll never get to tell you I love you.

I looked at Nathaniel, then, at the way he dominated the room.

I hated him so much.

'What's going on?' Emile spoke first. I squeezed my eyes shut for a split second then held eye contact with her, the apology in my eyes raw. She looked so bewildered. *I am such a bad person. Oh for Elysium's sake, what have I-*

'This may hurt your feelings a little bit, dear.' Nathaniel's voice carried throughout the whole room silkily, like the scales of a snake, a slight rasp growing. 'But Maximus and I have been keeping some things from the two of you.'

'What do you mean?' Emile said desperately. 'Maximus?'

I saw Nathaniel's smirk in the corner of my eye. 'Do you want to tell her, then?'

It wasn't as much of a question as it was a demand.

I swallowed the growing lump in my throat and began.

'I- I haven't been- I- entirely truthful with you.' I said shakily. 'I'm, um, I'm not here for the reasons you think I am. Some parts of what you know about my past are true. But I was not a slave to the Rendans. Nathaniel, a native Rendan, bought me off my also native Rendan father when I was only young.'

'I thought you were Kendran.' I couldn't bring myself to look at Emile.

'Let him finish.' Desmond said.

I really didn't want to finish.

'I am not going to be fighting with you in this war.' I figured I might as well say the hardest part as soon as possible. 'Nathaniel and I are going to be with the Rendans.'

'What?'

I looked at her, then. Her face was ashen, hurt, angry, everything and anything all at once.

I felt sick to my stomach.

'You heard him.' Nathaniel said mockingly.

'Why did you come here, then?' Emile demanded. I could see her eyes filling as she walked up to me, until we were standing only a few feet from one another. 'Hm? Oh, come on, just say it, you absolute moron.'

'I was sent here as a spy.' My voice was far too calm. I saw Emile's face fall. 'I was here to- to find out your weaknesses, the both of you, Kendra's strongest fighters. And, I believe I have. My job is done. Home is calling.'

The words tasted foreign on my tongue.

Home was calling.

But not my home back in Rendo.

My home there, with Emile and Desmond, in that stupid house in that stupid countryside in that stupid country.

'Are you kidding me?' Emile whispered. Then she repeated it, a scream this time. 'I have spent nearly the whole past year with you now, Maximus, I told you things I would never have dreamt of ever saying aloud. I trusted you. But do you know what's even worse? I loved you. There. I said it. And I know you won't say it back, with good old Nathaniel here watching your every move, but you loved me too, didn't you? Don't you? Gods, why am I speaking in the past tense? I love you. I love you, I love you, I love you.' She broke off, tears falling down her face.

Desmond had come over, then.

'Nathaniel.' he said. 'I think we best have a little conversation outside.'

Nathaniel looked at me. 'I won't be long. When I come back in, we're leaving.'

I nodded and watched the door shut as they left.

And I took the opportunity.

'Emile, I-'

'Don't go back with him.' she whispered. 'Stay with me. I'll forgive you if only you stay here with me.'

'You have no idea what he's capable of. I can't do that, Emile. I'm sorry. I'm so sorry.' I breathed, voice breaking.

'Then say it back.' she said. 'Three words. Say them and I'll find you in the midst of this war and we can run away together, and we can be happy. Please, Maximus. Tell me you love me like I know you do. Please.'

'He'll find us, Emile. I want nothing more than to run away with you, but I'm in an impossible situation, here.' I said desperately.

'Then just tell me you love me, if nothing else. Give me some closure. I won't forgive you for not fighting for me, but at least I'll know.'

I could hear the door opening. Time was running thin.

'I've already said it.' I whispered, rushed. 'Think about it. Hard. And when you remember, write to me. I'll wait for you, Emile.'

'And if I don't want to write to you?' she asked, face full of hurt.

'Then at least figure out when I said it.'

'When you said what?'

It was Nathaniel. Of course it was. My spine stiffened and any emotion dissolved from my face. I saw Emile scrutinising me, her pained reaction to how I looked in front of this damned man.

'Nothing.' I said coldly. 'Goodbye, Emile.'

She didn't speak. I turned to leave with Nathaniel, when she opened her mouth.

'I'll see you on the battlefield, Maximus.'

When I looked back, her eyes were hard.

Unforgiving.

I knew then that I had lost the last good thing in my life.

☆★☆

George was not on the boat, as I'd hoped he would be.

I was stuck with only Nathaniel to talk to. And I knew the only thing that he wanted to talk about.

'So, you really worked some magic on that girl then, eh?' They were the first words he said as we sat at the deck together.

'I'm not sure what you mean.' I said.

'Don't act stupid, boy.' *Boy. Oh, I had not missed that.* 'She's so in love with you that it's unbearable. I'll bet you any amount of money that if you go back there right now, she'll forgive you for all of this without even thinking.'

'She's very stubborn.'

'And she's very in love with you.'

I fixated my gaze onto my hands.

'You might be right. I don't know.' I mumbled

'What did you do to her? Gods, you must've learnt from the best.' Nathaniel said with a wink. I suddenly felt extremely exposed. And dirty. Really dirty. I subconsciously ran a hand through my hair.

'I was just… myself. And she liked it, so I carried on being myself. I didn't *do* anything to her.' I said, embarrassed.

'Okay, okay, if you say so.' Nathaniel said, raising his hands in the air defensively. He was in a scarily good mood.

I didn't respond, playing with my fingers uncomfortably. All I could think about was Emile. About the nights she'd spent comforting me as I healed, holding me tightly even as I threw up all my guts and could only lie around, unable to sleep, talk, even think.

'Shhhhh, it's okay, I'm here.' she had whispered into my ear one night as I trembled violently, waking from one of those awful flashback dreams. 'I'm here. It's alright. You're here. Look at me, please.'

I looked into the high colour of her cheeks and found myself getting lost in it.

'Did I ever tell you how beautiful you are when you're this close to me?' I asked distractedly.

'I believe you might have.' she smiled.

'Oh, I am being unoriginal. Terribly sorry. How about this; have I ever told you that when you touch me I go so hot that I feel like a volcano, like if I would only let myself explode, I could take down anyone willing to break your touch from me?'

Emile's breath hitched, and I heard it.

'You have not.'

'How on earth have we gone this long without you knowing such crucial information?'

'I was happy enough knowing that you think I'm beautiful. But I feel a lot more so after hearing that.'

'That's the effect I was striving to accomplish.'

'Should it not be me telling you such things, considering you're the ill one?'

'I find it takes my mind off it just to have you here, actually. Don't worry about me too much.'

'You're asking me not to worry but I've just witnessed you having a half-seizure over a dream.'

'You're being dramatic.'

'I am not.' Emile said crossly.

I only laughed in response.

It seemed so far away from where I was now, on a boat, riding away from the love of my life, so it felt, without even the possibility of her forgiveness.

I looked at Nathaniel and felt a deep and cold hatred burn inside of me.

Even if I went back to Emile, she wouldn't understand. I knew what this man was capable of. She didn't quite comprehend that even if I could best him, the years and years that had been spent ingraining a consistent and urgent fear of him into my head had done a number on me.

But, if it hadn't been for Nathaniel, I never would have met her.

At that point it felt like I would have much rathered not met her in the first place than deal with that burning guilt for the rest of my life.

I knew I could not kill her on the battlefield. It was preposterous to even suggest it. But I'd seen the hard glare in Emile's eyes when she looked at me; if I did not kill her, she would for sure kill me.

As I sat in my room on the boat a few hours later, I spent my time writing out the conversations we had had that stuck out to me the most. Of course, as of then I could remember every word we had ever exchanged, but I wouldn't forever, so I wanted to make note of all the ones I felt to be the most important in our relationship.

I wrote about the first time we met.

She chided me for calling her 'Your Royal Highness', chided me for bowing, chided me for practically everything I did. She showed me around the house. I have been in love with her since she first spoke. I have been in love with her for as long as I've known her. I was in love with her before I even knew what it meant to be in love.

About her cat's grin.

It was rare I ever saw it. Of course, she smiled all of the time. But there was a difference between every one of her smiles. This one, the cat's grin, I only saw it when she wasn't thinking. When she didn't care what she showed the world. That, I think, is why it was such an occasion to see it. I miss it. If I could draw, I would draw a portrait of her with that exact smile. It was the first thing to make me realise she was more than just my enemy, more than some lousy, pretentious princess, that she was more a raw and real human than I will ever be.

I described every shade of every colour in her eyes.

Of course, the majority of her eyes are a strikingly dark blue. Royal blue. It feels fitting that the shade of her eye colour is started with the word royal. Amusing, even. But, when you look closely, they're speckled with a golden brown, too, a particular splodge in her right eye more noticeable than the freckles over the rest of the two. The inner bit is lighter than the outer. I don't know why I noticed her eyes so much.

The specific heat of a flame that held the same as her hair.

Everyone always talks about how red hair is fiery, ferocious, all of that bull. It is fiery, really. But not any and every type of flame. Only the ones that hold dark and strong, when they've burned out for a few minutes and they're positively crackling with the heat. That's what type of fiery her hair was. Is. The type too hot to roast marshmallows, too large and daunting to grill barbeque food on. The type you strive to have on a cold and lonely night.

The way she made me feel, as well.

She made me feel real. And it sounds so odd when I say that, but she did. Sometimes, it feels like I'm so invisible that if I put a hand to my arm it would go straight through. She made me visible. Real. So real. Like an actual person, with feelings and thoughts and a real life pain tolerance, instead of just a machine coded for war. Sometimes she made me so angry that I wanted to scream, hit something, even, but I found that I never ever would have dreamt of laying a hand on her. Nathaniel always said to me that sometimes the people you love need a slap to put them in their place. That was just his way of consoling me as I looked at my bruised face the day before a battle, I think. I would rather kill myself than ever put her through the impossibility of being harmed by the one she loved, by not being able to escape, because a little slap becomes a big slap and a big slap becomes a big beating and it just progresses until it isn't really a game of discipline anymore, but a game of power. Testing the boundaries. Seeing how far you can go, how much you can get away with. I love her too much for that. I love her with every ounce of myself, with every gram of bone inside of me, every pound of blood in my veins. I love her with everything I am. But I love her enough to realise that I am not what she deserves. She would not hear of it any time I said it. I am not a good man, I would insist. No, but you are a good man to me, she would shoot back angrily. I did not like the way she spoke of that topic, so I dropped it with her almost immediately every time. But in the quiet of my bedroom, I would ponder over it. I am pondering over it now. Surely now, after what I had done, she would understand her worth. I am not enough for her, and not because she is royal and princess, but because she is whole. Unbroken. I am not whole. I am hardly half. And gods, if I am not broken then I am not sure if anyone else truly is. My soul is weightless, desperate to leave the fragmented body it is stuck with. I am the subject of my past. I am the subject of what I have been subjected to.

I decided that then would be a good time to stop writing.

⚔ Chapter Thirty Two ⚔

IN THE DAYS AFTER Maximus's painfully sudden departure, Emile made a discovery.

'Desmond,' she said, 'do you speak Rendan?'

Desmond had looked over at her with an expression of vague confusion and surprise.

'I- yes, I do.' he responded, pushing his glasses up his nose.

They both knew that this was bound to be about Maximus. Just the mention of the Rendan language had set him in both of their minds.

'Are you fluent?' Emile pressed.

'I think so.'

'You think so?'

'I was fluent a few years back. I have not spoken the language in quite some time.'

'Do you know what *te amo* means?'

Desmond started at the words, rearing back a little.

'Yes, yes I do.' he said, blinking too fast.

'Well then.' Emile said, growing impatient. 'What does it mean, if you are so sure you know?'

'Why do you want to know?'

'Just tell me, Desmond, for Gods sake.'

He thought it over for a few moments. 'It means *I love you.*' he eventually said.

Emile's insides suddenly felt both hot and cold at the same time.

'Are you positive that's what it means?' she said, forcing the calm into her voice.

'Yes. I'm certain.'

When you remember, write to me.

Emile stood frozen for a minute or two.

Then, she made way to the kitchen to grab something to eat.

She felt quite repelled by the idea of putting pen to paper, actually.

⚔ Chapter Thirty Three ⚔

I WAS FIVE YEARS old when Nathaniel hit me for the first time.

I remembered not thinking much of it. For the previous two years I had watched him do much worse to George, the unusually tall boy whom I'd made friends with rather fast. It seemed that a small slap was the least of my worries.

Of course, I still confided in George about it.

Even at the mere age of five years old I felt obliged to tell this boy everything that happened in my life.

Nathaniel was a tactical man. He waited another two months to hit me again, another miniscule slap. He hit me with a bit more force the day after. Then, he built up the force over a series of weeks, months, years, until if I were to be only slapped I would think of it as a grace.

I matured quickly for my age. By the time I was eleven years old, George and I were speaking as if we were eighteen already.

'Maximus,' he had said to me one fatal day from behind my door. 'Could I come in, please?'

I could hear the shakes in his voice and, immediately worried, I invited him in.

His dark skin was paled to a chalk white, lips swollen and eyes red.

I ushered him to sit beside me on the bed as an odd feeling of dread set inside of my stomach.

'I need to ask you a question.' George said.

'You can ask me anything you want.'

'Do you think that it's normal?' he mumbled. 'The stuff that my father does to us? To Adelaide?'

I had never thought of it before then.

'That depends on how you define normal.' I said slowly. I felt like Nathaniel was listening to my every word. It always seemed like he was.

'What I mean is, do you think that this happens to the people outside of this manor?' He paused, eyes flittering around as if he thought someone was in the room with us. 'Do you think this happens to the people in Kendra?'

I opened my mouth, and then shut it again.

'Your father cares for us.' I said curtly.

'He cares for you because you are the best fighter our world has ever known. Not because of some father-like need.' George said harshly. 'He cares for me because I am the heir to his throne. Not because I am his only son. And he cares for Addy because she is his ticket to alliances. As soon as he needs to partner up with someone, he will send her to marry their son. I have heard him talk about it. He loves nobody but himself.'

I didn't have any words left in my head to respond with.

We were twelve, at the time.

It is a shame that our childhoods were stripped of us so hastily.

The years most eventful in our relationship were the years we were fifteen and sixteen.

I remember George stumbling into my bedroom the night after his fifteenth birthday, eyes glazed and cheeks flushed red. His shirt was undone and his collar flicked up, hair a rumpled mess. He was not drunk, I realised as I inspected his pupils and his pulse. It seemed he was merely happy.

'What have you done? What is the matter?' I said urgently, pacing the floor as he lay on my bed, staring giddily at the wall.

'Do you remember that girl I met a few months ago?' George asked.

'I do.'

'She kissed me.'

My eyes widened, and I couldn't help but grin at him.

'You had your first kiss? Tonight? With that girl- Juliette, is that her name?- that you're so smitten with?'

George laughed so hard I thought he might be hysterical.

'Yes, yes, yes, yes! Oh, it was amazing.' George gushed.

'Did she say anything after?'

'She told me to meet her at that coffee shop downtown tomorrow at 2pm.'

I grinned, he grinned, we all grinned.

Juliette was found dead the next morning, with a knife wound to her neck.

'It was my father.' George whispered, his voice cracking. My heart broke for him. 'I know it.'

I think that was what made us realise what type of household we were living in.

To answer George's previous question; no, I did not think it was normal at all. The word for it in this language is abuse.

Nobody wants to admit that they're being abused. It's such a big, terrifying thing that it's ignored, not only by the abuser and the abused but the people surrounding them, too.

People knew what happened in the Flint manor.

But Nathaniel Flint was a powerful man.

He could end someone's life for an accusation sent his way with a click of his fingers.

People think that there are only two different types of people. Good and evil. I beg to differ.

I do not consider myself evil.

I do not consider myself good, either.

If I was forced to categorise myself, I would have to say that I'm more evil than I am good. But I was not born evil. When I was young, I was not evil. I was just a boy.

All evil people have secrets.

All evil men were once just boys, just as all evil women were once just girls.

Most of the time, the backstory of people who have committed the most terrible, hateful crimes do not make the crime okay. It only explains the motives behind it.

I commit the worst of crimes.

I openly admit that I am a murderer.

It isn't a good thing, but in a land of abuse and war and just boys and just girls, murder doesn't feel too much of a stretch out of the ordinary.

I was not a psychopath, nor was I a sociopath. I was empathetic, I felt love so strongly it devoured me, I was so remorseful it ruined my life.

In the end, I was really just a boy who had killed people.

I was not evil.

I was not good.

I was just Maximus.

Was that such a difficult thing to imagine?

You then have people such as Emile.

She is immediately placed in the evil section.

Why is that?- you might ask.

After all, she is a good person. She loves her parents and Desmond and even me. Anyone capable of making someone so terrible want to be, well, less terrible is surely a good person.

Ah, but that is only her basis.

Emile was as much of a killer as I was. She was not influenced by the abuse of other killers. Her sister was killed. That is the most tragic thing to have happened in Emile's life.

Ask her, and she will admit that her sister's death plays no part in the murders she has committed.

Emile killed out of a need to impress, a need for validation. Her motives were wrong, her backstory even worse. I killed to protect myself from the harshness of the real world. The things I did were evil, yes, but I was not an evil person. I was just a person who was forced into doing evil things. My brain was not evil.

Not to say that Emile's brain was evil, either. She was even kinder than I, so loving it was suffocating. She was just coddled. Spoilt. Not badly, of course. She was a great person.

But not everyone sees things in the light that I see them.

In the eye of the beholder, Emile and I are as bad as each other.

In reality, we are only as good as each other.

The things I have done are much worse than the things she has done, but does that at all lessen my goodness?

It heightens my evilness, yes, but it does not affect the good things I have done.

It's a little confusing, I know.

Maybe I really am insane after all.

Ask the eye of the beholder that one.

After all.

I am just a boy.

⚔ Chapter Thirty Four ⚔

WHEN I FIRST ARRIVED at the manor, I felt so calm that everyone's voices were unnaturally quiet. *Trauma response,* that voice in my brain whispered with a rasp. *You know that you don't want to be here.*

Of course I don't. Who in their right mind would?

George, apparently.

George? Oh- George!

The calmness became faint joy as I saw him running at me. I opened my arms in preparation as he bounded into the like an overly excited puppy, wrapping himself around me so tightly I thought he would cut off my blood circulation.

'I have missed you *so much.*' he whispered fiercely.

'I would say the same, but I'm afraid I've been quite preoccupied.' I responded with a slight smile.

'You need to tell me absolutely everything.' George said, his voice firm.

'I will. I promise. Come to my room tonight and I'll say anything you wish to know.'

George finally let go of me, his eyes glazed over with tears.

'Are you really so happy to see me that you're going to cry?' I teased, but I could even feel a lump in my throat.

'Shut up.' he snapped, voice cracking. I laughed until the tears fell from my eyes, grabbing his shoulders and pushing my forehead against his.

'So much has happened.' I murmured. 'You won't believe it.'

'I virtually cannot wait to hear it all.'

A hand clamped onto my shoulder. An icy cold hand. I flinched at the impact of the contact.

'Everyone!' Nathaniel's voice was slurred. He'd been drinking, clearly. But still, everyone was captivated by his words. His effect was haunting. 'Today is a momentous one, for sure. Maximus has returned! I propose a feast, in my manor, tonight. Be here for 8pm; it will be quite the occasion, I promise.' And then his lips were at my ear, the stench of alcohol wafting to my nose. 'Make sure you don't mess anything up tonight. Everyone is extremely excited to have you back and you will not ruin it before even 24 hours have passed.'

'I'm guessing I have to wear a suit?' I mumbled bitterly. I really hated suits.

'Of course you have to wear a suit. What sort of question is that?' Nathaniel said incredulously. He didn't bother waiting for my response, only stumbled away from me. I rolled my eyes.

'He's in a good mood, then?' George said.

'You could say that.'

He laughed humorlessly. 'I'm sure this dinner will be interesting.'

'I really do not want to have to deal with fawning old men and fangirling girls right now.' I groaned, starting to walk towards the manor. George walked at my left.

'I think the fangirling girls are quite cute.' he put in with a raised eyebrow.

'Not today they aren't. I want to sleep.'

'No chance. You're going to this dinner, and then after we're having a nice long chat.' George said, feigning innocence with a large smile.

'You might kill me for a few minor things.' I said. George was silent as we stepped in through the manor.

'Do I even want to know what you did?' he asked. 'No, I take that back. I want to know everything that you did. I won't kill you, promise.'

'Mhm. You're underestimating the extent of what I've done.'

'That doesn't sound very good.'

I collapsed on the sofa of George's living room, lying on my back.

'Can you not just tell me now?' he asked, pleaded, practically. I blew out a long breath of air.

'Hm. It's 6pm now, isn't it? We have approximately an hour and half until we have to get ready. So I suppose I could say quite a bit at that time.' I said.

'Please do.' George said, eyes wide. 'Look, we can go to my room in case someone's eavesdropping.'

'That would probably be a good idea.'

'Then, hey ho, let's go!'

He may as well have just dragged me out by my ear in his desperation to hear of my time away. We got to his room, locked the door and sat on his bed.

'So.' I said.

'So.' George repeated.

I was quiet for a moment.

'Should I begin with Desmond?' I said tentatively. I wasn't quite sure how to approach what had happened with Emile, so I decided instead to start with that.

'Go for it.' George said eagerly.

I started off by saying how much of a father figure he was. I could see the confusion in George's face; I was supposed to hate these people, not think of them as fathers! Oh, but if he thought that was bad, he was in for a shock.

'He had some good advice, actually, in our first lesson.' My voice felt foreign. It was odd to speak in Rendan again. I was so used to speaking in Astaxan- the main language in our world- for Emile and Desmond and all of the maids in the manor. I still didn't know why people were so against speaking latin; oh well, I supposed, it didn't matter that much.

'Would you mind sharing that good advice?' George asked with a raised brow.

'He said… to use work with our flaws and make them work in our favour.' I said, recalling that first day of fighting.

The softness of Emile's voice.

The way her eyes glazed over as she stared at me.

The way my breath hitched in my throat.

'By 'our', I suppose you mean you and the princess?' George asked. It wasn't rude, in any way, but it just felt odd hearing Emile being referred to as 'the princess'.

'Emile, you mean. And, no, he was just talking about everyone in general, I suppose.'

'Sure. But while we're on the topic of Emile, I want to hear about her instead.'

I stared at him.

He knew.

Surely he knew.

'Okay. What would you like to hear?' I said cautiously. I was going to tell him; I just wanted to know what he already knew, first.

'Something happened between you two, didn't it?' George said, his voice holding a note of accusation. He didn't look angry; just curious, really.

'Perhaps.' I said, my mouth tilting up in the corner.

'Gods, Maximus! Tell me, please, I need some amusement.' George said, rolling his eyes.

'Amusement in my tragic love story?' I said.

'Shut up. You know that isn't what I mean. I just want to hear about you swooning like a fool.'

'I do not swoon.'

'Oh, I bet you do.'

'...'

'I knew it!'

'Just shut up.'

George laughed and I pushed his arm.

'Okay, enough joking. Tell me about her.' George said. I chewed on my lip.

'I may or may not have forgotten the task.'

'The task?'

'I'm sure you heard about the Rendan's in the Kendran Sacred Forest?'

George's eyes widened. 'And about how they were all killed, too. What did you do, Maximus?'

'It was Emile and I.'

'Just you two?'

'Yes. Just us.'

'Okay...'

'We were travelling to the city that it's located in for two days.'

'Two whole days?'

'Five trains and a horse each throughout the journey.'

'Gods.'

'Then we stayed in a hotel for the third night.'

I saw the realisation dawn on him. 'Oh?' George said, trying and failing to hold back a grin.

'Yep. One room. One bed, too, surprisingly.' I said. I liked remembering it. I suppose it was a reminder that even though I was perceived as the most heartless being to walk the world, there was a heart in me somewhere. A heart that beat solely for one person.

One person that would never forgive me for what I'd done.

The guilt hit me like a trainwreck, right there and then.

See, I think that at first I was in too much shock to really comprehend the extent of what I had done.

It had been like poison. Travelling through my veins, avoiding my heart like the plague.

Until I was speaking about her, about Desmond, and I realised just what I had caused.

I remembered the hurt on Emile's face. The way her entire body seemed to collapse, her bones all breaking at the same time, eyes rimming red before she even started crying.

Oh, but when she did cry, it was so much worse than I had imagined.

I could hear it as she slammed the front door shut, sliding down against it. Screaming, practically.

Could I really blame her?

I'd spent so long pushing her away, and she didn't know why. The reason was so much worse than she ever could have conjured. But, really, was it such a stretch of imagination? Did she truly think that Nathaniel was a good man? She'd seen my hostility after he had left. Desmond had, too. Perhaps they had merely brushed it off as chance. But there was more evidence that, if only she bothered digging a little further, she would have easily found. Emile Elizabeth Elires was smarter than she let on. A lot smarter. Her brain was wired in the way mine was, only the lengths of the wires were shorter, less tangled, less complicated. She thought past the boundaries of normal human morality.

So why hadn't she thought enough to realise the pain Nathaniel had put George and I through?

Why hadn't she thought enough to see what I was plotting early on, before I fell for her, before she fell for me?

I have been in love with her ever since she first spoke. I have been in love with her for as long as I've known her. I was in love with her before I even knew what it meant to be in love.

I supposed if it had been so easy for me to fall for her, why should it not have been just as easy for her to fall for me?

'Maximus? Did you hear me?'

George's voice pulled me out of the depths of my mind, and I blinked a few times, bringing myself back to reality.

'Sorry, no, I didn't.' I mumbled.

'Are you alright?'

My scar burned. The one that I had gotten during that damned task, to be exact.

The other ones will remind you of all those terrible experiences you've just told me of in the years to come. This one, though,; it will remind you of me. Of what you did to save me. I would say that makes you sort of a hero.

She was right, fundamentally. It did remind me of her. Painfully. But it did not make me feel like a hero.

I was tempted to run away, grab a boat, and go back to her right there and then.

But until I'd proven to myself I could best Nathaniel, that would never happen. I knew it. George knew it. Even Emile knew it.

'I'm fine.' I mumbled. 'Just got a headache.'

'Are you sure you're okay?'

'I'm sure. I don't really feel like talking about Emile, that's all.' I confessed.

'I'm sorry.'

'It's fine. I think I'm going to go to my room now.'

'I'll see you tonight.'

'See you.'

As soon as I arrived in my room, my body crumpled in a series of sobs, the type of sobs that racked your soul and your body and everything else in you until you were empty.

A trembling fragment of a person.

☆★☆

I was not used to seeing myself in a suit.

I had straight black trousers, a tie that was much too tight around my neck, and an oddly fancy white button-up. I hadn't yet had the nerve to put on the blazer.

Emile would have said you look like a prince.

Must you torture me at every given moment?

I do not 'torture you'

Oh, I beg to differ. Why do I even talk to you? You aren't real. You're just a figment of my imagination.

Am I?

Of course you are. Now leave me be.

I checked the time. 5 minutes until 8. I figured I'd better be there a little early, so I pulled on the blazer

and set off down the smooth staircases and oak floors.

'Hey.' I stopped in my tracks and turned around, wincing slightly at who I saw.

'Anastasia.' I greeted stiffly. She was wearing a long dress, white, and she looked… happy. Her cheeks were full and her hair wild, skin a peachy tone.

'So it is you. Maximus. I believe you're home a month early.' Anastasia said. I shrugged.

'Yeah, well, I completed the task, didn't I? There was no reason for me to stay there any longer.'

'You didn't tell anyone about me?'

I shook my head sharply. She exhaled in relief.

'It's been tiresome in this place, what with Nathaniel on our case all the time. I think he was just worried about you.'

'Worried about me? That can't be.'

'I must have misphrased it. Worried about your task. About the future of Rendo.'

I bit down on my lip.

'Can I admit something to you, Anastasia?' I asked quietly.

'You know my deepest secret. You can tell me anything you like.' she said with a laugh.

'He should be worried for Rendo. Because I am not going to kill Emile Elizabeth Elires, and she is much too angry to let him kill her.' I said. I saw Anastasia raise an eyebrow.

'You fell for the princess of Kendra, didn't you, you big idiot.' she said, pushing me lightly.

'Don't tell anyone. Especially not Nathaniel.'

'Why are you still here? We both know Kendra is a much better country than ours, and the girl you love is over there. If I were you I'd waste no time in going back to her.' Anastasia said, watching me curiously.

'He would ruin me.'

'You are much more skilled than he will ever be.'

The world was spinning.

'Let's discuss this some other time. We have a dinner to attend.' I said curtly, walking off.

'You can walk away from me, Maximus, but you cannot walk away from yourself. I learnt that a long time ago, the hard way. Don't hurt yourself more than you have to.' Anastasia called after me. My cheeks were burning up. I burst into the dining room, checking my watch. 20:01. How had I managed to still be a minute late?

'Maximus. Took you long enough.' Nathaniel said. He had sobered up immensely. His face was back to it's rigid coldness, and his hands were clasped tightly behind his back. I figured he wouldn't be publicly drinking for a while after that charade.

'I'm hardly late.' I said.

'Just sit down, will you?' Nathaniel said irritably. How was it that I'd been in his presence for a grand total of 10 seconds and already he was sick of me? It was quite offensive, actually.

'Where am I sitting?'

'Right at the end.'

'This end or the farther one?'

'Farther. I'm at this end.'

I nodded and went to my seat, flinching as I slumped on it. I had forgotten how uncomfortable they were.

I tapped my foot against the floor impatiently.

At exactly 5 minutes past 8, everyone flooded in, filling the seats and the elongated table.

Luckily for me, George was at my right and Anastasia my left. Adelaide was at the bottom with Nathaniel, probably so he could show her off as some sort of prize. She was quite pretty, I supposed, but not in the sort of way that should be shown off. She still looked like a child, still had a babyface. Of course, I couldn't say the same for Anastasia; she looked alarmingly mature for her age. But Adelaide was still just a kid.

I wished I could save her from this life.

'Settle down, now.' Nathaniel wasn't trying to shout or anything, but his voice echoed throughout the room all the same. Everyone fell into a tense silence, watching him in anticipation. 'Now, as you all know, we are here to celebrate the endeavours of our very own Maximus Invictus Blare.'

The table burst into rounds of applause. George clapped the loudest, just to watch my embarrassment. I made a face at him.

'Now, as many of you may know now, I took in Maximus when he was only a toddler, hardly able to walk. I have to say, I am quite impressed at how well he has fared over these past 11 months. I admit openly that I have raised a genius, not only in the art of sword fighting, but as a means of his unnaturally clever mind.'

Everyone's gaze turned to me, before going back to Nathaniel.

'He has done what many of us never could.' He paused for effect. 'He has made our worst enemy, the Kendran princess, fall in love with him.'

My heart dropped to my ankles.

I could feel George's eyes burning into me as I smiled tensely at the people clapping for me and laughing in glee.

But, really, my mind was blanking everything out.

I was not too keen on talking about mine and Emile's love affair right there and then.

'Now, now, let's calm down. Of course, we're all very proud of our boy, Maximus, but this isn't the only thing he has achieved. He saved Anastasia Ivene, sworn companion of my youngest daughter, Adelaide, from death at the hands of those dastardly Kendrans, for a start.'

Anastasia did not look too happy to be put in the spotlight. Her lips tugged up in the slightest, a reserved sort of half-smile, but I could see the way her skin was tightening over her bones.

'And he has saved our country in this war. Without him, I am not sure what we would have done.'

Everyone murmured their agreement to one another. I felt rather pressured, actually.

'So, let us raise a toast. To Maximus. The boy of many talents, many wonders, and the boy who has done his country proud.'

I clinked my glass onto George and Anastasia's, avoiding their eyes. They were the only two people on that table who knew about how I really felt for Emile. For Kendra in general.

'Maximus, if you wouldn't mind sharing a few words with us?' Nathaniel said as he finally sat down. I coughed awkwardly and stood up, trying to keep my back as straight as possible.

'Good evening, everyone.' I started. I had made many speeches before; this one was going to be easy. 'I would like to say a huge thank you to my closest comrade, George Flint, who has been here for me in my darkest of times. It has been difficult for me, making friends in this place, but I have always found George to be a constant in my life. I cannot exactly remember the day we met, but I can remember the many days that came after it, all the memories we have, all the times we have shared. Sometimes you don't understand me, and sometimes I don't understand you, but that's alright. You try your hardest, you try so hard, and I appreciate you endlessly. If there is ever going to be a time where I have to choose the person in the world that I love most, the person who comes before anyone else, it will be you, in a heartbeat. No matter how many girls I meet, how many epic love stories I am a part of, you will always be my best friend, you will always be the first person I want to go to. This feels like a wedding speech. The conclusion of this thanks is that, George, I will continue to love and support you eternally, universally, no matter what happens, no matter how many people I have to kill for you-' Everyone laughed a little there. '-no matter how many times we fall out, and no matter what is thrown at us, even in our worst of times, even when our relationship is on it's last string, I will come back to you. I will come back for you, always.'

I let my eyes meet George's. I saw the brown glaze over, I saw him blink and look down. Everyone was speaking of how beautiful it was. I did not want to be remembered, though, as the man who gave beautiful speeches.

'Now that I have done that, I have more I would like to say.' I said loudly, captivating everyone's attention. 'I have been away from this house for nearly a year now. When you put it into perspective, it doesn't seem too long, but Gods if it didn't feel it. I've done things I never would have imagined doing. And now, I'm exhausted, I cannot lie. So, after all that I've been through, *I* would like to raise a toast to getting so drunk I forget my own name, thank you very much!'

Everyone laughed and raised their glasses, but my mind had transported me to a train with a girl months ago.

'When I get back to the house from this entire charade, I'm going to get so drunk that I forget my own name.'

'Mind if I join you?'

'Not at all.'

I shook my head slightly and sat down, pushing the memory to the back of my head as I took a swig of my drink. I wasn't sure what it was. It tasted strong, I knew that much. I carried on drinking until I'd nearly finished it all.

'I have some things I'd also like to say.' It was George, standing up rather unsteadily. I looked at his glass to see it was empty. He'd probably already refilled it a number of times, too, knowing him.

'Maximus. Maximus, Maximus, Maximus.' he said with a lazy grin. 'I don't even know where to start. You are something else, that's for sure. Most people would be jealous to have a best friend this much more talented than them. Me? I only recognise quite how lucky I am. What would I have done had we not been friends? You are the reason I am pushing myself to this war, Max. If we ever had any chance of salvation, I know it lies in your hands. You seem to be evil, I know, I know, but you are a good man. Believe me if you will not believe anybody else. You are a good man, Maximus. Yes, you kill people, but to me you are the best man you could be. The best *friend* you could be. You are merciless when it comes to your enemies, but when it comes down to your allies, your companions, I have never known anyone to be a greater man.' With that, he sat down, and everyone was clapping with all their might.

I grinned at George.

He grinned back.

Then I downed the rest of my drink and called a maid over for a refill.

☆★☆

I quickly realised that you can't, in fact, get so drunk that you forget your own name. Well, at least I couldn't. It got to a point where everything was spinning, where my knees felt weak and my tongue heavy and numb, but I could remember my name perfectly fine.

'Do you not think you've had enough to drink now?' George said, pulling me away from the table for a moment. I frowned. Why did he have four eyes?

'My name is Maximus.' I mumbled, words slurring. 'Damnit! Why can I still remember it?'

'Come on, we're going to your room.'

'I don't want to go to my room. I want to dance. Dance with me, George!'

George shook his head at me and I walked off.

I found a girl with bleached blonde hair and bright green eyes and extended a hand out to her.

'What's your- your name?' I yelled over the noise.

'Lilith.' Lilith said, her face bright with the excitement of my talking to her.

'Well, Lilith, would you care to dance with me?' I said. She smiled widely and took my hand, wrapping the other around my neck and pulling me in. I blinked before letting my spare hand fall at her hip.

'I would love to.' she said.

We danced for a total of 5 minutes peacefully.

But then I shut my eyes, and all I could think about was Emile.

It was wrong to use this girl to try and console myself, especially when I was so drunk. But I couldn't help myself. I squeezed my eyes shut and imagined it was her, moulded Lilith's strong collarbone to the soft curve of Emile's neck, feeling her hair as if it were that same red, the red that coloured my own blood.

It wasn't until I opened my eyes and saw a flash of brown, rather than that familiar flash of royal blue, that the pain really hit me.

I cleared my throat and muttered an apology before stumbling away, finding George.

'Can we go back to my room, now?' I asked. George didn't bother asking any questions. He grabbed my forearm and guided me away, up the stairs, through the winding corridors, and into my bedroom, where I fell into my bed.

'I miss her.' I said. George sat at the bottom of my bed silently. 'I really miss her, George.'

'I know you do.'

'I want her back. I want- I want to go back. Gods, I want to go back so much. But I know she won't forgive me. My- I hurt everywhere. Everything hurts. I feel like something's been ripped out from inside of me and it's- it's infected or something, raw and red, and it won't- this- this infection, it won't go away, and it's spread- it's spreading, it's spreading really fast, and I don't know what to do.'

There was a moment of silence.

'Go back to her.'

I wasn't sure I'd heard him correctly as I pushed myself to sit up.

'What?'

'Go back.'

I didn't know how to respond.

'Maximus, this country is ruined. You were never here to protect Rendo. You were here to protect me, to protect Adelaide, to protect yourself. Kendra is a good country. They deserve someone like you fighting for them.'

'But Nathaniel-'

'You could best him with your eyes closed.'

I shut my eyes.

'Go back.' I whispered.

'Sleep on it.' George said, turning my light off as he walked out.

The next morning, a war proclamation was made.

⚔ Chapter Thirty Five ⚔

I GOT OVER MY hangover before it had even begun. I woke up at around six the next morning, still a little tipsy as I went down the stairs and collapsed in the main living room. Nathaniel was there, watching me with cold eyes, sitting like a statue in his armchair.

'Hey.' I mumbled.

'*Bonum mane,* Maximus.' Nathaniel said curtly. *Good morning.* Ah. He was back to his usual self, bad moods and all.

'How are you?' I asked.

'Fine.'

There was an awkward silence.

'I have some news to share with you.' he eventually said. I raised an eyebrow, attention sparked.

'Oh? Do tell.'

'Early this morning, perhaps three hours ago, a war proclamation was made.'

I stilled.

'What?'

'You heard me quite well. In around two weeks, we are going to war.' Nathaniel looked pleased. I am sure that I did not.

'Two weeks? But surely- how did this- I am so confused.' I rubbed my brow with two fingers, forehead creasing.

'We'll set off for a battlefield in Kendra in exactly two weeks, aiming to try and take it over. We're starting with the small places, like that battlefield and the area around it. There'll be armies distributed around in Rendo and in other Kendran places, too, but the princess and Desmond Axel are going to be at that battlefield, so we are too. I should hope you are rather excited, considering the lengths you have gone to for this war.' Nathaniel said, examining his fingernails.

Oh, yes, I'm extremely excited to kill the girl I love.

George's words from the night before faintly flashed in my mind.

Go back. Go back.

I swallowed hard. I really needed to speak to him now that I was sober again.

'Um, yeah. Really excited.' I said.

'If you're nervous, really, don't be. You'll be fine, we both know it. You're an unnaturally gifted fighter, Maximus, truly.' I think he meant to be comforting. I did not find any comfort in hearing those words come from his mouth.

'Yeah, I know. Thanks. Is George awake, by any chance?'

'He's reading in his room.'

'Thank you. I'll see you...'

'Tomorrow night will be the first time we're alone. We're going to go over what you learnt from the princess and the old man.'

'Ah. Yes. See you then, I suppose.'

'*Vale.*' Goodbye.

My heart was pounding in my face as I set off for George's room. If I was going to leave at all, it would have to be before I told Nathaniel any crucial information. 'If' being the keyword.

'We need to talk,' were the first words I spoke as I burst into George's room, skin flushed and sunken.

'Well, hello to you too, Maximus.' George said, spinning around on his desk chair. I slammed the door shut. 'Please, take a seat.' he continued, gesturing to his bed. I did as he said, running two hands through my hair to try to console my nerves.

'War. Two weeks. Did you know?'

'I was awake when the proclamation was made.'

'Why were you awake at… three in the morning?' I said with a frown. George shrugged.

'*Pater* wanted me to stay up.' I was glad he was finally using the Rendan term for it.

'He definitely knew.'

George thought it over for a moment.

'Definitely.'

'Why did he not keep me up?'

'In case you went running off like you're planning on doing now?' My neck went bright red.

'It isn't running away from anything, necessarily. Not in the way that I see it. It's… moving towards something.'

'Or someone.'

'Something *and* someone.' I corrected myself. George sighed.

'I've only just gotten you back, too. I'm going to miss you so much.' he said mournfully. I froze.

'You aren't coming with me?'

'Gods, I could never. I'm the Flint heir, Maximus. I can't leave this place. I'm stuck here.' George said.

'But what if I don't come back? Scrap that, if I do leave we both know I won't risk coming back here unless it's absolutely necessary. What if I never see you again?'

'You'll see me on the battlefield in two weeks, will you not?'

I felt so heavy, and yet so light, everywhere.

374

'I can't go without you. I can't do it. I said that I would always come back for you, I promised, I can't just break that now.'

'You know you have to.'

'Don't make me go without you.'

'You don't have a choice.'

'Please. She won't- she won't forgive me. Desmond will, sure, but Emile is much too stubborn for that. I can't lose you as well as her.'

'You won't lose me. I'll write to you; I wouldn't risk writing back, but I can still speak to you.'

'It isn't the same.'

'Would you rather such a corrupted country win a war against one as beautiful and innocent as Kendra?'

'Stop it. Stop it right now.'

'Maximus.'

'George.'

My throat was swelling, tightening. It felt awfully cruel to make me choose between my bestfriend and the love of my life, as it seemed.

I could see that George was upset, too. He tried to hide it as he lifted his chin high and held his back straight, but his nut brown eyes were glistening in the dim light.

The sun was rising. I could see it in my peripheral vision, through the window.

It looked too beautiful for a day so miserable.

'Listen to me right now.' George said. His voice was dangerously quiet. 'You're going to find my father as soon as he is in his office. The only reason you're still here is your fear of him. And do you know what you're going to do? You're going to best him in a duel. He is going to be a difficult opponent, yes, but I know you've done worse. I know that you can do this. I believe in you. Then, after you have done that, you are going to grab the bag I'll have packed for you full of food and water and spare clothes and you're going to leave this country and find that stupid girl and that stupid old man and you're going to go to war with them. It's going to be odd. I know. And you are right; I might never see you again as my best friend. But it's alright. No, no, don't cry on me. Wipe away those tears. As soon as I am the man in charge of this manor, you are going to be free to come here whenever you please.' I could see some sort of internal war wage with George in the last sentence. I wondered what he could possibly be in conflict about. It was sure that as soon as Nathaniel died, which would hopefully be rather soon, George would take over everything. It was queer to think of him in control, but it was his birthright, his right by name, after all.

'And what if I don't best him?' I countered. 'It's too big of a risk to take. He'd either get me sent to death row for an unjust attempt on his life or I'd be held here like a hostage for the rest of my life.'

'Why do you think like that?' George said, lifting both his eyebrows. 'Why must you always doubt yourself? You will win. I know you will, and I know both you and my father better than anyone else. You deserve this. Emile deserves this. Even Kendra deserves this.'

I chewed on my lip until it spilled with blood, filling my mouth with a metallic tang.

'When will he be back in his office?' I asked. I saw George smirk in the very slightest. We used to watch Nathaniel's routines together so that we knew where he would be at any time. I figured that in a year, his routine would have changed.

'He's normally in there after lunch, for the whole afternoon. He spends his mornings in the arena.'

'I expect he will most likely want me to be in there with him?'

'I would assume so.'

'Such a shame.' I said dryly.

'We'll eat dinner at around eleven.'

'Eleven? We used to eat it at one.'

'Ah, yes, but that was when he used his office in the morning. Now that he uses it in the afternoon, we eat earlier so he has more time to work.' George pointed out. I nodded slowly.

'That leaves me five hours to do what I like.'

There was a pause where we both stared at each other.

'You never finished telling me about Emile.' George said slowly. 'Since this is the last time I'll see you, I would quite like to hear about her, if that's alright with you.'

'Of course it's alright with me.' I said, a little too quickly. I saw doubt flash over his face. 'No, really. I can pick up starting with the task, if you'd like?' I continued.

'Go for it.'

I took a deep breath.

'So, after a night in the hotel we spent the day walking through the woods. The sacred forest. Did you know that the city it's in is called Sancire? It's quite odd, I think, that a Kendran country has a name of Renan origin.'

George nodded his agreement.

'Anyway, when it got dark we set up a camp just a little bit off the path, and just… sat around the campfire for a little while before going to sleep.' I said carefully. Clearly not carefully enough. The look that had enveloped George's features was enough to send me into fits of laughter.

'Gods, you've been busy.' he grinned.

'Shut up. You're wrong.'

'Sure I am.'

'No, really. Swear down.'

George didn't respond. He simply rolled his eyes.

'So the day after we went to the core, where those thirty Rendans were. Um, as you know, we did kill them all but there was a little... difficulty throughout.' It felt very humiliating, still.

'Difficulty? Please say it wasn't bad.'

I didn't say anything at all. I just lifted the bottom of my top so he could see the raw and red scar there, stretching over the entirety of my lower abdomen. It was still sore to the touch. George gasped aloud, hand clamping over his mouth.

'What the hell, Maximus?' he hissed. 'How did that happen?'

'It wasn't because of the fighting. It was Emile. One of them was coming up behind her, and... he would've killed her. I was watching it. So I jumped in myself and took off his head. I was quick, Gods I was really quick, but clearly not quick enough.' I shrugged, dropping the fabric gently.

'Are you alright?'

'I am now. I certainly wasn't when it first happened.'

'What happened after he got that hit on you, then?'

I swallowed. It was hard to explain this part.

'I lost loads of blood. She got me to a hospital of course, and they did some stuff, so I survived, clearly. But I was... asleep for a while.'

Was asleep the right word for it?

I didn't actually know.

'How long is a while?' George said suspiciously.

'Nearly three weeks, Emile said.'

His eyes widened.

'That isn't even the worst part.' I said. 'You know about my dreams, yeah? Well, it took me about six weeks to heal after that, so of course she and Desmond were watching my every move, even if I was stuck in my bed. They even watched me sleep, just in case something happened during it. And, of course, things did happen. But they were even worse now that people were watching me. I had… like, seizures and stuff. I don't know. Emile says- said it was a trauma response, but she isn't thinking of the right piece of trauma.' I laughed, then. 'That makes my life sound so miserable. There's so much of it that she can't even pick out the correct bit.'

George didn't say anything for a few moments.

'I can't believe you risked your life- your *reputation*- just for that girl.' He looked at me wistfully. 'I hadn't believed that you felt about her to that extent until now. You wouldn't even go that far for me.'

'Yes I would.'

'You wouldn't. I know you wouldn't. Because I'm a Flint and my father would soon find out and that would ruin everything. Although, I suppose now that you're leaving, that changes things.'

'It doesn't have to change everything.'

'Just because it doesn't have to doesn't mean it won't.'

I looked down at my hands.

George continued speaking in response.

'The fates don't take our opinions into consideration. They have a line to follow; sure, that line can be split into different lines, with a whole range of different universes full of different possibilities, but in this universe, in this life, I know how we will end.'

'And how will we end, George?'

He looked pained by the question.

'You'll find out soon enough.' he said simply, looking away. 'Besides; I don't think we were finished talking about your lover.'

I laughed and threw a pillow off him, even though my insides were curling with confusion.

You'll find out soon enough.

I did not want to know what he meant by that.

☆★☆

It was immeasurably awkward at the dinner table.

Nathaniel, obviously, was not at all fased. He sat at his end, picking at his food like a little kid, apparently focused on something else.

'Maximus.' he said suddenly. 'I was expecting you at the arena this morning.'

George and I shared an amused glance.

'Sorry.' I mumbled.

'Be there tomorrow, will you?'

I looked at George once again. He was trying not to laugh.

'Sure.'

'*Gratias Agere.*'

'*Libenter.*'

The rest of the meal was spent in silence.

'I am going to be in my office.' Nathaniel said as he stood up to leave once we'd all finished eating. 'If you need anything, knock first.'

I looked at George.

He looked back at me.

Don't go yet, he mouthed. I nodded, clasping my hands together in front of me with a blank expression as I felt Nathaniel's eyes rake over me. He seemed pleased with what he saw, as he spun around and left, the sound of the door slamming echoing throughout the room.

'Adelaide. Anastasia. Maximus has something to tell you.' George said immediately. I looked at the two of them, still sat at the table, secretly holding hands, and felt a pang of jealousy. Even though their relationship was restricted to secrecy by the law, they were happy. They would never do anything to harm the other. I swallowed.

'I'm leaving this place. Like, now.' I said. Anastasia wasn't surprised; Adelaide, on the other hand, was.

'What? But you've only just gotten here?' she exclaimed in outrage. 'Surely my father is not going to send you away merely weeks before the war.'

'He isn't.' Anastasia said quietly.

'What do you mean?'

'She means that I'm going off my own accord.' I cut in. 'I'm going back to Kendra. I'm sorry, I don't know how to explain this to you, but please, if you ever need anything, tell George and he can write to me.' I said.

'Why are you going back to Kendra?' Adelaide seemed completely lost.

'Emile.' Anastasia said simply. 'It's because of the girl.'

'Emile?' Adelaide frowned. 'I thought you didn't like her.'

I stayed quiet, almost guiltily.

'Oh.' Adelaide said. '*Oh.*'

'Yeah. Oh.' I murmured.

'Do you love her?'

'Addy!' George proclaimed. I didn't even have to think about it.

'Yes.' I said. 'Of course I do.' *How could I not?*

'What are you waiting for?' Anastasia said with a raised brow. 'Why are you explaining yourself to us, of all people?'

'*Pater*'s going to kill you.' Adelaide actually looked a little worried for me.

'He isn't going to get to do that.' I said. 'I'll beat him in a fight, wound his pride, just to let him know that I am better than him. I always have been and I always will be. And now I'm going to prove it.'

'You're fighting him… now?' Adelaide asked slowly.

'Swords or fists?' Anastasia asked eagerly.

'Yes. And swords.' I said.

'We really should get going, Maximus.' George said.

'You're fighting him too?' Adelaide said.

'I'm just packing him a bag.'

'Oh.'

'You're right. Let's go.' I looked at Anastasia, my eyes saying what my words never could. She sucked her bottom lip in between her teeth and I gave her a small smile.

'See you.' Anastasia said, her voice quiet. Thick. I averted my gaze from her.

'Goodbye, Maximus!' Adelaide called after me as I left.

'Since when did Anastasia not hate you with a passion?' George mumbled as we sped to my bedroom.

'I don't know. I think she was rather fond of me while imprisoned in the house back in Kendra.'

'Why on earth was she fond of you then?'

I shrugged, not bothering to answer.

As soon as we got to my room, George started fumbling with my wardrobe, opening a backpack and throwing it on my bed.

'Go now.' he said breathlessly. 'Go!'

I nodded hastily, running off to find Nathaniel's office. Of course, I *did* know where it was; it was like I'd said before. I just hadn't been in the manor for an abnormally long time.

I got to the door, checking my sheath for my sword and pulling it out. It reminded me of Desmond. I didn't necessarily want to be reminded of Desmond, considering what I had just recently done to him.

I opened the door, not knocking as Nathaniel had requested, sword pointed out in front of me.

'Can you-' He cut himself off, eyes latching on the tip of my blade. 'Ah. I was wondering why you seemed so distant at lunch, Maximus Invictus Blare.'

The use of my full name was unnerving but I stayed deathly still, waiting for him to make the first move.

The air tasted of tension.

I fought to keep my eyes staring at Nathaniel unblinkingly, unemotionally, neutrally.

Luckily for me, he was the first to look away, standing up with his hands raised in the air.

'I did not train you to kill like a coward.' he said. He sounded cut off, annoyed, even. I vaguely wondered why. 'Would you truly murder an unarmed, innocent man?'

'You are anything but innocent.' I said finally. My voice was like satin, smooth and silky. Calm.

'Will you not at least give me a fair fight?' Nathaniel continued, ignoring what I had said.

'If you bothered asking, you would know that that is what I have come here to do.' I said.

Nathaniel's sword was out in a flash, his head tilted to the side.

'Such good morals. If it were me, I would've killed you whilst you were defenceless.'

His sword came at me, and I dodged the blow easily.

'I am not here to kill you, Nathaniel.'

I threw a hit at him, but he knocked it off.

'Oh? Then why are you here at all?'

I ducked down as he went for my head, my own blade going in the same rounding action. I ripped the material of his trousers, even cutting his skin a little, I realised, as I saw small prickles of blood run down his calf. I saw the faint surprise on his face at me landing a blow so early on in the fight.

'I'm only here to best you.'

We were in full swing, then. I was at the advantage on paper; younger and at the prime of my ability, I was the best I could be, technically. But Nathaniel was different. He wasn't some humble old man, retired from his days of fighting. He was constantly at his prime, constantly the best he could be, constantly unfaltering.

The winner, it seemed, would be determined by who's prime of fighting was better, I supposed.

'You do realise that you will only properly best me when I am dead by your hands? By your sword?'

He went to slice over my scar gained from battling with Emile, and I held myself from showing any sign of weakness. In fact, it propelled me to work even harder.

'Technically, no, I will have bested you today when you are at my mercy, sword on the floor with the tip of my blade at your throat. There is a war for killing you in.'

As I felt my energy increasing, my steps becoming lighter and my movements more precise, and less desperately placed, I could feel Nathaniel's decreasing, although in quite an odd way. It was like he wanted me to win. His moves were slow, sluggish, predictable, even, the sort of thing that he would usually never be.

Don't ponder on it too much, that voice in my head said, *take it and go. As soon as you've beat him, you can go back to Emile, back to Desmond, back to Kendra.*

That was really all the motivation I needed.

'Is this because of that girl?' Nathaniel asked mockingly. 'Are you going to go back to her, now? Don't look at me like that. It's obvious that you're hopelessly in love with her.'

I landed a rather aggressive blow to his knee with the back of my sword, sending him stumbling backwards and his sword flying in the air as he struggled to catch it.

For a moment, I saw panic in his face.

I savoured the panic with a sick sense of pleasure.

I caught the sword and pushed them both to either side of his neck; I hated hearing Nathaniel speak about Emile, as if he had the right to. He had no right to even think about her. She was so good, so... kind. She was everything that Nathaniel was not.

His biggest mistake was trying to use feelings that were so strong as some form of weakness.

No: if anything, they were my strength.

'You just wait, Nathaniel.' I whispered. I could feel his breath on my face. It was icy cold. Why was he always so cold? 'I'm going to make you regret everything that you ever did to me. To George. To Adelaide. Even to Anastasia. I'm going to ruin you until you have nothing. I'll ruin every aspect of you. I'll ruin this country, too. Your legacy that you are so determined to have? It will be gone as soon as I say it will. Your time is coming. I suggest you prepare for it.'

And, to my ultimate shock, he started laughing.

Not even one of those sad laughs you have when you know you've lost.

A full on cackle, as if something I had said was so completely amusing.

'Remember this for me, will you?' Nathaniel said. '*Ad vitam aeternam.*' *To eternal life.*

His words sent chills running through me, but I couldn't figure out why. It wasn't as if he'd said anything necessarily creepy. Well, I couldn't judge that, could I? I'd have to know the context first.

The thing is, I didn't really want to know the context.

'*Mors vincit omnia.*' I shot back, voice hard. *Death conquers all.*

We stood there like that for a few minutes, just staring at each other. His eyes, once a brown close to black, now pale and light, were lifeless, staring at me as if I was invisible. My pride did not like being looked at like that, especially not by the man who raised me.

Finally I took a step back, throwing Nathaniel's sword on the floor and pushing mine into my sheath. He stayed still, watching me carefully.

'I'll see you in two weeks.' I spat as I turned to leave.

'*Audentes fortuna iuvat.*' he said, his voice quiet.

Fortune favours the bold.

If there was anything at all, aside from George, that I had missed about the Flint manor, it was the casual use of old Rendan quotes.

As soon as I was a good enough distance from the office I broke into a run, bursting into my bedroom. The bag was packed, and George was sitting next to it. He stood up quickly at my arrival.

'Well? How did it go?' he said hastily. I simply grinned. He grinned back, pulling me in for some sort of embrace.

'I knew you could do it.' he whispered.

We broke apart, eyes glistening.

'I wish I didn't have to leave you.' I said, voice cracking.

'Grab your bag, Maximus. I have a boat out front for you.' George said simply. I pulled the bag over my shoulders and followed him out of my room, out of the manor, back onto the ledge I had walked down before I'd even known who Emile was.

That time felt so long ago.

'Be careful.' George said. I nodded again.

'I'll miss you.' I whispered.

'I'll miss you too.'

I stood there frozen for a second before boarding the boat, waving goodbye, setting off.

However, as I left the harbour, as I left Rendo, I could hear George say some final words.

'*Astra inclinant, sed non obligant.*'

The stars incline us, they do not bind us.

⚔ Chapter Thirty Six ⚔

EMILE USUALLY PRIDED HERSELF for her impeccable senses. And not in a smell, touch and taste sort of way; in a sixth sense sort of way.

And that's why when a piece of her heart shifted, when the weight lifted off it, she knew that something had happened.

Something to do with Maximus.

She could feel the change in everything she did; in the lightness of her steps as she pranced with a sword, in the way that her arrow pierced the target perfectly every time, the way that, for some reason, she simply could not stop smiling.

'What are you so happy about?' Desmond asked in faint amusement. Emile shrugged, spinning her sword around her wrist and arm in a sort of acrobatic way. It was a rather impressive trick, actually.

'Do I need a reason to be happy?' Emile asked.

'When you put it that way…'

She grinned, letting the sword come to a stop as she leaned backwards into a small lunge.

'Come on then; fight me.'

She lay awake that night, eyes staring at the dull black of the ceiling. It felt as though they were glued open, painfully so. Even blinking was like a chore.

Emile took her fingertips and ran them down her eyelids, shutting them as if she were a dead person. She could feel the persistent uncomfort of her pupils still moving, sticking to the skin they were covered by. A shiver ran through her, but she refused to open her eyes.

When she did eventually fall asleep, she had a very strange dream.

It was Maximus on a boat, a stuffed backpack on his shoulders and an excited look on his face. Emile recognised the waters he rode on. They were nearing Kendran waters.

But why would he be coming to Kendra?

When she woke up, there was a bittersweetness filling her lungs with every breath she took. The air tasted like disease.

For a brief moment, she considered telling Desmond what she had seen. But the possibility of it just being nothing was too big of a risk to take; so she stored it in the box in her brain reserved for Maximus, filled with all the other memories they had shared.

It was not a box she very much liked to look at.

But sometimes, just sometimes, she had to sneak a peek at it. Just to remind her of what she had done.

What she had had.

And even though it ripped her heart apart and threw it into the abyss, she couldn't help but watch through the memories, watch what had been stripped away from her only a few days ago.

Emile had come to the realisation that, actually, Maximus was technically never even hers to begin with. He'd been against her the entire time, thought of her as a rival the entire time.

Although she wanted to hate him with everything she was, she could not do it.

It hurt too much.

What they had felt too real, too raw, to just be... fake. How could he have faked such feelings? Yes, he was a good actor, but she had felt the racing of his heart as she pressed her hand to his chest, the dilation of his pupils every time she laughed. It was enough to fake a face, but to be able to fake bodily reactions? No, it was impossible.

Emile figured it would be a good time to write in her diary.

23rd November, 0070
My head is whirring. I can't even think through the noise. Maybe I'm going mad, but I think that something has happened with Maximus. I had a dream about him last night; he was on a boat, on the waters just before the Kendran Seas. Now, I don't know if it's just my mind playing tricks on me or if it was, like, some sort of vision, but either way it doesn't seem too good.
Oh, but I miss him terribly. I feel icy cold without him here, and yet so covered, so concealed. Maximus made me feel free. He made me feel like I could do anything and everything, no matter what people said, no matter what my parents and Desmond thought. But perhaps that was as much of a lie as everything else. I don't know what to believe.
There's a certain quote I can remember him saying to me consistently. 'Vita non est vivere sed valere vita est.' I'm not sure if I spelled it right. It took a few times to memorise it, but now it is ingrained in my mind. Life is more than merely staying alive. Perhaps Maximus uses Rendan when speaking to me so he can say what he wants without directly saying it. It for sure felt like that with the whole te amo.
Well, I have a little quote of my own.
It's from my favourite book; the Iliad.
'No man, against my fate, sends me to Hades.

And as for fate?
I'm sure no man escapes it.'

⚔ Chapter Thirty Seven ⚔

NATHANIEL HAD NEVER BEEN quite so angry in his entire life.

He could feel it coursing through him, infecting his thoughts, blurring his vision. His hands trembled with rage.

Bloody Maximus.

Always had to go and ruin everything, didn't he?

Nathaniel had had a clear plan in his head; he had Maximus back home and the war proclamation had been made. Everything was going completely right.

Until he burst into the office doors with a sword in his hand and Nathaniel knew that everything was over.

That stupid, stupid girl.

Maximus had never been… *soft*, per say. He had always been fondest of George, and even then everyone knew that Maximus would only go to great difficulties to protect himself, the selfish twat.

That is, until he met Emile.

Fighting Nathaniel was a great difficulty for sure.

A great risk, even.

So why would he do it for a single girl?

He did not make the decision by himself. No, Nathaniel knew that much as a definite. He was pushed along by somebody else, somebody who would do just about anything to save Maximus Invictus Blare from the life he was destined to lead in Rendo.

Mors vincit omnia.

Nathaniel slammed his hand down on the table, leaving papers to flutter around the room.

The words reverberated off the walls of his brain in an extremely unnerving manner.

Death conquers all.

If Nathaniel knew anything, it was that he was not going to let fate have it's way with him so early on. Maximus had shaken him a little, yes, but Nathaniel had learnt from his mistakes. Don't mention the girl. Clearly it was quite a soft spot for him.

He racked his brain for something. Anything.

Nathaniel was desperate to pin the blame for this on somebody, anybody, as long as it wasn't himself.

See, something inside of him, something deep inside of him, knew that it was all his fault. Nathaniel wasn't as clever as some, yes, but not totally oblivious. He knew enough to see what was going on in front of his own face.

He did not regret what he had done to Maximus for the entirety of his childhood.

He did not blame himself, either.

If anything, it was surely the fault of the fates.

After all, it was them who chose what happened in everyone's lives. It was them who decided to put the boy through the torture.

Nathaniel refused to believe that anything that happened in his life was in his own control.

He had this sort of image in his mind that he was not his own person, not really, that there was some higher source controlling his thoughts, his actions, his everything, and that the only part of Nathaniel that was truly, really Nathaniel was the body it inhabited.

He figured that out (or so he thought) after beating his own son for the first time.

The thought of his son made him wonder, actually.

What if George played a part in this charade?

It was not likely. The two were unusually close, and if anyone would want to help Maximus, it would be George Flint, for sure.

I can't let him get away with this.

If Nathaniel was known for anything, it was all but mercy.

He knew it was an absurd thought, conjured up on the spot to console himself from the fact that he'd driven away his chance at victory.

They could still win the war, Nathaniel told himself desperately. He would have to take out the three big ones early on; Maximus, Emile and that stupid old man, Desmond.

But who would have the nerve to help him defeat them?

Nathaniel could take down one at a stretch, yes, but all three of them were too much. He had not built up his image from being able to fight off such gifted people; he'd built up his image from taming them. And there was no way he could tame the people who already hated him more than he could even comprehend.

Nobody was the answer.

No one in their right mind would dare go against Desmond Axel, previous war hero, trainer of any great warrior you could possibly think of.

No one in their right mind would dare go against Emile Elizabeth Elires, warrior princess of Kendra, trained by Desmond himself, destined for things so bloody and great that it was any ordinary warrior's damned dream.

And no one in their right mind would go against Maximus Invictus Blare.

He was the most dangerous of them all.

At first, he seemed to be a nice quiet boy, perhaps a little shy, perhaps a little awkward.

Anybody from Rendo knew what he had done.

Everyone in Nathaniel's army had heard the people he'd defeated, the masses he'd brought down, the way he licked his hands clean of blood afterwards.

Maximus did not like to be perceived as a psychopath.

But, then again, does any psychopath want anyone to know who they really are?

No, Nathaniel knew he wasn't that bad. He'd seen the guilt on Max's face, the way he vomited until it was nothing but acid after his first kill, the way he choked on his own breath when he saw his lover, Rose, as known by his friends and family, hanged.

But he was something alright.

Nathaniel did not want to wait to find out what that something was, exactly.

He had found a blame.

He had found an opening for his wrath.

George Flint.

A man of very few fears.

But, for all George was not afraid of much, after being brought up around Maximus himself, he was certainly afraid of one thing, at the very least.

His own father.

Nathaniel Flint.

Nathaniel knew this better than anyone else, and hell if he didn't use it to his advantage.

He strode out of the office and along the corridor, making way for his only son's bedroom.

☆★☆

George Flint had not expected to feel quite so empty after Maximus's departure.

Not empty in the normal sort of way. It was a heavy emptiness, like there was a weight dropped in the middle of the hollow he'd come to call his stomach. He'd never felt anything quite like it.

He lay on his bed, staring at the book he was reading. He was hardly even paying attention to it, really. However, his eye caught on a certain sentence.

Fas est ab hoste doceri.
One should learn even from one's enemies.

It seemed to resonate with Maximus quite a bit.

George understood love very clearly; he found it interesting, if anything. How was it that it felt so forbidden to tell someone labelled your lover that you loved them, until the moment 'felt right'? Surely if you are going to call one another such things, you should be sure that you truly love them, first.

But as much as George knew about love, he could never understand how Maximus had managed to fall in love with the Kendran princess.

She was stunning, yes. Scarily so. Everything about her was just so imperfectly perfect that she felt unreal.

Yet, the two of them had been brought up despising the Kendrans. Now, even though George knew enough about the situation of the war to sympathise for the country, he still resented them from his upbringing, no matter how beautiful their princess was, in both looks and personality. He felt physically repelled by the thought of loving one, even if he knew that they were harmless.

It was kind of an internalised thing.

And so, if George and Maximus had learnt the same of everything, how was it that Maximus could feel so deeply for this girl and not feel, even in the slightest bit, hesitant about it?

Everything had changed in the past few days.

Everything had changed so much.

George could hear footsteps coming up through the stairs to his floor; rather heavy footsteps.

Rather angry footsteps.

George had memorised the exact sounds every person who roamed the manor made, and that sound would be none other than his father.

But what does he want up here?

George sat in anticipation after he put away his book and pressed his back to the end of his bed.

The door swung open and his heart dropped to his stomach, adding more weight to the already unbearable heaviness that was pulling him down.

A hand clamped over his mouth, slick with sweat.

He felt like throwing up.

'George, son.' It sounded as if Nathaniel's throat was full of scales, his voice running through them and cracking up before leaving his lips. 'We have a little talking to do.'

Seeing as George was presently unable to respond, he nodded once, only a slight gesture.

Nathaniel grinned and hooked his spare hand around the back of George's neck, pushing him forwards as a means of pulling him with him.

The grin was not like a smiling grin.

In fact, it was more of a grimace.

Or maybe it was just him baring his teeth like a damn lion.

There was a word for that comparison, George thought in a daze. Was it zoomorphism?

George was thrown into Nathaniel's office and he quickly sat himself at the chair in front of the desk, forehead hot and sticky.

'Now, then.' Nathaniel rasped, arranging himself in front of Geoge. 'Let us begin.'

George didn't say anything. His pupils had dilated to a point where the brown was hardly visible beneath the black; was that supposed to happen when in close contact with your own *pater*? George was not sure that he wanted to know.

'I am sure you know about Maximus's little... incident.' Nathaniel began. 'And I regret to inform you that I have realised you played a part in it. Don't look so shocked; you have messed up, yes, and now you will face the consequences.'

Consequences.

Oh, for Hades-

'Don't look so alarmed, boy. We're going to war in two weeks. As soon as we win, all will be forgiven.'

George was not relieved by that whatsoever.

'Yeah. As soon as we win.' he echoed miserably.

'But, until then... you have to realise what happens when you dare to go against me.'

There was a sharp pain in George's ear.

He pressed a finger to it and it came back bloody.

His eyes caught on the glint of a blade. The glint of a dagger.

A dagger.

Oh.

It seemed the consequences were going to be slightly more elaborate than he had been expecting.

☆★☆

Adelaide sensed a change in the atmosphere.

Her and Anastasia spoke about it in the darkest hours of the night, when everyone else was silent, when the two of them were free to be who they wanted.

'Did you see George's face today?' Adelaide asked, the worry prevalent in her voice.

'I saw the bruises. And the dried blood. And the-' Anastasia cut herself off as she shivered wholly. 'Something has happened.'

'Oh, I know exactly what has happened.' Adelaide said angrily. 'My stupid *pater* has brought it upon himself to blame my poor brother for Maximus finally doing what we all want to do and leaving, and now George is taking all of the blame for what father caused.'

Adelaide was trembling, in both fear and rage.

'I know that you're upset-'

'Upset?' Adelaide repeated. 'I'm more than upset. I'm afraid. I'm afraid of my damned dad.'

'You don't have to worry yourself with this. You're only a child yourself, you know. George can look after himself.' Anastasia said soothingly.

Adelaide swallowed.

'I know. I just feel so… I feel like I've been done so wrongly, being born into this life.'

Anastasia's lips pressed to Adelaide's for a moment.

'Don't think like that. Things will turn around, someday in the future. *Non est astra mollis e terris via.*'

There is no easy way from earth to the stars.

Adelaide let the words comfort her as she fell into a deep slumber, but even as she slept through the chaos she was shrouded in, her conscience was screaming at her, saying to wake up, wake up, wake up if you care at all.

A few rooms away, George was going through a few more punishments.

A few rooms away, life was coming increasingly close to death.

☆★☆

When George woke up, he was alone.

His brain felt like it had been cut from his head and battered about, then pushed back in as if nothing had happened.

Everything hurt.

There was blood everywhere he looked, even if there wasn't really. Red stained the walls, stained his clothes, his skin, his vision. Everything was so red that perhaps it was even a little black.

Nathaniel had carved his name into George's forearm, he vaguely remembered.

How sadistic did he have to be?
How sick was his mind that it had somehow justified carving his name into the skin of his firstborn child?

George felt ill.

Perhaps he had contracted some sort of infection from the knife; it had certainly been inside of his skin enough for that to have happened.

Either way, it didn't matter.

He still had a lot to come.

And while George was struggling with the unjust treatment from his father, there was a little boat, sailing out at sea.

A little boat destined to soon hit a storm.

⚔ Chapter Thirty Eight ⚔

I KNEW THAT THE journey was going to be restless. I knew it as soon as I stepped on that boat, as soon as the air went from a pleasant warmth to a greedy cold. I especially knew it when the murky water went clear as ice, so clear that I could see the contents of the Rendan Ocean spilling out before me. Fishes were common where I lived. Animals such as seahorses, on the other hand, were not as common. That's why I nearly jumped with joy when I saw a swarm of them appear from under my boat.

There was some comfort in long journeys, I supposed.

The first day passed fast. Before I knew it the sun was setting, and by Zeus it was the most beautiful sunset I'd ever seen. Perhaps even more beautiful than the sunset I watched with Emile once upon a time.

But the beauty in that was more than skin deep,

There is a word that means exactly that.

Kalon. That's what it is.

As I watched the ball of fire disperse behind the clouds, I realised the love I had for words. There was sort of a word bank in the back of my head, filled with unique words I'd heard and read from time to time that I felt as though I may use in the future. I picked a few out, then, and dove into them.

Not mentally, of course.

My brain did not have the capacity to hold all of what I felt, most of the time.

So I wrote instead.

Of course I did.

I found myself writing a lot, as of late.

I have been searching my mind for words that make me feel a very specific way in my boredom, and I believe that I have found some. The first is fanaa. It means 'the destruction of self, destroyed by love'. It quite reminds me of Emile and I.

I didn't fully destroy myself.

I am still happy and I am still well. Happy is a bit of a stretch, yes, but I'm not depressed. Why should I be? I'm going back to see her again, now, anyway.

But I feel as though I have destroyed quite a bit of my mind. I used to be so... cruel. So quick to put up the barriers. The barriers have been destroyed in love; these barriers, this massive part of myself and my identity, have been destroyed in my love for Emile.

So, when asked if I identify with the word fanaa, I will say yes. Just not in the way you primarily think.

The second word is nubivagant. It doesn't really sound very beautiful, does it? It means 'wandering in the clouds, moving through the air'. Very vague.

I don't know why this word is so intriguing to me. Perhaps it isn't that; perhaps it is only comforting. I like to think that, in those briefly euphoric moments I occasionally have, I am wandering among the clouds, my eyes blinded in the mist.

But, then again, all of these moments are spent with Emile.

Which leads me to my third word.

Virago. 'A strong, brave or warlike woman.'

Take a wild guess at who that describes perfectly.

Go on, take a guess. I doubt you'll get it wrong.

If you guessed Emile, then bingo! You are, unsurprisingly, correct.

I think I might be obsessed with her. Not in a creepy way. Gods, that sounds bad.

I'm obsessed with us, is the better way to put it. I'm obsessed with the way my heart flutters when I think about her, the way my pulse quickens just at the thought of the colour blue.

The colour blue is another thing that has been destroyed in my love for her. It used to be one of those melancholy colours, a bit sad, kind of boring.

Now the colour blue is a pit of memories.

I didn't have the strength to write anymore. My muscles felt weak, and my hands physically could not handle it.

I had found the journey to be reasonably peaceful up until then.

However, it was hastily going to take a turn for the worst.

☆★☆

In the midst of the night, the stars went pale. The light was vanquished and the breeze stolen from me, leaving my throat parched and sweat dripping down me. It was unnaturally warm for a day in winter, and the lack of wind was not helping.

I wished I could sleep, but I was nearing the Rendan base, and I knew it.

I was coming up with a plan to distract me from the heat I was shrouded in.

They couldn't see me leave the boat; if they did, they would notice me, and they would notice that I was not supposed to be on a stolen rowboat by myself at four in the morning, going through a Rendan base to get to the Kendran Channels.

No, I was going to have to be fast.

There was a certain part of the base with only two guards, distant from the rest, reserved for special cases only. It was expensive to get through there, considering it took you through the quickest and safest route to Kendra. The guards did not waste time giving second chances to people who went there without reservations; they discarded them, throwing their bodies into the deepest parts of the ocean.

Now, the guards were good fighters, yes, but I wasn't worried by them. I could take them out easily. It was after that that I was going to have to hurry.

The death of the first would set off an emergency alarm throughout the whole base, and the death of the second would send off a series of them. It would take the rest of the guards minutes to come and see me; for all I was a skilled fighter, I could not take out hundreds at a time in my current state, starved and dehydrated. I'd have to get through before they had the chance to take me out.

That was when I was going to take part in a little robbery.

There would be the boats of the guards parked up all in the reservation entry. I could take the keys of the guards I killed and then their boats, after. However, to know which boats were theirs, I'd have to watch them in the early morning as they took over the shift from their companions. I was nearly there, by then. I'd just have to watch carefully…

I was practically falling asleep.

How am I to fight when I am so tired?

I felt ill. My throat was raw, stinging with every breath I took, and my lungs simply would not fill, no matter how much air I took in. My vision was spinning.

If I didn't sleep soon I was going to start hallucinating. That was not what I wanted to happen.

I just had to get to Kendra as quickly as possible. The route took me through to the countryside where I had previously been, I knew that; Nathaniel had explained the entire way before sending me off before, in case I needed to go back to Rendo in an emergency. If I got the electric boat that I knew one of these guards were bound to have, I'd be back there within eight hours.

It all felt quite surreal.

Oh, so much had changed in only a few days.

I took my hand and ran it through the water beside me. It was getting warmer. I brought my fingertips to my mouth, tasting it. Chemicals. *Nearly there.*

Five minutes passed, and then I saw light.

Here we are.

I checked the time on my watch. 4:27. They were doing the changeover in three minutes.

I let my boat come to a stop, putting the oar next to me as I sat with my legs crossed, watching carefully.

4:28

4:29

4:30

Somehow those bloody guards were right on time. I stared at their boats, memorising the details. The better one was the dark brown one, the largest boat there. It would be easy to pick it out; just find the biggest one and jump straight on.

I decided to give it a few minutes before I showed up, let the guards have a slither of their life left.

Then, I picked up the oar and started moving.

It didn't take long to get there. Soon enough, I had my boat parked up at the side and the suspicious eyes of the guards on me. I discreetly pulled out my sword, holding it at my side.

'What's your name?' the first guard yelled.

'Get out of your boat!' the second commanded.

I did just that, jumping out lightly and pointing my sword at them.

'Hey.' I said. 'Gods, I haven't seen you two for a good while, have I?'

They stared at me in disbelief.

'Maximus? You- why are you-' The realisation dawned on them. I felt a smirk tug at my lips.

'Are you going to kill me, now?' I said mockingly. The look on their faces clearly said yes. 'Such a shame. I was going to give you a chance, too. It's quite sad that this is how it has to end.'

I took my sword and brought it down on the first guard, cutting through the top of his head. I could see his skull poking out as his eyes rolled back and he fell back.

The first alarm went off.

I wasted no time shoving my sword through the second's chest and plucking the keys from both of their pockets.

I hastily found the big brown boat and jumped on, pushing the first key I picked out into the ignition.

Please be the right one, please be the right-

The engine turned on and I let out a long breath and set off, putting on the self-driving setting and jumping out onto the front as I stared back at the guards on the base.

They looked furious.

Confused.

And a little scared.

A sick sense of pleasure ran through me at the sight of their fear.

Their eyes were trained on me, unmoving.

So I pulled my sword from my sheath and wiped the flat side down the left of my face, over my lips, up the right.

I saw a few of them jump, a few of them look away.

I licked the blood from my lips.

And then I grinned, all my teeth on show, just to watch them as their trembling knees gave way, and they fell to the floor.

As they fell before me.

☆★☆

I realised that if I didn't drink soon I was going to pass out from the absolute lack of liquids. I had a single water bottle in my bag, and George had said to save it for when I really needed it. Well, if my calculations were right I'd be landing at the countryside of Kendra in about an hour (the boat moved much faster than I'd thought it would, reducing eight hours down to four) meaning that it could be classed as really needing it.

I drank half of the water and saved the rest of it.

The chill of the frozen air had returned, even slight breezes racking through me unnervingly. I was positive that I had come down with something at that point. I listed off all the things it could be in my mind.

Pneumonia would be an obvious choice. But pneumonia is a silent disease, at least at first; if I'd contracted it during my time on the boat I wouldn't have known so soon.

I looked at my fingertips and was positive they were slightly grey. Perhaps I had frostbite. But it was most likely I was just hallucinating from my lack of sleep.

Hypothermia? I had plenty of symptoms. Patches of my skin were red and everything spun, not to mention the clumsiness and the consistent trembling.

I took a numb fingertip and pressed it against my neck to feel my pulse. It was hardly even there.

That was another symptom. Weak pulse.

Before long I would start losing my memory, losing my consciousness. I'd just have to pray that I'd get to Kendra before then.

I had read somewhere that in extremely severe cases people 'started to undress' when suffering with hypothermia. That did not sound very appealing at all.

I raked through my bag for food, coming back up with a bag of chocolate. I ate all of it in seconds, my breathing shallow and low after from the speed.

I got those horrible hiccups you get when you eat too fast, the silent ones that are so violent it makes you think you're genuinely going to throw up.

My already weak body could not handle that.

The hiccups and the chocolate, I mean.

I stumbled to the side of the boat and threw it all back up until there was nothing but acid erupting from me.

The edges of my vision had gone dark.

Was that really the way I was going to die? Alone, in the middle of the ocean, of hypothermia out of all things?

I shivered.

And then my eye caught on something.

Land.

Kendran land.

I was there, an hour earlier than I had expected.

I jumped to my feet and almost fell back over as I got closer and my vision was filled with guards.

Oh.

I'd almost forgotten about that part.

Well.

At least I wasn't going to die?

⚔ Chapter Thirty Nine ⚔

I PULLED THE KEY out and stuffed it in my bag before practically falling off the boat. The guards looked very shocked to see me.

'Maximus? Back so soon?' one asked, although he looked rather worried. 'Desmond said you were going to be away for quite a while, and blimey you look half frozen to death. Are you alright?'

'I- I' My speech was slurred, my tongue numb. 'Fine. I- fine.'

I faintly recognised that Desmond mustn't have told anyone about my situation for the guards to have said that to me, for them to have ushered me up the path to the house.

'Right, Desmond's in the living room, go speak to him.' that same guard said, smiling uneasily. I nodded, movements jerky, and staggered through the corridor, lurching into the living room.

'Maximus?' Desmond sounded confused, at first. I did not know what his face was doing. Everything was dark. 'What on earth is wrong? Your lips are- your lips are blue…?'

'I- I- back. Came back.' I stammered, blinking rapidly in panic.

'You've come all that way by yourself?' Desmond sounded hopeful, if a little doubtful.

'I don't- yes. I think.' *Memory loss.*

'Come on, you need warmth. Hypothermia. That's what you have, isn't it? Gods, why would you risk your life like that just to come back here? You could've just written a letter to me and I would have found you.' Desmond sounded proud, still, that I had come back, but extremely concerned.

'Wouldn't let me.' I mumbled. Desmond didn't have a response to that, apparently. He guided me up to my room and I collapsed onto the bed, feeling the warmth of my old sheets slipping in between my fingertips.

'Go to sleep, Maximus.' Desmond said.

I could hear him walking away.

'I- I missed you.' I said, as loudly as I could. My voice was hardly a croak. There was silence for a second.

'I missed you too.' Desmond said quietly. 'Now, sleep.'

My eyes shut and everything fell away as I felt myself drift off.

☆✭☆

Emile was sat in the clearing at the forest, hands clenching the grass. She looked down and was almost positive it was growing through her fingers. She jumped and picked up her hand, placing it on her leg gingerly.

Desmond ran out in front of her, eyes wide.

'He's back.'

Emile's stomach crumbled away.

'What?' she said in disbelief, hoisting herself up.

'Maximus. He's come back.'

'Already? But I thought he said-'

'I know fine well what he said. He's here, in the flesh. And he looks terrible, too. He has hypothermia, I think.'

If Emile was good at anything, it was holding a grudge. But through her resentment she couldn't help but feel a pang of worry.

'Hypothermia? How?'

'He came the full way by himself, on a boat I assume. And since he's clearly not meant to be here it will not have been a good boat. A little rowboat is my guess. It's the middle of winter, Emile. He's lucky he got here before his state worsened.'

Emile swallowed. Desmond was watching her carefully, cautiously.

'Would you like to see him?' he asked softly. She knew it was going to hurt her; even thinking about him after what he had done tore up her breathing and tied together the wires in her mind.

'Yes.' she said anyway. She didn't much care about the hurt; Emile Elizabeth Elires wanted to see the boy she loved and feel like she could truly love him in spite of his betrayal, even if just for a few moments.

She went up to his room.

And, sure enough, Maximus was curled up in his bed, snoring gently.

Emile thought that if she pulled out her heart and stood on it the pain would be bearable compared to that.

She took a few steps closer to the bed, letting her eyes trail over his face. He was unearthly pale, his lips teetering on the edge of a light blue. Her fingertips automatically reached out to touch them.

She yanked away her arm.

Maximus hadn't looked so vulnerable since the injury after the task, when he had finally found peace in being with Emile.

Now she understood why he was so afraid of it in the first place.

Emile hated him most for letting her fall in love with him, for breaking everything she had just with a few sentences.

She hated him so much that it blinded her sense of direction when she was around him, that she almost forgot completely about all the times they'd shared, about the conversations they'd had, and she just wanted to push a dagger through his chest and end her misery.

But the traces of the love that she'd locked away in the darkest part of her heart stopped her.

Emile shut her eyes for a moment.

Everything in her was burning up.

Everything in her was freezing up.

On a whim, she reopened her eyes and leaned forwards until her lips were practically touching Maximus's ear, feeling the coolness of his icy skin radiating off him.

'*Te amo.*' Emile whispered, her voice on the fine line of being non existent, so quiet it was hardly even a breath.

She pulled away, gulping down the lump that was forming in the core of her throat.

That would be the last time she admitted to loving Maximus Invictus Blare.

Or, at least, the last time for a long time.

☆★☆

When I woke up, everything was groggy.

I could see again, which was a good sign; clearly, too, in opposition to the blurred images I was faced with before my vision blacked out completely.

I pushed myself to sit up. No dizziness. I felt completely well.

It was only after a few minutes of confused pondering that I remembered Desmond's magic medicine that cured relatively minor illness.

I was in Kendra.

Gods.

I was in Kendra!

I'd done it. Gods. I'd really, truly done it.

Just as I was about to leave my room, Desmond burst in. His face split into a massive grin when he saw I was awake and alright.

'Maximus, son!'

He pulled me into a choking embrace, but even in my discomfort I couldn't help but let my arms wrap around him, too.

'Desmond.' I mumbled in response.

He let go of me and sat at the foot of my bed.

'Right. Now that you're awake and we've had our happy little reunion, we have some things to discuss.' Desmond said, his tone serious. I nodded sharply.

'For a start,' Desmond began, 'there will be no secrets between any of us any more. Emile has told me about your previous situation with Nathaniel, and I completely understand that you had no choice in the matter. However, I would like to know what has made you so unafraid as to come back to us, now.'

'I fought him. Nathaniel, I mean. My friend George urged me to do it, so I did. And I won, so now I'm here.'

'You mean to tell me Nathaniel Flint is dead two weeks before we go to war with his army?'

I could see the hope in Desmond's eyes.

'I couldn't bring myself to kill him.' I said quietly. 'I'm sorry.'

The hope disappeared, but Desmond was not put down by the news at all.

'Don't worry.' he reassured me. 'As long as you're here, safe with me and Emile, I'm alright.'

My breath hitched at her name.

'Can I see her?' I asked. I saw the conflict in his face.

'She isn't as willing to forgive you as I am.' Desmond said steadily, not daring to look me in the eye.

I knew it.

It didn't matter.

I had time.

And in time, she would forgive me.

Just knowing that she was here with me gave me peace of mind.

'That's fine.' I said, my voice wobbling slightly. I cleared my throat awkwardly. 'So, war soon, huh?'

'It's going to be amazing with you on our side, you know.' Desmond said with a grin. 'I'm using this situation to our advantage. You know Nathaniel Flint so well that it quite literally blows my mind. You can kill him for us, when you're ready and when the time is right. You are the key to our victory. You and Emile.' There was a pause.

'I know.' I mumbled. 'If we're going to win we're going to have to tolerate each other. It's just-' I cut off with a heavy and shaky breath. 'It's just hard being so close to the girl I'm completely and irrevocably in love with and just knowing what an awful thing I've done to her. I know she won't trust me ever again. I just hope that, in time, perhaps an extremely long time, but in time all the same, she will somehow learn to forgive me for what I've done.'

Desmond smiled at me.

'You have a beautiful soul, Maximus, I hope you know that.'

I raised an eyebrow.

'You are the first person I've ever met to think that, you know?' I said, laughing. 'Even George knows how ugly I am on the inside.'

'You're only ugly because of what you've been through.' Desmond paused. 'Through fire, we all come out a little scarred. But I'm sure you've heard the saying *igne natura renovatur integra?'* *Through fire nature is reborn whole.* 'You are as beautiful of a man as your soul can ever be. Through the fire that scars you, you are reborn completely. Truly. Honestly. In my eyes, you will always be beautiful, in an odd way.'

I found that, for the first time ever, I felt that the words someone spoke to me completely touched my soul.

And I think that's the most beautiful thing of all; to feel seen when being perceived in the way that you really are.

It must be because of how uncommon it is.

Nathaniel certainly never would have seen me that way.

Even George wouldn't.

Of course Desmond did, though.

Desmond saw everything that went further than the skin.

⚔ Chapter Forty ⚔

EMILE AND I DID not speak.

I was too focused on the upcoming war to care much.

I spent every second of every minute of every hour of every day training, until my hands were calloused and my knees weak. I was determined to win the war, no matter how much it took.

No matter how much it hurt.

No matter how much it killed.

I was going to win that war, and I was going to do it with pride.

But every now and then I caught a flash of blue.

I was still going to win the war, yes.

But I was also going to win back my girl.

⚔ Epilogue ⚔
TWO WEEKS LATER

EMILE HAD WENT HER whole life surrounded in talks of war. Of blood and death alike.

As a child, she'd thought of murder and love as vaguely similar.

But now, as she stood next to the person she loved, even if she hated herself for it, Emile found that murder was much different to how she felt towards that boy.

Her eyes caught on Maximus's grey ones.

Even if they were both as destructive as the other.

⚔ Acknowledgements ⚔

I WANT TO SAY thank you to every single person who has been on this journey with me. It still feels surreal to be able to tell people that I've written a full book at thirteen years old.

For a start, thank you to my Grandad Daz, for helping me throughout the full publishing process (which, by the way, was literally harder than writing the book).

Thank you a million times over to Danielle, for the beautiful cover of my book, which I wholeheartedly adore.

Thank you to my mam and my dad, who started me with reading before I ever knew that my love for words would inspire me to write a book. Thank you for introducing me to the world of fiction, to the world of my imagination. Thank you for being the best parents I could've asked for, and thank you for being the best parents I could ever have, in a thousand lives, in a thousand years, in a thousand millenia. Thank you for being the core reason that I ever wrote this book, going all the way back to the first lockdown when I started my obsession with writing. Thank you for being the fuel in that fire. Thank you for being my inspiration.

Thank you to each and every one of my friends, who've helped me have the confidence to write and publish this novel in ways they can't even imagine.

Thank you to Bella Spoors, for being my number one cheerleader and the best one around. Thank you for loving my book so much, and for giving me the motivation I needed, for being more excited over it than me.

Thank you to Bayleigh: even though I know you aren't interested in reading books, you've been nothing but interested in mine. I know that you aren't exactly a book person, but you have been constant in your support.

Thank you to Anna, for being a sun in the dark (and exceptionally tall sun at that). Thank you for being my best friend before I knew it myself, and thank you for being one of the first people to be that type of friend to me.

Thank you to Grace, for being someone I'm glad to share my name with, and for your consistent interest in what I've been writing. Thank you for making me, and everyone else, laugh without even meaning to make us laugh.

Thank you to Freya, for being the first person to ever love fiction and books as much as I do. I've always found that people who say they love books never really do in the same way I do, but you do, so thank you for it.

Thank you to Ruby, for always being there and for always listening to me ramble about my writing. Thank you for being one of the kindest people I've met, and thank you for bestowing that kindness upon me.

Thank you to Holly, for making me laugh even when I'm falling asleep, for being the funniest person I've met. Thank you for being the person I can talk to about anything and everything: for being the person that brightens my day, everyday.

And finally, thank you to Bella Petrie, for being my biggest and most enthusiastic supporter, for always encouraging me to keep on writing, for always reassuring me that you're going to buy ten copies of this. Thank you for loving this book even when I didn't, for not giving up on it even when I did, for believing it meant something even when I was sure it didn't, for saying it would go somewhere when I had convinced myself itn never would. Thank you for your terrible singing that, somehow, never fails to make me laugh, and for your fabulous ability to have conversations with me literally using our eyes. Thank you for being my best friend, for being someone I'm proud to say to everyone who's reading this, that you've been the best friend I could've asked for when I was doing this.

Thank you, everyone, for making sure that I was never alone during this.

Thank you to everyone for being a part of this massive milestone, even if you didn't really know you were a part of it.

Thank you to everyone for everything, always.

I couldn't have done any of this without any of you.

Printed in Great Britain
by Amazon